Pink Slips and Glass Slippers

Pink Slips and Glass Slippers

Handwritten inscription:

BROOKE,
THOUGH THERE'S A
DISCLAIMER ABOUT FICTIONAL
NAMES, WE ALL KNOW HOW
THE NAME OF THE HEROINE
WAS INSPIRED. ENJOY MY
DARE TURNED BOOK,

J.P. HANSEN

BESTSELLING AND AWARD-WINNING AUTHOR

P.S. YOU NEED THOSE SHOES

bliss career publications, inc.

Omaha, NE

PUBLISHER'S NOTE:
This is a work of fiction. Names, characters, places, and incidents either are the product of the author's imagination or are used fictitiously, and any resemblance to actual persons, living or dead, events, or locales is entirely coincidental.

Products and business establishments mentioned in the story are owned by their respective copyright and trademark holders.

Song "Wedded Bliss" by Chase N. Allman

ISBN: 978-0-9840934-6-5
LCCN: 2012950355

Design and production: Concierge Marketing Inc.

Published in the United States of America

Prologue

Charlotte, North Carolina

*I*f it's better to have loved and lost than never to have loved before, why did she feel so empty? Brooke Hart savored the Sweet Violet one last time, then stood and smoothed her hair. Now the tough part.

While rubbing the clinging soil off her fingers, she trudged toward Tanner's grave. He had left an indelible mark—one that she just couldn't wipe away. But today she would try. A swirling breeze pulled emerald leaves from the majestic oak tree's grip. June twenty-first had crept up once again.

Brooke paused, hoping to stifle the humidity and her tightened chest. She plunked down and removed her bag's contents. Her eyes fluttered as tears merged with droplets of perspiration falling onto his picture. Brooke stared at the photo of the strongest man she ever met, "Why did you quit?"

Holding the letter in trembling hands, she sensed his presence.

My Dearest Brooke ...

Her stomach churned.

Brooke slid the ring up the rose's stem and carefully positioned it on his stone. She closed her eyes and pictured the magical day on the beach when he dropped to one knee and changed her life forever. Brooke drew a deep breath. A sudden breeze soothed her overheated skin.

She ran her hand across the paper as if it was Tanner's chest. Her ring finger found the tiny watermark she imagined was from his last tear. She inhaled slowly to capture his fragrance on the paper. And as always, she raised her closed eyes to the heavens; but this time she didn't see his face. She lifted his picture from her lap and proclaimed for the first time, "I forgive you ... and I forgive me."

1

What am I doing here? Brooke had been asking herself that question for the past six weeks. The thirty-three-year-old vice president seemed to have it all, yet it felt as if her career ladder and life had crashed. Hoping to move on, relocating to the new company had officially backfired. All the blind dates set up by her well-meaning inner circle—her father, Melissa, Shane, and Todd—had fizzled before hors d'oeuvres. Online dating turned into *mis*-matched.com. *Damn Tanner.*

Feeling claustrophobic in this stuffy room, the corporate strangers eyed her like a piñata and they were clenching bats. The stiff dress code mirrored the culture, and both felt about as comfy as tweed pajamas.

Suddenly, the boardroom hushed. All eyes pointed to the entryway like canines at obedience training graduation. Except for Brooke, whose back faced the door. She craned her neck; a whisk of air drew her to the opposite direction, followed by a masculine scent of sandalwood and cedar. *Seductive.*

Mr. Smellgood looked striking from the side. His physique matched his fragrance. He set his fancy briefcase at the head of the table—mahogany on mahogany. As if revealing a game show prize, he slid off his navy suit coat. Brooke's eyes widened as he draped it over the high-backed leather chair. He had a rugged build she expected to see on a mountain climber or surfer, but not on an executive for a drug company. Brooke's instant attraction surprised her.

Without uttering a word, he headed to the refreshment area. Brooke figured he was either the president or CEO; she hadn't met either one yet. Quite a departure from the GenSense days that had faded like a winter sunset. As he stopped to pour a coffee, his backside didn't look too bad either. She straightened her posture, preparing for his return trip.

"Chase can't start a meeting without his coffee." The voice startled Brooke. She hoped the power tie next to her wasn't psychic.

Brooke uttered a half-hearted "ah" and nodded like a bobble head. She grimaced as she surveyed the unfamiliar faces. All of her previous coworkers she called friends had parachuted out after the acquisition. Now she felt deserted. Times like these made her question herself, something she rarely did, even after abandoning her early dreams of becoming a child psychologist for the more stable career in business.

She figured Mr. Caffeinated Smellgood had to be CEO Chase Allman, but he looked too young and much more attractive than the wooden puppet behind the podium of the "merger" announcement. Brooke recalled his bio: forty-one, yet he appeared her age—quite young to be running a multi-national company. *Impressive.* The only knock on him—Duke undergrad, then JD/MBA. To a North Carolina girl, usually a triple dukie meant three strikes against you, but this guy didn't have the look or attitude she'd despised. And too sexy for clothes.

On his return walk, he even exuded poise while balancing a full cup of coffee on a saucer. His monogrammed lavender shirt looked as if it was painted on all the way down to the cuff links. An expensive tie dangled at the belt line of his navy pinstriped slacks. But the clincher for Brooke: the shoes. She loved well-shined shoes—especially Gucci. This guy's look screamed success. He belonged on a cover of an expensive men's catalogue. A heat flash kindled as she pondered him without his shirt.

Damn, she caught the glistening band on his finger. Brooke's shoulders slumped, *figures.*

Brooke loathed formal meetings or maybe the concept of a boardroom—it didn't matter. This place felt pompous and sterile with its flamboyant furnishings and subdued culture. Though the buyout brought her riches, she felt like rags. Listening to the incessant chit chat, her stomach churned again.

Chase perched at the head of the table and all chatter ended. He had an alluring charisma, highlighted by piercing brown eyes with gold flecks. Flashing a smile that could melt a diamond, he said, "Good morning."

Brooke was mesmerized by his combination radio announcer voice and TV host good looks. Everyone else muttered, "Good morning," but Brooke just gazed with puppy love eyes. The last person to create such a stir inside her was Tanner.

"Let's get started. We have a full agenda today. Thank you all for being here, especially the new members of our team. For those of you who haven't met me, I'm Chase Allman." This drew laughter from everyone but Brooke—making her feel even more alien. "Why don't we begin by having each new person briefly introduce him or herself." He stared at Brooke. She flinched, looking like she was just tasered.

Big gulp. "I'm Brooke Hart. Let's see, I'm originally from Charlotte, graduated from UNC, then lived in Charlotte for a while, but moved back to Chapel Hill for the past few years. I'm happy to be here with y'all." She released a flutter of blinks—*did I just say y'all?*

Brooke fidgeted in her chair as twenty-two frowns descended on her. Pharmical Solutions was located just outside downtown Durham, North Carolina, one of the vertices of "Research Triangle," which also included Chapel Hill and Raleigh. So named in 1959 with the creation of Research Triangle Park, it was the Southeast's Silicon Valley. To residents of Durham and Raleigh, Chapel Hill was considered the weak link in the triangle. Sensing there weren't many Tar Heels in the room—Duke country now—she felt as welcome as a Red Sox jersey in Yankee Stadium.

David Greenberg, general counsel, vice president of Human Resources—and Brooke's new boss—though she rarely saw him, chimed in, "Brooke comes to us from GenSense and is vice president of our new Integrated Client Services department." *Yeah sounds impressive, but in reality, I'm an overpaid telemarketing babysitter—reporting to this android. Integrated Client Services even sounded robotic.*

Chase said, "Welcome to Pharmical Solutions, Brooke. I look forward to seeing great things out of ICS. Glad to have you."

"Thank you, sir, nice to be here." She felt relieved that she avoided another *y'all* and stifled the blinking. She stared as Chase mouthed the next introduction. She loved the way his lips moved. *Stop it, don't go there, no, not any further, she told herself—he's married and I work for him, he's forbidden fruit.*

Staring out the expansive windows and suppressing yawns as the new employees spoke, Brooke kept peeking at the man at the head of the table. As the final newbie, a vice president of something or other, rambled on about his background, Brooke noticed Chase staring at her. His swift glance away confirmed it.

I shouldn't have worn this dress. It felt tight, too low cut. I'm leaving the wrong impression.

Brooke adjusted her posture and returned her gaze to the wall of windows. Cumulus clouds battled the Carolina blue-sky backdrop. She recalled the GenSense days and how different it now seemed. The most impressive room at the start-up had been her cubicle. With no view. They didn't need fancy clothes or offices, let alone *bored-rooms* with refreshment stations. She felt akin to her old company like her sorority. She missed it.

Brooke remembered the feeling of elation when GenSense issued the IPO. Overnight, she was worth one point two million. On paper. At least for a few weeks—until the stock market tumbled, cutting her stock value nearly in half. Still not bad. And since the estate settlement, money had never been a concern. It seemed like once she quit worrying about cash, it poured in. She still would trade it all for what she once had.

Brooke realized the toll work extracted from her personal life. She had worn so many hats—sales, marketing, finance, operations, and even decorator. Now she was in charge of only one function and, for the first time in her life, boredom had set in.

Brooke sensed she needed change. For some strange reason, she got a second chance at life. But the recent changes only caused anxiety. *I have to be patient and give this place time. There has to be something more for me in life.*

A wave of unease churned inside—Brooke desired another man and didn't even think about Tanner.

The next few days passed like a rollercoaster. Brooke needed to decompress. The drive back home always did the trick. Brooke loved her Lexus HS Hybrid. She remembered the day she bought it. Brooke had applied her decision analysis course by, first, doing the research, then test driving all the luxury hybrids—BMW, Audi, Acura, and Mercedes. She made the mistake of consulting Weston Ingram, a brilliant trial lawyer and good father to her—most of the time—but on this one, he treated Brooke like she was twelve years old. His main objection that hybrids were an overpriced fad was a misnomer. She realized his true rationale stemmed from Pearl Harbor. If it were up to him, she would drive a Buick.

Lexus won hands down. In rare defiance, she ignored her father's calls, and with no regrets. Beyond having the best fuel economy and the quietest ride, it had a killer sound system. Once she closed the door, she was in her own cocoon.

Today, she felt fidgety—even in the comfortable leather seat that engulfed her like a security blanket. Brooke thought, *this isn't the company for me. I should have heeded everyone's warnings. Aside from Chase, nobody impresses me. And, my interest in Chase isn't professional.*

Instead of losing herself in her music, she pressed speed dial one on her cell.

"Hello Brooke," he said in his usual peppy voice. Surprised to catch her life coach live instead of voicemail, she drew a blank.

"You talked me into this high rise hellhole, now talk me down off the roof."

Shane sighed, "Uh oh. I know you well enough to know you've had a setback."

Why does he always say setback? It's irritating.

"Setback? I'm walking with the living dead here."

"Well, that sounds like it qualifies as a setback. What's wrong now? You've only been there a month." *Setback again. Argh.*

"Six weeks."

"Semantics."

"Well, it feels like six *years*."

Shane Gallagher, Ph.D., had been Brooke's life coach for the past three years. Though she had only met with him in person once—at his Boston office—most sessions were on the fly from her cell phone. Brooke marveled at how well he understood her. The majority of his advice had focused on personal growth and rarely on career—until he urged her to join Pharmical Solutions. Since then she had lost her playfulness he so loved. Shane clicked into therapist mode.

..is place sucks." Brooke rubbed the back of her neck.

sterile than a hospital and with more stiffs than a morgue."
.huckled, louder than usual. "At least you haven't lost your sen. .1umor."

"Seriously, my boss is up for *Anal Manager of the Year,* and it seems like everyone else is battling for runner-up. Aside from their CEO, there's nobody I can even talk to."

"Well, you met the CEO. That's good."

"I wouldn't say *met.* I propped my eyes open during a meeting he ran. Or tried to run. It was scheduled for four hours but lasted the entire day." She suppressed her true perceptions.

"You just miss GenSense." Shane had an uncanny directness in an East Coast way. A little too quick at times, but precise, decisive.

"You can say that again. I miss everything from GenSense's wear-whatever-you-please dress code to the I-make-a-difference attitude."

"It's natural. You miss the challenge. At GenSense, you guys created something you were passionate about. Plus, you were running practically everything there. Now you're in the ocean instead of a pond."

"More like drying up on the scorched sand. I'd like to leapfrog back to the pond before I rot away."

"How much of this anxiety is Tanner-related?"

There he goes again. Uncanny. "I don't know ..."

"I've been thinking about you the last few days. Did you make your visit on the twenty-first?"

"You know I did. I'm both a creature of habit and a glutton for punishment."

"Well," he inhaled a deep and audible gasp, "talk to me."

"This time you'll be proud of me." Brooke paused, but Shane remained quiet. She continued, "I finally followed your advice."

"What do you mean?"

"For the first time, I was able to forgive Tanner—and myself."

"Congratulations. That's the greatest accomplishment you could have achieved. And you certainly have an impressive resume." Comforting warmth enveloped Brooke. She had a familial respect for him: Shane was like a father to her—she craved his approval, but he treated her with compassion and empathy.

"You've been on me to move on, but you know me, it has to be on my own terms. I realize it's taken me too long, but I finally feel like I'm on the right path ... on that, at least."

"Don't be so hard on yourself. It's perfectly natural to grieve— actually, it's healthy. What's unhealthy is prolonged grieving. Only you can determine when you're ready to move on. And only you determine your happiness."

"Well, I'm nowhere near happy at work."

"Again, ease up on yourself. The perfectionist inside is going to strangle you. My advice is to meditate, find that place of peacefulness— your inner hammock—and put things in perspective."

"That's easy for you to say."

"When's the last time you meditated?"

Uh oh, here he goes again.

"You got me ... um, it's been awhile," she said.

"Meditate right after we hang up. Find your center. You've only been at Pharmical a matter of days. Practice patience—and focus on what you *like* instead of what irritates you."

Brooke blushed as the dreamy CEO popped into her head. And seeing him shirtless. Time stood still for a few moments and her agonizing memories of Tanner disappeared. She said, "I will," with a flurry of blinks.

"How's the blinking?" *Sheesh, this guy's good—does he have me on a camera?*

"Fine," she rubbed her nose.

"Good. Give it time. In six months, you're going to be happy you did. I'm proud of you."

As Brooke hung up, she wondered what Shane would be like as her father. She loved her own dad but Shane's fatherly advice always resonated inside. At times, the lawyer in Weston Ingram, Esq., smothered her. Once again, Brooke sensed Shane was correct. But she wondered if she could last six days, let alone six months. Why do life coaches always piece life into six-month quadrants? Do they manage their own lives in half-year increments? I wonder if he drives his wife nuts.

Discussing Tanner usually stung inside. But not today.

2

Chase drifted into a dreamy state, recalling the moment he noticed Brooke. His heart raced again as he visualized her luscious lips and mesmerizing big blue eyes, framed by long flowing blonde hair. And her body ... her body could stop a freight train. A real-life doll— and with a brain. She had an alluring yet carefree air about her. He wanted her to stand up and turn around as he introduced her.

After the meeting ended, he pretended to have to speak to one of his managers so he could catch her figure as she sauntered out the door.

He prided himself on his level-headedness—the proverbial voice of reason at the company he ran. Today, however, his equilibrium was off. Throughout the meeting, he had a difficult time concentrating, unable to keep his eyes off her. He kept thinking, *why couldn't I find someone like Brooke? My life would be so different.*

The BMW revved and yanked him out of his dream. It screamed like his private plane before takeoff. Uh oh. Chase's eyes widened at the dashboard. He lunged for the stick. After a growl, the engine breathed a sigh of relief. So lost in Brooke, he had missed shifting through second and third gear. His heartbeat raced faster than the tachometer. She was one intriguing and enticing woman.

Why does she have to work for me? With furrowed brows and eyelashes any woman would kill for, Chase squinted into the rearview mirror, hoping for an answer. The only reply was a radio host bantering about the problem with pro sports. He clicked off the talk noise, but the silence didn't help. The focused business whiz was smitten. He had reverted back to freshman homeroom, staring at a cute girl. Only now his crush was forbidden.

Pulling into Pharmical's campus-like office park, he said aloud, "Why does she have to work for me?" as he slammed his car door with a bit more force than usual.

Chase realized he couldn't cross the line in this day and age. She was off limits. He had to be professional—to act like a CEO. But Brooke was even more alluring than Heather had been, and Heather was a one in a million.

"Duke, Duke, Duke, Duke of Earl"—his ringtone—brought him back to earth. Chase answered, "Hello, Oksana."

"Hello Mr. Allman, I am sorry to bother you ..."

"It's no bother—and stop calling me Mr. Allman—it makes me sound old. Call me Chase. I was just about to call you. Tell my little man I'm sorry I'm running late again, but I'll be home soon."

"That is no problem. Take your time. That is not the reason I called."

"Oh."

"Mr. Chase, she called twice today and this time she spoke to me. She asked for Parker."

"No!"

—— ♥ ——

The elevator chimed open and Brooke froze. Chase's lips curled into that sensational smile. With broad shoulders in sturdy posture, he looked even better than in the boardroom.

"Hello. What a pleasant surprise." He extended his hand. While reaching her hand forward, her heel caught and launched her forward—right into his chest. Miraculously, she didn't fall. Instead, he managed to grip her in a bear hug. His fragrance dazzled her nostrils.

"Are you all right?" Chase freed a hand and flipped a switch on the elevator panel. Brooke was impressed he could support her one-hundred-twenty-pound frame with one arm.

A rush of embarrassment blended with a sudden flash of pain. "I'm not sure. I think I hurt my ankle." Her ankle had never fully healed since her running days in college. Judging from the burning sensation, she figured she re-injured it. *Oh great, now I won't be able to run this weekend.* The realization of missing the Run for the Cure amplified the pain.

"Hold on, I've got you. Let's get you off this elevator. Don't let go." Chase clutched her with a lumberjack's grip and then said, "Put your arm around my shoulder."

Brooke liked the way that sounded—and the way his strong hands held onto her. Manly, but with a gentle touch. Sliding her fingers across his firm back, she stopped at his muscular shoulder. Oh! She gasped as her breast pressed up against him. She wondered if he noticed. Brooke's heart raced.

"Oh my!" Ruth Shelby, Chase's overprotective administrative assistant, stood open-mouthed in front of the elevator door. With a sideways glance, she closed her jaw enough to smirk as she placed her hands on her hips.

"Oh, good, Ruthie, can you help us?" Chase ignored Ruth's body language and attempted to appear professional. He couldn't even fool himself, thinking this must look ridiculous. Brooke wanted to shoo her away.

Chase said, "I think she hurt her leg. Here, help me get her to a chair."

Ruth pinched Brooke's free elbow and yanked her away from Chase, causing another writhing pain. Brooke contemplated kicking Ruth with her good foot.

Chase and Ruth guided her to a nearby chair. As he attempted to lower her with sweaty palms, Chase's forearm pressed against her breast. His heart thumped as his groin tingled.

"You really should have that x-rayed," Chase said as he stared at everything but Brooke's ankle.

"I can take her," Ruth announced with a screechy voice that belonged on a corn broom.

"The nearest hospital's across town. I'm heading that way," Chase lied.

"Your car's not big enough." Ruth's eyes narrowed as she crossed her arms over her silicone chest. She had been envious of Brooke since the moment she saw her. She could tell her boss was infatuated with this newcomer. The last thing she wanted was to grant this Barbie doll a chance to flirt with her administrative property.

Chase creased his brow, "Well, it's big enough for me and the passenger seat has the same room." Brooke wanted to chime in *yeah, yeah, yeah*, but instead remained silent. She didn't realize her mouth hung open.

"You have a conference call with Marvin Wixfeldt in an hour. I'll take her."

"I can take that call on my cell."

"You'll lose the connection in a hospital."

"I want to get out of it anyway. Maybe I can blame the hospital for the lost call. I should take her since I'm responsible for her injury." Brooke raised her eyebrow.

"Very well. You're the boss." Ruth frowned, then spun and strode away.

"Can you stand up?"

Brooke loved how Chase's lips formed. *It's not fair that he has lashes like that.*

"I'm not sure. It's starting to swell up."

"Do you want some ice?" Brooke would have loved a frigid painkiller, but didn't want to invite Ruth back on the scene.

"No, if you help me, I think I can make it to your car."

Chase wiped his hand on the side of his fitted trousers and then reached out. Brooke didn't think she needed help—her butterflies could carry her. She grabbed his hand, noticing it was as moist as hers. With her opposite elbow, she struggled to push herself up, then stumbled. Her entire leg felt as if lightning had struck. Her grimace invited Chase closer—not pre-meditated, but enough to do the trick. Inhaling that intoxicating aroma, she eased onto his side again. Despite the excruciating pain, Brooke felt exhilarated and comforted. He had an alluring demeanor. Trusting. Confident.

And *married.*

Brooke felt naked, realizing her breast pressed against him again, but she didn't dare try to move away. I have to calm down she told herself but her heart defied her mind's request. She worried she might go into cardiac arrest in addition to a broken ankle if she didn't relax. Judging from the stink Ruth made, she wondered if Chase rode a Harley. Brooke pictured herself hugging his six pack abs as his strapping upper body guided the motorcycle. This didn't help bring her heartbeat down to human levels. She was looking forward to an intimate ride with this handsome prince, even if he was married.

The elevator door opened and this time—without heels—she managed to make it inside without incident. Chase pressed lower level, where she guessed his mystery mini-ride awaited in a private stall in the company parking garage. The plunge of the elevator felt like a freefall. Neither one wanted another employee to observe them arm-in-arm again. Both of their ears popped just as the floor felt that heavy sensation of stopping.

"I'm right over there," Chase nodded to the right. Brooke followed his gaze and noticed a shiny Harley. Her cheeks flushed. Passing the motorcycle, Brooke sighed. They kept hobbling several feet until Chase stopped at a red BMW convertible—it resembled a chariot. Brooke grinned. *No snuggling, but the ride would be intimate.*

"Hold on a sec," Chase pulled his key from his front pants pocket while holding Brooke. He pressed a button and the sleek car chirped and lit up. Chase opened the door, and Brooke's eyes widened. How can I possibly slide into that low seat without my skirt riding up to my belly button—or my top moving for a nipple shot? Or both. Brooke drew a deep breath then sighed.

"I've got you. Hang on." Chase glanced both ways as if preparing to cross a busy street. Nobody. He lowered his hand just below Brooke's derriere and before she could protest, he whisked her up into his arms. Brooke nearly fainted.

Brooke delighted in his warm sweet breath against her cheek—minty fresh. Their lips nearly touched. She liked this feeling. He clenched her and paused, amazed at how light she felt in his arms. They both smiled and he looked even more handsome up close. Brooke licked her lips.

Chase said, "Let's do this." Brooke closed her eyes, then unconsciously parted her wanting lips just in case.

He lowered her, dashing her desire for a romantic kiss. Her eyes flipped open. He was guiding her feet first into the car. As she sighed, he said, "Try not to move. I'll try not to bang your foot into anything."

"Kay," was all she could mutter. When her feet neared the carpeted floor, he slid his sturdy hand across her backside. Brooke whimpered, overcome with a flash of heat up her spine and back, settling below her waistline.

"Are you okay?" Chase's eyes curved like a concerned doctor about to perform surgery on a loved one.

"I think so." Brooke's eyes fluttered as guilt permeated inside—*how could I think of kissing my boss's boss? Plus, he's freaking married.*

"Try not to move. I promise I won't drive too fast," he smiled with playful eyes.

Chase pulled off his suit coat and set it across the back seat. Brooke's eyes widened. As he slid into his snug position in what resembled a cockpit, her nostrils inhaled his alluring fragrance. Brooke purred inside.

"I really appreciate your—."

The door shut before she could finish the sentence. She adjusted her blouse, realizing it didn't leave much to the imagination. She desperately wanted to pull out her compact to see how red her face looked. She guessed her makeup looked like modern art. *Calm down,* she thought as he opened his door.

The BMW had that new-car smell. She guessed Chase Allman always drove the latest models. The rich leather blended well with his natural aroma. Depressing the clutch, he turned the key. The engine fired up into a suppressed roar. Still fantasizing about running her hands across his chest on a Harley, she delighted in the prospect of observing this dreamy man operate his toy car. She hoped they missed every traffic light.

"Do you care if I lower the top?"

"Huh?" Brooke's stunned look screamed *no chance.* She didn't want one molecule of him to escape. Plus, she pictured her long hair turning into a bird's nest.

"It's such a nice day. I have to put the top down." Brooke bit her lip and frowned. Chase picked up on her hesitation and said, "I have a baseball cap if you're worried about your hair."

"Okay, thanks—you read my mind." Chase chuckled and flashed that wow smile. While reaching for the button to activate the automatic retractable roof, Brooke inhaled like a last breath before a platform dive.

"Would you like that hat?"

"Yes."

Chase reached behind his seat and pulled out a dark baseball hat. Handing it to Brooke, his smile matched the logo—Blue Devils.

Brooke gasped as if he had punctured her lung. "I can't wear this."

"Why not?" His smile remained frozen—cute in a teasing way.

"No North Carolina girl would ever be caught dead in a Duke hat."

Chase laughed so hard that she thought he'd break a rib. Brooke crinkled her eyebrows into a mock frown. He loved the way her eyes sparkled. With laughter tears forming on the outside corners of his eyes, he reached behind her seat and retrieved a Harbour Town Golf Links hat.

"Much better." Brooke flashed an inviting smile that rivaled his. Reaching to exchange it, his fingers brushed against her hand, sending a flutter up her spine. He truly had a magical touch.

"I guess I'll wear my lucky hat just for you." Reaching behind her seat, then sliding the Duke National Champions hat over his brown wavy hair, he released a hearty chuckle. The cap highlighted his eyes in a fresh youthful way.

"Isn't Harbour Town on Hilton Head?" Brooke asked rhetorically, still examining the hat in her hands.

"Yeah, it's one of my favorite golf courses in the world."

"Are you a pro golfer too?"

Chase snickered, "Not quite—I don't play enough to be any good." He opted against telling her about his low handicap, or that he rejected an offer to be an assistant teaching pro coming out of college. Sometimes he wished he had chosen that path—those guys *play* golf and still earn a living—serving as a CEO paid well, but was not child's play. He didn't want to bore her by whining about his past; he was interested in this woman who made his heart thump faster than his beemer's tachometer. "I'm guessing you're not into sports?"

"Why do you say that?" Brooke frowned.

"Oh, I don't know … your gracefulness maybe?"

The tone of his voice activated Brooke's brass ovaries. "Actually, I ran cross country at North Carolina—on a full scholarship." She said *full scholarship* with gusto.

"Seriously?" Chase almost blurted *you're too good looking to be a jock.*

"Why does that surprise you? Actually, I still run every day. Hey, you were able to lift me off the ground pretty easily …"

"We'll have to go running sometime." Chase hoped to shift the conversation and pull his size twelves out of his mouth.

"Where do you run?"

"Same spot as your hat. I have a place on Hilton Head Island. They have great beaches for running."

"Where on Hilton Head?"

"Sea Pines, of course." Brooke frowned, detecting that dukie snobbery in Chase's tone.

"I have a place on Hilton Head also, but I'm too young for Sea Pines." Brooke thought *touché.*

Chase raised an eyebrow. "Really, whereabouts?"

"I own a villa in Shipyard."

"I'm intrigued. What made you buy there?"

There's that condescending tone again.

"It's a long story, but the shortened version is, I wanted a real estate investment and love it there, especially the beaches. I rent it out most of the time."

"It's not too far down from Sea Pines. I run by it all the time."

"Well, I won't be running much for a while," Brooke glanced down, noticing her foot had ballooned to the point of exploding. She also noticed it hadn't bothered her—until now. She was absorbed in this man. Brooke felt carefree and alive near him, something she hadn't experienced for a long time. Then, it struck again—*he's married!*

Brooke rode a rollercoaster in her mind. When she forgot about his marital status, she sensed a strong attraction—the exhilaration of the downward rush of the ride. The understanding that he was off limits—both professionally and personally—resembled the abrupt, head-jarring stop at the end of the ride. But she kept jumping back in line for more.

"We're not far from the hospital. The top orthopedic surgeon is a close friend. I'll see if he's available when we arrive." Chase considered calling but feared missing out on the conversation with this amazing woman seated beside him. He postured upright like the alpha male, a super-hero rescuing the damsel in distress. She wasn't the typical damsel—or Chapel Hill girl. His computer mind churned: without a ring, she didn't match the paradigm of going there for the *MRS* degree. Did she break the mold or was she divorced? Her bio didn't say. He wanted to ask her all the questions but decided now was not the time. *Be professional,* he told himself for the umpteenth time.

"Thank you," Brooke said, sounding genuinely grateful.

"Here we are," Chase said, pulling in front of Duke Raleigh Hospital. His look of pride didn't match his inner feelings—he didn't want the ride to end.

"Oh God, please don't make me wear anything Duke," Brooke's eyes brightened.

Chase laughed. "I'm glad you're not in too much pain. You still have your sense of humor."

"I'm not kidding."

Chase laughed louder, then said, "I'll pull some strings and get a Blue Devils cast on your leg." His eyes dazzled. Brooke wanted to steal his lashes.

"Don't you dare."

Parking at the curb a few feet away from the emergency entrance, Chase set his parking brake, and said, "Sit tight." In a flash, he thrust the door open, jumped out, and jogged toward the oversized sliding front door. Brooke shamelessly stared the entire way. She removed the hat and brushed her hand through her hair. Chase emerged pushing an empty wheelchair toward her. Uh oh. Brooke feared presenting a panty show to her CEO, so she preempted his arrival by shoving the door open, then swinging her legs out. Like a gymnast preparing to dismount, she boosted herself up with both hands and placed all her weight on her good foot. Good so far. As she steadied herself upright, she fell against Chase and lingered for a moment.

"I thought I told you to sit tight?" Chase flashed that smile that could resurrect the dead.

"I'm okay," she blushed, guessing he caught the show anyway.

Chase slid the chair to Brooke's side and before he could move, she lowered herself and then nestled in. Chase marveled at Brooke's derriere. The wheelchair wasn't nearly as much fun as the Siamese twin hug—but she still looked sexy in a peculiar way.

Once inside, the receptionist took over, much to Chase's chagrin. They made Brooke fill out a small forest in rules and regulations—even though her ankle throbbed. Watching Brooke leaf through the countless forms, he wondered how many trees had fallen at the hands of HIPAA. At times like this, he didn't feel proud to be in the healthcare industry. This time though, he reveled in the red tape—he loved watching her slender fingers fondle the forms.

"Boa!" Chase craned his neck as he fixed his gaze on his old college roommate standing nearly on top of him.

Chase hesitated, then said, "Dixie-dawg!" Brooke broke from her paper pile and raised her eyebrow to see who she guessed was Chase's doctor buddy. *Boa?* Nice nickname—did he wrap frilly feathers around his neck? Or is he a snake? Or both?

Dixie-dawg was dressed in a typical dukie uniform—baggy khakis, overstarched button-down with white T-shirt, finished with nerdy glasses and a buzz cut, circa 1950s.

"Boa, you gonna introduce me to your pretty girlfriend or just stand there with your mouth open?"

Brooke thought, I hope this clod's not the doctor.

Chase considered strangling his buddy, but struggled to say, "I thought I left you a message."

"Oh, sorry. I didn't receive anything—but I was in surgery. When they said you were here, I came running out. Excuse me, I'm not used to seeing you in that monkey suit—doesn't look like you're here for another golf lesson."

"Very funny," Chase frowned, then said, "Dr. Dixon Carter, this is Brooke Hart. She works for Pharmical and she took a bad fall. I was hoping you could examine her. She's in pain and all those forms are making *me* sick."

"Pleasure to meet you, Brooke," Dixon said while holding her hand like a princess, then kissing it. He glanced back at Chase—who was wincing—and said, "Anything for you, Boa, or should I say, Mr. CEO?"

As Dixon spun and bee-lined to the reception area, Brooke marveled at how differently men sound when they're around college buddies. They enter a time machine and revert to childish frat boys. None of her girlfriends ever had juvenile nicknames—she was always just Brooke—the serious student and athlete. Brooke wondered what Chase was like in college and what stories were behind silly names like Boa and Dixie-dawg.

"I can wheel you into an x-ray room right now and then finish the paperwork later." Dixon gaped at Brooke as if Chase was invisible.

As Dixon whisked Brooke away, Chase said, "Thanks a lot." Brooke made him feel like a schoolboy—and in a completely different way than his college buddy.

Chase's ring tone startled him—Ruth. "Don't forget your conference call. Marvin made me promise I'd remind you." He frowned.

There's a fine line between forgetfulness and avoidance. In this case, both applied. Chase wished his personal administrative assistant protected him more often, but he was so smitten that his left brain shut down. Over the years, he had developed effective time management skills. Today he wondered what time zone he was in.

He dispensed a feeble, "I was just about to dial when you called." He had dreaded this call; consultants made him queasy—especially Marvin. He plodded outside, away from the crowded waiting area, and dialed.

The half hour with Marvin Wixfeldt passed like an eternal torture chamber for Chase. Marvin had a dictatorial edginess about him. He treated Chase like a pawn. Unfortunately, the high-powered consultant had the attention of key board members, and knew it.

Chase spotted Brooke through the doors—finally he had an out. Dixon wheeled her over with a grin like the Joker. Chase ended the call abruptly, then rushed inside. He noticed the cast on Brooke's leg and said, "That doesn't look good."

"The x-rays are negative, but I'm ordering an MRI just to be safe."

"Then why the cast?"

"When I heard she was a Tar Heel, I wanted to amputate," Dixon said with lips curled in a devilish grin.

"Hey, stop it." Brooke almost called him Dixie-dawg, but didn't want to push her luck.

Dixon continued, "Relax, it's just an air cast to stabilize her leg until the swelling dissipates. You should've iced it for her."

Chase ignored the scolding and said, "If it's not broken, why the MRI?" Brooke's eyebrow rose toward Dixon. Chase figured his college buddy just wanted to see Brooke again. And again, he was right.

"She has a bad sprain but given her previous injuries, I want to make sure there's no scar tissue. Brooke, you'll need to use crutches for a couple of weeks to minimize the pressure."

Chase and Brooke thanked Dr. Dixon Carter as Chase literally pulled the chair handles out of Dixon's hands. He shot Dixie-dawg a scowl, thinking, *you're done—go hump someone else's leg,* then wheeled Brooke out the door. He had parked his BMW just outside the entrance, illegal to anyone but a friend of the good doctor.

The air cast made the injury appear swollen and painful, but it helped stabilize the ankle. The ice pack had numbed the throbbing. Before Chase could walk in front of the wheelchair, Brooke stood up, opened the door, and climbed inside—without incident. She looked pleased to avoid panty peek-a-boo.

Starting the car, Brooke pulled on the Harbour Town hat and Chase slipped on his trusty Blue Devils cap with a smirk. There were a thousand questions he wanted to ask, but didn't dare. Instead, he asked, "How's the ankle feel?"

"Much better."

"Dixon's an interesting character." Chase accelerated, matching Brooke's heartbeat.

"You mean Dixie-dawg?" Brooke's eyes sparkled and almost caused Chase to veer off the road. She wanted to delve into how Chase earned the nickname Boa but thought against it. She wondered what was worse—being a dog or a snake.

"He'll always be Dixie-dawg to me. Around him, I still feel like I'm in college again. Is that weird?"

Chase suddenly had a sweet, vulnerable look—like a cocker spaniel approaching for approval, with tail wagging. Brooke loved the way his lips came to life when he smiled. She wondered if he kissed as good as his lips looked right now.

"That's not weird. Actually, it's funny." Brooke opted to let Chase off the hook, "Don't worry, I won't call you Boa at a meeting."

"How are you finding the transition from GenSense to us?" Chase changed the subject back to his comfort zone and Brooke's eyes narrowed.

"Fine," Brooke lied.

"Well, I'm sure you're impressed with the greater resources at Pharmical?"

Greater resources? More like a corporate death ritual, each and every day, Brooke thought, then said, "I'm starting to get acclimated to the new culture." She rubbed her nose.

"That's good. Well, if there's anything I can ever help you with, don't hesitate to ask."

Yeah, provided I can sneak past Ruth-the-pit-bull. "Thanks. I will."

The return drive passed quickly even though the talk remained work related. Pulling into the garage, Brooke directed Chase to her parking spot—quite a distance from the CEO's. Brooke said, "Thank you so much for taking me in—and getting me such quick medical help."

"My pleasure. It's the least I could do after causing your injury."

"You didn't cause it—I tripped like a klutz."

"You're no klutz. It could have happened to anyone. I guess I can't go running with you for a while now." He flashed that killer smile.

Was he going to ask me to go running? Brooke wanted to say, what about your wife? "Not unless you let me go in a powered wheelchair."

Chase chuckled. "Which one's yours?"

"The silver car on the left."

"Not the Lexus *hybrid*?" He sounded like a dukie and she didn't like the mocking way he said *hybrid*. Against her inner prodding, Brooke didn't take the bait. The last thing she wanted was to argue with the CEO, let alone a dukie who drove a beemer—especially after he so graciously helped her.

Stopping behind Brooke's car, Chase asked, "Can you drive?"

"I think so—I'm right footed."

"Let me help you to your car." Brooke had already opened the BMW's door and started to spring herself out of the low car seat, looking like a seasoned pro. As she hobbled over to her car door, Chase gripped her arm. His sturdy hands provided instant comfort—and heat—something she hadn't felt in a long time.

Brooke maneuvered into her familiar Lexus seat. Chase said, "Maybe we can grab a coffee sometime?"

"I'm not a coffee drinker." The moment Brooke said this—causing Chase's shoulders to slump—she regretted it.

3

He's married. He's married. He's married. No matter how hard Brooke tried, she couldn't expunge her feelings. Chase had it all—good looks, intelligence, plenty of money, incredible body—and a wife! Plus, he was the boss. Two huge strikes against her libido that raged like never before. But she couldn't get her mind off him.

Replaying their day together, Brooke's injury didn't bother her. Driving was a breeze, and even the short walk to her place seemed pain free. Normally, re-injuring her ankle would have ruined her day and zapped all her energy, but not today. He had such a way about him. Carefree, charming, witty and *married.* Her inner see-saw was leading her toward a nervous breakdown.

Brooke swayed in her favorite chair—the same one her grandmother had told her stories from as a little girl. She inhaled, then released a deep sigh. Brooke pondered, *I haven't felt this way in a while.* Most people flipped on TV or music when they arrived home, but Brooke turned to her chair. The rhythmic rocking motion always brought solace, her place of tranquility. Even if it was for a short while, it worked wonders for stress reduction.

While gently rocking, Brooke strained to reach her iced tea—and missed. With her good foot, she slowed to a halt and fixed her gaze on the nearby picture frame. As she gripped the chilled slippery tumbler, Tanner's face drew her out of her trance. A chill shot down her spine.

I'm sorry Tanner. Guilt swirled inside as she stared into the picture. Her stomach twinged and her throat dried. In an instant, her inner harmony shattered as if she had dropped her iced tea on her solid hickory floor. She sipped, yet could barely swallow. Brooke felt as if she had cheated on him.

Jake "Tanner" Hart was her soul mate, the man of her dreams, the love of her life. "I miss you." Tears stung, blurring his face—his handsome face. Brooke blinked hard, causing even more tears to rain off her crimson cheeks. He had been her everything, but nothing she could do would ever bring him back. She cursed the rare blood disease that destroyed him, destroyed their baby, and threatened to destroy her. When he finally gave up the fight, her heart ached as if it went along with him.

Inspecting her ankle, she sighed, realizing she would miss the Run for the Cure this weekend. Brooke felt her neck tighten as her entire leg flared up. The timer beeped for her Lean Cuisine, but she didn't flinch. Her appetite was shot once again.

The ringtone startled her. It was Todd. That's bizarre.

"Hi Todd. How did you know I was just thinking about you?"

"Because I've been thinking about you too." He laughed.

Brooke missed their talks. Todd Hollis represented more than a former boss and mentor, he was a close friend—someone she always felt comfortable around. She said, "Tell me you've changed your mind?"

"Nope. In fact, I have good news."

"Good, I could use some today."

Todd paused, thinking Brooke didn't sound right. "We finally landed an offer on the house. Suzette and I have to be outta here in six weeks."

"I'm happy for you," Brooke half-heartedly replied.

"What's wrong?"

"I miss the old days. This new job isn't doing it for me."

"I tried to warn you. Pharmical isn't for most people. Are they boring you to death or strangling you with rules and regulations?"

"Both. I just don't have the passion for it anymore. I think I need a change. A big one."

"Now you sound like me."

"Not that kinda change. I'm not ready to retire—but I'm happy for you and Suzette." Todd bit his upper lip. Brooke sounded off, just like last time. He considered asking about Tanner, but knew her well enough to hold off.

Instead, Todd said, "Mark Twain wrote 'the secret of success is to make your vocation your vacation.'"

"Easy for him to say. He wrote books about drifting down a river."

Todd chuckled. "Hang in there at Pharmical. You gotta give it at least six months."

"I know, but time there should count in dog years."

"You still have that sense of humor. Hey, Suze is yelling for me. I better see what she wants," he huffed, "talk to you soon."

When she missed Tanner in the not-so-distant past, Brooke always dove straight into her work. Todd had been a great friend, a shoulder to cry on, and a support beam for her. He had the ability to bring the best out of her, personally and professionally. She would have done anything for him. Suzette was one lucky woman. Now, as he prepared to move into his next chapter, Brooke realized she was losing an ally.

Brooke feared she was descending into the same dark hole as three years ago. She just didn't have the passion anymore. Not at Pharmical. Not for life. Staring at Tanner's picture, she pleaded, *Help me, Tanner. I need you.* The tears streamed along their familiar path. She desperately needed a vacation. A permanent one.

I'm not a coffee drinker. The words still stung.

Chase Allman wasn't accustomed to rejection, especially from a new vice president. After all he did for her—obtaining the head of orthopedic surgery at Duke—she shucked him like a bad clam. *She has some nerve.*

Chase rubbed his chin, considering the possibility that he came on too strong. He wanted to ask her to dinner, but his corporate inner guide flashed a bright red stop sign. Getting a coffee was harmless and politically correct. Even if his intentions were cloudy.

His ringtone jolted him. Who's calling this late? Fearing it was Heather, he reached for his cell. The caller ID made him chuckle. He jumped up to close his bedroom door and answered, "What's up, Dawg?"

"You are, Boa." Chase heard music in the background.

"Are you out carousing again?"

"I'm on my way home from another night of pure debauchery. Ladies' night. You should try it sometime." Dixon slurred the last words.

"Hey, thanks for seeing Brooke on such short notice."

"That's why I'm calling …"

"Oh." Chase bit his upper lip.

"You're not tappin' her, are you?"

"What?" Chase's eyes squinted into a glare that could scare Clint Eastwood.

"You're not tappin' …" Before Dixon could finish, Chase cut in, "No! She works for me. Are you nuts?"

"Good, then you won't care if I do."

"Dawg, you're drunk so I won't kick your ass this time. Let me be clear: stay away from Brooke Hart. Don't embarrass me. Act like a doctor for Chrissake."

"But, she's smokin' hot."

"I'm warning you. Don't even think about it. Besides, aren't you engaged? What will wife number three-to-be say?"

"Engaged means *I still have time,* Boa. That's why the woman wears the ring and the guy doesn't."

Ordinarily, Chase would laugh at his buddy's twisted perspective—even revel in it—but he felt a burst of jealousy. He pursed his lips so tightly that he could barely speak, but managed, "If you embarrass me and cross the line with Brooke, I swear I'll kick your ass so hard you'll need a team of doctors to surgically remove my foot."

"Relax, relax. I'm just playin' with ya. Sheesh, where's your sense of humor?"

Chase understood Dixon well enough to know he was serious as a heart attack. His intentions for Brooke were out of bounds. Since college, Dixon consistently earned his Dawg nickname. Though funny in the past, now it struck too close to home.

"Behave. Next time I kick your ass." Chase clicked the off button and silenced his ringer. He noticed tension in his neck and shoulders, hands shaking. He heard a rustling and snapped back to reality. He sat quietly for a moment, hoping he hadn't awakened his three-year-old son, Parker. The only sound he heard was his own heart thumping like a bass drum.

Chase laid down on his Tempurpedic mattress. The foam caressed his back muscles and he focused on his breathing. Thoughts of Brooke swirled in his head, replacing his angst for Dixie-dawg.

4

The elevator door slid open. Brooke whisked in—gracefully this time. He marveled at how her leg had healed in record time. He flipped the lock just as the door closed. Without uttering a sound, their eyes locked and their inhibitions melted. As their lips met, passion exploded. With tongues dancing in each other's mouths, they alternated moans of pure delight.

He had wanted her the moment he saw her. Now she looked even more amazing.

She pressed against him, drawing a primal moan. A rush of warmth enveloped her. As if reading her mind, he slid the straps off her shoulders, releasing the dress to the floor. The room blurred like a steam room. They kissed again with even greater passion. She caressed his slacks, causing his knees to buckle. He throbbed and had to have her.

He carefully lowered his slacks and boxer briefs and the belt clanked against the floor. Her slender fingers gripped him, then began gliding up and down. His knees buckled again but he managed to steady himself enough to unsnap her bra with the flick of his fingers. Their lips met, this time with slippery warm urgency. He was ready to explode as she melted into his arms.

He lowered his hands down her back, driving a tingling throughout. His thumbs slid beneath her thong and eased it off her hips, landing on top of her dress. He glided his strong hands across her firm derriere and gently massaged her. The titillating sensation caused her to coo in his ear.

Their eyes met; he stopped and gripped her. He swooshed her off the ground, as her eyes widened. After an instant where she felt weightless, her legs naturally settled on his hips. He plunged inside her …

Chase felt a strange sensation. He couldn't escape it. Something kept slapping his cheek and then his nose.

Chase shot upright. He rubbed his eyes, and then Duke came into focus. His tail wagged as his tongue bounced up and down on his lower teeth. Usually, this happy face brought a smile. "Aw, Duke, not now."

Damnitall.

Jogging next to man's best friend, Chase lowered his eyes and yelled, "You ruined a perfect dream. Thanks, buddy. I'm not sure who's worse—you or Dixie-dawg?" Duke's ears rose and twitched but neither one slowed from their aggressive pace. Chase shook his head.

He couldn't shake the forbidden dream though. Most of the time his alarm would awaken him and instantly erase his memory of the night's dreams. Duke's tongue bath couldn't wipe out this one. The dream branded an indelible mark—the kind that preoccupied a man throughout the day.

Both man and dog continued their sunrise run, this time with a touch of distance between them. The sun poking through the horizon usually caused Chase to take notice. However, this morning Chase was preoccupied and Duke allowed him his space—as only his golden retriever could.

Chase chuckled, then said, "Didn't mean to yell, buddy. You ever dream of little poodles?" Duke didn't respond.

Brooke's effect on him had become a twenty-four-hour phenomenon. Chase had never experienced a dream quite like this— even back when he was thirteen. It seemed so real. Brooke felt so real. And too damn good.

Grinning, he hummed the popular Aerosmith song, "Love in an Elevator"—he'd never regard the company elevator the same way. Or his new vice president.

Chase slowed to a walk three houses away and his gentle tug halted Duke. Sweat circled his chest and underarms beneath his faded blue and white national championship shirt. He surveyed his home as morning dew blended with the early morning sun, radiating golden prisms and adding heaviness to the air. In another hour, the humidity would overwhelm the Carolina outdoors. But right now, Chase felt euphoric.

He pulled his T-shirt from his abdomen and wiped his forehead. Glancing at his slobbering dog, he wondered if Duke experienced the same runner's high.

"Duke, why do you love running so much?" Chase marveled at how well his trusty dog understood him—except for dreamtime. Duke raised his ears but remained focused on the upcoming fire hydrant. At his usual spot, Duke raised his leg and glimpsing at Chase, he released a loud embarrassing sound—that reeked like week-old Mighty Dog.

Peeking both ways as if readying to cross the street, Chase scolded, "Will you behave if Brooke runs with us?" Duke trotted on.

After grabbing the newspaper off the skirt of his driveway, Chase spotted Oksana tiptoeing down the porch steps in her bare feet. He called out, "Good morning."

"Hi, Mr. Allman."

"Call me Chase. Anything wrong?"

"No, I just wanted to speak with you before I wake up Parker." They now stood within a few feet of each other. Chase stepped backward, hoping his sweaty clothes wouldn't bowl his nanny over. He marveled that even at this early hour, she still made a striking appearance. Nothing like Heather, but well-kept and feminine. He wondered if all Ukrainian women looked like her.

"What happened?"

Oksana turned her head slightly and flipped her brown hair out of her eyes. "She called yesterday." Chase felt a deep pang in his chest as his runner's high dissipated. He was so caught up in Brooke that he had completely forgotten Oksana's call yesterday.

"Are you sure it was her?" Chase bit his lower lip as he squinted into her deep brown eyes.

"I'm sure. She called twice. And this time, she spoke to me."

"What did she say?"

"She asked for Parker. When I said, 'Who's calling please'—like you told me to do—she hung up. But then a few minutes later, she called back." Chase cast an eerie frown. Oksana's lip trembled, and after a hastened breath, she continued, "This time, she asked for Parker again. When I said, 'Who is calling,' she yelled, 'Who do you think you are? You are not his mommy.'"

"What did you say?"

"Nothing. She hung up."

"What was the caller ID?"

"Both calls came in 'Restricted.'"

"That's her all right." Chase stared past Oksana, then asked, "Where was Parker?"

"He was taking a nap and I was cleaning up the kitchen. He did not wake up so I know he did not hear me."

"You did the right thing. I don't want to scare you any more than you already are, but keep an extra close watch on Parker, okay?"

5

What is she trying to do now? It had been eighteen months since Heather vanished. When she fled from the cocoon of Hazelden Treatment Center—after only three days—Chase feared the worst. He doubted his head-strong wife would ever heal on her own.

After a three-month intense courtship, they married with much fanfare. "Congrats, Heather. You got this thirty-eight-year-old corporate hotshot to finally settle down," Dixon Carter, his best man, toasted at their wedding. Heather was the most attractive woman Chase had ever laid eyes on. Stunning. He fell for her immediately.

Chase had completed the accelerated JD/MBA program at Duke in only three and a half years. With degrees from Duke Law School and the Fuqua School of Business, he had several career options. He decided to accept Pharmical Solution's offer for a fast track utilizing both degrees. He started as a corporate attorney, and then was rapidly promoted until becoming CFO within twelve years. With each rung of the ladder, Chase felt the pressure of Pharmical's culture—meaning, if you wanted a shot at CEO, you needed to be a good Baptist, with a wife and two and a half kids.

Heather appeared at the perfect time. Chase considered her more than a career enhancer. Others called her a "trophy wife," but to Chase, she was his everything. He even introduced her as spectacular.

Early on, the couple seemed happy. They were even tabbed "Raleigh's power couple" in the newspaper. However, soon the age difference of fourteen years plus the pressures of the new CEO post mounted marital challenges. The couple bickered over minor things at first, then as Heather became pregnant, they fought more often than they made love. Though she had agreed to raise their children full-time prior to their marriage, Heather never wanted to abandon her modeling career. At twenty-four, she was still in high demand—doing print and television ads for a major cosmetics company. She commanded top dollar and earned every penny.

Then she became pregnant and as her stomach grew for the first time, so did her resentment. She crossed from loving to loathing, and Chase was too busy at work to do anything about it.

By the time she reached her second trimester, Heather felt an emptiness that she never overcame. After giving birth to Parker, rather than feeling natural maternal instincts, Heather despised her new existence. All of her life, she had identified with her looks. She had plenty of admirers. Modeling was her outlet, her way of gaining—and then maintaining—acceptance. Unable to transition to wife and mother, she descended into deep depression. Then the drugs started. Her pity party worsened. More drugs. Her addictive personality compounded the addictions and destroyed her—quickly.

Chase witnessed his beloved, and now mother of his newborn, self-destruct. He pulled some strings to secure admittance in the top rehabilitation program in the country. Then he cut the check for five figures without batting an eyelash. She fought rehab at first, but then agreed she needed help. At least to him.

He never imagined it would come to this. When she ran away, she abandoned everything, including the man who was providing her everything she said she wanted. Chase was devastated.

After she was missing for a week, Chase feared she had relapsed. He understood the grave statistics. He knew relapse meant collapse—total collapse. After a month, Chase burrowed into defense mode. He realized the press would have a field day with the juicy story. He pictured the headlines: Drug Company CEO's Wife Addicted to Drugs. He knew his holier-than-thou board of directors—the same people who anointed him CEO—would oust him in an instant. His whole life, and Parker's future, stood at the whim of others.

At the twelve-month mark of zero contact with Heather, Chase leveraged his connections in the media to secretly file for divorce. It offered the only solution to the recurring nightmare. Heather had ripped out his heart, and he'd be damned if she'd stomp on it in public. He worried about Parker's development without a mother. Then he met Oksana.

The Ukrainian immigrant was a godsend. Twenty-six, educated, and in desperate need of a steady job, she was the perfect candidate to serve as Parker's nanny. He admired her strong family values—she still sent money back home to her parents. With what he was paying her, notwithstanding the nicest roof over her head she'd ever known, she earned more in three months than her father made in three years.

Chase appreciated Oksana the moment he met her. She had a great demeanor and felt passionate about raising children—believing it was her calling. Oksana became an integral part of the family, a surrogate mother. Chase needed her, but he feared that his estranged ex-wife-to-be would scare Oksana away.

The question continued to haunt him. *What is she trying to do now?*

Brooke's ankle throbbed when she awakened. After a fitful night of sleep, she felt as if she was in a war zone—and she was losing. Limping to the bathroom without the use of her crutches, she stopped in front of the mirror. "Yikes, my eyes look like eclipses." Brooke barely recognized herself. *I'm becoming my grandmother.*

There's no way I'm going in to work today, she said to herself. Her reflection actually horrified her. The foot ached so badly that she couldn't even cry, though her bloodshot eyes stung. She hobbled back to her kitchen counter and popped two over-the-counter anti-inflammatories, then wrestled trying to open a child-proof prescription bottle of pain killers. Brooke called out, "How do the elderly do this? It must suck being old."

Finally, she popped the small circular protector off. The contents spilled all over the counter and several landed on the floor. She scooped up three pills—three times the recommended dosage—and popped them in her mouth. In too much pain to grab a cup of water, she mustered enough saliva to swallow the pills, then limped back to bed.

She slept like a teenager.

"Whenever I see your smiling face …"—her ringtone—shook her out of a deep slumber. Usually, the upbeat song brought happy memories of Tanner and going to see James Taylor on their first date. Under the stars, so romantic. Right now, she wanted to stomp on the phone. Without looking at the caller ID, "Hello …"

"Brooke? Is that you?" *I know that voice. Oh shit.*

"Hi, Daddy."

"I was calling to leave you a message. What are you doing home?"

She wanted to say, *what are you doing calling me?* "I'm, uh, not feeling well."

"Oh."

"Actually, I hurt my ankle and I'm going in late today."

"I told you not to run those stupid marathons."

Why does he always have to auto-scold me?

"I didn't hurt it running and I haven't done a marathon in over a year."

"How'd you hurt it then?"

"Long story." The last thing Brooke wanted to do was recant the story of falling into her new boss's boss. *Think quickly.* "Listen, I'm out the door and it's illegal to talk and drive, so can I call you later?" That's it, hit him with the legal angle.

"Okay. But Billy's worried about you. He hasn't heard from you in over two years." *That's it, he's calling to rebuke me for not calling my brother. He didn't even want to talk to me.*

"I'll call him later, Daddy, I promise," she lied.

Brooke sensed her father's intentions were pure, but she felt as if her whole world was tumbling. She hated her job, her mentor was moving away, Tanner still haunted her, and she couldn't clear Chase out of her mind—even with her ankle in such pain.

A different pain shot inside her. Billy, her older brother, suffered from drug addictions and alcoholism and here she was, concerned about herself. She loved Billy. Early on, he was strange—picked on at school and did weird things at home. When they diagnosed her older brother with bipolar disorder, she prayed for him constantly and always thanked God that she was *normal*.

Now he lived in a trailer park and had a menial job, yet never complained. The last time he called her, he was out of it. She lost it with him. Brooke felt horrible afterward. She'd done everything she could to encourage sobriety, and when he failed again, she snapped at him.

After leaving a cryptic message on her boss David's voicemail, Brooke hobbled across the hickory floor of her apartment to the front door. Almost outside, she realized she had better grab her crutches. *I don't want to be yelled at by Dixie-dawg.*

The drive to the doctor's office stressed Brooke. The effects of the drugs lingered, but her foot still ached. She never recalled feeling this much pain in college. *Getting old sucks.* In her early twenties and especially her teen years, things seemed to heal much faster. Though she suffered from recurring stress fractures and minor sprains, she never missed a meet in four years at Chapel Hill. She had held the mile record until two years ago.

Brooke didn't hesitate to skip out on work; the ankle provided enough of an excuse, plus the CEO had advised her to get to the doctor today. She didn't recall ever missing a day at GenSense. Brooke hoped she could drag this injury out. *Maybe I did tear ligaments like good ole Dixie-dawg said.* She feared that he just wanted to hit on her again.

Pulling into the office building near Duke Raleigh Hospital, she rehearsed a pep talk on handling the Dawg if he strayed from professionalism. Dr. Dixon Carter shared an office with eight other orthopedic surgeons. The waiting area was packed with what looked like the walking wounded. Wheelchairs, crutches, slings—you name it. She recalled another time, when she brought Tanner to an office just like this—only in Chapel Hill. Surveying the room as she signed in, she figured this would be an all-day event. She was glad she had brought a book Shane had recommended over a year ago that she had never taken the time to read.

Brooke sighed, then opened *The Bliss List* to page one just as a child's coo rang out from behind her. She turned and met the eyes of an angel. Brooke said, "You're sooooo cute. What's her name?"

A mother in the full leg cast said, "Thanks. She's Marielle."

Without breaking her gaze, Brooke asked, "She's adorable. How old?"

Marielle reached out to Brooke as her mother said, "She just turned six months."

A voice called out, "Brooke." Brooke nearly fell off her chair. *I guess being associated with Chase Allman has its advantages.*

Brooke waved to Marielle while mouthing, "Bye cutie-pie." The infant's toothless smile froze time, until the nurse repeated, "Brooke Hart!"

Once inside, a heavy-set nurse weighed her, measured her height, then took her pulse, temperature, and blood pressure. She actually lost two pounds—not bad for my first day without exercise. It dawned on her that she hadn't eaten anything, so those two pounds were one drive-thru away.

The nurse, trudging as if she had a hip pointer, led Brooke down a bright, aseptic, tiled hallway to an exam room. Even with an air cast, Brooke thought she could beat her in a race. Once inside, she closed the door and handed Brooke a thin cotton robe and said, "Please strip down to your bra and panties. Ties in the back."

Brooke scrunched her eyebrows, holding the garment at arm's length. The nurse scowled, "Do you need help putting it on?"

"No, but is this thing necessary? I just have an ankle injury." Bile formed in Brooke's mouth. She hadn't showered and remembered she was wearing two-day-old panties.

"Ma'am, that's how Dr. Carter examines all patients." Nurse Kankles crossed her beefy arms and released a grunt.

"Okay, whatever. I can manage the robe on my own, thank you." Though Brooke could take her in a foot race, she didn't want to provoke a wrestling match.

Brooke lifted the skimpy robe again and winced. She figured she'd better hurry so doctor Dawg didn't barge in while she changed. She could just hear him telling Chase all about her unmatching bra and panties. Two-day-old panties.

She wrestled out of her clothes in record time—ignoring the pounding ankle—and hastily tied the string behind her as tightly as she could. Her shoulder popped while doing it. She glimpsed at herself in the mirror and gasped. The fluorescent lighting and her hasty makeup job wouldn't land her a Cover Girl offer.

Brooke eased onto the lone chair in the small room and crossed her legs like a tourniquet. The handle moved and the door whooshed open. Then, a feeble knock landed on the already open door. Just as she expected.

"Hi Brooke." Dr. Dixon Carter lunged toward her and extended his hand.

"Hello, doctor." She reached out and gripped his hand. He wore the same dukie outfit: starched white button-down, baggy khakis, boat shoes, and those nerd glasses.

Holding onto her hand a little too long, he said, "Call me Dixon," followed by, "Tough night?"

Brooke bit her lower lip. Hard. "Do I look that bad?" Her dark circles accentuated the narrowing of her bloodshot eyes.

Gulp. "I meant, err, the ankle. You ... you look great today," he fibbed.

"Dixon, I won't argue with you. I barely know you, but you're a bad liar. I look worse than my ankle feels."

"Well, let's take a look." He crouched down and started to fiddle with the air cast. Brooke froze and tightened her legs together. He glimpsed up at Brooke, asking, "Does this hurt?"

"No." At this point, she didn't care if he amputated her leg—he was not going to have a panty peek. Two-day panties. She held firm.

He deflated the cast and she welcomed the fresh cool air. The color of her foot resembled a losing rugby team. "Yikes," Brooke said.

"Not too bad, Brooke, I've handled much worse." He fondled her foot like he had a fetish.

"Well, I hope you washed your hands."

Dixon laughed and said, "You do have a good sense of humor. Chase was right." *Chase was talking about me?* Brooke raised her eyebrow as if begging more information.

"I don't like the swelling, but I think we should be able to get an MRI today. I'll have to ice you down first." Staring at her cleavage, he meant to say *ice it down*. He hoped she didn't notice. She did, but chose to ignore him.

"How long will it take?"

"To ice it?" He broke his gape, "a half hour. An ankle MRI is quick. Assuming you don't need immediate surgery, you'll be outta here in no time."

"Immediate surgery? I don't like the way that sounds."

"I don't mean to scare you. I doubt you need surgery, but I wanna take all the precautions. You're getting the FOD."

"FOD?"

Dixon smirked as he said, "Friend of Dixon. The friend of Dixon advantage."

As she glared into Dixon's flirty magnified eyes through his horned rims, bile returned to Brooke's mouth. Big gulp.

"Let me wrap an ice pack on your ankle. This will be cold for the first few minutes."

"I'm a big girl. I've iced an ankle before."

"When?"

"In college."

"Did you go to Duke?"

"You serious? I could take you criticizing my looks today, but now you've offended me." Brooke's lips curled into a devious smile.

"Don't tell me you're from the dark side?" Dixon crinkled his bony nose causing his glasses to slide down.

"Is that what you call a Tar Heel?"

"Oh my God, Chase didn't warn me. I guessed you were a Blue Devil since you worked at Pharmical. How did you get hired there?"

"That is the million dollar question I keep asking myself."

"Well, coming from UNC, you must be something extra special to work there then."

Most of the time, Brooke enjoyed the North Carolina/Duke banter. But coming from this nerd, she felt offended. Dixon Carter, *Dixiedawg*, gave her the heebie-jeebies. She opted to just stare at her ankle with pursed lips, hoping he'd go away. Dixon took his cue and exited as awkwardly as he entered.

Brooke perched upright with eyes trained on the door handle. She half expected doctor Dawg would barge in to sneak a peek. The ice pack settled on her ankle as little droplets ran off her foot, landing on the tile floor. The sensation shifted from torture to soothing in a matter of minutes. She sighed and remembered Tanner ...

It was raining that day. One of those intense Southern downpours that forces anyone with common sense to wait in shelter until it passes. Late for the appointment, she pulled up to the curb and dropped off her boyfriend. She watched him limp across the soaked pavement and hobble through the automatic door. Wounded and drenched, he still looked attractive.

Jake "Tanner" Hart was entering his freshman season as a highly touted linebacker for the North Carolina Tar Heels. A High School Parade All-American second teamer with good grades, he was heavily recruited and had his pick of Division One schools. He had it all—sprinter speed, vertical leap, strength, and toughness. The dirty blond may have looked like a Beach Boy, but he was one tough football player. Kurt Cobain with muscles.

Because he was a Charlotte native with a father who played varsity baseball at the University of North Carolina, it was a given he'd stay local. After an official visit to USC—mainly to see California—he committed early to the Tar Heels. Brooke Anne Ingram, his high school sweetheart and a successful athlete in her own right, accepted her UNC cross country scholarship soon after Tanner committed. Prom king and queen, they made a striking couple. People—even complete strangers—often stopped and smiled at them. Both from prominent families who actually got along, wedding bells were imminent.

Nearing the end of the grueling two-a-day practices, Tanner had suffered a broken hip during a brutal tackling drill. Brooke had missed it and was glad she didn't witness the injury. She winced when she heard how vividly the bone popped, how Tanner screamed in pain, how his teammates vomited instead of calming him until the paramedics shot him full of morphine.

Listening to the orthopedic surgeon, Brooke understood Tanner's suffering would fall just short of apocalyptic. The thing that amazed Brooke the most was how Tanner never complained. She realized he had to be depressed. It was the first injury he'd ever suffered—in an instant, his dream of playing pro ball shattered—yet he never let on that it bothered him. He hid his emotions. Always did. It probably festered in his youth, but his coach reinforced it: Never let them see you sweat. Ever.

To Brooke, she only saw Tanner in positive light. Even his negative qualities. She adored him. And he adored her. That day in the doctor's office, he looked so vulnerable—and so handsome. When the doctor said he'd have to redshirt his freshman year, he accepted it with grace. She fell in love with him all over again.

Why did it ever have to end?

6

While the hip slowly healed, the young couple grew closer. Brooke did more than merely excite Tanner, she inspired him. He loved her sense of humor, her love of children, and her enthusiasm for life. He was convinced that his hip mended ahead of schedule because of her spirit. They began discussing marriage at the end of their sophomore years.

With Brooke watching his every move on the playing field—even on the sidelines—Tanner started at strong side linebacker his junior year and was elected team captain as a senior. Though the hip still nagged him, he never let it show. Brooke's athletic accomplishments rivaled Tanner's. She lettered all four years and set three school records as a senior.

During graduation week, Tanner dropped to one knee and Brooke's eyes immediately welled up as she covered her mouth in astonishment. In a deliberate and serious tone, he said, "Brooke Anne, I can't even put into words my love for you. You have always been there for me. Through my highs and my lows. I can't promise you a life of highs, but I can promise you I'll love you always. You are my everything." His lip quivered as he whispered, "Will you marry me?"

Tears streamed down Brooke's creamy complexion. Too choked up to speak, she nodded rapidly, then drew a deep breath, smiled, and said, "Yes. Oh my God, yes!"

They married one year later.

— ♥ —

A loud clank shook Brooke out of her daydream. Even though it was so long ago, her memories of Tanner never faded, just like their dream love. She heard a knock, then the door swung open. There stood

Nurse Kankles holding a wheelchair. She eyed Brooke, then asked, "Are you all right?"

Brooke sniffled and swept her fingers under each eye. "I'm fine."

"Okay, I'm going to cart you to your MRI."

Brooke glanced away, still leery of her appearance, and said, "I can probably walk on it. The ankle doesn't even hurt."

"Sorry, honey. Doctor's orders. Take my hand." Her man hands matched her kankles.

The MRI lasted ten minutes, and Brooke clung to her tiny smock the entire time. Thankfully, happy doctor Dawg didn't come in panting; she just wanted to throw on her sensible sweatpants and unrevealing T-shirt.

The test results were ready after only twenty minutes; Brooke figured a few days. There definitely were some advantages to the FOD thing she thought, as long as he doesn't look at me.

Dr. Dixon Carter explained that she only had a bad sprain. Aside from some typical signs of wear and tear consistent with a cross country runner, she should heal in a few months.

"Great, that's good news. Thanks for everything, Doc. I can see why Chase thinks you're the best." The moment the words left her mouth, Brooke regretted it.

"I'm flattered."

"Is there anything I can do or some prescription you can write me to help it heal faster?"

Dixon's mouth curled into a fiendish grin. He said, "Sure, my hot tub tonight. I'll pick up a prescription for Moet & Chandon bubbly. Works wonders."

Brooke felt like hurling what little food she had in her stomach. Her expression caused Dixie-dawg to actually back up one step, nearly falling into the corner. Usually, Brooke's Southern manners trained her to be polite no matter what. Rather than a customary *no thank you*, she said, "Um, no, I'd like to keep this professional." She wished she had a rolled-up newspaper.

Dixon mumbled, "Well, if you change your mind ... maybe some other time when you're feeling better?"

Brooke's scowl propelled him out of the room without even attempting to respond. After scurrying out the door that shut harder than usual, she thought, *what kind of person has friends like this?* She pictured Dixie-dawg sifting through her personal records, causing a wave of nausea.

— ♥ —

Brooke's ankle still ached and she considered cancelling her appointment again. After pulling the ice pack from her freezer—the thought of Dixon touching it still repulsed her—she secured it around her ankle with an Ace bandage. The first few seconds felt especially frigid, even more agonizing than last time; she wished the pain would subside. And hopefully help ease the trip.

The throbbing dissipated as Brooke merged onto the I-40 onramp toward Greensboro. Though it was not too late to turn around, the trek to visit her father was long overdue. She figured he would want to spend more time than lunch today.

Though Weston Ingram still considered Brooke his little girl, he was tremendously proud of how she'd turned out. They had a special bond that survived life's phases. Brooke spent her first ten years idolizing him, the next ten despising everything he did and resenting him for ridiculing her dream of working with children—and the rest of the time since, regretting how she had treated him. If anyone could overcome suffering, it was her father. She still called him Daddy, and probably always would. In fact, Brooke enjoyed her father—and didn't know what she'd do if she ever lost him.

A good number of Brooke's friends had been raised primarily by their mothers, a reality of society's divorce rate. None of them had fathers in their lives like Brooke did. Though most people viewed the day Brooke was born as a tragedy, she didn't. She never knew her mother—never had the chance—yet she felt her loving presence through her father. Seated on his lap as a child, Brooke enjoyed hearing stories about her mom. She was a radiant woman who selflessly made the ultimate sacrifice. Brooke often wondered what her mother would be like today and how her life would be different if she hadn't died while giving birth to her.

Brooke realized her father must have grieved hard after Mary, his beloved wife and the mother she never knew, died so tragically. She understood the feeling of despair all too well. She wondered if he ever blamed her. If he did, he only let on once. On her sixth birthday, after he tucked her in, she remembered feeling scared. Clutching her blankie, she had wandered into his bedroom and caught him crying. As his eyes met hers, she asked, "What's wrong, Daddy?" He said nothing, then wiped his eyes and said, "Go back to bed, sweetie."

She scrutinized his hands, noticing their wedding picture and the tears smeared across the glass. With a tender voice like a little angel, she asked, "Do you miss Mommy?" He nodded with chin wobbling and trembling lips, unable to speak. After a long pause and another swipe at his eyes, he drew in a deep breath, then said, "I do … but I love you with all my heart. You're my princess. You're as beautiful as she was. Now go back to bed and dream sweet dreams."

That night was her earliest memory of her father. She guessed each birthday brought out the same bittersweet emotions. When she spoke of her ritual trips to Tanner's gravesite, he had a knowing that stemmed from experience. Today, she wanted to talk about moving on, but since he never remarried, she wondered if he ever had.

Brooke merged onto I-85 South heading toward Charlotte. She always dreaded this hour and a half part of the drive. The mundane highway lulled her to sleep. One of the few highlights of I-85 was the Lexington stop. Her mouth watered thinking about the Honey Monk— the world's greatest BBQ—especially since she skipped breakfast. She said, "Not today," her father would kill her if she showed up full.

Brooke dialed his landline. After five rings, voicemail—the ancient kind that played the message out loud on the phone. She left a message as quickly as she could. Most people could be reached via cell phone. Or, better yet, if they were out, they would forward their landline to their mobile. Not Weston Ingram. The media fear mongers had him convinced that cell phones caused brain tumors. With the ten minutes a month he'd use a cell phone, if cancer struck him, then the entire human race would end in Verizon Armageddon. She didn't feel like talking now anyway, he'd get the message.

Aside from outdated beliefs about the Japanese and irrational cell phone phobia, her father was a brilliant man. After winning the prestigious Morehead Scholarship and its free ride to UNC—where he met Mary—he attended Duke Law. The *Duke Law Journal* accepted him in his second year, and then he finished the following year with a perfect GPA. With those credentials, Weston Ingram could work anywhere in North Carolina. He chose the oldest law firm in Charlotte. After becoming the youngest partner, he rose to the top by age fifty-eight. Though he was still senior partner at sixty-two, he talked about retiring and making golf fun. Brooke knew he would never retire and, given his impatience, feared golf would kill him.

On rare occasions, Brooke didn't heed her father's advice. She had to admit, most of the time, he was right. But despite her own dreams, he always wanted her to be an attorney. His expectations were beyond merely obtaining a college degree; he wanted her to follow his career path and have what he had. She didn't dare tell him that many of her friends had doubts about her chosen path since it did not appear to involve children, which she had always dreamed of. Then, when North Carolina offered her a free ride, the conclusion was forgone. In the middle of Brooke's senior year in college, being a lawyer just didn't feel right.

Brooke had mulled over the legal profession, due to her father's not-so-subtle prodding and out of respect, but she ultimately decided against it. Analyzing career options, she simplified her choices: doctors diagnose, buyers haggle, teachers teach, businesspeople discuss and present, but lawyers argue. It boiled down to not wanting to bicker with people all the time. She couldn't imagine entering the profession with her *can't we all just get along?* attitude. And she couldn't imagine Weston Ingram, Esq., doing anything else.

Noticing the exits, the two and a half hour drive seemed to fly by. Glancing in the rearview mirror, she grimaced. Daddy's little girl looked like the before picture. Oh, well, he'll understand.

Turning into Myers Park, memories resonated. Happy memories. Myers Park served as a perfect place to grow up, and welcoming even after moving away. One-hundred-year-old majestic oaks imparted a sense of historic identity. Brooke turned onto Queen's Road, with its stately mansions on plush green one-acre lots separated by tree-lined dogwoods in the median.

While pulling into the semi-circle driveway, Brooke spotted her father perched on his front porch in his favorite spot—a rocking chair similar to hers. He grinned, then waved as he stood. He had dressed up for her once again. He glanced at his watch as usual and she wondered how long he had been sitting there.

With the car in park, but still running, Brooke lowered her window, and said, "Hi, Daddy."

Placing his hand on her car door, he said, "You're a little late. I was worried about you."

"I left you a message. Besides, I'm not late. I told you I'd get here in time for lunch. It's not even noon yet."

He squinted at his watch again, just to make sure, then said, "I bet you're hungry."

"Actually, I ate a big breakfast," she lied.

"Well, I'm famished. I have a reservation at the club. I want to go before it gets too crowded."

Brooke didn't feel like the country club scene—definitely not the Charlotte Country Club—especially in her outfit. "I'm not dressed properly."

"Nonsense. You look fine," he strained to inspect her ankle. "Plus, you have an injury. We don't have to go to the Mecklenburg Dining Room. We'll grab a sandwich at the Byron Nelson Bar."

When he furrowed his bushy brown brows, she knew it wasn't optional; he obviously wasn't going to take no for an answer. He wore his customary country club ensemble: light yellow slacks, striped blue Brooks Brothers' button-down, and blazer. He looked dead set on showing off his daughter. "Okay, we can go if you want. Get in."

He pulled her door open and grimaced. "You shouldn't drive on that ankle."

"I just did, Daddy. For two and a half hours and I made it here just fine."

"Let's take my nice big car. I don't think you should drive any more than you have to." Sick of driving, Brooke conceded. Her father didn't make senior partner at the law firm by losing many arguments, including with his little girl. She reached down and untied the bandage, flipping the slushy warm ice pack to the car's floor.

"Let me help you." He gripped Brooke's shoulder as she turned to step out.

"I'm okay."

"Where are your crutches?"

"I haven't used those things yet. They're more of a hindrance." Struggling to stand, she wished her father would loosen his grip. His rigid fingers dug into her shoulder like arrows. She wanted to tell him to let go, but realized he was just being a Southern gentleman. Brooke recalled Chase and his strong yet tender touch.

She slinked, favoring her good foot, with her father still clenching her arm too tightly—like a tourniquet. He led her to the key pad on the side of the three-car garage, punched in the code, then still clutched her as the door opened. She noticed the Arnold Palmer Cadillac license plate holder. He opened the heavy door for Brooke without loosening his grip on her.

"Thanks," Brooke swung her bad ankle in, then hopped up and slid inside. She appreciated the comfortable, wider seats, but smiled as she thought about the BMW. She settled, relieved he was driving—she wouldn't have to hear him try to drive from the passenger seat.

When he started the car, the vents burst warm air into Brooke's face. The stereo blared a classical piece that might have been recognizable at human decibels. He was oblivious. "I haven't seen you in a long time." He shifted the car into reverse.

"Huh?" Brooke hoped he would kill the turbo hair dryer and supersonic stereo—she didn't dare mess with his controls.

"I said, I haven't seen you in a while."

Brooke grimaced, causing her father to lower the music, but he left the air conditioner howling. As if screaming into a fan, she said, "I know. I've been busy."

"I thought I'd see you last week. Did you visit Elmwood Cemetery?"

That didn't take long. Brooke's eyes fluttered a flurry of blinks. "Um, yeah, I did."

"I thought you might stop by ..."

"Daddy, you know that's a tough day for me. I'm never feeling social on that day."

"I understand." He glanced away.

Brooke bit her lower lip and sensed her father's contemplation. The two remained quiet until they arrived at the pillared entrance of Myers Park Country Club.

"Here we are. I'll drop you off at the front." Always the Southern gentleman.

Standing at the curb, favoring her good leg, Brooke marveled at the parklike grounds. Rolling hills met magnificent oak and maple trees forming around the famous Briar Creek. She learned to swim, swing a golf club, and hit a tennis ball here. Happy times.

Brooke didn't feel like Charlotte Country Club today and was glad that her dad didn't persuade her to go there. In Weston's world, persuade meant demand. She didn't want to watch him work the room. But the real reason, the memories of her wedding, were too much for her to handle today.

Weston grinned as he ambled up the sidewalk, nearing his daughter. She truly was the apple of his eye. Even in her thirties, she still resembled the seventeen-year-old prom queen. Another couple strolled within earshot of Brooke as Weston called out, "My, you are one beautiful girl."

Brooke blushed, partly because both strangers glanced over their shoulders, but mainly because, even though she felt unattractive, her daddy made her feel good. As only her daddy could.

"Thanks. You're not so bad yourself—for an old man." They both laughed.

Weston grabbed Brooke's hand, kissed her cheek, and the two of them shuffled toward the door. "I think your leg's healed. You walk better than I." Weston smirked, then lunged ahead for the door. She smiled as she let go of his hand and entered, noticing her foot had improved.

The convivial Byron Nelson Bar rekindled Brooke's appetite. With the thoughts of mouth-watering barbeque still lingering from the drive, her stomach growled. They strolled across the stodgy room that resembled an old library more than a bar, settling on a table at the window. Her nose detected good grease, bringing her lips into a curl. Her father seated her.

A fifty-something career waitress weaved her way through the half-full lounge. She forced a tepid smile that matched her weary eyes while she scribbled their matching drink orders—iced tea, unsweetened. Brooke felt like a margarita, but didn't want the lecture about drinking and driving; Weston always waited until five o'clock for any alcohol.

Weston inhaled a deep breath and while exhaling, said, "It's good to see you."

"Good to see you too. Sorry I missed last Saturday."

"I understand. You've been busy and what, with the injury and all. What are you doing with your spare time, now that you can't run?"

"It's only a sprain. Even though it's painful—more painful than any of my stress fractures in college, I'll be running in no time." She nodded toward her foot as her ankle started to ache.

"Well, don't push it. Let it heal this time. Hey, this is one of the few times I could beat you in the mile." He laughed at his own joke while Brooke smirked. Glancing out the oversized window wall, she spotted a few golfers on the putting green. She recalled her earliest memories of golf. Brooke and Billy would tool around on the practice green before Daddy pulled up in the cart. Then, she would perch on his lap as he drove them to the first tee. Though too little to play, her dad let her putt on the real greens alongside him.

From her early teens, they used to jog together. At first, it was around the block, then a few blocks, then around the neighborhood, until they would run for five miles. She still remembered beating him for the first time.

If it weren't for her father, she never would have set records in cross country. Brooke had fond memories of running with him as she conditioned for a new track season. After running five miles at a brisk pace, they'd play a best-of-five tennis match—right outside where they were now seated. The courts seemed bigger then, but rekindled the same warm memories.

Weston surveyed the surrounding tables and nodded to a man nearby whom Brooke didn't recognize. Always working the room, Brooke thought. "How has your shoulder been?" Brooke drew her daddy's gaze back to her.

"It still hurts when I swing a golf club."

"That's probably a blessing. Makes you slow down your swing." They both laughed.

"How's work?"

Brooke sighed, "I'm not sure." Weston's bushy brows furrowed as his dark brown eyes intensified.

"What do you mean?"

"I miss GenSense ... this new place just isn't right for me."

"I warned you about Pharmical."

Brooke hoped he wouldn't do this. "No you didn't."

"You know I battled against that company."

"Oh come on, it was what—four years ago?"

Weston Ingram represented three wrongfully terminated employees of Pharmical: a general manager fired two days after his sixtieth birthday, a sixty-two-year-old scientist, and a fifty-eight-year-old sales manager. None of the dismissals was "performance related"—like the company claimed. All three had been replaced by much younger outsiders. "It wasn't that long ago."

"Well, I'm not worried about age discrimination. I'm the youngest senior manager they have."

"It's not age discrimination. It's the way they treat people. Pharmical just doesn't follow the golden rule. They should have settled those cases out of court without smearing three good people in the process."

"It's a whole different company today."

"Not as long as that CEO is still there. That guy could scare a great white out of the water."

Brooke's eyes widened. First, his college buddy called him a snake and now her father called him a shark. She'd perceived an entirely different side. Now's not the time to defend Chase Allman, she decided.

"Look, I'm their youngest vice president, they pay me a ton of money, and though it's not my dream job, it could be worse." She couldn't believe she was now defending the company she loathed. Daddy could draw her into any debate.

"Excuse me, are you ready to order?" Weston shifted his eyes from Brooke to the waitress.

Ordinarily, Brooke would have asked the waitress to come back later, but she was thrilled by the interruption. "I'll have the Reuben."

"Would you like to substitute a salad for the fries?"

"No, I'll have the fries. And can you bring ketchup?" The waitress smirked as she jotted on the small pad. Weston frowned.

"I'll have the blackened grouper with rice. And can you bring me an ice water with a fresh lemon?"

"Right away, sir."

"Hungry? Thought you had breakfast." Weston raised one eye brow at Brooke.

"Actually, I'm starving. I haven't been eating right lately."

"You've got to take better care of yourself."

Here we go again with a food debate. "How come you never order a Reuben?"

"Well, I don't like corned beef or Swiss cheese. And sauerkraut gives me gas."

"Ewww. Too much information."

Weston chuckled, then eased into a fatherly grin, "Well, you asked. Don't expect me to misrepresent myself."

Brooke glanced away. *Does he always have to sound like Perry Mason?*

Weston continued, "You never told me about your visit to Elmwood Cemetery."

I can see why he is so good in court—he's relentless. "Actually, I'm glad you asked. For the first time, I feel like I'm ready to move on."

"That's great. Are you seeing someone?"

"No, Daddy, I'm not." Brooke's lips pursed as if she bit into a lemon.

"Well, it's been long enough. It's time you dated."

"I'm not going through this with you again. I've *been* dating."

"You've never dated anyone more than once."

"Sheesh, enough already. It's not like flipping a switch and voilà, there's Mister Right at my doorstep."

"You're not even trying though."

"Look who's talking?" Brooke paused and bit her lip as her father's expression darkened. She gritted her teeth, wanting to retract her lack of tact.

"I've been meaning to say this to you since Tanner died."

Brooke's eyes widened, mouth opened. She wished her sandwich would arrive right now. It didn't. Weston continued, "The day your mother died was the saddest day of my life," he paused, having to breathe, "if it weren't for you, I wouldn't have ever made it." His voice cracked. She understood what he meant all too well.

Weston closed his eyes tightly, then popped them open, "But there's a reason for everything. We all die. I just couldn't figure out why God had to take my Mary when He did." He swallowed hard, "But, I knew you were His gift in return. I wallowed for a long time, then I poured everything into you. I tried to be your mother and father all in one. Sometimes, I failed, but I kept on trying. You turned out okay. Hell, you turned out better than just okay. But now I see so much of myself in you. It's almost like you're me thirty years ago. I shut down then. I wouldn't let anyone in. There were plenty of chances, but I didn't take 'em. Now, I'm an old man without a partner to share life with. Don't make the same mistake I made."

Brooke gulped so hard she almost choked. She'd never heard her dad ramble like this. She almost didn't recognize him. The usually stoic facade had cracked, leaving only his heart. He glanced away, chin wobbling. Brooke widened her eyes as tears clouded the already dim room.

After a long pause, imbued with emotions that swirled like a hurricane, Brooke said, "I won't—"

The clanking dish startled father and daughter. "Reuben for the young lady. With fries. I brought you extra ketchup."

Brooke's appetite had gone from unquenchable to invisible in a matter of seconds. She stared at the Reuben she had so craved as if it was suddenly covered with mold. The fries she would have killed for earlier now smelled repulsive. She sipped her iced tea, then eyed her daddy. He cut a piece of his fish and forced it into his mouth. He reached for his water and gulped. She could tell his mouth was too dry to eat properly. Just like hers.

Neither one of them spoke while they struggled to eat. Brooke managed to consume half the sandwich and hardly touched her fries. For the first time in as long as she could remember, her daddy left food on his plate.

"Would either of you care for dessert?"

Both Brooke and her father replied in unison, "No." Weston said, "Please just charge this to my account."

"Right away, Mr. Ingram. Have a nice day. Hope to see you soon."

During the short drive back, with the air conditioning still blasting in her face, neither of them spoke. As Weston pulled into the driveway, he said, "You wanna come in for a while?"

"Not today, Daddy. I have a long drive and my foot's hurting."

Weston shot a look of dejection, "At least let me grab you a fresh bag of ice."

"Sure." As much as Brooke just wanted to bolt out of there, she had to allow her daddy to be the gentleman. And her ankle throbbed.

After Weston shuffled into the house, Brooke stepped out of his Cadillac. She hobbled over to her car, jumped in, and started the engine. Within a minute, her father emerged from the garage carrying a gallon-sized cellophane bag packed with crushed ice. As he handed it to her, he said, "Are you sure you have to leave so soon?"

So soon? The last hour felt like an eternity. She wanted to say something wise like, it's Saturday, Daddy, how am I going to meet a guy hanging out with you, but instead, "Thanks for lunch, Daddy. I'll see you soon."

"Remember what I said."

"I will. Don't worry about me. Take care, love you."

Driving away, Brooke felt drained. Her emotional tank ran dry. Visiting Tanner's grave, Todd moving away, the job she dreaded, and her aching ankle, all descended on her like a landslide. Between Shane, Todd, and her father, she had plenty of advice about life. She realized they were all right—in their own ways—but she also understood life had to be on her own terms.

It's not that I don't want a man—it's that Mister Right is my boss— and he's already taken.

7

The shrill ring startled her. Her office landline still sounded foreign to her. And Monday mornings were never Brooke's high achievement intervals as her life coach liked to call them. She had been thinking of calling Shane and hoped it was him, but caller ID revealed a local number. "Hello, this is Brooke Hart."

"Good morning, Miss Hart. It's Ruth Shelby from Chase Allman's office. Do you have a moment?" Brooke shot upright in her chair. She hated being called Miss Hart, but thought against arguing.

"Yes, of course. Hi, Ruth." Brooke almost called her Miss Shelby but bit her lip instead.

Bypassing the return hi and small talk that usually ensued, Ruth said, "Mr. Allman would like to schedule a meeting with you today."

Big gulp. *Why? Am I getting fired?* "I'm free most of the afternoon."

"Mr. Allman has an available time slot at 2:15 p.m. Does that work for you?" Brooke sensed it was a rhetorical question since her company Outlook was blank all day.

"Yes ma'am."

"Good, he'll see you at 2:15 p.m. sharp."

"Ruth?"

"Yes, I'm here. Do you have a question?"

"What is the purpose of the meeting?"

"You'll have to ask Mr. Allman." Ruth sounded like the wicked witch in *The Wizard of Oz.*

"What should I prepare for the meeting?"

"I don't know … prepare to answer his questions. You may want to bring a progress report on Integrated Client Services."

Brooke wanted to slap Chase's surly guard. "Thanks for your help," Brooke said with saccharine coating, "I'll be there at two-fifteen." Right after hanging up, Brooke said, "Beee-atch." She ducked her head into slumped shoulders and hoped nobody heard.

Peering out her fifteenth floor window, Brooke's pulse pounded. Adrenaline surged for him as hackles rose from Ruth. Her petty insolence reminded her of the *bitches and backstabbers* in high school. And it all stemmed from jealousy. She wondered why Ruth felt threatened. Is it because I'm younger? Or because I'm a vice president? Or is it something else?

GenSense never had a real pecking order. Everyone felt important. It extended far beyond the company-wide profit sharing—people just followed the golden rule and worked with a sense of purpose. Pharmical was too big and profit hungry. Perhaps not sharing equitably in the wealth created a monster. Whatever the case, she sensed Ruth couldn't be trusted.

A tendril of panic formed in Brooke's stomach—how am I ever going to prepare a progress report for a division that had made little or no progress since I joined?

"Excuse me, Chase." He dropped his hands from the back of his head and gripped the sides as he spun around on his ergonomic leather chair.

"Hi, Ruth." He smiled that warm smile that made her melt.

"Brooke Hart is scheduled for 2:15 today."

"Great, thank you."

"Oh, and she was all worried about the purpose of the meeting." Ruth raised her eyes.

"She shouldn't be. What did you tell her?" Chase hoped Ruth didn't press him. The fact of the matter was he couldn't shake Brooke from his mind. He used the ankle injury as an excuse to see her.

"I said you just wanted to have an informal discussion."

"Perfect, thanks. Can you shut my door on your way out?"

Chase waited until Ruth settled her petite torso at her cubicle. With the door closed, she would hold his calls. *I'm lucky to have Ruth. I don't know what I'd do without her.*

He lifted the telephone off the receiver—the actual landline. This call couldn't be made from his unprotected cell or office speakerphone.

He had used speakerphone on so many conference calls lately that the real phone felt strange. It matched his insides.

The call was answered on the second ring. Chase lowered his head almost between his legs, and said, "Can you hear me, Max?" The call lasted less than a minute—nothing new to report, as Chase had feared. Listening to the gruff private eye, Chase questioned Max's competency. This was different than chasing around a philandering spouse with a high-powered zoom lens. If exposed, Chase Allman stood to lose it all.

Chase had been dreading the next call. But he didn't dare ignore him. Nobody blew off "The Butcher."

Brooke scrambled to pull up and print reams of reports. She had a tough time asking Cheryl, her shared assistant, for help—Brooke still didn't understand the inner workings at Pharmical; plus, it wasn't in Brooke's nature. Back at GenSense, she had served as her own assistant—answering her own calls, drafting her own letters, even getting herself her own iced tea. She wondered if Chase treated Ruth as his coffee gopher. As much as she loathed Ruth, Brooke hoped he wasn't *that guy*—the one who thought his time was more important than someone else's. CEO or no CEO, he was no different than another human being.

Though hunger pangs growled, Brooke had no time for even a drive-thru. And she couldn't imagine asking Cheryl to fetch her a chef salad, without croutons, and fat-free dressing on the side.

At 2:06, panic extended well beyond tendrils. She drew a deep breath. *I don't know what I'm doing ... and I don't even care. How much could he expect me to know? Is he following up on my injury? What was he really interested in?*

Another deep breath. Time to find out.

Though the ankle still ached and, carrying a full briefcase didn't help, she advanced without wincing. Brooke had always had a high threshold for pain. She followed orders, icing it at nighttime—when it hurt the most—and attempted to stay off of it. The whole experience actually helped her avoid unnecessary tasks. She sensed this meeting would be anything but unnecessary.

Entering the elevator, she felt a whisk of relief as she slinked inside without incident. It was empty and she rested on the wall while pressing the button for the top floor. She laughed, thinking she didn't even know which office was his—or if it was on the top floor. Hey, maybe he's not the guy who has to play king of the hill at the top of the corporate kingdom. She doubted it—he wasn't the communal, cubicle type.

The elevator bumped to a stop and the door slid open. She stood for an awkward moment, then lunged forward, feeling lost. This floor didn't resemble hers—it was much nicer. Pharmical had its own C-floor—so unlike GenSense. Like walking into a Hyatt from a Holiday Inn. Her face scrunched into a sour expression.

Brooke strode to the double glass door and nearly rammed right into it. The door failed to open like every other door in the building. She spotted a mini box that required a card. She cupped her hands and peered inside through the darkened glass. Brooke spotted a receptionist several feet away, engrossed in her monitor. Brooke waved. Nothing. She knocked. Nothing. Growing impatient, Brooke knocked harder. Still nothing. Finally, she noticed Miss Screensaver broke her trance and glared her way. A buzzer sounded and the door whisked open.

Brooke shook her head while stepping inside. She felt as if she was on the set of *Star Trek*. She half expected to see guys with pointed ears running around. She laughed as she visualized dukies at a basketball game, bouncing up and down in their courtside seats—with Spock ears and their little Blue Devil shirts.

Brooke plodded toward the desk of the C-floor gatekeeper. Nope, her ears were normal. "Hi, I'm Brooke Hart. I'm here to see Chase Allman."

"Where's your tag?"

"I work here."

"Where's your tag?"

Brooke frowned, "I don't have one."

"And you work here?"

"Yes, I'm new … vice president of Integrated Client Services."

"I'll phone Mr. Allman's administrative assistant."

"Thank you." Brooke sighed.

After speaking into her headset, the gatekeeper glared at Brooke and said, "Ruth—Mr. Allman's assistant—is on her way. You really need to carry a pass for security purposes." Not, I'll get you a card of your own. So much for Southern hospitality on the C-floor.

Brooke spotted Ruth and was mildly surprised she could travel without a corn broom. She guessed Ruth was in her late forties, with a weathered face but a nice figure. Brooke was puzzled by Ruth's jealousy. Ruth scurried right in front of her and in a voice much too loud for the short distance, said, "Well, I can see you're walking just fine. I guess the injury wasn't so bad after all."

Brooke forced a smile, "It's still a little sore, but I'm much better, thanks." *How about hello or would you care for some iced tea? Was Ruth this pathetic? What's Chase doing with a witch like her?*

"Chase is still on an important call. It should end soon. Follow me."

Brooke struggled to keep up and hoped to slow her by asking, "How long have you worked here?"

Ruth peered over her shoulder, turned her chin upward, "I've been with Chase for six years now." Ruth's tone rubbed Brooke the wrong way, almost sounding possessive. *Is she attracted to him?*

"Well, I'm sure you're good at what you do then." No response. Even to a compliment. Brooke tried hard to connect with this woman, but she seemed more distant than the North Pole—and twice as cold. Shane's psychological profile tabbed Brooke as having "predominant interpersonal skills." Or, in plain speak, a people person. But Brooke wondered how Shane would characterize Ruth—probably suffering from interpersonal setback.

Brooke shifted gears, and asked, "How long have y'all been in this building?" Brooke didn't mind that she let another *y'all* slip—aloof to the impression it left with Broom-Hilda.

"As long as I've been with Pharmical. I moved to the top floor with Chase three years ago. I can still remember the day we were promoted to CEO."

We? Okay, I give up. This woman's got some Chase issues. Ruth could outdo Kathy Bates's character if they ever filmed a remake of *Misery.* Brooke followed without uttering a word. Ruth bee-lined to the corner of the floor and asked Brooke to take a seat in yet another boardroom, adjacent to what she guessed was Chase's office. Settling in to the expensive-looking leather chair, Brooke heard Chase's voice. She guessed he was on the phone. Even muffled, he still delivered a manly radio announcer's voice. She blushed, then repeated to herself *married, married, married.*

After what sounded like a phone slamming, Chase's door flew open. Brooke thought she heard Ruth say, "Miss Hart is in the conference room."

"Hi there."

Once again, with back turned, Brooke missed another dramatic entrance. She spun the chair and he stood right in front of her like a Greek god. He reached out his hand. Brooke lost control of the chair and it spun, inches away from hitting him where it counts. Red faced, she struggled to gain her balance—and keep her legs together. "Hello again." He eyed her carefully.

Still seated, Brooke grabbed his hand—firm, yet not overbearing, matching his grip. She hated people who gripped too tightly or offered the limp hand. Or people who held on too long—but she didn't want to let go.

With a look of genuine concern, he gazed deep into her eyes and asked, "How's the ankle doing?"

Brooke felt a hot flash. She thought, *if I were a teenager, I'd scream. And if I didn't fall off the chair on my own, his eyes alone could knock me to the ground—I had forgotten those lashes.* She inhaled his fragrance and felt tingly. Brooke managed, "It doesn't bother me much. I've been staying off of it."

"It doesn't look like you're staying off it now. I'm sorry—I should have met with you in *your* office. That was inconsiderate of me."

"It's no problem. It's not like you made me run up the stairs. I took the elevator—and didn't even fall ..."

He laughed, then grabbed her briefcase, handling the overstuffed bag with ease. He offered his upturned hand, and said, "Let me help you into my office." She almost said, I'm fine on my own, but the urge to touch him again overwhelmed her. Then, as his hand met hers again, a buzz flowed through her. She thought, if I melt anymore, I could just flow into his office like a stream.

She stood up and he grasped her shoulder the same way as before. They shuffled a few steps, until just past the door. Brooke saw Ruth and could almost smell her stink eye. Chase was oblivious, focused on Brooke and her sweet fragrance.

Brooke glanced away but could feel a burn from Ruth's searing eyes as she strolled with Chase. Passing through the door, her eyes widened. In addition to an impressive view from two window walls, it looked presidential. Mahogany plaques and picture frames matched his oversized desk. On a table, a picture of him arm-in-arm with George W. Bush, flanked by two other guys she didn't recognize. They were each holding putters in their white-gloved hands. Just as she tabbed him a right winger, she surveyed the adjacent picture—Chase and Bill Clinton, again arm-in-arm. Brooke caught Chase viewing her out of the corner of her eye, and said, "Impressive company you keep."

"That's no big deal." Brooke faced Chase, who smirked and said, "This is the one I'm most proud of."

Chase lifted a picture from the front of his desk: Duke Basketball Coach Mike Krzyzewski shaking Chase's hand. Brooke said, "I hope you washed your hand after that one." Above his autograph, Coach K scribbled, "Dear Chase, Thanks For Your Support."

Brooke hated to admit she was impressed, so she said, "Oh God, I better sit down before I get sick." They both laughed.

Brooke followed her own cue and while easing onto one of the two chairs in front of his desk, she asked, "Where's the one with you and Michael Jordan? Or Dean Smith?"

"In the dumpster." They laughed again, his noticeably louder.

Brooke surveyed all of his artwork: a Duke University painting, a blown up shot of an aircraft with Chase and a small boy—a son? Another Duke basketball picture, and a plaque:

People have to be given the freedom to show the heart they possess. I think it's a leader's responsibility to provide that type of freedom. And I believe it can be done through relationships and family. Because if a team is a real family, its members want to show you their hearts.

Coach Mike Krzyzewski

Interesting, she thought, no picture of a wife? Just before she could ask about the photo on the wall with the small boy, Chase said, "Brooke, I wanted to call you here to see how Integrated Client Services is doing?"

She reached down and searched for the stuffed folders as if picking a card from a deck crammed inside her briefcase. She spotted it and nearly broke two nails pulling it out. Placing it on her knees, she opened it, and said, "Well, so far, we're on budget."

"That's great."

"It's a bit of a misnomer though. I have twelve openings in my division, so my P&L is skewed."

"Why so many openings?"

"I guess they all thought I was Attila the Hun." She laughed, but noticed Chase's furrowed brows. Brooke gulped, then continued, "I'll shoot to you straight—I tend to be brutally honest rather than politically correct."

Chase nodded while he watched her lips move as she spoke. Brooke inhaled, then said, "HR hasn't been as helpful as I would have liked." Brooke felt relieved for stopping short of saying *dragged their feet* or *useless*—or worse. Maybe I can be PC, she thought.

"We need to secure the right team to deliver the number this year. What does David Greenberg say?"

Brooke pictured the absentee android and nearly blurted, can you introduce me to him? "I haven't bothered him with this. He seems like he has a lot on his plate right now. His HR department works at a snail's pace and the few people they've sent me have all been duds. I've had more luck on my own."

"Well, if you're not getting the support you need, you've gotta get in Greenberg's face. I'll back you to the hilt."

"Thank you, sir," she bit her lip, "but I'd rather you didn't say anything. I don't want anyone thinking I'm a tattle tale—running to the CEO. I don't want to scare any more people away." In truth, she wanted to nuke the entire division and start fresh. The people who bolted were the marketable ones; the employees who remained needed a perpetual cry towel dispenser. Such a difference from before—nobody ever left GenSense.

"How's our fill rate?"

Brooke marveled at Chase's understanding of her world, a microcosm of the greater whole he oversaw. *No wonder he's CEO—he has a nice grasp of all elements of Pharmical.* He admired his ability to grasp the macro, yet understand all the micros. Plus, she loved his enthusiasm—and his chiseled features. *That face belonged on a magazine cover.*

"My department's customer fill rate's in the eighties."

Chase frowned.

Brooke said, "It's not where I'd like it, but without a full staff, I feel like a Band-Aid on an amputated leg." Chase grinned for the first time in a while, sending a wave through Brooke. Though even handsome with pursed lips, when he flashed his smile, she melted.

Similarly, Chase enjoyed Brooke's spirit. Her lips mesmerized him as they formed each word. In addition to brains and wit, she had unmistakable beauty. Heather had pretty features, but Brooke's beauty stemmed from within. She was the total package. Examining her bio earlier, he wondered why she was single. Was she ever married? Did she have any kids? He realized he couldn't go there, but craved more information. Imagining her in college, she would've been scooped up in two seconds at a Duke party.

"Where would it be if you were at full capacity?"

"In the high nineties. Focusing solely on Stabilitas, there's no reason our numbers dropped to the low eighties."

Stabilitas? The word shattered Chase's dreamy gaze. His eyes burst as a wave of paranoia mushroomed inside like a nuclear implosion. *Did she find out? How could she know? She couldn't know.* He drew a deep breath, and realized his anxiety still lingered since the earlier call. His voice of reason resonated—*she couldn't have heard anything. My door was closed the whole time. I've got to settle down.*

Brooke sensed Chase's unease; he'd lost that sparkle in his eye. "Am I boring you with these numbers?" *I hope I'm not leaning too far forward.*

"Not at all, Brooke, I love numbers." He slightly furrowed his brows. Brooke had always been perceptive with body language—especially obvious signs like crossing one's arms in the middle of a negotiation or glancing at one's watch. Chase's change was more subtle, but detectable. She hankered for a peek in her compact without him noticing.

"I brought a whole stack of numbers, but I'm still trying to learn 'em all. What would you like to discuss next?"

"There's no need to continue beating a dead horse, Brooke. I have all the confidence in the world that you'll have ICS running smoothly soon. You'll fill your openings, just be patient." He peered at her hands, and she folded her left hand on top of her right.

Chase switched gears and asked, "Did Dixon take good care of you?"

"The ankle's fine—the MRI was negative. And it feels much better. After having said that, can I be honest?"

"Please."

"After what he said to me, I'd rather amputate my leg than see him again."

Chase grimaced, wondering how Dixon crossed the line this time. He knew from experience how off the wall he could be. Chase made a mental note to have it out with Dixie-dawg. He decided to avoid discussing him with Brooke, but his scowl spoke volumes.

"Do you have any questions for me?"

Yeah, tell me about your wife? Why don't you have her picture up? Is that your son next to you? Why are you friends with a creep? Who did you vote for? Why do they call you Boa? Did you get your own coffee this morning? Boxers or briefs?

Instead, "What is happening with GenSense?"

"What do you mean?"

"An old client called and said he couldn't re-order any of our products."

"Listen, GenSense was a strategic acquisition that the board believed would fit well with our five-year strat plan. Pharmical was intrigued by gene therapy, but it's new for us—and we still see it as futuristic. I'm pushing for a division dedicated to genetic treatment, but for now, I'm afraid GenSense is on hold."

Futuristic? Brooke's brows scrunched. "On hold? Millions of people die from leukemia each year. GenSense provided hope for so many people—real hope. We had an incredible remission rate. I was expecting Pharmical to obtain FDA approval by now."

"Don't get me started with the FDA. It's a wonder anyone can stay in business with those clowns."

"We already had enough research data from Canada and Mexico. Our little company secured the green light from the FDA for a test market. Why isn't Pharmical pushing for a rollout?" Brooke felt her jaw tighten.

"Like I said, we're going to walk before we run. I'm not at liberty to discuss specifics, but M&A is actively pursuing other companies to buy and integrate."

Brooke's stomach churned. Her divine calling had been trampled, now sitting in corporate purgatory, waiting to be *integrated*. Everything she fought for and believed in was now tossed in a company closet. She realized if GenSense existed five years ago, Tanner would still be alive—by her side—rather than a memory lingering like a haunting shadow. She'd return everything ... all the money ... if only GenSense's revolutionary treatment could reach the dying masses in time.

Brooke's face turned ashen; with white lips, she said, "Excuse me, Mr. Allman, but I think I'm going to be sick."

He started saying, "I'll do my best to try to salvage GenSense—" but Brooke had already lunged toward the door. He asked, "What's wrong?"

Brooke advanced beyond his door. Stunned, he remained silent as he watched her. He wondered why she looked so distressed, but marveled at her faultless figure.

Did I make her sick? Recalling his answers, he didn't think so. Her reactions seemed peculiar, like an obsession. She definitely cared about GenSense—and he loved her passion, but didn't realize her rationale. *Women.*

Admiring Brooke's final steps before the elevator, Chase noticed Ruth wasn't at her desk. He slid his bottom drawer open and removed the picture. He glanced up once more, hoping Ruth wouldn't just pop in. Coast clear. He spun in his chair and slid the Coach K photo over to the side and set the framed picture in its spot. He breathed a sigh of relief, but while glancing at Heather, he felt a thud. That same face could light him up in the not-so-distant past; now, she looked like a ghost. What a waste. Chase's hackles rose, causing him to spin back around. He hiccupped in surprise. "Hi, Ruth, you scared me."

"I'm sorry. Are you finished with your meeting with Miss Hart?"

"Yes, did you need me for something?"

"I was just going to put your messages in your in tray."

"I'll take 'em, thanks." He reached out and grabbed the sizable stack of papers—so much for the electronic age. The small pink reminder slip flashed at his eye like a neon Vegas casino sign: "Call Max Molini. He says it's important."

With panther speed, Chase closed his door, then lifted the receiver. On the first ring, "What the fuck took you so long?"

Huh?

To a guy accustomed to people kissing up to him, there were few who could get away with *this* greeting—especially in his office—but Max Molini was one of them. Chase didn't hire him for his social graces. "Sorry, I was in a meeting."

"A meetin'? Man, I wish I could just jack around in a meetin'. Well, one of us has to work."

"You left a message. You said it was important?"

"Are you on a secure line?"

"Yes."

"Well, I have some good news and some bad news."

"Go on." Chase hoped Max didn't say which one you wanna hear first?

"Well, the good news first. Your little Heather surfaced."

Chase gulped and the words struck like a sucker punch. Though he had been searching for her for so long, hearing the news brought a wave of apprehension. Life had become easier with her gone. Now that she surfaced, the game changed. And Chase's risks ran high. "Where is she?"

"I got this second hand, but I'm ninety-nine percent sure it's accurate." Max paused for effect.

Chase held his breath.

"She's in Minneapolis."

"That makes sense," Chase exhaled, "Hazelden's in Minnesota and I think she had a cousin in the twin cities area."

"Not so fast, Chief. I haven't told you the bad news."

"What's that?"

"She's shacked up with some low-life scumbag in a not-so-nice area."

"She has a boyfriend? Are you sure?"

"Like I said, I'm ninety-nine percent sure, but I'm only one-hundred percent if I see it with my own eyes. Unless you wanna fly my ass from New York to Minneapolis."

"It doesn't sound like that would be necessary. What do you have on this guy?"

"You don't wanna know."

"You're talking about my wife. This information is exactly what I need to end this marriage once and for all. Don't worry, I'm a big boy. I can take it."

"From what I hear, this guy's lucky he's still walkin'. About a year ago, he crossed the wrong person, and his enemy list is impressive."

"Drugs?"

"Bingo! He got busted dealin' meth and did time. He's gotten into other shit too, but he's a small time punk."

"Well, there's nothing I can do on my end. It's her life. Or death, in her case. After all I provided, I can't believe she'd just throw it all away like this."

"She's a junkie my friend. And junkies do crazy shit."

"Well, keep an eye on her. She tried to call Parker once and gave my housekeeper a hard time, but for now, the only threat is to herself."

"Hey, for what it's worth, my friend, you don't deserve this. I'm sorry you gotta go through this. I know it's hard, believe me, I know. I'll keep an eye on her for you but try to forget about her." Max's *forget about her* blended into one word.

Chase set the receiver back on the hook and stared at his wall. Not the pictures with former presidents, not the Coach K memorabilia. The blank wall. His eyes blurred—not from tears, he was past that—from shock. As the words hit like a punching bag, he felt like he was having an out-of-body experience. In hell. Max reinforced his gravest fears.

He recalled the day his life fell apart. First, the call from Mary, Parker's best friend's mom, wondering where Heather was, and why she didn't answer her cell. It wasn't like Heather to be late. Chase knew better. He'd discerned her erratic behavior, listened to her rant and rave about small things, and observed how she coped—by popping pills. Then, racing home, his intuition screamed trouble. Noticing her car in the driveway, he feared the worst.

While yelling her name to the empty house, he ran upstairs. There she was—comatose, sprawled out on the bed with a note next to her. The paramedics told Chase that if he'd gotten there an hour later, she would be dead. In many ways, she did die that day.

Beyond the bottle of sleeping pills she swallowed, Heather's blood work revealed how deeply her addictions extended—Vicodin,

OxyContin ("hillbilly heroin"), Demerol, Percocet, and cocaine. But the most damning drug was the trace of Stabilitas.

The media would have a field day with that one. He could picture all the talking heads declaring that the new age anti-depressant caused suicide—even for the CEO's wife. Fortunately, he knew the right people who squashed the information before it landed on the front page or became the top news story. And, so far, he had managed to keep his pending divorce private.

Being forced to live two lives tore at him. All the cover-ups to deceive the public. Lying about the divorce to maintain that good bible-belt image—and his job. Lying to his son about where mommy is. Lying to himself. His conscience tore at him. Chase loved Parker and turned his full attention to his son. He enjoyed tossing a ball back and forth, wrestling on the family room rug, and reading him bedtime stories. But he missed going on a romantic date, sharing his love, his passion. He accepted his fate that he couldn't date while living his lie. Even though he had every reason, he still felt guilty and hesitant about divorcing Heather.

Hearing Max describe Heather's new life tore Chase apart. The woman he loved with all his heart and soul—the mother of his child—was a junkie all along. *Maybe I should have been there for her? I placed my job ahead of her. Were there signs of her illness, but I was too wrapped up in me to notice?* And the realization stung—she wasn't coming back; his life would never be what he wanted it to be. He felt like a modern-day Job from the Bible, guessing his suffering would pale in comparison.

And now, Brooke Hart popped into his life—literally. Convinced everything happened for a reason, Chase didn't believe in coincidences. He had been awakening in the middle of the night wondering why Brooke entered the picture. *She came into my life for a reason. But why now?* Since his dream, he couldn't get her out of his mind. He wanted to know everything about her, to share life: running together, walking the beach hand in hand, enjoying a romantic candle-lit dinner, serenading her with his guitar, and to awaken to her natural beauty at sunrise. But he realized he couldn't, thanks to his double life.

8

The vice grip on Chase's temples tightened. He was beat and it had nothing to do with the pressures of the job. Usually, he turned to a round of golf or a vigorous run—without Duke. But today he decided he'd do something different. Glancing at his Omega watch, he decided he'd surprise him. Chase tossed the clutter from his in-tray into his briefcase, grabbed his suit coat, and darted past Ruth. "I'll see you tomorrow."

Ruth raised her eyebrow. Chase didn't have any scheduled meetings and he wasn't traveling anywhere. She sensed something bothered him. Though she wanted to pry, she decided not to ask why he was leaving early. She realized her job description—the unwritten one—meant protecting him at all times. From the tidbits of information she'd overheard, she felt for Chase. She observed he had aged more than a U.S. President during the past year and realized it wasn't from work.

Outside, Chase fired up the beemer, then pressed speed dial two on his cell.

"Hello, Mr. Allman, I mean Chase, is that you?" Oksana sounded surprised.

"I've got good news for you."

"What do you mean?"

"I'm giving you the rest of the day off."

"Are you okay?"

"I'm more than okay. I'm on my way to Angel Academy. I get to pick up my son and spend the rest of the day with him."

"Oh, Parker'll be thrilled to see you. He keeps talking about how you're going to take him deep sea fishing."

"Well, not fishing today, but we'll do something fun. I've been so busy lately, I think we're due for some father-son stuff. I might take him mini-golfing."

"He'll love that. You want me to call Mrs. Stanton?"

"No, Betsy will remember me. I want to surprise the little guy. I love seeing Parker's eyes light up when he sees me."

"Oh, you know he will. Want me to make you a dinner tonight?"

"No, I'm taking him out to Chuck E. Cheese or wherever he wants. You take the rest of the day off. Go treat your boyfriend to a nice dinner and use my charge card."

Oksana giggled. Chase knew she adored Parker and relished the role of housekeeper and part-time chef. He made her feel like a family member and awarded her time off when she may not have needed it. "Thank you. Tell Parker I'll see him tomorrow morning."

Set on a peaceful wooded lot in an upscale area, just a few miles from Chase's house, the entrance sign read: "Angel Academy Learning Center …Where Young Minds Grow." After Heather fled, it served as the answer to Chase's prayers. He feared leaving his son in typical daycare where the kids cry in a sound-proof room while the adults plopped down in their own area, eating donuts and gossiping.

Angel Academy was the exact opposite, thanks to owner Betsy Stanton. She exuded a grandmotherly air. The kids loved and respected her and the other teachers, and the center provided a safe and enriching environment. Betsy read stories and occasionally made up her own. The kids looked forward to going to preschool and never wanted to leave. It was exactly what three-year-old Parker needed, and Chase felt better knowing his son was happy there.

Pulling his beemer into the parking lot, Chase couldn't remember the last time he'd picked up Parker. He was excited to surprise his little guy and hoped Betsy didn't mind him arriving a half hour early. Pulling the front door open, he marveled at how quiet it was inside. He guessed the kids were playing out back on the jungle gyms. The reception desk was vacant, so he entered his code in the keypad and advanced toward the main room.

He faintly heard Betsy's voice through the door. He opened the door and realized it was story time. All the kids were sitting in a semi-circle on the floor in front of Betsy. He spotted Parker's curly head, seated front and center, and smiled. A chip off the old block. He hated to interrupt, so he just stood in the back listening. Her calming voice captivated the kids. He wished more teachers could teach like her.

Without a book, Betsy was telling a story about dragons and elves. He listened, not wanting to interrupt, and enjoyed watching the children and Betsy's animation as she told the story. When she spotted him over her wire-rimmed glasses, Betsy paused, smiled, and said, "Parker, I think you have a special visitor."

Parker turned and his eyes lit up, "Daddy!" He glanced back at Mrs. Stanton with adorable puppy eyes. When she nodded, Parker jumped up and darted to his father's outstretched arms.

As other kids began rumbling, Betsy said, "Story time isn't over yet." It was all she needed to say. She held court without raising her voice, and in an instant, the room of twenty or so kids fixed their gazes back on her. Chase marveled at her uncanny ability to hush a bunch of three- and four-year-olds. He wanted to bring her to his next board meeting.

Holding Parker in one arm, Chase waved to Betsy with the other, marveling at how much he'd grown just in the last couple of weeks.

"Where's Oksana?" Parker asked.

Chase lifted his free hand and crossed his forefinger over his lips, then lowered the hand to open the door. "Shhhh. Let's not disturb story time, son."

Once outside, he said, "I wanted to pick you up today."

"Yippee! Can we go shark fishing? Can we, Daddy?" Parker's brown eyes with hazel flecks lit up as he spoke. Chase melted.

"Not today. That's for a weekend when we have a full day."

"Do you promise?"

"Absolutely, I already talked to the captain of the boat, and he says he'll take us where all the sharks are."

"Are there any dragons?"

"No, I think dragons are only on land."

"Nah ah. Dragons are in the water and they breathe fire out of their mouths. And only the elves are safe from them."

Oh to be young and to believe in dragons and elves, Santa, Easter Bunnies, and Tooth Fairies. Rather than dispelling the myths—and facing the wrath of Betsy for spoiling her story—Chase shifted gears. "You wanna play mini-golf?"

"Can we?" After drawing a big nod from Chase, Parker said, "Yayyyyyy!"

"And maybe afterward we can go to Chuck E. Cheese."

"What about Oksana?" Parker's expression shifted to concern.

"Nope, I gave her the night off. Just you and me kiddo."

"Will she be back?" Parker asked.

"Of course. Oksana said to say hi and she'll see you for breakfast."

Though the heat index dictated air conditioning, Parker insisted they drive with the top down. Chase played his MP3 file named "Parker Tunes" on the stereo, drawing a beaming smile from his energetic son. "Shake my Sillies Out" and "Baby Beluga" were quite a departure from classic rock but the silly sing-a-long with Parker was just what Chase needed. He didn't realize how uptight he felt until he sang, "I gotta shake, shake, shake my sillies out, and wiggle my waggles away." Chase occasionally listened to Raffi when driving alone to remind him of his son—and to lighten up his mood, but nothing beat the real thing. Moments like this were father-son bliss.

Parker wanted to play mini-golf at Pirate's Cove, a miniature golf treasure that offered two eighteen-hole challenges. Parker chose the Blackbeard course because it went through a cave. Fortunately, majestic oaks and mist machines made the outdoor activity tolerable on a hot day. Hokey pirate themes abounded. Parker mimicked his dad's putting touch and actually did well for a three-year-old. He made a hole-in-one and his joyful squeal stopped time. Chase marveled at Parker's hand-eye coordination, wondering if he might be golf's next child prodigy. Though Chase had an opportunity to earn a living teaching golf, he chose a different path. The corporate world paid off well, but it had its own hazards.

After their golf balls were swallowed by the last hole in the course, they relaxed together sipping root beer next to the big pirate ship.

The root beer hit the spot, but spoiled Parker's appetite. Chase needed another activity to entertain his son before dinner. Too blistering hot to play catch, especially in wool dress slacks, he remembered the two bags of stale bread in the trunk. Perfect.

"What are we going to do now? Can we go shark fishing?"

"I told you we need a full day to go fishing, but I've got something I know you'll love."

"What is it? What is it?"

Chase realized he made a serious parental faux pas, opening the can of worms too early. Parker played the guessing game for the duration of the drive. Even flipping on the next Raffi song didn't help. Chase finally pulled off to a gravel parking spot next to the pond. Parker said, "Can we feed the turtles?"

"Yep. I've got some turtle food in my trunk."

"Can I feed 'em?"

"Absolutely." Chase popped the trunk and handed Parker the bag of bread; they headed to a big rock on the water's edge. Parker wound up and threw the first bread piece as far as he could. Seconds later, a couple of turtles surrounded the floating bread like sharks on a wounded seal. Several turtles floated toward the ripple. Parker enthusiastically pointed out the biggest turtle. Chase grinned.

The turtle feed lasted for close to thirty minutes. An alligator that had been sunning itself on the far banks splashed into the water and, in a slow but deliberate motion, headed toward their feeding area. Game over. Parker protested, but "Don't Feed the Alligators" was one rule Chase would never bend.

Hand in hand, they bee-lined back to the car and jumped in. "Can we watch him from the car, Daddy?"

"I guess so, but if he gets too close, we're outta here."

"Yippee." Ah, the simple things, Chase thought. Who needs to take their kid to Disney World for a good time?

After a few minutes of slowly floating in the middle of the pond, the alligator's curiosity waned and it retreated to the other side, out of view. "You hungry for some dinner, buddy?"

"Can we still go to Chuck E. Cheese?"

"Sure, whatever you want."

"I like this. Can we do it tomorrow?"

"No, this is a special treat, son. I have to work. That's why Oksana usually picks you up from Angel Academy. I'm glad I could surprise you today though."

"Me too."

The Chuck E. Cheese was located on Mayfair Street, about twenty minutes away. Chase flipped on "Parker Tunes" again and father and son sang "More We Get Together," "Down by the Bay," and "I Wonder

If I'm Growing." As they pulled into the parking lot of minivans and SUVs, the sleek BMW turned a few soccer moms' heads. Parker wanted pizza but Chase couldn't stomach it. He opted for the healthiest thing on the menu: the salad bar. He ordered Parker a six-inch cheese pizza and a soda. Surrounded by moms and dads seated with their children, Chase and Parker ate in silence. After finishing half a slice and two sips of soda, Parker said, "I'm full." *Typical.*

Chase had only finished half of his salad, but could part ways without remorse. "You want a Cinnamon Stick?"

"No, I'm full." Chase nodded then chomped one more bite. Still chewing, he stood to leave.

"I miss Mommy." Parker's simple statement hit Chase like a drive-by shooting, causing him to choke on the remnants of his iceberg lettuce.

Chase gulped, then said, "I know you do, son. I do too."

"Is Mommy ever coming back from her trip?"

It had been almost a year since Heather deserted her son without so much as a call. Chase despised lying to Parker, even if it was for his own good. Max's words resonated inside as Chase's usually lucid mind went haywire. *What could he say?* Parker believed in dragons and elves, but somehow, seemed to figure out his mommy's return was a myth. It was time.

Chase drew a deep breath, then said, "Buddy, I'm not sure. Your mommy's sick and needs to keep going to different doctors."

"When's she gonna get better?"

"I don't know, son. I don't know." Chase glanced away, eyes stinging. He rubbed his eyes, brooding, then regained his composure. He said, "We'll say a prayer for her tonight. Which reminds me, we better head back home, mister. It's going to be your bedtime soon."

The question dampened a great day like raindrops on a beach. Even Raffi couldn't ease the heaviness in Parker's heart. Chase sensed Parker was confused about things. Parker liked Oksana and, in many ways, treated the affable nanny like a mother; but Chase realized there was no substitute for his mommy. Now that Heather was trying to call, he wondered why. *What could she possibly say to her son?* Life would never be back to normal for Parker and it sickened Chase more than the deception.

Back at home, Parker put up his usual battle for a delayed bedtime. Chase compromised by agreeing to read a story before light's out. "This one." Parker handed his father *The Boy Who Cried Wolf.* Aesop's message of always telling the truth hit Chase hard. Thinking there are no coincidences, he glanced up, wondering if this was one of those not-so-subtle times.

Chase set the book on the bedside table, and said, "Let's say your special prayer."

Parker looked exhausted as the fun from earlier caught up. Chase said, "Lord ..." and waited for Parker to join in, "Help me be the best I can. Help me to do what's right and treat other people like I want to be treated. Amen."

As Chase stood, Parker said, "What about our special prayer for Mommy?"

"Oh, sorry." Sitting back down on the bed, Chase brushed his son's curly hair back and said, "What do you want to say?"

"Lord, please help Mommy get better and come home to play with me. Amen."

Chase stood up and turned away so his son wouldn't see his tears. Parker's sweet voice—the voice of an angel—played on his heartstrings. He missed his mother. No matter how nice of a day Parker spent with him, he missed Mommy. *How could she ever do this to such an innocent child?*

With slumped shoulders, Chase trudged back to his bedroom. He approached the bed, the same bed where Parker had been conceived, and dropped to his knees. He said his own prayer, *Lord God, thank you for all my blessings. I'm not here to question your will, but for some reason, you're testing me. I accept it even though I don't fully understand. Please bestow me the strength to raise Parker, to be his father and his mother all in one. I really tried today but feel I've failed. Please help me.*

9

*B*rooke tossed and turned all night until her alarm rang like a sonic boom. She needed caffeine this morning, thinking maybe this was divine intervention. Today would be a perfect day to run. As each inactive day accumulated, she felt flabby and lethargic. Inspecting her ankle, the black and blue appeared light gray with blue highlights. Improvement. She was nowhere near ready for a run, but she desperately needed exercise. She clutched the ankle supports as if weighing them. Brooke then studied the padding on her running shoes. Why not? A short jog couldn't hurt.

The clincher loomed on the wall—Tanner's *Sports Illustrated* photo delivering a bone-crunching tackle while still recovering from a major injury. *If Tanner could play like that on a bum hip, I can jog.*

Brooke began with a brisk walk, then started jogging. The ankle responded well so far. Her mind shifted from focusing on the injury to what had really kept her up all night. She still wanted to strangle Chase for putting GenSense—and everything she had worked so hard for—on hold. How dare he call it futuristic. Genetic research had progressed to successful gene therapy, and Pharmical had the life-saving treatment stuck in meeting abyss. They had enough interest to buy it up, but lacked the guts to advance it. Without innovation and backbone, no medical advances would have ever happened. Remorse seeped inside for letting Chase off the hook, and for storming out. *He must think I'm an emotional wreck. Well, I'll find out soon enough.*

The jog lasted twenty minutes, and it was the best she'd felt in weeks. The ankle tightened but the rest of her relaxed. Nothing a little ice couldn't cure. After a nice hot shower and quality mirror time, she was good to go. For the first time since the injury, she wore heels. Not her sexiest ones, but still much more appealing than flats. With one last inspection in the mirror, Brooke smiled at her knee-length tan skirt and sleeveless blouse. Not exactly Pharmical code, but perfect for a hot summer day. With a nod, she headed out.

Her palms moistened, making it harder than usual to steer her Lexus. Glancing at her speedometer, her eyes widened—*I better slow down*. She wasn't exactly sure why she felt nervous. There was a good chance he wouldn't be there, after all. Ruth could have been his gopher. But, if not, how would he respond to seeing her? How would she react? As long as he didn't say *futuristic* again, she'd be okay; if he did, anything could happen with steaming hot liquid in her hand.

Brooke parked out of sight across the street from Starbucks. She could still picture the two oversized Starbucks cups on his desk—a dead giveaway. She slid on her oversized sunglasses and floppy hat, looking more like Lady Gaga in a grocery store than a vice president of a major corporation. She laughed at her reflection in the rearview mirror. I can't believe I'm actually doing this.

Ten minutes passed like ten years. Brooke had decided if he didn't show up within thirty minutes, she'd pop into work. While applying fresh lipstick for the umpteenth time, she noticed the unmistakable red car barreling toward her from two blocks away. She ducked, pulled off her ridiculous hat, then shut off her ignition. She counted to ten, heart pounding, then peeked up. Coast clear. She wondered if he whizzed by, then she spotted him striding into Starbucks.

After a final glance in her rearview mirror, she drew a deep breath, then opened her car door. She figured she had time and he couldn't see her hiding spot. Brooke strode with the best posture she could manage on a still-sprained ankle that officially ached right now. Nearing the entrance, she drew a deep breath and whispered, "Showtime."

Brooke pulled the glass door open and paused at the entrance to allow her eyes to adjust. A burst of ground coffee drowned out any remnants of his aroma—*pity*. Most of the chairs were taken with paper readers and writer wannabes. Surveying the narrow store, she spotted Chase standing in line conversing with a young lady in front of him. She didn't think it could be his wife since he drove up alone. Just Chase being friendly. And he looked magnificent from the side—even better than in the boardroom.

She sauntered up behind him still unnoticed. Brooke inhaled his delicious fragrance as she eavesdropped his small talk. *Mmmmm,* she thought, wanting to slide her hands under his suit coat and across his chest. A tingling sensation eased her trepidation about the other day. She wanted to speak but enjoyed hearing his voice—and the chance to eye him up and down at such close range.

A guy in a business suit entered and headed over to the line. Brooke panicked, thinking what if Chase knew him? She pictured affable Chase spinning around to say hello while she stood there drooling. Still at a loss for words, she tapped Chase on his shoulder. He stopped speaking and glanced back over his burly shoulder. Recognizing Brooke, his eyes widened and fell back a half step, nearly bumping into the woman in front of him. "Hey, Brooke. What're you doing here?"

"Same thing as you, sir."

His brows furrowed. "I thought you didn't like coffee?"

Brooke marveled at how attractive he was, even frowning. "Um, hello, Starbucks sells tea also."

"And good tea," the woman in front of Chase said, hoping to rejoin the conversation. Chase remained fixated on Brooke's aqua eyes, and said, "Either you've grown or I'm shrinking." Chase chuckled.

Brooke realized he hadn't ventured below her cleavage and said, "I'm wearing heels for the first time since my injury."

Chase leaned back and stared at her feet, then slowly ran his eyes up her body, admiring every inch.

Brooke slid her front teeth against her lower lip as her knees buckled. It was as if his lashes tickled her skin to allow his x-ray vision to penetrate. The pain in her ankle magically subsided.

The line edged forward like dominoes, temporarily breaking their spell. Chase said, "You healed fast. Does it still hurt?"

Before Brooke could answer, the girl behind the counter said, "Are you having the usual, Chase?"

Chase spun around, startled, and said, "Oh, hey, Tonya. I'm sorry. You're fast today. The usual it is—you know me." The purplish-black hair and multiple piercings on the young girl looked more like Berkeley than Durham. Brooke wondered if she leaked when she drank and laughed inside as she imagined her applying for a job at Pharmical. Chase nodded at a nearby twenty-something black man with tight cornrows and facial scars that resembled the singer Seal who said, "What's up, A-Man?"

"Same ole, same ole, Marcus. You?"

"Ditto dat. Ditto dat." They both shared a hearty laugh.

Brooke stood wide-eyed, mouthing *A-Man?* She couldn't believe Chase befriended these workers—to a CEO, they were truly the little people. Yet, Miss Piercings was on a first name basis and Mr. Cornrows sounded like a college buddy. Her father always said: *Character is best revealed by how someone treats another who can do nothing for him or her.* These words of wisdom rang true about Chase. *And to think my daddy called him a shark.*

An even greater revelation struck Brooke: Chase waited in line, bought, and picked up his own coffee. His status elevated above the clouds. *Is this guy real or am I dreaming? Does he have at least one fault?*

Tonya placed two cups on the counter and said, "Anything else before I put these on your account?"

"Oh yeah, please add whatever my friend is having." Chase wrapped his arm around Brooke's shoulder and pulled her up to the counter beside him. Her heart ran like a jet before takeoff. Tonya said, "What can I get ya?"

Oh shit. Brooke's face flushed—she had never been to a Starbucks. She didn't understand why anyone would ever wait in long lines for overpriced and overrated coffee. Now she had to sound like a regular. The overcrowded menu on the back wall read like a foreign language, especially while blinking like a hummingbird's wings. She almost blurted *give me your Coffee Breath of the Day.* Miss Piercings's stare didn't help.

Brooke said, "I'll have a tea."

Piercings said, "Um, we have like a bazillion teas. Which one, ma'am?"

Ma'am? I'm not old enough to call me ma'am. "What's y'all's most popular?"

Tonya rolled her eyes. "I don't drink tea … but, our most popular is chai tea latte."

"Perfect."

"What size?"

"Large."

Piercings shifted her weight as if she had broken a leg. "They come in tall, grande, and venti."

"Uh, the same size as he's having." Brooke looked like she was attempting to rob a bank with her finger and thumb.

"Venti?"

"Sure, whatever."

Marcus wheeled and started preparing Brooke's order. He didn't want to keep Mr. A-Man waiting. Tonya pulled the receipt and set it in front of Chase. After signing, he dropped a five dollar bill into the tip jar. Brooke smiled at him. Chase grabbed his two cups and Brooke saw something strange—no wedding band. *That's a first. Did he slip it off?*

Chase carried his coffee over to the side where the creams and sugars were located. Brooke stood at the counter. Tonya pointed her eyes toward Chase and said, "You wait over there for it. We'll bring it to you."

Brooke felt like screaming, thinking *why didn't he have to wait?* Rather than saying something—and looking stupid again—she bit her lip and sauntered over to Chase's side. He looked like a scientist devising a secret potion as he added nutmeg, cinnamon, and two packets of Splenda to each steaming coffee. Marcus set Brooke's tea on the side counter and said, "Chai tea latte for the lady. Did I leave you enough air on top, A-Man?"

"Looks good."

Marcus flashed his grills then said, "Sorry about the other day."

"No problem—I'm just very particular about my coffee."

"It's all good, A-Man. I'm just here to please."

Brooke's eyes bounced like she was tableside at a ping pong match, unable to keep score. Chase popped the lids back on each coffee and turned to Brooke and smiled. "Would you please join me?"

"Sure." She spotted an open small table in the corner and hoped he'd nab it.

He waited, then said, "Don't you put anything in your tea?"

"Uh, no. Not usually."

"Really? Okay, let's go sit down, there's a table." Holding the coffees like bombs about to detonate, he motioned with his eyes for her to lead. Brooke realized she was staring at his lashes again, then bumped herself forward. Her ankle throbbed each time her heel landed on the hard floor. She realized her slight limp, but was still happy she wore the heels. She felt Chase's eyes like a magnifying glass burning a leaf.

Nearing the table, Chase slid around beside her and set his coffees on the table. Brooke inhaled and closed her eyes for an instant that she wanted to savor—his scent blended well with the aromas of fresh-brewed coffee. Even though coffee breath repulsed her, she had to admit it smelled inviting. Chase pulled the chair out and held it for Brooke. She smiled as she gracefully lowered herself on the chair—without falling this time.

After sitting across from Brooke, Chase sipped coffee number one and Brooke sampled her tea. "How's your tea?"

"It's fine, thanks." Brooke pursed her lips. "How's *your* coffee, Mister Picky?"

"Not as hot as usual. I prefer 175 degrees exactly and this is closer to 170. I hope the other one is 185."

That explained the "H" written on top of the lid of the untouched coffee. Brooke wondered if he had a thermometer chip in his mouth. "You seem pretty particular about your coffees, Mr. A-Man?" Brooke smiled as she emphasized *A-Man*.

Chase chuckled, then turned serious and said, "I can't drink coffee when it's lukewarm. Also, I hate it when they fill it too full." Brooke frowned. A thistle in the daisy patch popped up—Chase had quirks. *If he's this anal-retentive about coffee, I can only imagine how impossible he'd be to cook for. Or live with.*

"Can't you just mic it?"

"Never. It ruins the flavor."

Brooke peered to the side as she considered this. *He'd never appreciate my freezer-based menu.* She wondered if he popped his popcorn on a stove-top. Or cooked a Lean Cuisine in the oven. "Do you *ever* use a microwave?"

"Not if I can avoid it. Those things turn bread into hockey pucks and destroy most anything else."

Considering his V-shape, Brooke figured he was no bakery expert. This rendered his logic moot. *Did his wife have to wait till he left to thaw something out? And, where's his ring? I'm dying to ask.* Instead, "Well, I went running this morning for the first time."

"So, you're ready for our run together?" It sounded more like a command than a question.

Brooke smirked, then said, "Actually, it was more like a slow jog. I think I pushed it too much. My ankle's sore."

"Didn't Dixon tell you to stay off it for at least eight weeks?"

"I don't remember. He creeped me out and lost all credibility with me last week. I won't go back."

Chase choked and barely avoided a coffee catastrophe. His eyes narrowed, "I remember you saying that. What did he do?" Even upset, he still looked cute with those collector's lashes.

"Every time I go in there, he hits on me." Brooke had worked hard on her tact—Shane would be proud—but she couldn't hide her contempt for Chase's college buddy.

"You're kidding me?"

Brooke shook her head back and forth in robotic motion.

"Worse than the first time you saw him?"

Brooke nodded.

"I'm sorry, I really am. I think when he sees me, he reverts back to college."

"I understand. I don't hold it against you. Some of my college friends make Dixon look harmless." Brooke hoped she didn't sound like a prude. A side of her felt honored that a well-respected physician—who no doubt had his pick of young nurses—found her attractive. The sterile patient's room just wasn't the place to start a romance. Judging from Chase's reddening face—still cute when angry—Dixie-dawg would receive a well-deserved scolding. She'd love to listen in on that call.

Chase glanced at his watch, then said, "I have an early conference call so I better leave."

"Thanks for the tea."

"You're welcome." Chase heaved a sigh, then said, "There's not enough time in the day."

"I'd better head to work too. I don't want to upset my boss." Brooke twirled a few strands of hair and licked her lips. Chase forgot his own name.

"Let me know when you're ready to go running?"

Brooke smiled and nodded as Chase stood to leave. She lingered for a moment to catch his strut from behind one last time.

— 💜 —

"Why do you have to be such a fuck up?"

"What're you talking about?"

"You know exactly what I'm talking about."

"I'm heading into surgery in a few minutes, so quit beating around the bush."

"I told you to behave around Brooke."

"I did."

"You most certainly did NOT."

"I don't know what you're talking about." Dixon's voice cracked like a pimpled teenager.

"I can't believe you—you really are a fucking dawg. You crossed the line for the second time."

"Hey, if I did, I'm sorry. But you can't blame me."

"What?"

"She's smoking hot. And just cuz she's off limits for you, she's fair game for me."

"Would your fiancée agree?"

"Don't go there ..."

"Do you hit on all your patients?"

"If they look like Brooke, absofuckinglutely."

"You're unfuckingbelievable, you know that. If you weren't my best friend, I'd run you over in the parking lot and leave you for road kill."

"No, you wouldn't—not with that beemer. I'd wreck your engine." Settled at a traffic light, Chase realized the wide-eyed people in the car next to him heard his squabble. He brooded, unable to laugh at his buddy's feeble attempt to lighten him up.

Dixon broke the silence, saying, "There are two types of women: the ones I'd do and the ones I'd probably do."

"*Probably?*"

"That's what alcohol's for—to eradicate the *probably.*"

Chase snickered, amazed that Dixon could flip his mood switch so easily. The light changed, and as Chase sped away from the eavesdroppers, he said, "You really are a dawg. If I hit on my staff like you, I'd be toast."

"If I had *staff* like Brooke, it'd be worth it."

"You have plenty of hot ones who land in your warped range in that hospital."

"Not like Brooke. In fact, I have to add another type just for her—she's a *must* do." Silence. Then Dixon said, "Tell me you don't agree?"

"Okay, you're done. Do me and Raleigh-Durham a favor: try to keep it in your scrubs—for once!" Chase pressed the end button and flung his cell on the passenger's seat, right where Brooke had sat. He shook his head, then winced, *with friends like Dixie-dawg, I'm glad I don't have a daughter.*

As upset as he became, Chase couldn't completely lose it with Dixon. He had to admit Brooke was one special woman. *But, must do? That was a new one.* Though he couldn't clear Brooke from his mind, he recognized his differences with his best friend. He didn't need legal training to know that employees were off limits. Period.

Why couldn't I have met Brooke before Heather? Why does she have to work for me? And how do I keep her away from the dawg?

10

*B*rooke felt guilty she hadn't visited Melissa since starting at Pharmical. As usual, work replaced her social life. But Melissa had been busy each time Brooke tried to meet up. Her college roommate was finally tying the knot with Eddie Racer, her on again–off again boyfriend of the past eight years. Melissa's father, Clifton, called Eddie his "son-out-law." Though Brooke never cared much for Eddie either, she was happy for Melissa and was flattered to be her maid of honor.

The wedding crept up—now only a week away—and part of the reason Brooke delayed visiting Melissa had to do with her ankle. No need to limp in front of a bride-to-be who counted on her maid of honor to be strutting down the aisle on her special day. Her friend was a nervous wreck by default. Brooke didn't want to raise Melissa's anxiety any more than necessary. Though hush hush, especially to Clifton, Brooke knew Melissa was three months pregnant.

The main reason Brooke avoided Melissa was the painful memories. The wedding, the vows, the husband, the baby—Melissa had everything Brooke had lost. The memories haunted Brooke and she had to suppress her angst. Or at least try. She had to be there for Melissa. After Brooke lost the baby at the six-month mark, Melissa was the first person she saw—aside from Tanner. Melissa and Brooke grieved together as if they both had suffered the same loss. Deep down, Brooke realized that the day their baby's heart stopped, so did Tanner's will to live.

Tanner was already in the advanced stages of Chronic Myelogenous Leukemia (CML), so the miscarriage was lightning striking in the same place twice. When she first learned of Tanner's disease, she remembered staggering around in a daze. Beyond denial, she suffered from acute depression and refused medications that could have helped. She blamed everyone—the doctors, Tanner, and even God.

Tanner's death sentence appeared out of nowhere. CML mainly struck the elderly but rarely a man in his twenties. Especially not a major college athlete who could bench press twice his weight. By the time the signs appeared, which Tanner ignored—fever, loss of appetite, weight loss—it was too late. The disease had already reached the "accelerated phase."

Tanner had been dieting to shed the extra weight that followed his football career and the gold band on his finger. Figuring he was just overzealous in his endeavor to reach his high school weight, he never even visited a doctor until he had lost over eighty pounds. Always the big, strong man, to Tanner leukemia was the furthest thing from his mind.

Though CML was not curable by standard methods of chemotherapy or immunotherapy, new treatments were being tested by scientists in Canada and Mexico. These new gene-based treatments attacked the disease with advanced computer technology. Brooke offered to quit her job and find a new one in Canada; Tanner's company allowed him to transfer from outside sales to telesales, which he could do anywhere in the world. Then Tanner's doctor eradicated his enthusiasm, calling the treatment "unproven and unstable."

Despite the naysaying MDs, Tanner fought it with the same intensity he brought to an opposing running back. With a baby boy on the way—Jake Tanner Hart, Jr.—he had an even greater will to defeat cancer. Though his weight dropped, he kept his spirits above the clouds. Until the day Brooke lost the baby. Their baby.

One month later, Brooke found Tanner dead in the garage, collapsed on the steering wheel with the motor still running. Then, she saw the note.

> *My Dearest Brooke,*
>
> *I'm sorry you found me like this. I couldn't tell you because I knew you'd talk me out of it. But I can't go on. Please understand and forgive me.*
>
> *I know I didn't always tell you, but I love you with all my heart. Always have, always will.*
>
> *For all the things I meant to say, but was too shy or too*

stupid, here goes. *You are everything beautiful to me ... I love your smile, how your eyes light up when you look at me, how you held my hand when they told me my hip was broken, the way you kiss with your tender lips. I love how your eyes flutter when you're nervous. Most of all, I love how you love me, even now.*

Please don't remember me like this. Remember me as the shy boy who fell in love with you in Biology class, who couldn't take his eyes off you, who tried to find a way to talk to you but took till the end of the year to ask you out, who didn't know what beauty looked like before I met you. From the moment I saw you, I knew I'd spend the rest of my life with you or my life wouldn't be worth living. Then you said yes to being my girlfriend and I knew we'd be together forever. I marveled as you grew prettier every day. The easiest thing I've ever done was to ask you to marry me. When you said yes, my heart filled with tremendous joy. You may think I'm leaving you too early, but I know I was the luckiest person on earth.

I still remember how happy you made me when you said we were pregnant. I was on cloud nine. I had felt lousy all day and then you magically lifted me up with the news. You could always make me feel better and all it took was your smile. We always dreamed of having a baby together.

I apologize that I'm so stubborn. I should have listened to you and gone to the doctor. Who knows, maybe they could've made it go away. It doesn't matter now. The day they told me I was going to die, our future died too. I could see it in your eyes, and feel it in your heart. I'm sorry I let you and our son down.

If there is a God out there or up there, I hope He's the forgiving one we read about in church together and not the vengeful one in the Old Testament. If there really is a hell, I've already been there. Whoever said God works in mysterious ways had it right.

I'm sorry I didn't make us rich. But as my dream shattered, God gave me you. Your love was more than any NFL money. I don't think I'd have made it without your love. I'm not sure moving to Canada would have made a difference.

I felt so helpless that day our baby died and you really needed me. I wanted so badly to dry your tears, but I didn't have the strength to even hold you up. Instead, all I did was make it worse. You said you were afraid of dying during delivery, like the mother you never knew. You'd make the greatest mother and I want you to be some day. Kids are drawn to you. My biggest regret is that I couldn't give you the room full of children who adore you and your beautiful eyes and radiant smile, in the place we dreamed of by the ocean, living a life of love.

I guess I'm not really good at dying. I've shriveled up enough to know it's my time to go. I'm heartily sorry if it hurts you, but I can't go on like this. I don't need some doctor lying to me about how long I have. I died the day our son died. You made me strong in so many ways. And now I want to go out on my own terms. This has nothing to do with you or your love; it's just my time.

As God is my witness, I'll find a way to help you in the afterlife like that movie Ghost. I'll protect you and even help you meet someone who loves you, though it's not possible to find anyone who could love you more than me. I want you to have the things we dreamed about.

Please forgive me. I'll always love you even if I'm not by your side.

Goodbye My Love,
Tanner

— ♥ —

Brooke's fingertip touched the smeared word on the final page where Tanner had cried his last tear. Sensing his presence, she surveyed the area like a strobe light. Brooke gazed at his picture and said, "I forgive you. I'm so grateful you came into my life." She carefully folded the letter, slid it back into the original envelope, then tucked it in her purse. Just like before. Brooke drew a deep breath, then glared at her watch. *Oh shit, I'm late.*

Brooke sped away from the curb, then hit speed dial three on her cell, rather than texting while driving. Voicemail: "Hey you've reached Melissa's cell. Eddie and I are probably busy with the wedding plans. Please leave us a message." Brooke laughed, noticing her new message included Eddie and ended with us—that meant the wedding was still on.

After the beep, "Hey Melissa, it's your absentee friend Brooke. I'm running a little late, so what else is new? I should be there in fifteen minutes. See ya soon." Brooke wasn't sure if Melissa would hear the message before she arrived, but felt good she logged a message.

Brooke's relief lasted about one traffic light. She couldn't erase the lingering hurt inside. Her stomach churned again and she hadn't even eaten lunch. Brooke realized the symptoms that eluded her doctor had nothing to do with food; she yearned for the life she now feared she'd never have. All she wanted was to raise Tanner's kids and yearned to fall in love over and over again.

Pulling into Bistro 221, and though a homemade soup sounded good, Brooke wasn't sure if she could stomach any food. Or if she could keep it together. She vowed to shelve her emotions and focus on calming Melissa. Having lived together at North Carolina, she knew Melissa's good qualities and her flaws. Brooke understood her better than anyone. She could make high-strung Melissa laugh at will.

Brooke shut off her car, peeked into her rearview mirror, and grimaced, "Yikes." Stress always did a number on her. Brooke lacked the time for even a minor makeover. She opened the door and spotted Melissa's yellow VW bug, with the Tar Heels sticker, and wondered how long she'd been there.

Brooke yanked the oversized wooden door open and, like a coiled up rattler ready to strike, Melissa pounced on her. "Hey girl, sorry I'm late. Have you been waiting long?"

"Seems like it." Melissa pointed her eyes to the podium with the "Please wait to be seated" sign, then said, "They wouldn't seat me until 'everyone in my party was present.'"

Brooke noticed the forty-something hostess glaring. "I'm so sorry. I've been crazy busy, but probably not like you. Let's grab a table. I wanna get all caught up."

Hostess from hell attempted to appease Melissa by blaming "restaurant policy," but Melissa rolled her eyes. As a minor consolation, they were seated in a private booth.

"You look fantastic! I haven't seen you in what, over six weeks now?" Melissa said.

Brooke's head shot back like an air rifle just went off in her face, "Are you joking?"

Melissa had always been brutally honest, especially when on edge—which was most of the time. "I don't know how you do it. I mean, balancing being a big wig in business and still looking incredible—"

"I think you need glasses." They both laughed and Brooke sensed Melissa's stress level returned to the human range.

"So take my mind off this wedding and tell me something fun. How was your date with Tobin?"

Brooke's eyes narrowed, "Um, quid pro quo. Forget Tobin."

"What do you mean?"

"Let's just say, of the guys you've set me up with, he was a new low."

"I thought he was perfect for you. He's witty and handsome, plus he makes great money. What happened?"

"Well, you're one-for-three: he makes good money. After he bragged about himself throughout dinner, I had to order an oxygen tank just to be able to breathe." Melissa released a nervous giggle. Brooke said, "I don't think I said boo—until he asked me to go back to his place."

"Oh my God. Seriously?"

"Serious as a heart attack."

Melissa bit her lower lip, then said, "Did you?"

A waiter appeared like a pop-up window and smirked. They ushered him away with a quick order. Melissa had her usual heirloom tomato salad with fresh greens; Brooke ordered a bowl of the soup special. Even though escarole with white bean didn't sound appealing, she always loved their soups. Plus, she knew Melissa would share her salad.

Brooke lowered her voice, "C'mon, give me a little credit. Sex with him would've required headphones."

"He was probably just nervous. Eddie thought you'd like him. When Tobin stared at your picture, he nearly fell off his chair."

"I wish he had fallen. I would've been spared another date from hell." Melissa laughed; Brooke nearly blurted something derogatory about her hubby-to-be, but suppressed it. Brooke continued, "Why do guys always self-destruct during dinner? And then they think I owe them nookie."

"I'm sorry."

"Enough about my dating dilemma. Are you ready for the big day?"

"I've been ready for, like, the last eight years. I already feel like Eddie and I are married—I wish the wedding was over. Was yours this stressful?"

Brooke felt another pang in her stomach. She remembered the glorious day each time she gazed at the picture beside her bed. Tanner made her so happy and she couldn't have imagined a more fairytale wedding. Rather than add to her friend's obvious anxiety, Brooke said, "Don't worry, enjoy it cuz it flies by."

"I'm worried my belly's gonna pop out any day now."

"You look great. I can't even tell you're pregnant."

"Well, I feel pregnant. I'd like to run over the person who wrote that 'morning sickness only occurs in a small number of women and is usually mild discomfort.'"

Brooke laughed, "Definitely written by a man."

"Did you have morning sickness?" The moment Melissa asked what she considered a harmless question, Brooke's expression soured. As pregnancy memories ran through her head, Brooke felt an incredible ache inside, worse than before—and much worse than morning sickness. Her eyes welled up, disabling her speech. Melissa filled in the awkward silence, saying, "Oh, I'm so sorry ... I didn't mean to ... sometimes, I say stupid things."

Stupid things actually lightened Brooke's heavy heart. But the unhealed pain lingered. Brooke dabbed her eyes and shifted her posture upright. As if by a divine act, the waiter who appeared at the wrong time earlier, rebounded this time, "Lunch is served, ladies." He dropped the bowl and the plate like a lightning flash, then vanished.

Brooke tasted her soup and her mood improved by the second spoonful. *Who says soup's not comfort food?* She suppressed her gloom and focused on Melissa, asking light, open-ended wedding questions.

After most of the salad and soup was consumed, and Brooke paid the check, Brooke said, "I'm sorry. I didn't mean to lose it."

"Don't say another word. I understand."

"And I didn't mean to bite your head off about what's-his-name."

"Brooke, don't worry. Tobin isn't coming to the wedding. I'm glad you are though. You're such a great friend. Hey, wouldn't it be funny if you met someone at the wedding? I'd better get credit."

"Don't count on it. The online services set up a new website for me: un-match-able dot com."

"You always make me laugh."

Brooke felt relieved. In Melissa's eyes—at least on the surface—Brooke rallied and accomplished what she set out to do. Her earlier outburst could have easily pulled the bride-to-be into her pity party. Brooke hoped her spirited side showed up on Melissa's day, leaving Miss Depressive in the closet where she belonged.

After a hearty hug, Brooke returned to her car. She pressed speed dial one on her cell.

Shane picked up on the third ring—a minor miracle—and said, "I've been thinking about you. It's funny you called."

"Happy thoughts?"

"Should they be?" he asked.

"Yes, and no."

"Start with the yes."

"Why doesn't that surprise me?" They both laughed. Brooke marveled at how relaxed she felt talking to her life coach—much easier than Melissa. Brooke said, "Well, I'm making progress on my work goals. I'm actually enjoying Pharmical and finally giving it a chance—"

"That's fantastic! Congratulations. Doesn't that feel great?"

"Yes, but not so fast. Don't you wanna hear the 'no'?"

"If you must."

"I'm having a hard time with life." Brooke's eyes fluttered.

"What do you mean?"

"My stomach's aching like never before."

"Did you go to a new doctor?"

"Yes. It's the same old, same old. They can't find anything and the medicine only upsets it more."

"How much of it is related to the past?" He hesitated to say Tanner this time.

"As you know, my old roommate from college is getting married."

"Melissa, right?"

"Yes. I don't know if I told you, but she's pregnant. I can't help but think about Tanner and the baby."

"That makes perfect sense. You still have survivor's guilt. I'm guessing it's a combination of remorse from your mother's death in addition to your experiences."

"I don't think about my mother at all anymore and I've worked to forgive Tanner."

"You may not think you're mourning your mother, but subconsciously you are. As for Tanner, you're still grieving but it's more on the surface and easier to recognize."

"Now you sound like a shrink."

Shane chuckled. "I do have my PhD, but I'm not trying to shrink you."

Brooke returned a half-hearted laugh. "I reread that book you sent me, *On Grief and Grieving*, for the zillionth time. But the more I read it, the less I understand."

"Kessler and Kubler-Ross would be the first to caution you about attempting to simplify grieving. Each person's grieving varies. In your case, your loss is complicated."

"What do you mean?"

"Well, just because you read a book, it doesn't eradicate your grief, Brooke."

"You told me the book would solve my problems."

"No, I most certainly did not. I told you that book would help you understand the grieving process, and allow me to help you through each phase. Grief is a healthy emotion. Prolonged grieving is not. I suspect you still suffer from all five phases of grieving—though not as much as when I first met you. Today, you're struggling with acceptance and that ties your stomach in knots."

"So basically, you're saying I've made no progress?"

"That's not at all what I'm saying. Your grief spans three decades and includes complicated dynamics. I'm saying you've made tremendous progress, but aren't there yet."

Complicated dynamics? Brooke was glad Shane hadn't used the word *setback* on her—that's progress. "What should I be doing differently?"

"Change your thoughts. Said another way, change your perception of your thoughts."

"Huh?"

"You view the deaths of both your mother and Tanner with the same emotion: guilt—as if you caused it; Tanner's view of ending his own life was likely one of relief, saving himself from suffering and saving you from suffering by watching him die slowly. In his eyes, he was doing a noble thing, yet you see it differently. Your mother's death wasn't self-inflicted and you didn't cause it. You shouldn't feel guilty about it, but you do. Clinging to the past rips you apart, just like worrying about the future strikes fear."

"Here you go again with that live-in-the-now stuff."

"The past is history, the future's a mystery, but right now is a gift. That's why we call it the present."

"That's a great quote on paper, and one that I do believe, but I'm having trouble with practicing it."

"You're looking through a blindfold rather than rose-colored glasses."

"Okay, enough about Tanner and my mom. Let's go to the present. My best friend's getting married *and* having a baby—the two things I wanted so badly, but will never have. To make matters worse, I'm supposed to stand in front of four hundred people as her maid of honor and act normal, like it's not being flaunted in my face. How can I fool myself into seeing roses with that scenario?"

"Listen to yourself. The answer's in your own words."

"Sorry, I flunk this test. You're gonna have to dispense the *answers*, Shane."

"How old's Melissa?"

"What's that have to do with it?"

"Look, if you want my help, you're going to have to give me a chance. Just answer my questions, then I'll make my point." Brooke pulled into a parking spot at Pharmical and kept the car running for the air conditioning. She studied her gas gauge and grimaced.

"Okay, Melissa's thirty-three."

"Great, and is this her first marriage?"

"Yes."

"How long has she been dating this guy?" he asked Brooke.

"She's been dating Eddie for eight years."

"And she's pregnant?"

Brooke's frown blurred her vision. "Yes, I just told you that."

"Ah ah ah. Just humor me and answer the questions. I'll make my point soon."

"God, you sound like my father. Are you sure you don't have a law degree?"

"Very funny. Final question: do you like Eddie?"

"Not really, and Melissa's dad thinks he's a loser. In fact, he calls Eddie his son-out-law."

"Here's my point—please have an open mind. And please don't interrupt me until I've finished," Shane explained.

"No objections. You have the floor, counselor."

"Stop it, or I'll hold you in contempt of court." They both laughed and it was enough to silence Brooke during Shane's soliloquy: "Melissa's thirty-three, never married, dating a loser who wouldn't commit for eight years until he impregnates her, and feeling societal pressure, they're getting married."

"Pretty much." Brooke rested her chin on her fist.

Shane continued, "And you had the man of your dreams for fourteen years, and you still feel an amazing love for him today?"

Brooke's eyes stung. She struggled, "Yeah."

"Let me finish before you say anything. My point is: who's better off? A wise man once said, 'It's better to have loved and lost than never to have loved at all.' But the wisdom lies beneath that love, for it's being grateful for the experience of life's greatest pleasure—to love someone with all your heart—that brings happiness. This ignites a universal law of like attracts like. From that happiness, from that feeling of pure gratitude, comes renewal—the ability to love again." Shane's musical tone sounded like a poet performing a dramatic read.

Brooke dabbed her eyes and pondered this for a moment. She wished she took notes, afraid to ask him to repeat it. "That's beautiful. That's one of the most profound things you've ever said to me." After a pause, she said, "I think I get it."

"You're grasping more than you know. Go easy on yourself. You're on the upswing—you're starting to enjoy your job and you've forgiven Tanner—and yourself. These are enormous steps. Plus, I haven't even heard one *y'all* out of you in a long time," he chuckled. "Now, just practice gratitude each morning."

"Thanks." Hanging up, Brooke's shoulders and neck relaxed. Shane had an uncanny way of connecting with her. When she felt like a derailed train heading for a crash, he always set her back on the tracks and guided her at the right speed. She did feel gratitude—for having such a great life coach, who appeared magically at her time of greatest need. And she felt guilty for not sharing her deepest secret.

11

*B*rooke shot straight up. She was there, floating at the foot of the bed. Exquisite radiance illuminated the dark room, casting a welcoming glow. An overwhelming feeling of love emanated from the snowy translucent figure—with a kaleidoscope of brilliant colors sparkling around her outline. Though their communication was instantaneous, Brooke reached out and said, "Mommy?"

Their hands converged in the air; a wave of comfort overflowed Brooke. The aura's lips were closed, but she was communicating to Brooke. A soft voice was singing, "I love you. I love you. I'll always love you." Brooke said *I love you* in return and experienced a comprehensive knowing—a serenity with this mystic that extended well beyond her sparkling eyes.

Brooke's eyes fluttered and as they popped open, the image vanished. Brooke flailed her arms and called out, "No, come back!" But her desperate pleas only met emptiness in the bedroom. Brooke attempted to reenact her dream, but the harder she tried, the further the memory faded.

Brooke reached over to her nightstand and grazed Tanner's picture as she flipped on the lamp. Her pajamas soaked with perspiration, she surveyed the room, and shivered. It looked empty, but she wasn't sure. The euphoria was replaced by anxiety.

Mother, Mother, please come back. Silence. Her teeth clattered as a chill permeated inside. Leaving the light on, she reached for the comforter at her feet. While lying down, she pulled it up, holding it tightly against her chin. She stretched her peripheral vision with saucer-like eyes and surveyed the room one more time, then asked aloud, "Are you still there?"

Brooke recalled having visions in previous dreams, but never with such clarity. They usually included Tanner and how she imagined her mother. Tanner looked healthy, a vibrant boyish college student. Never the feeble man at death's doorway. Her mother always looked the same: mid-twenties, thin, curly strawberry blonde hair, and bright blue eyes—just like the picture in her photo album.

After lying awake with the light on long enough to settle her nerves, Brooke clicked off the bedside lamp. With wide eyes, she searched the darkness once again. Realizing she was alone, Brooke closed her eyes. Sleep evaded her as she tossed about while replaying the lucid dream.

Brooke's alarm jolted her out of a deep trance. Though it seemed as if she had been up all night, she slept hard just before the sun peeked up. Although Brooke could have slept till noon, thoughts of her day's tasks began awakening her. She looked forward to a busy day of interviews—her department was nearing full strength.

Brooke replaced her damp pajamas with a fresh Tar Heels T-shirt and matching shorts, then laced up her running shoes. The jog revived her body, but her mind remained fixated on the dream. The more she replayed it, the more ingrained it became, as if possessing her. *I wonder where this one fits in the grief book?*

She had decided to don the brace and her ankle complained in its familiar way, diverting her attention to the present. *When's this thing going to heal?* Her thoughts shifted to Chase, and she picked up her pace. The questions began flooding in: *Why does Chase want to run with me anyway? Is his interest professional or does he want something more? Does he run every morning? Mmmmm, I'd like to see him in running shorts—especially short ones. God, am I back in high school? Okay, now I'm wide awake. I know where I have to go.*

After a quick but vigorous shower, Brooke sipped her Weight Watchers strawberry-vanilla shake—only four points and quite tasty— as she readied herself in the mirror. The drive to Starbucks flew by in spite of the ice bag wrapped to her throbbing left ankle. Thinking about Chase eased the pain, as if in a magnetic pull. Every once in a while, the magnet weakened as the word *married* flashed in her mind; she wondered if the wedding band would be missing again. It didn't matter—today, she just had to see him.

Pulling up to Starbucks, this time Brooke parked across the street. She surveyed the area and spotted a few BMWs, but no red ones. Her watch read 7:34, about ten minutes earlier than the other day. She guessed he always arrived at the same time, because anyone so anal about his coffee temperature had to be OCD about time. Rather than wait like a stalker, she decided to enter.

You could always count on a line at Starbucks. She'd never entered an empty one. This morning was no exception—except no Chase. She considered the bathroom, but opted against knocking. If so, given this procession of snails, he'd emerge before she reached the counter. Miss Piercings wasn't working; instead, a cute younger girl with a New York Yankees cap held court behind counter. Brooke wondered if she knew Chase also.

The coffee aroma teased her senses even more than last time. At 7:44, she'd moved up three spots, still no Chase. At 7:50, now second in line and still no Chase, she breathed a sigh of relief—at least he's not OCD. She wondered if she should knock on that door after all, as an image of him washing his hands in 175-degree water popped up. She giggled.

"Well, you're in a good mood today."

Brooke startled, "Huh?"

Marcus flashed his golden grills and Brooke said, "Oh, hey, Marcus."

"You want the Chai tea again?"

"Good memory, I'm impressed."

"Any friend of A-Man is a friend of mine. You missed him though. He was early ... but I was ready for him." Brooke's shoulders sank, contrasting Marcus's triumphant grin.

Perky Yankee chick said, "What can I getcha?"

Brooke rubbed her temples, then said, "I'll have what A-Man orders, but only one."

"A-Man?" Yankee chick's glare looked like a Red Sox pitcher just beaned her. Marcus said, "You know, Chase Allman."

"Oh, my bud," she beamed, "I love him. He's my favorite. Why didn't you say so?"

My bud? Love him? Favorite? Who is Chase Allman anyway? He's more interesting by the minute.

Marcus asked, "You gonna drink it right away or take it with you?"

Figuring this meant the difference between 175 and 185 degrees, Brooke said, "Now."

Marcus said, "Quad expresso, extra dry, extra hot," coming right up for the pretty lady. Brooke smirked and nodded. Though she recognized some of the lingo, she still felt like a foreigner, and grateful for Marcus.

Brooke paid the bill—realizing his two coffees cost more than a movie pass—then headed over to the counter and waited. She completed this step on her own, without having to be scolded by Chase's *bud*. Baby steps. *I wonder if Shane would call this progress.*

"Here you go," Marcus placed the coffee on the counter like a trophy.

"Thanks."

"My pleasure. I gave you an extra cup and a sleeve. Be careful though—it's hot." As Marcus said this, she laughed at the pun that popped in her head.

Setting the scalding cup on the creamer area, Brooke tried to remember what Chase added. As she surveyed the choices, she scratched her head, then added nutmeg, cinnamon, and three Splendas. She stirred like a magic potion and then dipped her finger. "Ouch." *How the hell does he drink this?* Not wanting to request an ice cube and look like a rookie, Brooke realized she'd have to let this cool. But she yearned to taste it, to sample Chase in an odd way.

The guy following her in line at the counter stood behind her again at the condiment stand and stared, until finally grunting a fake cough.

"Oh, I'm sorry. I'm waiting for this to cool."

He smiled and while keeping his eyes on her derriere, said, "Take your time."

Brooke gripped her smoldering cup and bee-lined across the room to the open spot, realizing it was the same table where she and Chase had sat. She blew on the coffee, but could still feel the heat through the cups. Still ouch. After blowing on it again, this time for several seconds, she pressed the steaming liquid to her lips and sipped.

Brooke's expression resembled a kid's first sip of beer. Like the inviting aroma of coffee, the beer commercials misrepresented the first taste. She sipped again. *How does he drink this motor oil? I hope he keeps mints on hand.*

Brooke winced, looking like a kid who learned Santa was a hoax, then capped the coffee and headed to her car. She considered tossing the whole thing out, but her father's voice rang in her head. *Damn the poor starving people in India—this cup's hot.*

She took a sip. The temperature had dropped to near human range, but it still tasted like mud. Upscale mud, but mud all the same. She couldn't part with the Chase memento just yet, so she placed the hot cup between her legs, grinned, and headed to Pharmical's headquarters. Her ankle didn't bother her for the entire ride.

After finishing half of the quad espresso, Brooke felt a rush. She wondered if it was the caffeine or residual from her thoughts of Chase. Either way, she felt alive, ready to interview the day's roster of candidates she'd found, without any help from HR or her boss. *Why can't Chase be my boss? I bet he's a great boss ... married.*

The boardroom felt colder than usual, and Chase sensed it had nothing to do with the air conditioning—or his coffee temperature. The youngest board member by sixteen years, Chase felt like a kid who wandered downstairs into a roomful of adult guests at his parents' party. Today, to make matters worse, the great Marvin Wixfeldt held court, dazzling everyone except Pharmical's young CEO. Wixfeldt, aka The Butcher, had earned his moniker the old-fashioned way: chopping off employees heads—and getting paid for it. But Marvin's habit of calling Chase "kid" at these meetings bugged him most.

Beyond Wixfeldt's Ivy League pedigree—Harvard undergrad, Wharton MBA—the high finance guru and infamous consultant had a penchant for chumming inside the real lifeblood of corporate America—the boardroom. He earned his lofty price tag by convincing key board members that he could inflate the stock price—and everyone's wallet—through two magic words: "workforce reductions." Mere mention of those words made Wall Street sharks salivate, and twenty-four/seven media pundits banter. The board sat up like Pavlov's dogs.

The Butcher had spoken with Chase twice via "conference calls" that felt more like courtesy calls. Chase despised lip service, and he didn't trust the information that fell past this man's lips. Beyond personality conflict, likely from the north/south thing, Chase had fundamental ideological differences. Chase prided himself on building and that ability helped him claw his way up the corporate ladder to what he thought was the top spot at Pharmical. Until he plunked down at his first board meeting, the kid interrupting the grownups.

Chase believed successful business required two elements: great people and a competitive advantage. The concept of cutting people in order to grow was like cutting off your left hand because it slowed your right. But the reality was, no matter what Chase thought or said, Pharmical headed toward a workforce reduction. And The Butcher, who relished his nickname, was in the back room licking his chops while sharpening his blades.

Chase felt queasy as he listened, knowing The Butcher's recommendation was near. With Chase as CEO for three years, the company experienced record profits and even exceeded the lofty revenue targets of outside analysts. For the most part, Pharmical was on pace to deliver their five-year strat plan number, which dangled a big payout carrot in front of Chase and his management team. Most of the burden fell on the laps of the gifted mergers and acquisitions team that Chase had assembled—always the builder.

Ironically, the board's compensation was tied to stock performance. Though you'd think the two went hand in hand, they usually never did. In the corporate turtle versus the hare race, the short-term pop squashed the five-year opponent every time. And now the fashionable buzz words were *workforce reduction*.

True to form, The Butcher rounded the table, handing his fancy packaged pitch to each board member, which Chase hadn't viewed but feared it was already pre-approved. Chase frowned as he leafed through the tidy stack and stopped on the final page. There it was. He shook his head as if fire ants had climbed in his ears. As he reread it, he felt like a human punching bag.

Chase gulped, then mumbled, "Excuse me," and darted to the door, hoping he could make it just a few more steps.

Thrusting the men's room door open, he splashed cold water on his reddened face. He trembled and his insides churned. The sinking feeling stung like a sucker punch to the gut. It was the worst he'd ever felt. Staring in the mirror, he knew he wasn't returning to that meeting.

— ♥ —

Brooke's day blossomed into her best yet at Pharmical. She extended three job offers—and all three candidates accepted on the spot. With five remaining finalists and only two slots remaining, she liked her odds. Today made up for all the other days. The coffee actually improved as it cooled. Though it made her breath bad—the main reason she didn't drink coffee—she appreciated the caffeine boost. It left tea in the dust.

She had an open time slot due to an applicant calling in sick. She lifted her landline.

"Brooke, is that you?"

"Hi, Melissa, got a minute?"

"Are you okay? You're not cancelling on my wedding are you?"

"No, what're you crazy? I'd never do that to you. Listen, I wanna take you out tonight and celebrate. I'm having a great day. I felt lousy about the other day and I'd like to make it up to you. Happy hour and dinner is about the wildest bachelorette party I can throw for you. Sorry, I hope you weren't counting on boy toys in only cuffs and bow-ties, feeding you berries."

"Yeah right." Melissa laughed out loud and said, "Wow, you do sound great—like yourself. I was worried about you." Melissa bit her upper lip and decided to break away from another night of worrywart wedding planning. Plus, Eddie wanted a guys' night. "Yeah, I'd love to. Where do you have in mind?"

"I'm thinking Santiago's."

"Oh my God, perfect. I could so use a lemon-drop about now."

With Melissa's enthusiasm propelling her, the rest of Brooke's day felt magical. She missed Chase, but thought of him each time she sipped her Starbucks.

Brooke drove back to Chapel Hill and met Melissa for happy hour at Santiago's Tapas & Martini Bar. Opened a few years ago, the place was quite the hotspot. A lively atmosphere and entertaining staff made

Santiago's a perfect place for the two college friends to unwind. And nothing like their famous lemon-drop martinis to jumpstart the night. Never much for the bar scene, Brooke enjoyed Melissa's company. They reminisced about the college days with jovial conversation that matched the festive ambiance.

Melissa's cell buzzed. "Oh, it's Eddie. I better take this."

"Yeah, go ahead." Brooke pulled her cell out of her purse and noticed Shane had called, but didn't leave a voicemail. He was the type who counted a missed call as a voicemail—something that bugged Brooke. With Melissa hunkering on her cell, she decided to call him back, even though she guessed he wouldn't still be working.

After five rings, voicemail, "Hi Shane ... it's me, Brooke. I saw you called. You'll be proud of me. I musta had rose-colored glasses today. I had an awesome day. Filled almost all my openings—and all by myself. I had a great dream—not a nightmare—a dream. My mother and Tanner visited me but it wasn't bad—it was a nice dream. Even though it kept me up all night, I went running and then went to Starbucks to see Chase and had the coffee Chase drinks and kinda liked it, then I ..." Oops, Brooke pressed #, realizing in her happy-hour happiness she rambled about Chase. She listened, hoping for a prompt to re-record. Nothing. *Dammit—why do they call these smart phones?*

As she set her cell down, Melissa stared at her with that famous look of girlish amusement. Later at dinner, in the middle of lemon-drop concoction number three, Brooke told Melissa all about Chase.

Chase realized that he had to pull himself together, but the harder he tried, the worse he felt—and looked. He couldn't remember the last time he vomited; his mouth tasted like raw sewage. Staring into the mirror, he realized the water he splashed on his face didn't help. His eyes resembled red fire balls—the kind he used to eat as a kid. His stomach flared like a brick oven. *How could I possibly have anything else to puke?* Just then, he hurled into the sink.

I have to get back in there. Chase rubbed his face with a paper towel that felt like sandpaper. "Are you okay?" Chase snapped his head to the right, unaware that Henry Stoddard, Chairman of the Board, had even entered.

"Uh, yes, sir. I think I have a touch of the stomach flu."

"You don't look good, son. Why don't you head home and rest? It's probably only a twenty-four-hour thing. I can fill you in on the meeting tomorrow."

Chase realized he had no choice but to follow his mentor's advice. He couldn't tell him the truth. He wanted to sneak back in the room and grab his copy of The Butcher's report, but knew he couldn't. Besides, he'd already seen enough.

Driving home, the wind running through his hair usually invigorated him. Today, it irritated him. Oblivious to the inviting blue sky, he didn't even consider golf. The lingering acidic aftertaste—that even toothpaste couldn't remove—had him queasy about his next cup of coffee. Though the lunch hour had passed, he didn't have any appetite. Driving past eateries that usually made him hungry, made him cringe. He contemplated stopping, but decided to speed home. I hope I don't hurl all over my leather interior.

Pulling into his driveway provided relief, but his stomach still churned. Inside the three-car garage, Oksana opened the house door with wide eyes.

"You're home early, sir."

"I think I have some sort of flu. I feel lousy. Act like I'm not even here—I don't want to make you sick too."

Duke sidestepped Oksana, practically knocking her over, and bolted to Chase, tail wagging, and mouth huffing. "Not now, Duke. Heel. Heel Duke." Reluctantly, Duke plopped down, but his eyes begged for a petting. "Not now, Duke. Sorry."

As Chase slogged through the door, Oksana covered her mouth and backpedaled into the kitchen, bumping into the granite island. Rubbing her back, she said, "You don't look so good. Can I get you anything?"

"No, I think I'm just going to crawl into a hole and die."

"Don't die!"

Chase realized that even though Oksana was fluent in English, she still missed some of the nuances. Usually it was funny, and he would explain the concept of slang. Now, with patience waning, he said, "It was a joke."

"Oh," Oksana released a nervous laugh, "I can get you some ginger ale—I hear that helps."

"No, thanks. I'll be fine. I don't think I can stomach anything right now. I just need to sleep. If I'm not out in twenty-four hours, call an ambulance." Oksana's eyes widened again and before she could say anything, Chase said, "Another joke." As he plodded away, he said to himself, "Sort of." But he wasn't joking.

Chase trudged the winding stairs to his master bedroom and closed the wooden double doors behind him. He eyed his guitar, but decided to listen to music instead. He plopped down on his bed and sighed as his muscles relaxed. After the cushioning settled, he breathed deeply, then reached for his iPod and Bose headphones. He clicked on his "Relaxation" folder. The recordings of his own original guitar playing always soothed him. Though it required several minutes, he finally closed his eyes and let his mind drift.

His eyes fluttered as the nightmare intensified. *I can't reach the control panel. How can I maneuver this plane? A luminous cloud swirled—where did that come from? I can't see anything. Where's the damned hurricane anyway? Why aren't there any warnings on my radio? I'm frozen but I can still see. I've got to find Parker. Son, I hear you—where are you? Dammit, why can't he hear me? Brooke, is that you? Have you been here the whole time? Grab Parker for me. Hurry, before we hit the storm. Oh shit, the plane's going down, down, down. We're gonna crash—brace yourself—and help me pull Parker inside. A clearing in the clouds … oh no, we're heading freefall into the heart of a storm. Why can't I scream? Brooke, help … I've got to pull Parker inside … help … Brooke? Heather! What did you do to Brooke? Brooke … Brooke … Brooke!*

"Daddy … Daddy … Daddy—"

"Huh, what." Chase's eyes popped open, revealing terror.

"Wake up, silly, it's Parker."

The sweet chirpy voice pulled Chase back to reality faster than his eyes, which still maintained a glassy stare. "Oh, thank you. I was having a nightmare."

"Oksana told me to wake you up. You're too old to take naps."

"Is that what she said?"

"No, but wake up before it's too dark to go fishing."

Fishing? As the word registered to his still groggy mind, he felt a sinking sensation. "Oh son, I'm sorry. I don't feel good."

"Do your ears hurt?" Parker was still taking medicine for another ear infection.

"No, bud, but my tummy hurts. A lot."

"Are you gonna throw up?"

"I did before, but I'm okay now."

"So we're not going fishing?"

Chase squinted at his bedside digital clock—6:07 p.m.—and realized he hadn't eaten anything since breakfast. His stomach still ached, mouth and lips parched. "Parker, I can't take you fishing now. I just don't feel good, okay? But I'll make it up to you this weekend."

"Can we go shark fishing?" Parker's eyes sparkled instant enthusiasm.

"That's for me to know and for you to find out, mister."

"Goodie! I get to go shark fishing." Parker bolted for the door, yelling, "Oksana, I get to go catch some sharks with my daddy!" As Parker's voice trailed off, he felt grateful for Oksana. She'd obviously stayed late once again, sacrificing her own personal time, for him. Parker adored her. Though grateful for Oksana, a part of him envied the time she spent with his son, who seemed to change each time he saw him. Going fishing was a great idea and he considered the perfect surprise for Parker. But given his nightmare, he wouldn't book it right now.

Chase remained in bed and slept well, but awakened earlier than his six o'clock alarm with Duke lying on the floor. That's odd, he usually sleeps with Parker. As Chase slowly stepped over Duke, his dog shot up—out of his own doggy dream—and caused his master to stumble.

"Dammit Duke. What are you doing in here anyway?" Duke cocked his head to the side and then stretched out on the floor, releasing a sigh through his wet nose. Chase shook his head and lurched into the bathroom. After relieving himself, he turned and almost fell into Duke, who was now wide awake, wagging his tail. Chase knew that look.

"Duke, I don't feel like running today." Duke's head bowed slightly in a pose, while his tail thumped against the tile. He stared back at his dog, and, standing there in his underwear and T-shirt, he had a change of heart. Chase said, "Okay, we'll compromise. Let's go for a quick walk."

Duke's ears shot straight up and his posture followed. "Sure, you know the word *walk*, but *no* doesn't seem to be in your vocabulary." Duke jumped up and pressed his paws against Chase. As Duke slobbered on Chase's face, Chase burst out laughing. "Okay, you win. I know. I know. Let's go … but no running. And quick! I gotta eat something soon or I'll miss work today." *Work*. The word hovered in the air and stung like a hornet.

After a surprise pancake breakfast with Parker, Oksana, and even Duke who coaxed more than leftovers with his eyes, Chase checked voicemail—realizing he'd gone twenty-four hours without it. Of the five messages, Ruth left one informing him of a lunch meeting with Henry Stoddard. *Good, just the man I wanted to see.* Craving caffeine even though his stomach still churned, he decided on Starbucks. The pancakes had sounded good and tasted even better, but never felt the same one hour later. He hoped the 175-degree espresso—only one today—would agree with him and dilute the buttermilk glue inside. He needed his A-game with Henry.

Henry Stoddard mentored Chase Allman into the corner office. He lured him away from a competitor with promises of upward mobility, and promoted him up each rung until convincing the stodgy board to elect his young prodigy Chief Executive Officer. Chase understood the board preferred an outsider with CEO experience, but Henry Stoddard could be convincing. Henry was Chase's guardian angel, and as long as the aging chairman perched atop Pharmical's board, Chase Allman could do no wrong. Henry had been more supportive of Chase than Chase's own father, Nathan Allman.

As Chase drove to Hope Valley Country Club, he wondered how his dad was doing. He hadn't seen him since he remarried and escaped to Mexico with his senorita. After his wife's death, his dad washed away his grief with premium tequila. Henry and Nathan both graduated from Duke, possessed similar mannerisms, and were both lousy golfers who used more mulligans than tees. They differed now, in their golden years. Henry remained golden and Nathan turned to liquid gold—with the worm.

Nathan always thought he'd die first. Then Barbara—"Babs" to everyone, but "mom" to Chase, died after a short bout with lung cancer; Nathan fell into a perpetual pity party. Since childhood, Chase suffered from asthma due to a severe allergy to cigarette smoke, which doctors linked to a smoke-infected womb. Babs thumbed her nose at the Surgeon General and dissenting doctors during her first pregnancy, then blasted the medical community when she delivered a ten-pound boy—while puffing away.

Growing up with constant headaches, Chase winced each time his parents lit up. Even when Babs found out she had lung cancer, she scoffed and refused to relinquish her lifelong habit. Nathan stopped cold turkey the day of Babs's diagnosis, hoping his wife would follow suit. She didn't and died six months later with a cigarette smoldering in her hand.

It hit Nathan hard. Chase felt depressed his mother chose cancer sticks over life. The day she died, Chase took up running; Nathan ran the opposite direction. Chase begged him to seek professional help, but instead, his stubborn father started smoking again and began self-medicating. First with whiskey, then gin, now tequila—or, as Chase called it, *to-kill-ya*.

The visit to Mexico still stung and Chase wondered if it would be his last. He couldn't imagine flying all the way down there to pick his old man off the floor each day. He wasn't sure what was worse: Heather killing herself with illegal drugs or his dad doing it legally.

Chase pressed the end button until he was certain his cell phone turned off. Beyond punctuality, Henry's leading pet peeves were "people gabbing away in a restaurant" or "pushing on those damn buttons while you're trying to eat with them." He owned an outdated cell phone—the number a secret—and Chase had never received a call from Henry's cell. Verizon must love him.

Henry refused to use Outlook; instead, the Luddite kept a bulky Day-Timer—the paper kind. He hated his company email—delegating "all that e-junk" to his personal secretary. In Henry's world, technology was a burden, a distraction to interaction. In some weird way, it worked for Henry. He was that rare breed who could compute without a spreadsheet; his mind's microchip churned out brilliant results—even though he typed with his forefingers. Henry could grasp the big picture, then fill in the blanks—without technology.

Henry arrived ten minutes early as usual—"Henry time." Chase also admired punctuality, viewing it as respect for the other person.

After exchanging pleasantries including the obligatory "are you feeling better?" question, Henry glanced at the maître d', who said, "Afternoon Hank, I have your table ready."

"Very well, Jean-Claude, we're ready."

Following his gray-haired, distinguished mentor, veteran of countless power lunches, Chase thought, I've never heard him called *Hank* before. He didn't look like a Hank—he was always Henry. To him, calling Henry "Hank" was like calling his dad "Nate." Jean-Claude led them to a private table in the corner.

Henry, not one for small talk, dove right in, asking, "Have you read Marvin's report?"

"Yes sir, I studied it this morning."

"And?"

"I know with you I can be brutally honest, sir."

"Go on." Henry crossed his arms on his tie clip.

"It goes against everything I believe in."

"Be more specific."

A waiter appeared and Henry and Chase paused. He said, "Excuse me for interrupting, but would either of you care for a cocktail?"

Henry said, "I'll have a dry gin martini, up, three olives please." Chase frowned, thinking maybe he's more like my father than I thought.

Chase said, "Ginger ale, please." Henry's eyebrows crossed, Chase said, "I'm still a little under the weather."

The waiter said, "Right away," glanced back at Henry, and took his cue to leave.

Henry hit right where he left off, saying, "What don't you agree with?"

"Sir, you brought me in to build Pharmical. I'm doing that. I think The Butcher is going to destroy this company."

"Don't call Marvin that name! I hate that. He's doing exactly what I asked him to do."

"With all due respect, he's doing the opposite and you know it."

"Bullshit. His plan will drive our stock price to the moon."

"I disagree. I'm sick and tired of management by buzzwords like *workforce reduction*. He wants to dump a brand new division before it gets a chance to demonstrate why we added it in the first place."

"Are you talking about that ICS anomaly?"

"Yes, as a matter of fact, I am."

"My astute protégé, in case you haven't read anything lately, outsourcing's the wave of the future and Wall Street loves it."

"Then why have any people in Durham? If it were up to Marvin, he'd ship us all to India," Chase countered.

"I'm not sure why you're fighting this. Outsourcing a broken division saves us forty percent and drives our stock to a record high."

"What about our total quality initiative?"

"What about it?"

"It starts with building rapport with our customers. That's what ICS does. Our customers don't want to be put on hold by some guy named *Achmed*."

"Listen to yourself. You sound like a racist relic. We aren't turning our business over to a bunch of illiterates. Outsourcing allows us to go global, to communicate in all languages, and extend beyond the U.S. market. Besides, ICS's fill rate is not cutting it."

"The division's only five months old and isn't even fully staffed."

"Whose fault is that?" Henry asked.

"It's nobody's *fault*. Building a division takes time. Hell, our strat plan takes five years."

"So?"

"So why cut it now?"

The waiter had been hovering with the tray in the air. Both men ignored his not-so-subtle tactics. He finally set both drinks on the table and decided not to ask for a food order until they asked.

"See the bigger picture. The only number that matters is our stock price. I don't need Marvin to tell me Todd Hollis sold us a bill of goods with GenSense. Plus, I'm not a fan of that gal he duped us into taking."

"You mean Brooke Hart?"

"The blonde with more T & A than brains?"

"No, the woman who's been busting her butt ramping up a brand new division."

"She doesn't fit in at Pharmical," Henry said.

"What's that supposed to mean?"

"From what I'm hearing, she's a lightweight."

"Henry, I've observed Brooke Hart in action and I like what I see." The moment the words left Chase's lips, he winced.

"I'm not sure what you *see* beyond the obvious. Now that you mention it, I heard you were carrying her around the parking garage." Henry pressed both fists against his temples and fixed a glare.

The words hit Chase hard. Though Henry had stepped out of the day-to-day operations, he obviously maintained his gossip mongers. He could only imagine what was said to the old man. "That's absurd. I'm not sure what you heard, but she fell and injured her ankle—on company grounds. I was the only one around. What was I supposed to do, abandon her?"

Henry gulped his martini, then with an exaggerated swallow, glared into Chase's eyes. Chase lifted his ginger ale and sipped while locking his gaze with Henry.

The stare down looked like O.K. Corral to the fidgeting waiter perched tableside, pad in hand. "Excuse me, gentlemen, are you ready to order or would you care for another cocktail?"

Henry held his stare until Chase glanced down at the menu. Neither man felt hungry, but Henry said, "I'll have a Reuben."

"Very well, sir. And you?"

"Huh? Oh, I'll have a roast turkey on wheat and an iced tea."

Henry flicked his finger above his long stemmed glass and the waiter nodded, then fled as if the table needed an exorcism.

"Chase, I've known you a long time and have always been able to count on you. I'm going to impart some advice and I want you to pay close attention."

Chase gulped, but didn't utter a word. He maintained eye contact, but with less intensity, like a student listening to a professor.

Henry said, "I need you on board with these changes, plain and simple. Trust me on this one. You don't have to like it, but you have to stop fighting it. And watch yourself with Marvin."

Feeling bile in his throat, he swallowed hard. Chase paused, then, as if raising a white flag, replied, "You win." Chase felt internal combustion. The pancakes burrowed inside like a flaming bowling ball and his temples pounded. For the first time since joining Pharmical, he felt paranoid.

The duration of lunch remained somber and tense. A series of questions rattled inside Chase's head—he didn't dare ask to spare Brooke Hart from the gallows right now. He still didn't understand why she was on The Butcher's block but decided to approach Henry after things settled. His ally would agree with his proposition, just like always. Chase felt relieved Henry didn't ask about Heather. He didn't know how he'd handle that question.

Driving back to work, Chase was crestfallen—like his hot air balloon had an ice pack clinging to it. He hated battling Henry, whose diatribe bit like a rabid dog. *Am I just overly sensitive because of the flu? No, something bugged him beyond his stomach. His paranoia intensified—did The Butcher now aim his cleaver at me? Recalling the board's wish for an outsider, did Marvin Wixfeldt battle Henry's recommendation?*

The innuendo about Brooke Hart stung. Chase recalled *All the President's Men,* wondering who played deep throat to Henry. He didn't see The Butcher that day, but who knows.

Beyond the constant job pressures—which included making the tough calls—Chase Allman was being asked to go against his instincts. To rip up his plan, toss it in the air, and expect it to land with a better picture. It felt rotten.

With three new hires in tow like ducklings, Brooke ventured to the company's cafeteria. Though the menu reminded her of dorm food, she thought lunching there would make a positive impression. Plus, the deep employee discount would keep Greenberg off her tail. She hoped her invisible boss wouldn't be upset she didn't invite him. Brooke thought of her expense report hound as a diaper—always on her and full of you know what. Surveying the choices on the wall made her draw a similar conclusion.

The newbies didn't seem to mind. Brooke's three hand-picked client service representatives beamed, flashing enthusiasm that only new hires could. They all followed in their new boss's footsteps, ordering salad bar and diet sodas. A good sign, Brooke thought.

Though salad bar wasn't a dream lunch, all four women seemed to savor every bite. Brooke led upbeat conversation, hoping to offset the boredom of filling out all the forms on day one. She still remembered that day, though it seemed longer than five months ago. As they finished, Brooke felt a twinge in her stomach—that time of the month or bad hard-boiled eggs. Or both.

She said, "I know you have plenty of paperwork to sift through, so I won't keep you any longer. Good luck and try not to get too many paper cuts."

After a chorus of thank yous, Brooke excused herself and headed to the nearby bathroom. She slinked into the handicapped stall at the end, deciding the leg room was worth the risk. Relieved she made it in time, she relaxed and started marveling at how much she was enjoying her job. She no longer stared out her window, feeling emptiness; she finally felt like a contributor. New hires always rejuvenated her. Going to the employee cafeteria provided a boost of company pride, even though the salad dressing left a sour taste that lingered like stale coffee.

Coffee? Her mind wandered. *I wonder when Chase made his pit stop at Starbucks. I hope Marcus didn't tell A-Man I ordered his coffee. Or that he saw me the other day. Would Chase care?*

The door to the bathroom whooshed open, startling Brooke. She heard two women giggling and waited until they entered their stalls. Standing to exit, Brooke heard the voice and froze. "C'mon give me a break, he's my boss."

The other woman replied, "Ruthie, don't tell me you don't drool all day. He's got to be the most eligible bachelor in Carolina."

Ruthie? Eligible bachelor?

"Oh stop it—someone'll hear you."

Brooke held her breath like Houdini under water.

"Relax, I don't think Chase Allman is coming in *here* anytime soon."

While both women cackled, Brooke released her breath one molecule at a time. With eyes wider than the toilet seat, Brooke feared she sat in a danger zone, but guessed they didn't see her feet. As far as they knew, judging from their carefree banter, she was invisible. But she couldn't take any chances. Brooke did what any grown woman would have done: she plopped back down, lifted her legs up and out of sight, and cupped her ear. Brooke then covered her chest, hoping they wouldn't hear the sound of her pounding heart reverberating off the tiles.

Ruth's turn, "Well, he's not a bachelor." Brooke nearly gasped.

"Oh come on, Ruthie, his wife's completely out of the picture and you know it."

"Lucy, you're not supposed to know that. You're the only one I've told."

"Why does he still wear a ring?"

"With this company—are you kidding?"

"True. I feel bad for him though. He's such a nice guy—he deserves better," Lucy said.

"I do too. I know he blames himself, but he shouldn't. I wish that gold-digger would go away for good and let him get on with his life."

"Aren't you dying to find out what really happened?"

"I know enough already. I also know not to ask too many questions—he asks me for advice all the time. He trusts me." Giggles.

The bathroom door slid open again, and both women suspended their booth chat as someone else entered. Brooke felt like Janet Leigh in the shower, hoping the footsteps wouldn't land in front of her stall door. Maybe the handicapped sign would divert the new visitor. Through blinking eyes, Brooke gasped as she viewed the lady's shoes clicking below. Oh, God, no! She closed her eyes and clenched her teeth. Then, she heard the door next to hers open and swing shut. Her eyes popped open and fluttered like a hummingbird's wings as she exhaled and mouthed *thank you*.

Brooke heard two flushes within seconds of each other and heard the clacking. This was too much excitement for one bathroom break. Brooke shook and feared she'd fall. She gripped the handles tightly, mouthing another *thank you* to the ceiling. Even though her backside tingled like a funny bone, she didn't dare move.

Once the coast finally cleared, Brooke escaped. Her head never felt cloudier.

—— ♥ ——

"T.G.I.F." The words from the radio announcer hung in the air like Carolina humidity. Chase had forgotten what day it was and considered ordering three quad espressos. Usually, Friday meant high day, but today, his head spun. Scanning for parking, a car pulled out from the curb. Chase hit the brakes and ended his daze. Front spots always brought a smile to his lips. After a hurried parallel park, he exited while peering inside the tinted windows.

Chase was early. He wanted to see Brooke, but he didn't want to see her. Glancing at the line inside, coast clear. Standing by Marcus? Nope. He sighed while wiping his brow. He hadn't seen her all week and definitely didn't want to run into her today. Still unable to connect with Henry, the whole mess made him queasy.

Chase ordered his usual, and Tonya and Marcus both thought he looked tired. Chase said he looked forward to relaxing this weekend, which brought, "Amen to that, A-Man," from Marcus.

Back at the office, he dialed Henry's line again. Lucy answered and said, "He's in another meeting, but I've given him your messages. I'll remind him you called again," with a little too much enthusiasm.

"Chase, Dixon's been holding on line one."

Dixon? "Oh, thanks, Ruth. Send it in."

After one ring, "Dixie-dawg, what's up?"

"You are, Boa. I landed the usual prime tee time with your name on it."

Chase rubbed his temples, glancing at his calendar, then said, "You know, dawg, you're timing's perfect. You're on. See you then."

"Bring your wallet this time."

"Whatever. Later, dawg."

After the week from hell, Chase needed an escape. His best friend possessed uncanny intuitive abilities today. He still had a call to make, hoping she'd meet him for lunch.

"Yes." Brooke's voice broke through the office silence like a shout in a library. The cubicle heads shot frowns at her. "Finally, full strength," she said with a lowered decibel. Brooke couldn't wait to inform Shane that she nailed her goal—and with two weeks to spare. He'll be so proud.

She sipped her espresso and grimaced. *How does he like this stuff? I put in extra Splenda and cinnamon, but it still tastes like mud.* She couldn't believe she missed him again this morning, even though she arrived a half hour earlier.

As Brooke reached for her cell, her ringtone exploded in her hand. This would be weird, she thought, as she checked for Shane's name on the screen. *Oh shit.*

"Melissa, uh, hi. I've been meaning to call you." It was partially true.

"I'm freaking out! The wedding cake's destroyed."

"What?"

"I knew we shouldn't have used that place. Was it up to me? Nooooo, I'm only the freaking bride—what do I know? Once again, we had to do what *Eddie's* mother wanted. I'm so pissed."

Brooke grinned and strangled her laughter. Melissa's voice sounded like an auctioneer on Red Bull. She expected her friend to be wound up with one day to go. But Melissa sounded so upset, Brooke considered calling a zookeeper for a tranquilizer gun. Instead, Brooke made the mistake of asking, "What happened?"

Chase fidgeted all morning; paranoia coursed through his veins. The question haunted him—is Henry avoiding me? He glanced at his watch and grimaced. With the meter running at five-hundred dollars per hour, he didn't want to be one second late for his meeting.

Pam Moliere was recommended by all the local judges—many of whom she knew from Duke Law School. She graduated five years earlier than Chase and, from day one, built her reputation as one tough cookie. Though Chase considered divorce lawyers the dregs of the profession—tied with ambulance chasers—he respected Pam. Brilliant, engaging, tough on opponents, and bottom line: successful. The stakes were high and he had to hire the best. Recognizing the mother had the upper hand in custody battles, and sympathy from judges in high income settlements, he needed to act fast. He couldn't risk losing Parker.

Though steadfast in his decision to divorce, it still gnawed at him. Why did it have to come to this? He had moved beyond the initial shock, then the sadness, and most of the anger, but he knew the mother of his child less now than he did when he met her. Hearing Max describe the life she had chosen versus being there for Parker—and for him—still stung. And probably would for the rest of his life.

Unbeknownst to Pam, he tilted the deck in his favor. Chase had paid a retainer to each of the top-rated divorce firms in Durham, blocking Heather's chance to even hire a competent opponent to Pam.

He guessed she'd file a motion for legal fees; if Heather used his own money against him, it may as well be a win-win for him. Some would call it playing dirty, but he was just playing smart; he didn't care at this point. Chase wanted the whole mess over as quickly and quietly as possible. So far, he had impressed Pam with his media connections—it wasn't easy to keep a story this juicy out of the headlines.

Though confident in Pam, he noticed she did the thing he despised—procrastinate. Why are divorce lawyers slower than a romance novel in finishing? So far, Pam had dragged her feet enough to unnerve her even keel client. He understood the squeaky wheel got the grease in business, but that it backfired in divorce law. Applying unruly force broke the chain. But Chase had an intangible on his side: Pam truly admired Chase—she empathized with him.

Pam's admiration for Chase stemmed from her own childhood. Raised by her mother, after the father she never knew abandoned his three young children, she respected Chase's undying devotion. His love for Parker contradicted her pessimistic paradigm. In a world where so many kids didn't know their fathers, she appreciated her client's commitment to break the cycle, to never waver on what mattered most—his own flesh and blood—even when his wife went AWOL.

Pam sensed Chase hurt inside. She understood all the destructive phases and behaviors of divorce; her client fell in the middle of the uphill emotional battle. Stress revealed character and, in a selfish world of cut and run parenting, Chase was truly a good guy.

Pam realized the pre-nuptial agreement would hold up—lawyers understood how to do contracts—and though his differed from her template, it worked. Heather had signed all the dotted lines. Most divorce cases settled anyway—usually just before the scheduled court date. The procrastination strategy billed maximum hours, then it ended with a slice down the middle—unless there was a pre-nup.

When Chase handed Pam his financial spreadsheet, her eyes widened. For such a young guy, he'd done well. *Those corporate lawyers earned so much more.* Hoping to avoid a public spectacle, Chase was willing to offer Heather double the amount of the pre-nuptial. Also, Chase was open to allowing Heather visitation rights with the son she deserted—if it came to that. Pam wished all her clients were like Chase.

Chase prayed to close the divorce loop without more heartache, especially for his young son. Right now, Chase handed Pam a no-brainer case to win—Heather had violated at least three of North Carolina's grounds for divorce:

Abandonment of family. *Easy to prove.*

Becomes an excessive user of alcohol or drugs. *Hazelden's notes and finding her bags of legal and illegal drugs—including cocaine and pot.*

Commits adultery. *Tricky to prove, but Max promised to snap the right photos.*

The only thing working against the divorce was Father Time. The court dockets were packed thanks to the skyrocketing divorce rate and post-divorce squabbles that overburdened the fragile system. Unable to serve Heather since her last known address was Chase's house, and officially file the divorce, they turned to Hazelden, but Heather wasn't there long enough. Pam mentioned other ways to commence, but, when pressed further, went into ambiguous divorce lawyer speak.

But now that Max found her—with ninety-nine percent certainty, Chase wanted a SWAT team to serve her divorce notice, taking no chances. Once that simple document was delivered—even if she refused to sign it—Chase and Parker could move on with their lives.

Chase arrived five minutes late, but still beat Pam to the same restaurant. Once she was settled, Chase covered his entire checklist with Pam before their meals arrived. He handed her the most important piece of information—confirmed with Max during the ride over—Heather's whereabouts. The whole meeting lasted just under an hour. At five-hundred dollars an hour, it was the most expensive burger he'd ever eaten. He didn't worry though. If Pam could deliver him a happy ending to this unhappy story, it was priceless. Leaving Pam, he hoped she'd act fast; he applied enough of his own grease to the wheel.

Though the week passed like a decade, Chase noticed his mood brighten. He hustled to change his corporate costume to his golf gear. Though he desired an hour on the practice range, he just didn't have it today. Didn't matter: Dixie-dawg's trash talking always fueled his A-game.

Chase barreled out of the clubhouse and, true to form, spotted Dixon loading a cooler into the cart. His madras pants made Rodney Dangerfield look conservative. Chase chuckled while Dixon monkeyed with the golf cart as if preparing for a safari. He wanted to snap a picture.

Hearing Chase's laughter, Dixon spun; he donned prescription Vuarnets, circa 1980s, but so Dixon, "Hey, Boa. You made it."

"Of course—I wouldn't miss kicking your plaid ass for the world."

"Hey, do you have to return your grandpa's pants later—or can you wear those khakis all weekend?"

The introductory insults ended with disparaging comments about Dixon's frayed hat as the two buddies drove over to the famous first tee, lining up behind an antique foursome. Both Chase and Dixon frowned and then made enough racket to rouse their hearing aids. The blue-hairs didn't notice the speedier twosome. Chase hoped Dixon's pants would scare them away. No avail, so much for golf being a gentlemen's game.

Instead of griping, Dixon bolted up from the cart, and said, "Ready for a cold one?"

Chase, not a big boozer, rarely drank before nightfall. But, after this week, didn't hesitate, "Sure, why not."

The two best friends polished off an entire Heineken each before the group from hell hit their mulligans. The beer that looked so relaxing in the ads had the opposite effect on Chase. He couldn't shake the stiff neck that he'd had since Tuesday's hurl-a-thon. Even Dixon's banter, which usually elevated his spirits, irritated him.

After scrutinizing the senior foursome, on pace to break the course record for slowest play, the college buddies settled into the cart on the third tee in silence. Finally, Dixon said, "Chase, I've never seen you double-bogey two holes in a row."

"Don't remind me." Chase stared straight ahead.

"All kidding aside, dude, what's buggin' ya?"

Chase turned, and the pain shot from his neck down his side like a taser. Dixon peered over his Vuarnets. Usually, all kidding aside, coming from Dixon's mouth, meant Three Stooges time. Not now. "I had the week from hell."

"Join the club. I had a guy puke all over my operating table this morning. So much for a routine scope. I'm not sure that's what they meant in residency when they said, 'Ya never get used to the smell.' I've been around morgues that smelled better."

Chase's silence struck Dixon like a stun gun. Dixon said, "You need another beer!" then popped up to the cooler.

Chase said, "No thanks, not yet. I think I need some water."

"So do those geezers in front of us. They've been searching that pond for hours. Sheesh, did they die looking for a lousy ball?"

Chase just stared at the cart path. Dixon said, "I've never seen you this quiet. You all right?"

"Huh. Oh, I'm just thinking."

"You look like a Rodin sculpture." Still no response. Dixon continued, "Talk to me—what's up?"

"I'm having a come to Jesus week. They brought in some chop-shop consultant who wants to cut everything I've done and hang me out to dry."

"That's why they pay you the big bucks."

"No, they pay you to cut, they pay me to build."

"Good one. What are they chopping?"

"An entire division. Sending it over to India. A bunch of my people lose their jobs so we can help a bunch of maharishis buy bigger hookahs."

"That sucks. Sorry about that. What about your girlfriend Brooke. Is she getting axed?"

Brooke? Dixon pressed the button that finally brought Chase back to life. That's what friends are for. "First of all, she's not my freaking girlfriend. Will you guys stop calling her that!"

Dixon opted to ignore the *you guys.* Instead, "So, is she getting canned?"

"Looks that way. But the thing that irks me most is I'm totally out of the loop."

"And here I thought CEOs had all the fun."

Chase surveyed his reflection in Dixon's glasses—one of those moments when Dixon unwittingly hit the nail on the head. Chase said, "It used to be fun. I used to love what I did. Building this company into something. You wouldn't think I'd hit a roadblock now. Hell, our board of dinosaurs couldn't build a bridge across a dried up creek."

"Think of it on the bright side."

"How's that?"

"Now you can bang Brooke, Boa."

"Quit calling me Boa! I still can't believe you called me that in front of her."

"Well, you called me Dixie-dawg. And she was a patient. C'mon man, listen to yourself. Plus, Boa's a better nickname than dawg any day."

"Says who?"

"You kidding me? Why? Did she ask how you earned the name Boa?"

"I'm surprised you didn't tell her."

"Wah, wah, wah. Here, use this cry towel," Dixon said, unclipping his golf towel from his bag and flinging it in Chase's face. Dixon continued, "You know how many times that nickname got you laid? And do I get any thanks? Nooooo. You owe me—big time, Boa."

Chase chuckled. "Are you ever going to grow up?"

"Not till you have another beer. You won't let me smoke a cigar, and the way you wasted a perfectly good Heineken just doesn't cut it. You need to get laid, big time."

"Wah, wah, wah, yourself. Throw me a beer—and a cold one this time. And I'm doubling our bet." Dixon nearly fell over. *He's back.* Neither of them realized the geezer party in front of them had a full hole lead.

After Dixon's duck-hook drive, Chase made a quacking sound, then stepped up to the tee. Feeling a burst inside, Chase tightened his golf glove, then launched his drive straight down the middle, well past Dixon's. Sometimes it took a good berating from a guy like Dixie-dawg to pull you off the floor. Snapping the icy beer can open with a spray, Chase strutted like a matador and said, "Take that!"

"Where'd you go? I didn't see it down."

"You'd need binoculars. They're building a Walmart between our shots." *Take that—that's what friends are for.*

For the next three holes, Chase put on a clinic, beating Dixon like a drum. And Dixon didn't mind. Chase was a much better golfer anyway and should win. Dixon was just happy to have his buddy back. Now even in their match, Chase yelled, "What do I have to do to get another beer around here?"

"He's back—I love it. You didn't even need a nipple on that one." They laughed.

At the turn, the geezers called it quits. Feeling giddy from three beers, marveling it was before five o'clock, Chase slogged to the window to re-stock the cooler with green cans.

With smooth sailing in front of them, Chase and Dixon raced around the scenic back nine, laughing and heckling each other on every shot. Buddy golf.

By hole 13, Chase's beer muscle faded; his swing looked more like flailing while Dixon could have performed brain surgery. Chase still scored well enough to tie Dixon through 17. Then, on 18, Dixon sank an impossible putt to win bragging rights, worth much more than the cash. Chase smirked and, before Dixon could say it, handed him his wallet, and slurred, "Take it all, ya cheatin' bastard."

"Better luck next time, Boa," Dixon said while leafing through the green bills like a deck of cards.

"Enough with the Boa!"

"Wah, wah, wah. Hey, since I own your wallet after that ass whooping, the least I can do is buy you a cocktail. You up for the nineteenth hole?"

"Ah, thanks, dawg, but I can't tonight. I haven't seen Parker all week and I've gotta set up our fishin' trip this weekend."

"This weekend? Have you forgotten about tomorrow?"

"Tomorrow?"

"Don't give me that look. You better not bag on me like last time."

"Help me out here. I'm sure I have it on my Outlook. What's tomorrow?"

"Hello ..." Dixon removed his sunglasses and studied Chase's face, then said, "Charity for Children."

"Oh."

"You know I'm on the board and bought two tables at five grand a pop. I need you there."

"Why do you need *me* there?"

"Because if you bag on me, I'll write, 'BOA' all over your name tags."

"C'mon, seriously? I don't wanna go to a freakin' charity event."

"This is no ordinary charity event—this is Charity for Children. Do you know how many babes are gonna be there? Last year was insane. Of course, I'm on the invitations committee."

"I promised Parker—"

"Take Parker Sunday. He can go to a sleepover Saturday. Problem solved. Besides, I'm letting you off the hook tonight, so it's a fair trade-off."

Chase's eyes swam circles, the final effects of the beer setting in. With shoulders slouched, he said, "Do you always think with your pants?"

"Is that a 'yes'?"

"What time?"

"Cocktails at six sharp. And you gotta rent a tux."

"I own more tuxes than you have ties."

"Oh, excuse me, mister CEO. I wear pajamas to work so I have to rent one."

"Oh, you poor doctor."

"Orthopedic surgeon. Especially tomorrow. Hey, and no Dixie-dawg please."

Chase shook his head, thinking *why do I like this guy so much?* The seven beers didn't help him solve the mystery. *Maybe he's my alter-ego?* Though not easily led, Chase felt like a sheep being herded by Dixon.

Standing beside his BMW—more like swaying—Chase called a cab, by far the wisest thing he ever did with his smart phone. Chase said to no one in particular, "I'm not drinking tomorrow."

12

Question: what's the worst way to cram diametrically opposed families into one room? Answer: The Racer–Brenner Rehearsal Dinner.

At last, Melissa Brenner's long-term relationship with Eddie Racer headed toward the finish line. Before the checkered flag, there were plenty of red and yellow ones. Amid the scenic backdrop of Raleigh's Pine Shadows Country Club, the love in the air felt like a Hatfield–McCoy reunion—only with shoes.

Clifton Brenner, Melissa's father, had thrown Eddie out of his house three years ago when Eddie asked for Clifton's daughter's hand. *No-good scumbag* was the nicest term said during the ensuing exchange from Eddie's souped-up car that looked like it missed the cut in *Joe Dirt*. Someone would have called 911, but they figured Eddie would outrun the cops.

It took Melissa two and a half years just to be able to say "Eddie" in front of her father without causing a tantrum. When the EPT displayed positive, she pressed Eddie Racer for a speedy wedding. Even withholding the pregnancy news, Melissa faced a wrath from her father—not helping her nerves on their special night.

Clifton had been warned to behave so many times. He still called Eddie his son-out-law, but it was an improvement from the words yelled from the porch. Thanks to the invention of elastic, Melissa wasn't showing—or the night would have rivaled the real Hatfields and McCoys.

Eddie's parents wanted to have the rehearsal dinner in their backyard. Clifton drove by once and said, "No chance. I'm not going to make my relatives eat white trash." Melissa threatened to elope and run away. He told his daughter either it's at a nice place or he wouldn't pay for the wedding. Melissa used this as leverage to force her father to pay for half of the rehearsal—she agreed to cover the other half. Not exactly a great kickoff for two families to join in marital bliss.

Eddie's parents pulled into the stodgy country club looking like they were attending a NASCAR event. You didn't need to draw a dividing line, there were three:

1. Brenners: Jewish, sophisticated, rich, educated.
2. Racers: Atheist, Klan, trailer park, schooled at Boys Town.
3. The Wedding Party (except for Eddie's brother, all Melissa's friends): attractive, thirty-something, North Carolina alums, Generation STBR (Soon-To-Be-Rich).

Fortunately, no lines crossed, and dinner eventually ended.

Pacing to her car, Brooke thought the Jewish-Atheist ceremony would rival the millennium fireworks show.

Brooke did as well as anyone to keep Melissa calm and ignored Eddie whenever she could. It helped her through the Tanner baby anxiety. Arriving home as thunder and lightning alternated with the darkened sky, she collapsed on her bed. *Tomorrow should be interesting.*

"Whenever I see your smiling face ..." boomed from Brooke's bedside. Usually, the upbeat song made her smile—as she guessed James Taylor had intended—but, today, her first thought was Tanner. The memory of their first date together hung in the air like the ominous clouds visible through her window. Even with constant lightning flashes last night, she slept with the shades open.

Guessing it was round one of Melissa's wedding-day meltdown, she lunged for the phone and missed, spilling her purified water all over her dusty end table. *Oh shit.*

There are plenty of great ways to start a weekend morning—a nice smile, a deep invigorating breath, watching the sunrise, even ignoring the sunrise with an exaggerated turn in the opposite direction. *Oh shit* wasn't how Brooke wanted to open an emotional rollercoaster day. She grabbed her phone and ignored the spilling water.

"Hi, Daddy." *Oh shit.* Saturday. She completely forgot.

"I called you last night. Are you okay?"

"I've never been better." A lie, but it held some truth.

"Have you left yet?" Brooke hated when Weston Ingram, Esq., did this; she swore he could secure a book deal for *The Book of Rhetorical Questions*.

"Didn't I tell you? It's Melissa's wedding today. She's finally getting married—can you believe it? I'm in the wedding party."

"Oh. So, I guess that means you're not coming for lunch?" There he goes again.

"No, they're getting married in Raleigh at four o'clock."

"Oh."

Before he could say, *you can still make an early lunch,* Brooke went on the offensive, "I'll come next Saturday—I promise."

"I hope so. How's work?"

"Actually, I'm glad you asked. I'm really starting to love it. I finally have a full staff and I hand-picked each of them."

"That's great, congratulations."

"I've had a chance to spend time with our CEO Chase Allman. He's actually a great guy. He's sort of taken me under his wing." Brooke blushed as the pun hit her—*how would Freud interpret that one?*

"Well, I probably saw a different side back then. It was a couple of years since that case and maybe he's matured with the new job and all."

"Anyway, I better go. Love you. See you next Saturday."

Brooke lay down while gazing at Tanner's picture, the bottom of the frame still moist from her water spill. And the memories began flooding in. Her tender ankle was the least of her worries. She told the picture, "I hope I hold up today."

Brooke closed her eyes and allowed the silence to quell her nerves. Brooke propped up on her elbows and glanced away from Tanner's smile. Spotting the pink dress and slip dangling from her closet, she wondered if she needed a shoehorn. Brooke pondered a brisk run—a nice sweat wouldn't hurt. She slid out of bed, and her voice of reason stopped her before she made it to her running shoes. The threat of Melissa killing her if she re-injured wasn't worth the risk. Plus, it looked like rain.

Brooke did an about face and headed to the dress. Holding it up to her frame, she frowned, then eyed her Nikes, deciding on a compromise—a power walk. She remembered Shane's live-in-the-now advice, and for the next thirty minutes, Brooke marched pain free and carefree—as close to the elusive *now* as she could get.

Back inside her apartment, Brooke's voicemail alert beeped—three missed calls. All Melissa. Uh oh.

"The wedding's off!"

Brooke half expected this. "What? Why?"

"Eddie's an ass. I can't possibly marry an ass."

Bachelor party? Brooke suppressed her natural instinct to throw Eddie under the bus. Today her role was to hold the net under the rooftop. Being Melissa's friend meant loosening her strings at times. This was one of those times—but she had to assess it fast. Rather than ask *what happened?* and invite a four-hour diatribe, Brooke asked the rifle shot question, "What did he do?"

"Where do I begin?"

"I know Eddie's past. What bugs you the most?"

"He's pigging out at some brunch right now."

"So?"

"He's not following any Jewish customs. We agreed to fast today."

"How do you know?"

"His dumbass brother just texted me."

"How do you know he's eating and not just being social?"

"Hello—he, like, emailed a picture of bacon hanging out of Eddie's mouth. He thinks it's funny."

Brooke, raised Catholic, considered the issue. She recalled those Lenten days as a girl and remembered how religious Melissa's parents were, just like her own father had been. At eleven, he caught her eating meat on Friday during Lent—pepperoni pizza—and she thought he was going to perform an exorcism. No mention of bachelor party, no DUI or even drunk and disorderly, no fleeing the country; Eddie surpassed her expectations. "He's just acting out. Plus, he's not Jewish."

"If my father knew, he'd have a conniption."

"He won't find out, and if he does, so what? He'll love Eddie *less*? Look at the bright side. Imagine how your dad would be if he knew you were knocked up?"

"That's not funny."

"I'm not being funny, but I know you. You love Eddie. I think he loves you so much it scares him and he acts out. You've been wanting to get married for the last ten years. Relax. Take a deep breath. Everything's going to be fine. I almost called off my wedding like three times."

In hindsight, marrying Tanner fulfilled Brooke's dream; although she had some doubts, most moments felt magical, especially their wedding day. Brooke liked her answer—Shane would be proud.

Brooke heard sniffles on the other end and, after a few seconds, said, "You there?"

"Yeah, you're probably right. Do I sound crazy?"

The question stopped Brooke cold. After a deep breath, she said, "We're both crazy."

Melissa's amusement had a nervous twitch, much more subdued than normal. She said, "Okay, I get it. I'll calm down now. I think I'm just hungry."

"You and I both know how short life can be. And today's going to be the greatest day of your life—I can feel it. Settle down and enjoy some of it. I'll see you in two hours. You're going to look amazing. I'll be so jealous."

"I seriously doubt that. But, thanks—you know how to lift me up. I don't know what I'd do without you."

"Ditto, girl." As Brooke hung up, she heaved a sigh of relief, then considered a trip to Waffle House. Discussing fasting made her hungry, and blueberry waffles sure sounded good. Her mouth watered, then she noticed it again—that damn pink dress. As a compromise, she enjoyed a bowl of berries—including blueberries, but without the waffle. Then, she thought she'd kill two birds with one stone.

Brooke packed her makeup essentials into an overnight bag on top of her pajamas and Sunday's sundress. The intimidating pink dress would remain wrinkle-free on its hanger. She checked her email one last time. Aside from the company email announcements she'd ignored yesterday, two new ones caught her eye.

Late Friday, David Greenberg scheduled a meeting for eight o'clock Monday morning—*ouch*. So much for ever catching Chase at Starbucks. The other one: "Brooke, Congrats on hitting your goal. I'm so proud of you. Enjoy the wedding and the weekend—you've earned it. I'll have my cell if you need me. Kind Regards, Dr. Shane Gallagher, PhD."

As she reread her life coach's email, warmth spread inside. Still feeling hungry, Brooke craved coffee. She smiled. Starbucks—the infamous one—was on the way from her apartment to the wedding. Brooke carefully lifted her dress and headed out.

During the fifteen-minute drive, Brooke pressed speed dial one. "Good morning."

"That was such a nice email."

"The one from yesterday? Oh, yeah, congrats again, I really am proud of you and your accomplishment."

"You'd be proud of me again today."

"Why's that?"

"I sounded like you with Melissa."

"Your friend Melissa? The one who's getting married today?"

"Yep. She's either going to have a massive stroke or get married today."

"And I'm guessing you managed to keep her out of the ER?"

"I did. I sounded like you today and even threw in the *now* stuff, but in my own words."

"Congrats again. So, you do listen to me sometimes?"

"I always listen; I just don't always hear you."

"Touché."

They both laughed, then Shane asked the question he'd been holding back, "How are *you* doing today?"

"I'm holding up so far," Brooke bit her lip, "all I have to do is keep it together during the ceremony. Listening to their vows at the rehearsal, I almost lost it."

"That's perfectly normal. Most of the church loses it during the vows and *Ave Maria*."

"Well, they won't be in a church or singing any *Ave Maria's*—Melissa's Jewish."

Shane laughed even louder and Brooke cut him off, "And, it's a blessing for me. Their ceremony's quite a bit different from mine so it won't bring back the memories. Plus, they're having it in the hotel. If I ever walk down that aisle again, I'm converting to Judaism."

"Well, *mazel tav* and try not to drink too much *l'chaim to life* then."

"Not bad, even with your Boston Irish accent," Brooke laughed, thinking he sounded like the Lucky Charms leprechaun trying out for *Fiddler on the Roof.*

"You are making such great progress. Keep it up."

You are making such great progress. Brooke allowed the words to reverberate after hanging up. She felt another warmth. Whenever someone offered praise that resonated inside, Brooke lit up. When Shane praised her, it felt heaven sent.

The Starbucks sign pulled Brooke back from her dreamy state like a deployed air bag. A rush of panic hit—what if he's here? This'll look really weird. He'll think I'm a freak. No, I can just say I was stopping in the office. But, it's Saturday. I hope he's not a workaholic—the type who works all weekend. *Why would an eligible bachelor wear a ring?*

Brooke sped past the storefront. No sign of that red car, that's good. She glanced around, then parked in her original hiding spot with the motor running. She raised her eyebrow as "Every Breath You Take" rang out—*isn't this song about a stalker?* She drew a deep breath.

Inside Starbucks, a whole new set of faces came into view. Besides that enticing aroma, the only thing similar was the line. No Marcus, no Tonya, no Yankee chick—and no Chase. Brooke sighed, then stood in line.

"What would ya like?"

"Has Chase been in yet?" Brooke fidgeted.

"Who?" Two unfamiliar faces behind the counter glared.

"Chase? Mr. Allman? A-Man?"

"Does he work here?"

Perfect. Brooke had her answer—one of them, at least. Holding the hot cup, she inhaled the quad espresso, unable to stifle her giddy grin.

The drive up to Raleigh lasted longer than normal due to road construction and a steady rainfall. Well, they work on Saturdays, rain or shine I guess. Brooke hoped her pink dress didn't slide too much in the trunk. And she wondered for the umpteenth time if it would fit. *I sound like Melissa now.* And, just as the thought hit, so did Melissa's ringtone.

"Where are you?"

"I'm almost there. What's up?"

"Hurry up. Everyone's here. We're gonna get dressed. I'm not doing anything without you." It was Melissa's not-so-subtle way of granting Brooke the honors—in front of the others.

The RTP Convention Center looked majestic, even in the rain. After a major renovation, it featured meeting rooms of all sizes—including a ballroom big enough to host the wedding—a hotspot nightclub, spa, and two luxury hotels adjoined. The self-contained village resembled Las Vegas casinos in grandeur, yet offered a southern charm. Early check-in was a breeze. Clifton Brenner had picked up the tab for the wedding party—nice touch. The receptionist handed Brooke a message, unsigned, but definitely not unknown, "Hurry up to the wedding suite on the twenty-fourth floor." *What a basket case.*

Brooke decided to head up to Melissa's room first. As she entered the spacious suite, she noticed all the familiar faces from last night, most already in their pink dresses. No Melissa. Both Amber and Brandi bee-lined to Brooke, looking as if they survived *Survivor.* "Don't you two look sexy! Where's Melissa?"

"Thank God you're here," Amber rolled her eyes as Brandi pointed to a closed door across the lengthy marble floor.

"Ah," Brooke wondered how many times Melissa ran to the bathroom.

"Hey, at least she's here."

"Hasn't been easy. Get her dressed *please*—I think I need a drink." All three women giggled, as if back in the sorority, gearing up for North Carolina's Formal.

Melissa had her hair and nails done earlier, and including Brooke, it required seven women to alternate dressing, applying makeup, and calming Melissa.

Brooke said, "You look stunning. Time to go." As the sorority sisters proceeded down the hall, Brooke started singing, "Goin' to the Chapel" and even Melissa laughed and joined in.

During rehearsal, the ceremony had appeared hasty to Brooke, but today, peaceful divinity—in spite of Eddie's haggard-looking family tree. Under the Chuppah—the magnificent white canopy where the couple stood with the Rabbi—Melissa and Eddie became one. The vows of the ancient rituals of the Ketubah filled the room with rhythmic Aramaic scriptures; for Eddie, it might as well have been Pig Latin.

After the traditional commitment of the husband promising to be attentive to his wife's emotional needs, Brooke strangled her laughter. Seeing Eddie adorned in a white traditional robe, Brooke enjoyed God's sense of humor. Brooke just couldn't see Tanner doing any of this with a straight face. Brooke settled in and started enjoying the wedding. The hard part—getting Melissa there—was over. Except for the toast, which Brooke still wasn't certain she could deliver.

Brooke had endeavored to understand the Jewish wedding ceremony. Even though she still didn't grasp the lingo, she understood and appreciated the symbolism. Unfortunately, Eddie didn't even make an effort, and Brooke realized this caused plenty of her best friend's wedding-day jitters.

Brooke attempted to focus on each element of the wedding, but she kept drifting. First, recalling Shane's words, about the love Brooke had—that Melissa would probably never feel. And the loss Melissa tried to feel for her friend. As much as she feared this day, her gratitude lifted her up.

Later, after the champagne flowed and the wedding guests had taken their seats, Clifton Brenner delivered a droning toast.

As everyone sipped, Melissa eyed Brooke. It was time. This should have been easy, given Brooke's training in public speaking. But no course could prepare her for this.

Brooke rose, Clifton handed her the mike. She surveyed the enormous room, put the mike close to her lips, and drew in a deep breath that hushed the crowd. She fixed her gaze on Melissa, and said: "I don't know if anyone could love this beautiful woman more than I do. Sorry, Eddie, but, if it weren't for her, I wouldn't be here."

Brooke ambled over and kissed Melissa's forehead. Four hundred people were silent—like a video—and Brooke just pressed pause. Melissa's eyes welled, Eddie just stared ahead. Brooke faced the crowd, then reached out toward Melissa, "She's my angel. None of you know this but … a couple years ago … many years ago, Melissa stopped me from … from doing something to myself that I was, well, that I was too sick to stop myself from doing. When my husband—the love of my life—when Tanner ended his life, I didn't think mine was worth living. If it weren't for her being there that day ..."

Brooke's eyes fluttered, then released the pent-up tears, not tears of pain, but tears of love. With crackling voice, "It wasn't just one day either. Melissa was there for me when I needed someone the most. Eddie, you have no idea how lucky you are. You have one special bride. I hope you really understand that. I hope you cherish her each and every day."

Eddie was ready to break out in hives. Brooke turned back and faced Melissa, whose tears streamed down her face. "When you asked me to be your maid of honor, I nearly lost it. I love you *so* much."

Brooke placed the mike down and hugged Melissa as if they were Velcroed together. In more ways than even a marital bond, they were. Finally, Brooke excused herself and strode briskly toward the side exit. The microphone sat forlorn. Nobody dared to pick it up; it would be like following John, Paul, George, and Ringo onstage—not even Yoko would have tried.

Inside the bathroom, Brooke eased into the handicapped stall. This time, nobody entered. After emptying her tear ducts for nearly twenty minutes, a calm enveloped her. *Tanner? If that's you, ya coulda helped me a little more up there.* Brooke inhaled as gratitude replaced isolation and spread serenity through her like transcendental meditation.

Nearly two hours later, Brooke realized she had better return, hoping she didn't spoil the party. She practiced her apology to Melissa. Trudging back like she was heading to the executioner, she heard music ... and laughing. She smiled.

Men and women, children, dresses, ribbons, and tuxes flailed around the dance floor, looking sillier than the Chicken Dance. Melissa stood in the middle of the loose giant circle and waved Brooke over. *How did she see me?*

They danced, drank, spilled, danced, drank, spilled, and when the band finally quit, drank once more. Then, as Melissa and Eddie—whose bow tie was now wrapped around his head—waved goodbye, Amber and Brandi grabbed Brooke and said, "C'mon, we're all going out."

Back in college, Brooke's energy would have outpaced the alcohol, at least until last call. But tonight she just couldn't do it. The maid of honor's feet hurt, her ankle hurt more, and emotionally, she needed to bring the rollercoaster in for the night. A familiar Dave Matthews song started. As her friends started singing, Brooke seized the chance to escape. She quietly ducked out to the bathroom.

In the hallway, safe from peer pressure, Brooke was lost. She staggered down a long corridor and rounded a corner, wondering if a piece of cheese rewarded her effort to locate the elusive elevator. She wanted to rename the place *Labyrinth*. Adrenaline mixed with champagne, morphing into turbo bubbly. She wandered another hallway and sighed—*there has to be an elevator in this place.*

Brooke leafed through her purse but couldn't locate the hotel's number. Punching 4-1-1, she pressed the phone to her ear. Nothing. Brooke stared at her cell in a hypnotic trance, then realized, *crap—* dead battery. *Great, now what?* Brooke heard a ding and froze. She recognized that sound—it never sounded better. She spun around and spotted the elevators. *How did I miss that? I shouldn't have had that last shot.*

Brooke advanced toward the blurred sign, then entered a corridor holding four elevators, just as one was closing—*crap.* She slapped the up button, causing the door to reopen with a loud ding. While lunging toward the door, she glanced over her shoulder, paranoid that her wedding mates would spot her. One of her spaghetti straps dropped, but she didn't care—*I'm all alone, thank God.*

Humming "Crash Into Me," she jumped in front of the opening elevator door, then stepped forward. "What the …" As her eyes focused, she slipped and barreled into the stranger in black. He grabbed her— *oh shit, I'm gonna die.*

Clutching her in his death grip, time stood still, and his devilish laugh terrified her. She heard the door close, ending all hope. Feeling faint, Brooke gasped, petrified, unable to move. *I have to scream—or lash out—but I can't move my lips.* She inhaled hard, a last ditch effort to muster the strength to shout … *wait a minute.* That scent.

"Tanner? Is that you?"

But the man in black laughed louder, taunting her. He was enjoying it, the sicko.

She felt an upward force, as if being pulled to the light. Then, she landed on her feet—

"Huh!"

The man in black loosened his grip, but still clutched her, and said, "Oh my God. Brooke Hart—on an elevator! Imagine that?" She recognized that gorgeous smile, then the lashes.

"Chase, what're *you* doin' here?"

"I was going to ask you the same question. We have to stop meeting like this."

His eyes sparkled and his voice was playful. The man in black looked stunning in his tuxedo—the new James Bond. *Am I dreaming*? Brooke's head spun, her knees buckled. "I didn't see you at the wedding?"

"Wedding?"

The elevator door closed. Chase said, "Can I let go of you now?"

"I wish you wouldn't ..." Chase's eyes widened. Brooke considered rephrasing while noticing he wasn't wearing a ring.

The elevator lunged upward. He released Brooke, but she stood closely, grazing him with a slight sway while searching his eyes. Chase gulped, raised his eyebrows, and asked, "Which floor?"

Brooke inspected the panel—nineteen was illuminated—then said, "Nineteen."

Chase's brow rose.

Damn I love those lashes.

Chase said, "Were you in a wedding?"

Brooke glanced at her dress. "Can ya tell?"

"You look ..." Chase noticed her hair had extra flair, flowing across her soft shoulders. He closed his eyes tightly and shook his head, then said, "Wow."

Wow? "You look better than the groom." *I didn't just say that. I love him in that tux. He looks sexier than Clooney.* Brooke inhaled once more and purred as her eyes spun a slow circle.

Quick laugh, "I was at a charity event."

"For *GQ*?"

"You're funny." Brooke couldn't stop staring, imagining his 007 pose on the cover. *Did I just say GQ?*

The elevator thumped, jolting Brooke forward. Chase hugged her, this time with a gentle touch. He sensed she wasn't going to fall, but had to embrace her.

With a ding, the door slid open. Chase smirked, and said, "I better help you off." Without waiting for a response from Brooke, whose eyes shot open, he shifted his grasp from her arm to around her shoulder. His aroma had a stronger effect than the shot of Patron. Her legs went numb as he led her off the elevator. Brooke quivered and then felt a sudden rush.

They faced the guide board, the floor's fork-in-the-road. "Which way?" Brooke noticed he slurred his words, guessing he was tipsy too.

"Huh?" Brooke stared as if studying a math formula, "I think I'm that way."

"Me too. C'mon, I'll walk you to your room. Which one's yours?"

"I dunno. I think I'm in … 1944. Where are you?"

"Perfect, I'm in 1950."

He tightened his grip around Brooke, warming her, leading her. She felt a hot surge inside. Feeling giddy, neither had the slightest fear of being noticed. Their pace slowed as the tight carpet snagged her heels on each staggered step. They barely avoided the obstacle course of room service trays that popped up like booby traps. Though painted in upscale earth tones, the hallway was bright—too bright for Brooke. She wanted a peek at her compact, but she didn't dare let go. They held on as if their lives depended on each other; neither wanted the feeling to end.

"Did you say 1944?" Chase released her, and she jolted awake.

"Huh? Oh yeah, I think so. Lemme grab my key." Brooke opened her purse that seemed sensible earlier, but now looked ridiculously packed. She pulled out a white plastic card, then stared at it as if it contained the secret of the Holy Grail. Looking in Chase's eyes, she said, "I never know how to use these things."

Brooke struggled to fit the key in the slot. She slid it in slowly and held it still, causing a red light to illuminate. "Dammit." She tried again—red light. One more time in slow motion—red.

"Here, lemme try." Chase's hand slid across Brooke's as she handed him the key. He drove it in and out like a punch card—red. One more try—still red. "Are you sure this is your room?"

"I dunno. I was hardly in here—I got dressed with Melissa."

"I bet the front desk—"

"No way I'm walking anywhere now—my feet are killing me. Plus, this place is a freakin' labyrinth." Chase glanced at Brooke's open toe heels and smiled. *She even has cute toes.*

"We should call someone."

Brooke opened her purse again, then remembered. "My cell's dead."

Chase said, "My cell's broken too—someone spilled on it."

So much for smart phones. Both thought *alcohol decreases your IQ, alcohol decreases your IQ, alcohol decreases your IQ* Chase broke the silence, and said, "Here, follow me. We can call from my room."

Before the phrase registered, Brooke was being transported by Chase, slightly trailing him, savoring his intoxicating aroma like Dom Perignon. Even tipsy, Chase still looked machismo—like a matador and she was his flag. Chase stopped in front of room 1950, the "Hawthorne Suite." Brooke raised her right eyebrow and grinned.

Opening the door on the first try, he shot Brooke a playful smile. She shuddered, enjoying the way his lips glistened. And though he meant to tease Brooke about the key, he felt her gaze—that unmistakable look. He loved the sparkle in her blue eyes against the pink dress. *I've never seen her in pink—she should wear it more often.*

The door swung open and Chase whisked Brooke inside. He paused and twisted to find the light switch as Brooke bumped into him. Their eyes locked. As both hearts pounded, Brooke gripped Chase's neck and pulled, until her lips met his—and time stood still. Brooke's legs trembled.

He pulled back. His eyes flashed as if entering hers. Chase returned the kiss with a softness in his lips that surprised her. With mouths joined, their tongues danced. The fresh sensations felt exhilarating. They embraced; neither one wanting to leave the dream—or risk returning to earth.

Finally, Brooke broke and gasped. She softened her gaze as if searching for answers; Chase's eyes revealed a wanton desire. He slid his hands across her back, the silk providing a titillating shield against her tingling skin. She ran her hands under his tuxedo, across his chest. Brooke said, "We shouldn't be ..."

Chase's lips smothered hers. Brooke released and allowed the fire to explode. Their kiss propelled a deeper desire. His hands probed up and down her back and slid across her curves. He smelled so good. She ran her fingers up his abdomen to his chest as he found her zipper.

He shifted, gently nibbling on her moist lips, while carefully sliding her zipper down her side. Tension released, her pulse quickened. She opened an eye and caught his gaze, a flicker piercing the darkness. He slid his hand inside her half-opened dress, across her matching slip and brushed his lips against her ear. The warmth of his breath tickled her neck.

As if reading her mind, he sprinkled kisses in just the right spots. He cupped her breast through the slip, and nibbled on the moist skin. Brooke shuddered, releasing a dormant primal moan.

Brooke slid her hands under Chase's tuxedo with familiarity, only this time, she sent the coat to the floor. Her fingers uncoiled his silk bow tie, as Chase's eyes widened. She then slowly unbuttoned his shirt. He loved watching her concentrate on each button as if it contained some top secret. Brooke's delicate fingers gradually descended, heightening his arousal.

Brooke's fingers teased the last button open, then she opened his shirt. She bit on her lower lip, contemplating the best way to approach his well-toned front. Brooke slid her finger across his beltline, then ran her hands to his backside. Cupping his firm derriere, she purred, then slid her hands around his bare front, ending with circles on his chest. His skin felt warm and smooth, his chest muscles like their own island hidden by dark curly thick hair. She could spend hours on his island. He undid his cuffs and swung the shirt to the floor.

Chase reached out and glided Brooke's straps off, exposing her upper torso and her silk lace slip. He slid the slip off her shoulders, then worked his way down. As his fingers danced across her silky skin, Brooke's entire body warmed. She marveled at his touch—strong yet gentle. Each time he explored a different spot triggering a greater level of arousal.

Chase wrapped his arms behind Brooke and kissed her. His hands wandered, warming her hot zones. He broke the embrace, then kissed her chin, then the front of her neck, until lowering his lips to her aroused breasts. The gentle flicking of his tongue made Brooke's knees weaken. His fingers edged the dress off, revealing the thin silk slip. Brooke wiggled the dress down and tossed it aside, leaving her in the lingerie.

Chase gently caressed her skin through the slip, then lowered it to the ground, tangling it in Brooke's heels. She kicked it away and stood still. Her naked body shimmered in the darkened room, clad only in pink thong and high heels. Chase's eyes bulged, revealing hunger.

Chase moved closer and engulfed Brooke's ravenous lips. His fingers wandered, then tweaked her thong. Brooke moaned, then gripped the front of Chase's slacks. Slowly, she slid up and down, cupping the bulge—with widened eyes. Chase groaned as his knees buckled. She picked up her pace slightly, causing him to groan louder each time. She varied her tempo and his moans followed along. Brooke's excitement intensified with each moan.

Chase wrestled with his belt while Brooke continued to torment him. As his buckle opened, Brooke dropped to her knees and unzipped him. Chase's slacks hit the floor; Brooke placed her thumbs on both sides of his boxer briefs, then carefully lowered them. Gripping him, her lips engulfed him—he groaned an octave lower, begging her to continue.

Chase's heart raced with squinted eyes, close to the point of no return. He wanted to prolong the euphoria, to reward Brooke in his own way. He gripped Brooke's shoulders and guided her up. Brooke gasped for air as their eyes locked, revealing a new longing—a belonging.

Chase wrapped his arms around her, then whispered, "You're amazing, Brooke." Enraptured by the sound of her name purred from his lips, Brooke said, "You drive me wild."

Chase murmured, "No, you drive me wild," with warm breath sizzling Brooke's hot zones. Chase descended, whisking the flimsy thong down. The tingling chill from his whispers titillated Brooke's skin. She reached to remove her high heels, but Chase gripped her backside—then overwhelmed her. She gasped as his moist motions warmed her. Her foot pain faded, and she let go, taking pleasure in his magic touch. With muscles convulsing throughout her body, she forgot about her nakedness.

Brooke's moaning followed Chase's rhythm: she shuddered, then released, delighting in each ecstatic spasm. Chase groaned, then shifted, and fresh sensations burst inside Brooke. Her bliss resembled an out-of-control carnival ride—the ride of her life. She never wanted it to end. She dug her fingers into Chase's head—and pulled. Clutching his thick wavy hair, she pulsed and threw her head back, exploding into orgasm.

Chase gasped for air as Brooke's internal frenzy settled into numbing pleasure. She pulled him up, then stared deeply into his eyes. Gripping his arms, she gasped, "Oh God!"

Chase's lips curled, eyes wanton. He said, "I have to have you." Brooke's eyes widened as she said, "I want you."

Brooke felt a whoosh. Her heels flew off. She felt weightless like a hot air balloon as Chase's firm hands suspended her in the air. Feeling frenzied, she searched his eyes. Then, his groan blended with her moan as he entered her. She shuddered and time stood still—fullness, a belonging. Chase slowly began thrusting; Brooke moaned with each plunge, a combination of pleasure and pain. Soon, the sensation became pure pleasure, an erotic ride. She marveled at Chase's sheer strength and delighted in his deliberate motions.

Chase clenched and gazed into her eyes. They kissed with abandon. Brooke's numbness dissipated, replaced by a fresh pleasure, reaching depths beyond her wildest fantasy. Brooke marveled at this man's mastery. His thrusting deepened, breaking the kiss—each lover gasped for air.

Brooke groaned as Chase moaned, and each sound elevated their desire. Brooke purred, "You drive me wild." The combination of her sexy voice and breath titillated Chase's ear. He said, "You feel sooooo good." Moans became screams—they exploded at the same time, releasing a bursting sensation that connected the couple as one.

After the tremors turned to quivering, Chase carried Brooke over to the bed and lovingly lowered her. With eyes locked, he said, "Wow." After a prolonged gaze, he asked, "You thirsty? Can I get you something?"

"No, only you." Chase smiled, and ran his fingers through Brooke's hair, then on her cheek. His affection warmed her. He said, "You are amazing," then crawled in beside her. They snuggled in silence, soaking in their oneness, enjoying the serenity.

After a lover's doze, Chase began tracing his finger along Brooke's outline. She still marveled at his strong yet tender touch. She smiled lazily at him, and said, "Mmmmm, that feels good."

"You're gorgeous." The way he said those words could melt a girl's heart, but Chase's tone contained a new tenderness, which rekindled Brooke's warmth.

"You're so sweet." Brooke kissed Chase's cheek, then said, "I'll be right back, loverboy." Brooke sprung up and headed to the bathroom. Chase squinted, but missed viewing her naked body from the back—his vantage point from across the king-sized bed. He propped himself up on his elbows and prepared for her return.

Brooke arrived carrying a large bottled water. Her walk commanded attention, head high with self-assured eye contact, shoulders upright, fluid pace. She ambled around the bed, noticing him watching her. Chase found confident walks sexy, and Brooke sauntered as if she owned the room. Posture up, she stopped beside the bed and turned the cap, then drew a big sip. Chase perched upright, mouth wide open. The dappled moonlight illuminated Brooke's alluring body.

Chase was instantly attracted to Brooke; first, the boardroom, but now, every time he saw her, he melted. But now, naked, posing for him, she enflamed his animal desire.

Brooke's lips slid off the bottle with a popping sound, then she faced him, and said, "You want some?"

Chase said, "Yeah—but leave the water on the table."

"Sassy boy." Brooke liked the way he gazed at her, causing a tingle inside. Brooke sipped again, then said, "Here, you earned this earlier. Have some. It tastes good."

"You taste good." Chase grinned, then reached for the bottle. His arm motion flung the sheet open, exposing him. Now, it was Brooke's turn to stare.

As Chase finished a long sip, Brooke crawled in and straddled him. Now lying on his back, Chase tossed the bottle on the table, knocking the phone to the floor with a loud clank—a clank that both barely heard.

Brooke slid on top of Chase as if he was a hammock. Their naked bodies melded, warming, contrasting with the air conditioned chill. Chase wrapped his arms around Brooke's back, then gently massaged her neck, then explored further. Brooke purred, moving her hips up and down. He hardened, causing her eyes to widen.

Brooke shifted and reversed direction, sliding her hand down. Chase groaned, igniting a spark deep inside Brooke. She slid down while gazing into his wanting eyes. Chase throbbed in anticipation.

She slowly slid her tongue along her lower lip, and said, "I think I know why they call you Boa."

Chase prided himself on a quick wit—but he had no comeback. He could only groan his approval for her handiwork. Brooke's passion surged—she enjoyed teasing him. Slowly and deeply, she straddled him. They both groaned. The different position allowed Brooke to control the pace and maintain a slower, teasing rhythm. Chase's eyes were full moons, mesmerized by Brooke's every move. Earlier, there was a sense of urgency, but now, both wanted it to last forever.

Several strands of her wavy long hair slipped in front of her face. The moon's light framed her creamy skin, revealing exquisite lips and wanting eyes.

"You're so beautiful." Chase's eyes sparkled.

"I bet you say that to all your vice pres ..." Brooke cut herself off, then said, "I can't believe I'm sleeping with ..."

Chase pressed his finger to her lips, "Shhhhhhhh." Their eyes met, and Brooke regretted her snafu, fearing she spoiled the mood. Her eyes fluttered, trying desperately to find the right thing to say—to no avail.

Chase broke the awkward pause, saying, "Tonight, we're just two people sharing each other, both wanting the same thing—and having the best night of their lives."

Well put, thank you, Brooke thought, deciding to hush herself and enjoy this incredible man. Her guilt-ridden vocals fell silent to the passion. Brooke captivated Chase with her sensual rocking. When Brooke broke her gaze, she shuddered with delight, heightening Chase's arousal. He loved watching her take pleasure in him. Her varied rhythms unleashed new sensations, leading to continuous euphoric trembles and releases.

Chase's passion reached a boiling point; he gripped Brooke's sides with eyes revealing untamed hunger. He thrust with animal intensity, causing a flood of heat inside Brooke. Chase groaned, Brooke's head bounced back, then rocked back and forth as her screams joined him in ecstatic harmony. After their sonic explosion, Brooke collapsed in Chase's arms. She inhaled his scent, now mixed with passion's sweat, and savored it like fine wine. Smiling, she fell asleep in his arms.

—— ♥ ——

The sun's first ray replaced the full moon's glow piercing Brooke's eye through the blinds. She gasped and froze. It wasn't a dream after all. Glancing at Chase, she delighted in his half-covered naked body. Chase lay on his side facing Brooke with those famous lashes protecting his sleepy shut eyes. She watched his bare chest rise and fall. With tousled hair and lips closed, his nose fluttered with each breath. He looked like a teddy bear: part of her wanted to squeeze him; the other part wanted to pinch herself to make sure he was real. He had ignited a dormant passion inside her. Missing for so long, she recognized it and cherished it once again.

Brooke hated to leave the image, but she knew she must. She slowly withdrew while gazing at her mate, a warm kindling inside. Brooke maintained her stare until she entered the dark bathroom, then inched the door until it latched shut. She clicked on the light and placed her hand over her mouth as if strangling a scream. Brooke desperately wanted her makeup bag. She tousled her hair, hoping to revive some form of human shape, but frowned.

Thoughts swirled in her head. The dreamy night crash landed into a sobering realization—passion replaced by guilt. She needed an out, but couldn't think beyond her pounding head. The question hushed by Chase earlier returned like a recurring nightmare—*I can't believe I slept with the freaking CEO.* She stared at herself in the mirror, winced, and decided to quietly leave before he awakened. After one last look.

Brooke tiptoed over to the bed and tilted her head—he hadn't moved. His lips parted slightly and his breathing had picked up. She noticed his eyes were fluttering beneath the closed lids—*I wonder what he's dreaming?* Brooke felt a warming inside, that magnetic pull back to his arms. Weighing one more session with the lights off, her mind played tug of war. *What time is it? What time's breakfast? God, he looks so handsome.*

She sauntered toward him … then jumped. A loud noise startled her. Standing still, she heard clanking coming from the hallway— maid service—her out. Chase swallowed a few times as if his lips were reaching for air, then settled back to his slumber.

Brooke wanted to kiss his forehead, caress his hair, peer under the covers. Instead, she turned and darted away. There was just enough light under the door, and Brooke slipped her dress back on and bounced up and down while she tugged on her zipper. She reached down for her purse, then grabbed each high heel. She inhaled, wishing for a hat and sunglasses and quietly eased out the door.

Brooke squinted into the unflattering brightness illuminating her in the hall. With eyes adjusting, she spotted a man in a hotel uniform walking toward her. Clutching her heels and purse like batons, she sprinted to him, and gasping for breath, said, "Excuse me, do you work here?"

The man stopped and turned around. "Excusa me, senorita?"

"My key doesn't work. Can you let me in?"

He raised his eyebrow while scrutinizing her, "I'm room service, senorita. I don't have keys to the rooms."

"Can you do me a big favor?"

"Sure, anything, senorita. You want me to call someone for you?"

"Yes, thank you."

"Right away," he pressed on his walkie-talkie and spoke in Spanish. He inspected Brooke again, and asked, "Which room are you in, senorita?"

"I, uh, I'm not sure … nineteen something … near 1950."

"Ah." He flipped his hand-held radio again and rambled in Spanish. Brooke glared, wondering what he was really saying. She wanted to crawl in a hole, anywhere but this bright display in the hall of shame—clad in yesterday's garb. She hoped he wouldn't paint an "A" across her forehead. She feared the noise would rouse Chase—*he's the last one I want to see me now.*

The man said, "Sit tight," then left. Brooke hovered near 1930, then remembered her room number—1944. She tiptoed over and plunked down with her back against the door. The more she tried to will the maid, the longer it seemed to take. A door swung open down the hall and she turned her head the opposite direction. Brooke froze, hoping the guests would stop soon. They paused. Brooke glimpsed, then her eyes bulged as the pink intruders giggled—*oh shit.*

"Brooke?" Louder giggles.

"Hi, Amber. Hey, Brandi." The duo still donned wedding party pink dresses—now wrinkled—but they had fresh makeup and acceptable hair.

"We wondered where you went last night," Brandi lilted. Brooke pressed her finger to her lips, hoping to avoid answering. Amber chimed, "Why are you sitting there?"

"My key doesn't work. I'm waiting for...long story."

"I bet," Brandi said, mouth hanging open, "Looks like you had some fun, girl. Do tell."

"Brandi, shhhhhh. Keep your voice down," Brooke said while eyeing room 1950.

Amber said, "We ended up in a hot tub at some big-shot doctor's mansion. That's all I remember—until we woke up next to him in his waterbed." Amber glanced at Brandi, who giggled. "What was his name again?"

"Dixon from Duke," Brandi said, "but that's all I remember too. Hey, you think that creep drugged us?"

Brooke's eyes rolled to the back of her head. "Dr. Dixon Carter by any chance?"

"Yeah, that's it—Carter—like the president, he said. Hey, how'd you know? Were you there?"

Brooke froze, looking like she'd just been tasered. "No."

"How do you know Dixon from Duke then?"

"I don't really ..." Finally, Brooke noticed the housekeeping cart. She said, "Looks like they're here. I'm okay, thanks for your help, ladies." Brooke wanted nothing more than to crawl into her room alone. She whimpered, "What time do we need to be downstairs?"

Brandi said, "In, like, twenty minutes. We're supposed to decorate the room."

—— ❤ ——

"Brooke Hart, get over here." The voice nearly bowled Brooke over.

Pressing her hand over her heart, Brooke said, "You scared me. Good morning, Mel ... I mean *Mrs. Racer*. How was your night?"

Melissa rolled her eyes, then pulled Brooke aside, "Fast Eddie set the quickie record, then passed out on me. Needless to say, my *magical* night wasn't like yours I bet."

"Were you talking to Brandi and Amber?"

"Umm hummm," Melissa hummed in an evil pitch.

"Don't do this. I'm soooo tired right now."

"Do I know him?"

"Don't do this."

"Brooke, you have to tell me."

"Okay, if I tell you, will you stop asking questions?"

"Yes, for today, at least."

Brooke smirked, then cupped her hand, and whispered in her ear, "Chase."

Melissa's eyes darted back and forth like ping pong balls, "You mean the guy you work for?"

"Shhhhhhhhhhhhhhh. No questions, remember?"

Melissa gripped Brooke's shoulders, then said, "That is so not fair. You can't tell me something that juicy and expect me to just play dead. I'm your best friend, remember? Tell me."

Shaking her head, she said, "One final question, then you're done?"

Melissa nodded, bit her upper lip with her lower teeth, then said, "How was it?"

"The most amazing night of my life," Brooke's eyes welled up, bringing a loving sigh from Melissa. "You have no idea how hard it was to leave that room."

— ♥ —

The thump startled him. "Huh." *Where am I? What time is it?* Another clack, clack, clack on the door. He said, "Who is it?"

"Housekeeping."

Pulling off the sheet, he frowned at his nakedness, then frantically searched for his clothes. Chase darted toward the door like an antelope, saying, "Not right now. I'm in here. You'll have to come back."

No answer, but as the cart wheeled away, Chase sighed; he flipped on the light and rubbed his besieged eyes. *Shit, not another dream— it seemed so real. What is it with me and elevator dreams?* His foggy mind trailed his movement, then he spotted it.

Chase nearly fell, then regained his balance, and scooped it up. He caressed its silkiness, pressing it to his face. Chase inhaled deeply, as if enjoying a vintage cognac. Exhaling, memories flooded in. No dream. He returned to bed.

Admiring her pink laced lingerie, he closed his eyes and inhaled once more. He pictured her skin, as silky as the garment, but holding so many mysteries. She made him feel like a worldly explorer, responding to his every touch. She was the sexiest woman he could ever imagine. And she made him feel like the sexiest man alive. The way she gazed into his eyes, as if connecting to his soul. Her wavy hair, luscious lips, the way she kissed—all over. He felt a stirring. *Where is she?*

Chase flipped on the bedside lamp, then drew the shade open partially. He surveyed the entire room for a note or some sign. Nothing. He checked the bathroom—maybe she showered? Dry. Scanning the counter, he noticed lipstick on a half-full water glass. Lifting the cup like a chalice, he pressed his lips against the red semi-circle and imagined another embrace. He yearned to taste her lips one more time. *I hope she feels the same.*

Chase figured Brooke must have somehow gotten into her room. Thinking she left a voicemail he darted back into the bedroom finding the hotel phone unhooked on the floor. He returned the receiver and stared at the tiny orange message waiting box. No flash. He dialed the hotel operator for messages—none. Cell phone—where is it?

He ambled to his slacks crumpled on the floor next to his boxer briefs. He paused at the spot where he had hoisted Brooke up in the air. Chase closed his eyes and pictured her look of surprise as they became one. She felt so light—and so right in his arms—his muse, familiar yet stimulating. She brought out an inner beast he didn't know existed.

With cell in hand, Chase vaguely remembered the lady spilling champagne on it. Though he dabbed it with a napkin, then aired it out, it failed to work. He pressed the on button, and after a second, it lit up. He dialed voicemail—four messages. The first was from Ruth 4:47 p.m. Friday—that could wait till Monday, then two from Dixon: 12:37 a.m. Sunday, "Answer your phone ya wussy. This freakin' bar's hoppin' … It's like babe land … I'm in the can—get your ass down here!" Followed by: 2:06 a.m. Sunday, "Where the fuck are you? I got two babes following me home … They wanna hot tub. They're in sexy bridesmaid dresses, but not for long. Even you could get laid. If you get this, get over here. Otherwise, call me doctor ménage." Chase frowned, wondering if the dresses were pink.

The fourth message: 8:18 a.m. Sunday, "Hi Chase, it's Mary. Hope I'm not calling too early. Parker asked me when you were coming to pick him up to go shark fishing."

Shark fishing? Oh shit.

The last twelve hours came in like a breeze but left like a hurricane. Speeding to Mary's house, thoughts of Brooke raced through Chase's mind. Good thoughts. Naughty thoughts. He desperately wanted to call now that his cell worked, but didn't even have her number. Directory assistance was useless. He nearly crashed his BMW, then wondered how he'd ever be able to fly.

"Daddy!" Parker squealed, then sprinted and dove onto Chase's legs in a monkey hug.

Feeling lucky to avert serious injury, Chase rubbed his son's head, saying, "Hey little buddy—I guess you missed me," then glanced at Mary and said, "How was he?"

"He's always so well behaved. He's so excited to go shark fishing— what a great dad you are."

Raleigh East Airport was owned by a college buddy—a perfect place to fly in and out hassle free. They housed only thirty single-engine planes and bypassed a big airport's post–9-11 bureaucracy. Chase ran a little late but hoped they'd understand. He hadn't flown in over three months so he needed the flight time. Though the memories of Brooke ignited a special adrenaline, he was exhausted, in need of a boost for the flight to Hilton Head. *Starbucks is on the way.*

Parker kept Chase's mind on overdrive, peppering him with questions about sharks for the entire twenty-minute drive. Pulling into the parking lot, Parker said, "Do we get to fly in your plane, Daddy?"

Chase hadn't informed Parker of his plan. After a smooth takeoff, Chase caught a second wind, thanks to his spunky three-year-old. He marveled at his son's enthusiasm and the unfiltered questions he kept rifling.

"Are we high enough yet?"

"Yes, do you wanna help me with the wheel now?"

"Yippee!"

Clear visibility and, aside from the occasional wind gusts, the flight was smooth. Hilton Head Island Airport was mainly used for small crafts, but included commercial puddle jumpers—the big jets flew into Savannah or Charleston. On approach, he was directed to circle once, then cleared to land.

As the plane touched down, Parker's eyes nearly popped out. While taxiing, he asked about shark fishing for the millionth time. Chase just smiled. The guilt from not spending enough time together was replaced by anticipation. Although he thought about Brooke during most of the flight, he looked forward to a great father-son day. *Who needs Disney?*

Hilton Head Fish Stories specialized in sport fishing, boasting catches of line-sizzling king mackerel, acrobatic sailfish, and a South Carolina record barracuda. But Chase chartered a private boat and guide to catch the big one. Captain Carlos Rodriguez couldn't guarantee a shark, but he had a photo album that would have made Captain Quint envious.

The sun smiled down on the three as their twenty-six-foot boat cut through the waves, heading out to sea. Parker looked adorable with his life jacket pressing up against his chin while sitting on his father's lap, eyeing Captain Carlos. Suddenly, Chase pointed to the right and said, "Look." Parker turned just in time to spot an adult dolphin curve back into the water, followed closely by another.

"Wow. Is that a shark?"

Chase laughed, "No, those are dolphins—a mommy and a daddy." As the words left his mouth, Chase braced for the mommy question.

Instead, Parker asked, "Can we catch one?"

Captain Carlos said, "We're not fishin' for dolphin today. We're huntin' sharks," sounding a bit like Ahab.

"Yippee."

Carlos said, "You ready to get us some?" Parker nodded with wide eyes in an exaggerated motion. With that, Carlos slowed the boat, then dropped two already baited lines into the water, leaving a bloody trail across the phosphorescent water. Carlos set the poles in their holders. Chase was relieved they were trolling—Parker was too young to hold the poles. Carlos handed Chase a beer and a juice box to Parker. Chase returned the beer and said, "Sorry Carlos, I'm flying. Give me a juice box too."

Parker asked Carlos, "Is this where the sharks are?" Chase grinned at Carlos, who caught the hint. For the next hour, Carlos captivated Parker with tales of landing sharks. He handed them a photo album containing pictures of an assortment of interesting sharks caught—a thousand-pound tiger, a blacktip looking like a *Jaws* remake, a bull, and the intriguing hammerhead.

With Parker immersed in the photos, Carlos said, "You've got a bright boy. Most kids his age get confused by sharks."

With admiring eyes, Chase said, "Thanks, he keeps me busy with the questions."

"I wish more kids were like him. Seems all they want to do is sit around watchin' TV or playin' video games."

"Not my Parker. He sure is—"

One of the lines popped up and down, then buzzed as the line released. "Got one!"

Carlos yanked the pole out and pulled it high in the air as the reel screamed. Parker's eyes bulged, "Is it a shark?"

Carlos said, "Hard to tell—it sure feels like one though." He pumped the reel for several spins, then clutched as the fish outran the effort. This continued for thirty minutes and held both Chase and Parker spellbound. The fish jumped out of the water and twisted as if showing off, before plunging angrily in the water. "Tiger shark, about five feet." With sweat gleaming across his ruddy dark complexion, Carlos said, "You guys wanna try it?"

Parker's head twisted and froze on his dad with laser-beam eyes.

Chase said, "Absolutely. Come on buddy."

He lifted Parker in his arms as his son clung tightly to his neck. Chase set the base of the pole in his fishing belt and for the next twenty-five minutes did some serious deep sea fishing with Parker at his side. Not making much progress but enjoying the feeling of man versus beast, Chase glimpsed at Carlos with weary eyes. Carlos said, "You guys tired her out. Want me to bring her in?"

Chase nodded, then handed the pole to Carlos. Ten minutes later, Chase and Parker spotted the tiger shark surface beside the boat. It floated like a shiny canoe. Then, it thrashed, splashing water into the boat. Carlos said, "Look at her. She's a tiger shark all right."

Parker raised his chin and said, "Wow. It's big."

Carlos cut his line, releasing the shark. As it slowly disappeared back into the translucent water, he said, "You guys wanna catch a bigger one?"

Chase mouthed, "We better get back," but Parker cut him off, "Yay!"

Parker glanced back at Chase, "Can we? This is fun, Daddy. We're gonna catch a big shark!"

Chase said, "How much time do we have?"

"You're my last client today. We're already out here and I'm having a blast. I'll go out some more—where the big ones are."

Chase rubbed his chin and frowned, then looked at Parker. His son's eyes rivaled a Labrador puppy. "Sure."

"Yippee. Can we fish tomorrow too?"

"No, not tomorrow. But we'll do something fun. I'm thinking of taking the day off."

"Can we make a sand castle?"

"Maybe."

"Yippee." Parker's hug could melt dry ice.

Carlos set a new hook with a whole bonita fish, saying, "This is for the big sharks, Parker." While allowing Parker to touch the live fish, causing a burst of giggles, Chase left a message for Ruth that he'd be off tomorrow. Then he called Oksana and gave her the day off.

Two hours later, as the sun hovered above the horizon, Carlos reeled a ten-foot hammerhead right next to the boat. The giant fish lashed back and forth, then broke free. Though the lengthy battle didn't result in a picture, it didn't matter—Parker would always remember this day.

Heading back across the waves while stars sprinkled the darkening sky, Parker fell asleep in Chase's arms. Chase gently combed his fingers through his son's soft hair and gazed up, thanking each star.

13

Brooke woke up with an aching neck from a fitful night. *Monday morning, ugh.* Relieved the wedding ended, and surprised Melissa kept it together better than she had. Brooke couldn't stop thinking about Chase. Yesterday yin-yanged, as guilt and passion alternated on her psyche. Half expecting him to call, she wondered if he had any regrets.

Chase had enflamed Brooke's body in unimaginable ways, igniting her soul. Hoping he wasn't the type to wait three days, she had kept her cell nearby all day.

I have to go to Starbucks to see if Saturday was a fluke, or if it was real. I wish I didn't have that stupid meeting first thing this morning. I'll stay as long as I can—lately, he's been going earlier, so who knows? Either way, I have to see him today. I can't wait three days.

— ♥ —

"Can we build a sand castle?"

"Huh?"

"Wake up." Chase's eyelids lifted as his dream faded into realization. "Oh, hey little guy. You're up early."

"Can we build a sand castle?"

"You have quite the memory, son, you know that?" Chase rubbed his eyes.

Parker held his stare like a puppy waiting for a walk. After a pause, Chase said, "Sure we can. Today, we'll build the biggest sand castle ever."

"Yippee!"

Work had lost its fun lately and now, with the sticky situation with Brooke, Chase was relieved. He loved the beaches of Hilton Head and could think of nowhere he'd rather be than playing hooky with Parker.

No Migraine Monday today, thank God.

"Good morning Brooke. Take a seat."

"Good morning, Mr. Greenberg." Brooke raised her eyebrow while setting her Starbucks cup on the desk.

"This is Mr. Stuart Jacoby and he'll be sitting in on our meeting."

"Hello." Brooke smiled at the unfamiliar man sitting rigidly beside her; Jacoby feigned a smile.

"Brooke, Pharmical is in the process of some changes."

"Okay."

"We feel we have to stay one step ahead of our competitors." Pause. Greenberg continued, "We've made some tough decisions and I'm afraid they affect you and your department."

"Oh." Brooke's eyes fluttered, unmet by Greenberg, who stared down at the papers on his desk.

"Pharmical has decided to outsource Integrated Client Services."

"But, what about all those people I just—"

"They'll all be offered fair severance. That's why we've hired Mr. Jacoby and his firm."

Brooke gulped and the room spun out of control.

"I regret to inform you that we're terminating your employment, effective today."

"You're what?"

"Listen, I understand you're upset."

"Upset? I'm stunned!"

"I'd like to discuss some of the terms of your severance."

"I need to talk to Chase Allman first."

"Miss Hart, please don't make this any harder—"

Brooke's eyes narrowed, "Does Chase know what you're doing?"

"Mr. Allman is well aware of our decision, but he doesn't get involved with these types of things. I'll cover the terms of your severance …"

Well aware is the last phrase Brooke heard. The words saturated her brain like lithium and she was now floating in an out-of-body experience. The tears trickled from her fluttering eyes. Greenberg muttered something about taking some packet home. Numbness engulfed her body.

Greenberg and a security guard escorted her by the arm like they were placing her in a straight jacket. She said, "I can walk on my own." But they maintained their grip. She wanted to scream, to lash out. With heavy steps, she marched like an inmate en route to solitary confinement.

Just past the exit door to the parking garage, the men let her go, then stared while she headed to her car. Shock morphed into anger. Brooke slammed the Lexus's door, then glared back at the two frowning men, still scrutinizing her. *Do you really think I'm going back in there?*

Hackles rose as she started the car and squealed her tires, taking small delight in making the two wooden watchdogs scowl. She considered waving goodbye with her middle finger, but muttered into the rearview mirror, "You're not worth it."

Once outside the garage and out of view, she stopped and dialed. After the receptionist answered, Brooke said, "Chase Allman, please."

"Mr. Allman's office." The hair on Brooke's neck bristled.

"Is this Ruth?"

"Who's calling please?"

"It's Brooke Hart. I need to speak with Chase."

"Mr. Allman is unavailable. Would you care to leave a message?"

Brooke frowned and suppressed a grumble. "Yeah, please have him call me on my cell as soon as possible."

"Does he have your cell number or would you like me to take it from you?"

Brooke drew a deep breath and provided her cell number, then poked the off button like she was squishing a bug, nearly losing her nail—and accidently deactivating her phone.

Brooke pressed the on button—this time with less intensity—then hit speed dial one.

"Hi Brooke, I'm getting on a conference call. What's up?"

"I won't be able to afford you anymore."

"Come again?"

"I just got fired."

After a long pause, Shane said, "Hang on a second. Let me end this other call. Don't hang up." Brooke dabbed her eyes. A few seconds later, Shane said, "What happened?"

"They're dumping my department and outsourcing it to India I guess."

"I don't understand. Didn't you just hire a bunch of people?"

Brooke lost it. Sobbing uncontrollably, Shane tried to pacify her by uttering phrases like: "It's okay," "Take all the time you need," "I understand," and "Let it out." This only increased Brooke's sorrow.

Brooke blew her nose, then drew a deep breath, and said, "I feel so bad for all those people I hired—they're all losing their jobs. Ginny has a sick baby and really needed this job." She wiped her eyelids as a new batch of tears formed.

"Didn't you say they just let you go?"

"Yep."

"That company is messed up, Brooke. You're better off somewhere else. And do not, I repeat, *do not* blame yourself for the people in your department. It's not your fault. You didn't let them go."

Brooke sighed, then said, "I know, I know. I'm sorry I lost it—I guess I just needed a shoulder to cry on."

"That's better. Give yourself a day to grieve, then we'll talk tomorrow."

As Brooke pressed the off button, she stared at the phone. *Why hasn't he called me back? Is he avoiding me? What an asshole.*

Parker looked so sweet snoozing on his towel. Building the sand castle had been an all-day event that exhausted both father and son. Chase wished he could just nap like that. He could never sleep on a beach or an airplane. Chase glanced at his beach bag, but resisted the temptation to turn on his cell. He didn't want to wake Parker up just yet—loving the way his son's breathing blended with the gentle waves.

Today had provided the day off he and Parker deserved. He noticed that his son hadn't asked for his mommy once, hoping his son's concerns faded like the outgoing tide.

Tomorrow, I'll face the inbox flood, but I'm not spoiling the perfect day.

"Hi, Daddy, sorry to bother you at work."

"Don't be silly, Brooke. I always love to hear your voice. How was the wedding?"

"Fine."

"What's wrong?"

Brooke sniffled, "You were right. I should've listened to you."

"What's the matter?"

"They fired me."

"I ... I don't understand."

"Pharmical fired me today. They're dumping my whole division. All the people I brought in too."

"That's the craziest thing I ever heard. They just hired you. Why would they do such a thing? Can't they find you another VP slot?"

"Nope. Chase Allman turned out to be worse than a shark. He's a ..." Brooke almost said boa constrictor. Instead, "Weasel with a fin on his back."

"Well, I'm sorry to hear that, but it's probably a blessing in disguise. We'll find something better. I'm going to call Bill Barrister over at GDK. He'd love to have you work there."

"Hold off for now. I just found out and I can't think straight. Give me a few days."

"Well, honey, I just hate hearing you so upset after everything you've ... hey, why don't you come to lunch with me tomorrow and stay home a few days? We can map out a job search together."

Ordinarily Brooke had an excuse ready, a quick no-can-do, but now she felt a surge of gratitude. "I'd really like that, Daddy. Tomorrow, I have to tie up some loose ends, but I'll plan on lunch Wednesday."

Brooke hung up, set the phone down, and flipped on the radio— "Build Me Up Buttercup"—the song instantly brought memories. She recalled convincing Tanner to take a dance lesson before the wedding. "Buttercup" was the song they practiced with—over and over. She could still picture him trying to swing her around with that silly grin on his face. She cranked it up and sang along.

After the song ended, she considered the irony in the lyrics with her current situation as rain began pelting her Lexus. She flipped on the wipers, but they barely kept up. Brooke slowed and leaned forward, but continued driving. Her happy Tanner memory had washed away like an August storm, and her mind returned to Chase. She checked her phone—nothing. *I guess the big CEO is nothing more than a weasel. I can't believe I slept with that asshole.*

The flight back seemed long. A storm hovered up ahead in central North Carolina, holding unexpected gusts and thunder and lightning. Though Chase figured he could land, he felt queasy. Parker's eyes popped as each bolt of lightning descended from the clouds. He asked, "Will lightning hit our plane, Daddy?"

Nervous laugh. "No, son, we're safe. Our plane has special stuff outside so lightning won't hurt it." This was a partial lie, but Chase didn't want to discuss the real answer and cause his eyes to really pop out.

Chase decided to divert to the east and allow the storm to pass. He also diverted Parker's fears, asking, "You wanna fly over to the ocean and look for dolphins and sharks?"

"Yippee." He loved how his son's face lit up. Parker's enthusiasm was contagious, bringing a huge smile to his father's lips.

Flying low, they observed the fraying white tops of the lazy waves, directing the ocean toward land. Seagulls were dive-bombing a darkened area of blue water. "Daddy, look—what are those birds doing?"

"They're called seagulls and they're fishing."

Parker eyed his father, "Where are their poles?"

"They use their mouths and dive in far enough to catch a fish."

Parker pondered as his three-year-old microprocessor spun. Chase delighted in Parker's curiosity. Betsy Stanton at Angel Academy had marveled at Parker's intellect and verbal skills—developed well beyond his age. Chase needed a *Tell Me Why* book to keep up with Parker's inquisitive mind.

Chase noticed the storm had moved west. He asked Parker to check one more time for dolphins and sharks. After a full scan, Parker cheered as another bird plunged underwater, returning with a fish wiggling in its beak. Moments later, Chase brought the plane down with a bounce, then slid to a stop on the wet jetway of the tiny airport.

Unfazed, Parker asked, "Can we go to Chuck E. Cheese?"

"Sure, but then it's bedtime, mister." *Daddy has to go back to work early tomorrow.* He hadn't worried about work in four days.

After splitting a cheese pizza, they returned home. Duke greeted them at the garage doorway with wild licks and a tail that nearly knocked Parker to the ground. Chase wondered when Oksana had last walked him and motioned outside for a quick yard relief.

They brushed teeth together and washed up just enough to avoid Oksana's scorn the next morning. Chase tucked Parker in. Duke jumped to his usual spot in the bottom corner of Parker's bed then posed with mouth down, eyes slightly raised. Father and son recited Parker's special prayer and a warm glow spread inside Chase.

The weekend had been quite an interesting ride—exactly what both father and son needed. As Parker's eyes fluttered into sleep, Chase brushed his son's hair back, reminiscent of his carefree childhood.

As Parker drifted off, Chase headed downstairs. His mind flashed back to early Sunday morning. He could still picture Brooke—how incredible she looked—in light and dark, clothed and unclothed. *Hmmm, that reminds me.*

Chase bee-lined to the garage and popped the trunk. There it was—rolled up in the corner. Carefully gripping the lingerie, the feeling returned—her smooth skin, her delicate touch. Smothering his face with the silky garment, he inhaled deeply, groaning as her sweet alluring fragrance aroused him. Holding the small slip like a feather, he headed inside while pressing it to his nostrils each time he needed to breathe.

Once in bed, he inhaled the lingerie one more time, smiled, then placed it beside his pillow. Though physically exhausted, his mind was playfully awake. He replayed the night with Brooke with crystal clarity. She had ignited his mind, body, and soul—and now, even the memory thrilled him. He fell asleep thinking about her and awakened early the next morning to her aroma.

After inhaling once more, he called Duke from Parker's room. "We gotta do a quick run today. Can you handle that?" Duke's head cocked slightly.

———— ♥ ————

The drive to Starbucks flew. Chase peered at the lingerie on the passenger seat and grinned. Parking nearby, he glanced in the rearview mirror and slid his finger back and forth against his front teeth, then patted his hair. He glanced at the lingerie and decided to leave it in the car—a good excuse to get her alone. Chase then jumped out and scanned the street for the Lexus. *Crap.*

Once inside Starbucks, he did a quick search—no Brooke yet. He squinted at the counter and caught Marcus's eye, drawing a nod. The line was lighter than usual. With one more person to go, still no Brooke, Tonya said, "Hi Chase, where have you been?'"

"Hey Tonya, took some time off with my family."

"Looks like ya got some sun."

Marcus strode over carrying the usual two coffees, and said, "Damn, A-Man, you trying to look like me?"

"Hey Marcus. Did I get that much sun? I wore thirty."

"No, you look good. I'm just messing with ya."

"Remember the young lady I was here with a couple a weeks ago?"

Marcus said, "You mean Brooke *the babe*?"

Chase noticed Tonya's frown. "Yeah, Brooke. Did she come in yet?"

"No. I haven't seen her since last week. You supposed to be meetin' her?"

"No."

"I'll be glad to give her a message?"

Chase considered Marcus's question longer than usual, then said, "No, I'll see her at work."

One 175-degree espresso down—and still no Brooke. Chase decided to leave. Scanning the street one more time, he wanted to return her lingerie so he could remove it again. Bringing it into work was out of the question; he wanted to keep it anyway—at least until her fragrance faded.

Even though he lingered at Starbucks longer than usual, Chase was still early for work. The parking lot was fairly empty, but he circled the garage, searching for the Lexus—*nothing*. Each time he realized she wasn't where he was looking—first Starbucks, now the parking lot—he sighed. He passed the entrance and glimpsed over his shoulder, hoping to catch her pulling in, but still no Brooke.

I hope Ruth didn't set up any lunch meetings.

Chase loved this time of day. Empty office, one quad espresso down and still one to savor—at the ideal temperature. He whistled while flipping on his light switch, then winced at his inbox. He spotted Ruth's neat deck of notes on top of his chair. He leafed through each one as if checking his hand in a game of cards. Then, he spotted the ace of hearts: *Brooke Hart called. Please call her on her cell (704) 555-5309.* Dated yesterday, 9:07 a.m.

Chase tossed the other notes across his desk, then sprang from his chair. He peeked his head out. *Coast clear. Perfect.* Chase clicked his door tightly shut and twisted on the lock.

He drew a deep breath, but couldn't impede the heartbeat thumping into his throat. Realizing his time alone was limited, he dialed ... *please answer, please answer, please answer*—his cadence matched each ring.

"Hello."

"Brooke? I've been dying to talk to you."

"I was wondering when you were going to finally call ..." Chase didn't pick up her sarcastic tone. His hands trembled like a nervous sixth grader calling his first crush.

"I looked for you this morning ... I wanted to give you your pink slip."

The silence sounded like a lost line.

"You still there?" Chase's voice cracked.

"Oh yeah, I'm here all right ... I can't believe you just said that. You're an asshole!"

Silence.

"What? Brooke? Brooke? You there? Brooke? Brooke!" Chase squinted at the screen on his phone and the realization struck like a flaming arrow to his chest. *What is up with her? Asshole? I can't believe she just called me an asshole.* Chase began redialing, but hung up and stared into the earpiece.

Chase's head spun. Thoughts of rabbits boiling on the stove from the movie *Fatal Attraction* came over him. He gulped his coffee and grimaced—and not because it was too cold. He clicked on his email and scanned for something from her—maybe her guilt infected her heart and she sent me an email. He scanned his inbox and spotted her name. *What the hell?*

From David Greenberg: "Brooke Hart has elected to pursue another career opportunity. We here at Pharmical Solutions wish her well in her new endeavors." Chase detested the template send off. He glanced at his watch and wondered if his HR SVP was in yet. With waves of dread and confusion pulsing, Chase dialed.

"Good morning, boss. Where've you been?"

"Hi David. I, uh, I took a few days off."

"That's what I figured—smart of you with what's going on. Don't worry though, I handled it all yesterday. After Brooke Hart, the rest of the day was a snap."

"What happened with Brooke?"

"Well, she didn't handle it well. I had to call security. But you'd be proud of me—I offered her a lowball severance and she didn't balk. I still haven't heard from her so we may have gotten by cheap. I dispensed pink slips to her entire department by noon and handed it over to outplacement. So far, so good."

Pink slips? Chase's eyes rolled to the back of his head; if it weren't for his chair's sturdy backing, he would have fallen to the floor.

"Chase, you still there? Chase? Chase, can you hear me?"

Chase had dropped the phone and could hear Greenberg squawking through the earpiece while he raced through his emails. Then he spotted it—Greenberg's email to Henry Stoddard, cc: Chase Allman: "Good news, Mr. Stoddard. As of noon, I have personally met with the entire   Integrated Client Services department. Aside from Brooke Hart, I don't anticipate any issues. Phase two is now in Stuart Jacoby's hands."

Phase two? What is phase one? Why wasn't I aware of any of this? I need to make a call—she can't possibly think I meant …

After five rings, a generic voicemail, then a quick beep, "Brooke, it's Chase. Listen, I really need to talk to you. Please call me as soon as you hear this. Even if I'm in a meeting, tell Ruth to interrupt me. Please call."

I wish she'd pick up. She couldn't possibly think I meant … I have to talk to her.

Chase's temples pounded as he picked up his cell. Maybe she'll answer if she doesn't recognize the different number. He dialed Brooke. *I'll straighten this out before it gets blown out of proportion. I'll explain the misunderstanding and get her a job in another department.* Five rings, same voicemail. *Dammit, why won't you pick up? She sure is stubborn.*

An email flashed in the bottom corner of his screen—from Henry Stoddard. *He's in early. I'll ask him what's going on.* Chase pulled up Henry's empty Outlook calendar and sighed. Chase remembered his boss never used Outlook.

Chase opened his door and Ruth's desk was still empty. He considered leaving her a note, but didn't want to waste the time—he had to hustle over there.

Henry's office towered on the other side of Pharmical's campus, about a ten-minute walk. The building was used for Research and Development, and Security; Henry occupied the penthouse. Chase hoped he'd catch Henry early enough to grab breakfast together. He needed another coffee—even if it wasn't Starbucks.

Once outside, birds chirped lovely harmonies. A strong breeze from behind whisked like a wind tunnel on another humid Carolina day, lifting a sweet blend of jasmine and magnolia into the air. Ominous clouds swirled, shielding the sun's early rays. Chase power-walked with head down, oblivious to nature's delights.

Inside the building, sweat beaded on Chase's temples around windblown hair, causing the security guard to take notice. Chase retrieved his handkerchief and wiped his brow, then proceeded to the elevator. Security cameras scanned his every step like birds in a Hitchcock movie.

At the sixteenth floor, Chase marched across the dimly lit corridor, then advanced toward the light in the corner. Henry's door was closed but Lucy stood guard—*she's here early.*

Lucy peered over her reading glasses and bolted upright, "Chase, what a pleasant surprise. My, you look tan." Lucy's cheeks flushed.

"Hey, Lucy. Looks like he's in a meeting."

"He's been on the phone with London for a while."

"I was hoping to catch breakfast with him."

"Oh, he's already eaten—I brought him take-out from Le Peep."

"Wow, you need to train Ruth for me."

Lucy laughed and removed her glasses. "Henry's been dying to talk to you. He's been looking for you the past couple of days—"

"I took a little time off to spend with my family."

Lucy's chest tightened. Ruth had gossiped the scoop and Lucy realized she couldn't let on—even though she wanted to probe in the worst way, thinking he looked so boyish and cute with his hair mussed up. She wished she worked for Chase just for the view.

"He should be off soon and he'd kill me if I let you go before he saw you. I've never seen him this happy. Can I get you something?"

Chase smiled and said, "A Le Peep chocolate croissant and espresso would sure be nice." His grin bordered on laughter as he considered his request.

Lucy read his face, then raised her eyebrows, and said, "Seriously, it's no problem. I'd be happy to do it for you."

"I was just teasing, Lucy—"

"Can I at least get you a coffee? It's not espresso, but it's good and hot."

"I'd love a coffee—if it's no problem?"

Lucy practically jumped from her chair, saying, "It's no problem at all. I'd be happy to get you that croissant ..."

"Just coffee. Thanks though."

While Lucy was away, her phone buzzed and then Henry's voice boomed, "Lucy, can you bring me the Stabilitas folder? Lucy? Lucy? You there?" Henry burst through the door and nearly fell into Lucy's desk.

"Chase! I've been looking all over for you. Ruth said you were away."

Chase wondered what excuse Ruth used—she covered for him better than he could himself. He said, "I took a few days for family time."

"Well, you should do it more often. Have you seen the news? I can't stop watching that CNBC piece." Henry looked animated.

"I missed the CNBC piece. Good news?"

"Good news? I'd say so. The stock popped three bucks before the CNBC babe turned it over to Joanne's closer—that Wall Street guy she found was perfect. They practically read the script verbatim. Joanne's PR firm sure earned their pay."

Chase's stomach roiled every time Henry bragged about Joanne. One of Henry's hand-picked board members, Chase sensed she had his boss's ear—and more. Henry spent an inordinate amount of time in New York, and Chase guessed it wasn't all business.

"I missed it. What did they say?"

"I sent it out to all employees on email."

"I, uh, I just returned to work this morning, so I haven't gone through all my emails."

"Well, hang on. You gotta see this one. I can't stop watching it—and hell, I wrote it."

Henry resembled a Stone Age man at a computer seminar plopped in front of his monitor. Chase figured Henry needed Lucy to help him with the on/off button. Chase said, "Did you save the file to your desktop?"

"Huh?" Henry looked uncharacteristically bewildered.

"Never mind. Check your sent file for the email and just click on the link."

Instead of another *huh*, Henry just stared at Chase. Chase said, "Did Lucy send the email?"

"Of course. You know I hate doing those goddamn emails."

Chase wondered if Henry needed Lucy to say "right, left, right, left, right, left," when he walked. Chase shuffled around Henry's imposing mahogany desk, then in a few clicks, hit the file, standing as Henry remained seated.

The video opened with an attractive brunette woman in a dark blue business suit: "Though Hurricane Katia continues heading toward the Florida coast, a Carolina company isn't evacuating just yet. Some *great breaking news* out of Pharmical Solutions today. The drug company announced plans for a strategic workforce reduction which will allow them to globalize their reach while still cutting costs. This will pave the way for new markets like Asia and Europe. Leading the charge is Stabilitas, a breakthrough anti-depressant drug. Many analysts have upgraded the stock. Joining us now is Michael Pratt, president of Pratt Securities. Michael, your firm recently upgraded Pharmical to strong buy. Tell us what you see."

"Pharmical should see unprecedented growth, both domestically and in emerging markets. Their new globalization initiative is brilliant and we like their next generation of drugs. The anti-depressant market has tremendous upside potential, making Pharmical the shining star of Research Triangle."

"Thank you, Michael."

Though Henry had viewed the video a dozen times, he looked ready to salivate. He turned and stared at Chase with Doberman eyes. Chase just glared at the CNBC logo on the blank screen.

"Not bad, huh? Joanne and I spent all weekend in New York writing that. I never thought she could get it on all the news shows by Monday. She never ceases to amaze me. Oh, I could just kiss her."

Chase pondered the time it would take to write that short script and guessed Henry had enough time left over to kiss her all right— and then some. With his love-struck boss behaving like this, he didn't feel as guilty about his couple of glorious hours with Brooke. *That reminds me.*

"I was blindsided by the mass firing yesterday."

"What do you mean?" Henry frowned.

"I was off for a day and a half and when I returned, an entire division was obliterated. Why wasn't I in the loop?"

"I looked for you Friday and Ruth said you couldn't be reached. She made it sound like you were on a flight. Didn't matter—Greenberg and I hashed it out with Jacoby."

"I think we jumped the gun."

"How so?"

"Well, you and I discussed these changes, but you knew I wasn't in agreement."

"Bullshit. You said you were on board during our lunch."

Chase stepped back and furrowed his brows. Henry's narrowed eyes met Chase's like a bull eyeing a matador. He strangled a scream. "I don't agree with handing everything over to India this fast. There's too much at stake. I would've liked to test outsourcing first. What if it backfires?"

"See the big picture. Our stock just soared to a record high—better than a takeover play. And only because of the news of our downsizing. My net worth jumped to eleven digits in one day. Hell, I can finally retire. You made millions. We all did. The board's giddy, everybody wins. Why are you so down?"

"Why couldn't we have discussed it more? Most of those people let go were just hired. They all have families."

"C'mon, listen to yourself. You're not making sense. We provided those people outplacement. Don't let the board hear you whining like this. They'll lock you up in the *Ha Ha Hotel*."

"You didn't have to fire Brooke Hart. With her talents, and the way the media loves us, I could use her in our PR department."

"PR? They're the next to go. If it weren't for Joanne's New York PR firm, our stock would still be stuck in the mud. Besides, Brooke's not right for Pharmical."

"What do you mean?" Chase raised his eyebrow.

"She's the only VP we have without at least an MBA and she went to a *state school*."

"Why does everybody have to go to Duke around here?"

"Coming from Mister Blue Devil himself," Henry coughed into his clenched fist. "Besides, she's a lightweight ... apparently Greenberg had to call security to remove her from the building."

"Greenberg's afraid of his own shadow. He calls security if someone sneezes near him."

"I don't understand your fascination with that girl, but take my advice—stop thinking with your dick and see the big picture." Henry's eyes cast a ghostly glow.

Chase gulped and flared his nostrils. His head throbbed. Henry's comment struck like a sucker punch. Chase opened his mouth, then suppressed his return strike, but the question burned inside—*did Brooke say something to Greenberg?*

The intercom buzzed, "Excuse me, Mr. Stoddard."

"What is it, Lucy?"

"A Mr. Little from *Money Magazine* is holding for you on line one."

Chase seized his cue before Henry even spoke, pacing toward the door. He had wanted an excuse to leave—without speaking his mind. He paused at the entrance and glimpsed back.

"Oh, tell him I'll be right with him." Henry lifted his eyebrows, then lowered them as he pressed line one—without Lucy's help.

"Mr. Allman?"

"Oh, hi again, Lucy. Please call me Chase."

"I have your coffee, Chase. Would you still like it?"

"Thanks, coffee sounds great right about now."

He strode back to Lucy's cubicle. Henry's voice resembled a snake-oil salesman in the background. He reached for the oversized Styrofoam cup. "Thanks again. You're the best."

The coffee was lukewarm, but when Chase reached the elevator, he peeled off the lid and gulped. Before hitting the ground floor, he had drained the entire coffee. Chase tossed the empty cup into the trash receptacle, then nodded as he passed the security stand.

Once outside, the wind whipped his hair back and flung his tie up and over his shoulder. He clasped his tie down, then buttoned his suit coat, before trudging ahead. Though it smelled like rain, the air was dry. The walk back seemed to take forever as thoughts swirled faster than the gusting wind.

Inside his building, Chase felt a wave of angst. He considered jumping into his BMW and heading to Starbucks, but he needed to speak with David Greenberg. He combed his fingers through his gnarly hair, but only managed to make himself appear more disheveled. People he passed didn't recognize him.

He pressed the elevator button for twenty—Greenberg's floor, one below his own. He scraped one more hand comb—to no avail. Stepping off the elevator, his stomach churned. He wondered what Greenberg knew and wondered how he could get him to talk. Greenberg had worked for Chase for the past seven years, yet Chase had never been able to connect with him. He found Greenberg cagey and never felt he could trust him. Now elevated to SVP in charge of Legal, Human Resources, Customer Service, and Public Relations, David Greenberg held the same position as Chase, right before being named CEO. Paranoia flooded Chase—*did Greenberg want my job?* Brooke Hart could furnish Greenberg the keys to the corner office with just one comment.

Chase noticed Greenberg's door was shut, but his light was on. He inhaled, then plodded over to Janet, Greenberg's secretary. Glimpsing up from her keyboard, she looked as mousy as her boss. Chase considered office osmosis—like dogs that resembled their owners. "Hello, Mr. Allman, are you here to see Mr. Greenberg?"

"Hi, Janet, please call me Chase." Chase wondered if Greenberg let Janet call him by his first name.

"He's on the phone. Would you like me to tell him you're here?"

"No, that's okay." Chase maneuvered so Greenberg could spot him through his glass partition. David raised one finger in the air, and then stood with phone pressed against his ear. Chase said, "I think he saw me."

"You look like you got some color. Have you been out in the sun?"

"Yeah, I took a little family time this past weekend."

"Well, you picked a good time to get away. It was crazy here yesterday."

The door swung open, causing the partially open metal blinds to clank. "Are you here to see me?"

"Hi, David, you gotta minute?"

"Sure," he stepped back, bumping his foot against the door, and then stumbled toward his desk. Greenberg plunged into his seat and grabbed some loose papers. With trembling hands, he tried to straighten them against the desktop like an overstuffed deck of cards. After three failed attempts, he flung them on top of another stack. Chase guessed it was Greenberg's version of an inbox.

Greenberg noticed Chase's eyes, and then glanced away, saying, "You wanted to see me?"

"David, I read your email to Henry and I just wanted to talk to you in person about a couple of things."

"Okay."

"I just left Henry's office and he said some things about Brooke Hart that seemed unsettling."

"How ... how so?"

"I don't think she got a fair shake."

"Did she call you and complain?"

Chase rubbed his chin, then said, "I spoke with her, yes."

Greenberg crossed his arms. "Mr. Allman, sir, I asked her not to call you. I did. You can even ask Stuart."

"Relax, David—and call me Chase."

Greenberg gulped then flared his eyes, and paused. He looked like he was about to pee his pants. "What ... what did she say? Did she complain about her package?"

"I haven't even seen what we offered her."

Greenberg reached down and pulled a file drawer out. He lunged forward, then began leafing through with both hands while twitching his wire-rimmed glasses on his nose. Chase checked his watch. Greenberg set a file on his desk, opened it and with shaking fingers, handed Chase the top page.

Chase scanned the document, frowning three times in ten seconds. He glared at Greenberg, and said, "This is a disgrace. No wonder Brooke's so upset."

"Oh, I could tell she was upset. I had to call security after I, uh, after *we* terminated her. She didn't say anything to me about the severance though. I thought I saved the company a bunch of money."

"We can't just throw people under the bus and hope they'll go away. We need to do the right thing. She was a vice president after all."

"Well, I don't have the budget for anything more."

"To hell with the budget. This was done so fast, I don't think anybody thought this through." Though Chase was directing the criticism at Henry and his Butcher board, David's lips turned pale.

"I was only doing what I was told, Mr. Allman."

"Call me Chase. Don't worry about the stupid budget. Besides, I sign your budget. Just take it out of T and E."

"I'm over on T and E, sir."

"Stop arguing with me. We can't treat people like this. If I have to take it out of my own paycheck, I will. Find a way and I'll sign it!"

"Tell me what you want to offer her."

Chase's cheeks and ears were flush. He flipped over the paper and scribbled, filling the page within thirty seconds. Tossing the paper at Greenberg, he said, "Have this drafted and email it to me today. I'll handle it with Brooke."

14

"Shane, I feel like such a loser. I can't believe I got fired and then pulled outta there by frickin' security."

"Brooke, I know you're upset—and you have every right to be—but let's focus on the bright side."

"Okay, mister bright side, shine some light on this one."

"Up until the last few days, you were miserable at Pharmical. With the severance, you can take your time and look for a job you really want to do."

"Severance? I wouldn't call it that—it's more like rape."

"What did they offer you?"

"Two weeks' salary and outplacement."

"Tell me you're joking?"

"I'm serious as a heart attack. They gave me two frickin' weeks."

"You didn't sign anything, I hope?"

"They didn't afford me the chance. Plus, it's tough to write with your arms restrained behind your back by some flunky mall cop."

Shane grinned, imagining tiny Brooke making Pharmical's security officer sweat.

"This just doesn't add up. There has to be more to the story."

Brooke had been restless the night before, and even a brisk run didn't clear her mind. Her head pulsed from caffeine withdrawal, but she'd never go to Starbucks again—the thought of drinking the same liquid as Chase Allman repulsed her. Beyond her resentment, she felt a guilt that she couldn't shake—or explain. She'd hidden her transgression from everyone except Melissa, yet somehow she felt compelled to open up to Shane. She always felt comfortable with him and respected his wisdom.

Brooke drew a deep breath, "If I tell you something, will you promise not to tell a soul?"

"Of course, you don't even have to ask."

"Will you promise not to think poorly of me?"

"I'm your life coach. You need to share everything with me."

"I do, but this is different."

"Whatever's bothering you, we can talk about it later, if you'd like …"

Brooke inhaled deeply, then said, "I slept with the CEO, then he shitcanned me."

"What?" Shane's voice hit two octaves.

"I said I had sex with the CEO, then I got fired."

"That's textbook sexual harassment. They can't do that. Tell me what happened—everything."

"It's not like it sounds. It just happened."

"Were you two at the office?"

"No, long story, but he was staying at the same hotel where Melissa was married. I think he had some charity event."

"Go on."

"We met in the elevator—just by chance."

"Was he following you?"

Brooke giggled, "More like the other way around. He was already in the elevator, leaving his event, I was trying to just go to bed and, poof, there he was. I actually fell into him on the elevator again. Our rooms were on the same floor."

"Did you say *again*?"

"Longer story—not important."

"Did he coerce you into his room against your will?"

"No, not like that."

"What happened?"

"My key didn't work and he offered to call down … the champagne and shots at the wedding. Everything's kind of a blur."

"Did he kiss you?"

"More like the other way around. I mauled him. I've never been so attracted before in my life. I just … lost my mind. I couldn't control myself."

"And you slept with him?"

"Yes. I realize I made a huge mistake."

"Stop it right there, Brooke. First of all, what happened, happened. You can't do anything to change it. Second, you're not alone—forty percent of employees have dated a coworker."

"Is that supposed to make me feel better?"

"It should. And that statistic is for workplace dating. In your case, yours was offsite and off hours. Plus, alcohol was involved and that lowers your IQ at least thirty points. I'm sure he's attractive too."

"Not any more. After my robotic boss canned me, Chase had the audacity to call me the next day and rub it in my face."

"How so?"

"He told me he wanted to meet and hand over my pink slip."

"What?" Two and a half octaves this time.

"He told me he wanted to give me the pink slip himself."

"The day after they let you go?"

"Yep."

"That's harassment too. That guy's begging for a lawsuit. Have you told your father any of this?"

"Oh, God, no. He's the last person I'd tell. Look, I'm not interested in suing them. I know what happens in that type of case—the victim gets trashed and leaves with a scarlet letter tattooed across her forehead. I'm not a victim, believe it or not. I'm a big girl who slept with a guy who turned out to be a Class A Creep—but not a criminal."

"You really fucked me up!"

"Who is this?" Chase demanded into his cell phone.

"Who do ya think this is? For a friggin' CEO, you're not too bright, pullin' a stunt like this."

"Max?"

"Yeah, it's Max, hotshot. I'm not the friggin' tooth fairy—and I'm not your PI no more. I'm done."

"What are you talking about?" Chase rubbed his temples.

"Your little girl's flown the coop, thanks to you sending in the friggin' cavalry. You still owe me for my wasted time."

"Max, speak English."

"I'll spell it out for you. You used the address I gave you—without me knowing, and without my friggin' blessing—and sent in three bozos from Minneapolis PD. Your girl Heather took off with her little boy toy."

Chase pulled on the hair above his ears. "Shit."

"You wanna tell me what the fuck you were thinkin'?"

"My lawyer has been trying to serve Heather divorce papers for months. All they had to do was hand deliver an envelope. It's my fault—I said to make sure they sent enough manpower—I didn't want to take any chances. I didn't think she'd escape from three cops."

"Well, she did, dumbass. If I was there, I'd kick your ass. She's not hangin' out with nice people. They spot those cop clowns a mile away. My guy was babysittin' the front and could see the side door. When Barney Fife and his two side humps started waving badges, calling for Heather Ann Allman, she spooked and musta got out some other way. Now she's gone—and so is he."

"I ... I don't know what to say."

"Well, my guy's pissed and wants his money—and then some. You're lucky I'm level headed or you'd be missin' too. You owe me big time."

Chase gulped, "I told you I'm sorry. Of course I'll pay you. Can your guys find them? It should be easier to spot two of them."

"Nope, guess again. My guy's out. I don't even wanna tell you what he called me—be thankful I don't have a big mouth like you and your friggin' lawyer. If you expect me to make more calls, you gotta come up with double."

Chase bolted upright, eyes wide, "Done. I'll wire the money into your account right after we hang up. Do you know anything about this guy she's running around with?"

"Of course. I thought you'd never ask. Name's Douglas John, goes by 'Rusty.' He tells people his uncle's Tommy John—the big league pitcher. Rusty's no big leaguer, lemme tell ya. This guy's a loser with a capital L. He's a minor league washout who's been boozin' and snortin' away his whole crummy life. He's forty, six three, about two thirty, been convicted of small time stuff, did a little time. Basically, he's a pretty boy punk. Your girl picked a real winner."

Chase's pen ran out of ink. He leafed through his desk drawer, then grabbed a new pen and scribbled furiously in silence. Max tapped his fingers into the mouthpiece, then said, "You there?"

After a pause, Chase said, "Yeah. I'm trying to write down everything you just said."

"Well, write this down. Before you pull another bonehead stunt, do me a favor—call me first. And make sure you don't forget your little deposit. Oh, and one other thing."

"What's that?"

"The rent-a-cops got inside that crack house and found a bunch of stolen shit. The guys in there tossed your little girl and Rusty under da bus. So on top of my guys, the cops are lookin' for her too."

Brooke merged onto the highway as a fog enveloped her car like a gray netherworld. She drew a deep breath, leaned forward, flipped on her lights, and switched the wipers on. The air conditioning worsened her visibility and the lights illuminated the eerie mist. She felt unsure both inside and out.

The drive to Charlotte always brought out mixed emotions. Both her mother and Tanner were buried there, but in separate cemeteries. She feared she couldn't stomach visiting either one this trip. This would be all about her father. She couldn't imagine what she'd do without him. With Tanner and her mother gone, she never took her dad for granted. She looked forward to seeing him and spending time doing nothing. He always wanted to offer fatherly advice and Brooke usually listened. Brooke figured she could never tell her father the same information about Chase.

"Whenever I see your smiling face ..." startled her. The familiar ringtone sounded foreign today. Her first instinct—Chase—made her stomach sink. She reached for her cell on the passenger seat buzzing on top of three dimes. That's odd—I keep finding dimes in weird places. Not wanting to take her eyes off the already hard-to-see road, she answered without viewing caller ID, and cringed, "Hello, this is Brooke."

"Well, hello stranger. You're tougher to reach than the president."

The voice sounded vaguely familiar—definitely not Chase. She exhaled a sigh, and said, "Who's this?"

"Oh, I'm hurt. You never call, you never write. Now you forget—"

"Travis, is that you? I'm driving in a Carolina cloud right now and couldn't see your number on caller ID."

"How are things?"

"You have impeccable timing. I swear you're psychic."

"I've been called *psycho* but never psychic."

Brooke laughed, then said, "Have any jobs?"

"You know I always do. Why, you looking?"

"You could say that. Pharmical just eliminated my entire division and let me go Monday."

"I'm sorry to hear that. You've only been there a few months. What happened?"

"Long story." Brooke bit her lip, then said, "Basically, they brought me in to build a new division—which I did—then they decided to dump everyone and outsource it to India."

"That's messed up. Didn't they offer you something else? Pharmical always has openings."

"Apparently not, and with what I saw from that place—good riddance."

"Have you updated your resume?"

"Are you kidding? I didn't even have one when you placed me at GenSense. I hate doing those things."

Travis inhaled, "I don't have anything now, but I can probably get you in front of Pfizer. With your background, they're bound to find a place for you. I'm afraid you've gotta send me a resume first."

"Thanks, but no thanks, Travis. I'm not looking for a big drug company. I'm still stinging from Pharmical. Are you working on any more startups?"

"Not right now, but that can change in one phone call. GenSense was a magical placement, wasn't it?"

"You have no idea."

"Well, I've gotta grab this call—somebody I paged—but I'll call you later. I have some ideas."

Travis Bodady had run Bodady Search Partners, a one-man recruiting firm out of Richmond, Virginia, for sixteen years. Brooke recalled the day he called her as if it just happened. He termed it magical, but words couldn't describe how he affected her life. She marveled at his timing, half-wondering if he found her through the obituaries. He never did divulge his source, but it didn't matter—she said "yes" right on the spot.

Brooke noticed the fog clearing and sunshine ahead on the horizon. Shutting off her lights, she felt uplifted. Travis breathed new hope into her. She wished for another GenSense. *It would be funny if Travis worked his magic again.*

The ringtone sounded. She picked up on the first ring, "That was fast."

"Huh?"

Brooke recognized that voice with just one syllable. "Oh, hey, Melissa. I thought you were somebody else."

"Thanks a lot. Did you think I was Chase?"

Brooke cringed—the mention of the word *Chase* sent shivers down her spine. "He's the last person I want to talk to right now."

"Wait a minute. I thought you said he was this most amazing something or other?"

"Not anymore. He turned into a real creep."

"What happened?"

"How much time do we have?"

"As long as you need. Talk to me."

Brooke glanced at the clock in her Lexus, then scratched the back of her neck. "I'm meeting my daddy for lunch. Almost there. Basically, that guy used me on Sunday, then had someone fire me on Monday, then called me and rubbed it in my face yesterday."

After a silence, Melissa said, "You're kidding, right?"

"I wish I was. Hey, I'm pulling into the parking lot. You know how my daddy is about being punctual—I guarantee he's pacing. I'll call ya later."

Melissa said, "Don't you dare—" as the phone line went dead.

Though still a mile away from the Charlotte Country Club, Brooke needed to clear her head. The last thing she wanted was Melissa peppering her with questions as her father opened her car door.

Brooke entered the historic Plaza-Midwood neighborhood, providing a nice diversion for her cluttered mind. Majestic trees lined the streets, guiding her toward the sprawling grounds at Charlotte CC. Though recently remodeled, the clubhouse still maintained its historic Southern charm—with unique moldings and millwork, grandiose chandeliers, priceless murals, and antique furniture.

Weston had said "wear something nice," and she feared he was planning on parading her around to his network. Driving up the circular path to the great white clubhouse, Brooke felt uneasy. She craved BBQ, but figured she was in for a formal lunch.

She didn't spot her father, so she parked several yards away, near his car. As she trudged up the hill, she realized how well her ankle had healed—in spite of that tacky doctor Dawg.

Once inside the clubhouse, she spotted the distinguished Weston Ingram already working the room. Even at sixty-two, he was debonair in his charcoal suit and red tie. Brooke snuck up behind him. Weston sensed she was near and spun around. "Brooke, you made it. You look great."

"Hi, Daddy," Brooke leaned in and kissed him on the cheek.

"Let me introduce you to my friends." He turned and extended an open hand, "Gerald Wilton, this is my daughter, Brooke." They shook hands.

"Ron Weller, Brooke." Handshake and nod.

Weston said, "Ron's on some prestigious boards. I think the two of you should talk."

Brooke feigned a smile. Still mourning Monday's events—even if it was Pharmical—she wasn't ready to play the interview game. "It's nice to meet both of you."

Ron smiled and inhaled deeply, "I've gotta run, but here's my card, Brooke." Digging in his suit coat, he handed her a shiny card, "Let's have lunch."

"Thank you. It's nice to meet you." Treading away and behind the maître d', she glared at her beaming father and lowered her voice, "Daddy. I wish you wouldn't do that. Can we just have a normal lunch?"

Weston frowned, "Ron Weller is on the board of a bunch of big companies here in Charlotte. He was once vice chairman of a major tobacco company."

"Great, maybe I can start smoking."

The gray-haired maître d' pulled the chair out for Brooke as Weston plopped down on his chair and said, "I'm only trying to help."

"I know. I know. Everybody's trying to help. But I'm not ready to even think about what I want to do next."

"Well, don't wait too long. The economy's still in rough shape. We've lost three thousand jobs just in banking. There was a time when Charlotte gave Wall Street a run for their money in banking."

"That's banking. I'd rather kill myself than work in a bank."

Weston raised his eyebrow and curled his lips down.

After a long silence, Weston said, "Well, it looks like your ankle's better?"

"Much better thanks. I knew it wouldn't take as long as that doctor said. I've been able to run again. I'm entered into the Run for the Cure in another month."

"Don't push it. It may feel fully healed, but running a marathon will probably reinjure it."

"I know, I know. Believe it or not, I'm a big girl now."

"Do you have any job leads?"

Brooke suppressed a shriek. *He won't stop—I don't want to talk about it.* Instead, she drew a deep breath, and said, "As a matter of fact, I do. My recruiter called me this morning and said he had—"

"Whenever I see your smiling face..." That's probably him. I gotta take this, Daddy. Before allowing Weston the chance to voice his disproval for cell phones at the table, Brooke jumped up, turning away. Pressing the cell to her ear, "Hello, I was wondering when you'd call back."

"Brooke?"

Brooke froze, and her knees buckled. She recognized that voice. "What do *you* want?"

"Brooke, don't hang up," Chase gulped, "I really need to tell you something."

"What?"

"I've got a nice big package I wanna give you ..."

After Brooke heard *big package,* a sea of red overtook her. "What? I can't believe you just said that. You're no different than Dixie-dawg. Oh my God ... what an asshole!" Brooke nearly broke her cell as she slammed it shut.

Cheeks flushed, eyelids fluttering, and her heart raced faster than a king's cook beating eggs. Brooke pressed the off button as if strangling her cell to death, then after it shut down, she glanced up—all eyes glowered at her. *Oh shit*. Brooke felt as if she was standing in front of a Pharmical boardroom meeting, naked.

Brooke caught her father's scowl and decided against heading into that furnace. She wheeled around, lowered her head, and dashed to the ladies room.

After ten long minutes, Brooke peered around the corner. No eyes, except her father, now perched like a wooden tennis backboard.

Brooke moseyed over to the table. Weston had an empty martini glass in front of him. He didn't stand as his daughter slithered into the chair across from him. After a silence, Weston said, "Well, that was a fine show for the entire club. I'm guessing that wasn't your recruiter. If so, you can kiss that job goodbye."

"I don't want to get into it."

"I'm glad, neither do I, but the rest of the restaurant might. I've never felt so many stares."

The waiter appeared, causing a truce, asking, "Would you care for another cocktail, sir?"

"Yes, and make it a double."

He scribbled on his notepad, then said, "Would the lady care for anything to drink?"

"Sure. I'll have a cosmo."

Weston's eyes bulged, Brooke turned away.

"Very well, can I take your food order?"

Brooke ordered a cup of soup and a small Caesar salad. Weston frowned and said, "You need to eat more."

"I had a big breakfast," she lied.

Weston ordered a steak sandwich, and raised his eyebrows at Brooke, who mouthed *I'm not hungry*. The waiter hovered for a moment, then scurried away.

Weston cleared his throat, "Did you bring the severance for me to take a look-see?"

"It's not much. I could've written it on this drink napkin." Brooke reached into her purse, then unfolded an envelope and handed it to her father.

Weston pulled his reading glasses out of his front pocket, then scanned the crinkled paper. He grimaced, then fixed his gaze on Brooke. "I hope you didn't sign this?" It sounded more like a command than a question.

"No."

"Don't. This is absurd. I've never seen anything like this in all my years."

"It is what it is."

"You can't really mean that. They have to expect you to fight this. Let me blast them a nasty memo on my letterhead. I'll get you a real severance package."

Brooke fidgeted, then said, "No. I just want to be done with them. It's time to move on. I don't care about the money—I have plenty from the buyout."

"Honey, you're not thinking clearly. I know this company—they play dirty. I fought 'em and won, even with that shark Chase Allman."

Chase Allman. Hearing the name—especially out of her father's mouth—sliced through her. Brooke sighed, if he only knew the rest of the story. As much as she would have loved to dump on Chase, she decided against it. Weston was perceptive and she felt susceptible after her outburst heard round the club. Her father was understanding—to a point—Brooke's little tryst could never reach her daddy's ears. She feared he'd sue Pharmical with glee and disown her with disdain.

Brooke gulped her cosmo as Weston inhaled his second martini, then gobbled his two olives. Thankfully, lunch kept her from ordering another round. Brooke remembered the last time she had two cosmos and where it landed her.

Weston said, "I have a surprise for you back at the house."

Brooke smiled, "Don't you have to work?"

"Not today—I get to spend the day with my beautiful little girl. Besides, after those martinis, I'd probably sue Pharmical and watch that All-shark squirm."

Brooke hoped her daddy wasn't psychic. "No lawsuits daddy. Promise me."

"Yeah, yeah, I know. C'mon, let's go home before I order another drink."

"Can you drive?"

"I'm fine—I can handle my liquor." Hearing the way he slurred the last phrase, Brooke raised her eyebrows. She searched for the waiter, hoping to ascertain the actual martini count. Glancing both ways, she frowned.

Weston clumsily slid his chair back, then wavered as he stood. Brooke scanned the room one more time—still no waiter.

"I'll follow you home just to be safe."

"I'm fine, really, you're making another scene." Glaring, he said, "You ready?"

Weston gripped Brooke's arm as they ambled from the restaurant to their cars. Descending the hill, Weston shuffled in slow motion. Brooke noticed her father struggled and she wasn't sure how much of it was martini related. She hated to see him age, the thought of losing him made her stomach ache.

Brooke followed at a safe distance and her father seemed in control, unlike herself after a couple of vodka shots. She replayed Chase's call in her head, igniting another sharp pang in her stomach. How could I have been so stupid?

Inside the familiar home with all its dated furnishings, Weston led Brooke to the kitchen. He opened up the almond refrigerator door and said, "Look."

Brooke spotted the plastic bags with reddish lobster etchings on the side, "Lobster lasagna? My favorite. I've been craving it—how'd you know?" Her mouth watered as memories of cooking beside her daddy flooded in. She recalled the recipe by heart, though he always pulled out the withered paper from his "Meals" folder and followed step-by-step.

"Want me to buy the wine?"

"Nope. Got it covered." Weston reached behind the lobster bags and retrieved a bottle of Pouilly Fuissé.

"Wow, you even remembered my favorite white wine."

"Of course. We should start making it in two hours. Do you want to watch a movie in the meantime?"

Brooke smiled, picturing him planning all this. Always great with details, though he may not walk too well, there's no problem with his mind. She wondered how many times he'd gone to this much trouble for her and then she would make an excuse to scurry back to Chapel Hill.

"Sure, I haven't watched a movie with you in a while."

He led her to the family room, then strode to the oversized rear-projection TV with the DVD player she had bought him. "Wanna watch an old Cary Grant film?"

Brooke's eyes looked like Janet Leigh's in the movie *Psycho* as she focused on the cover: *An Affair to Remember.* "Oh God, not that one!"

"I thought you liked Cary Grant?"

"I just feel like watching a comedy …"

"Suit yourself." He lunged around the TV, then opened his video drawer. Leafing through the stack like library cards, he said, "How about *Forrest Gump*?"

Relieved he didn't suggest a romantic comedy, she said, "Perfect."

They both laughed at the now-famous scenes, evoking memories of growing up in the South. Brooke recalled their trip to Savannah when she was seventeen. Her father loved the tour of the set used in the movie and talked about it often over the years. Tom Hanks was brilliant as the lead, and she had forgotten how good Sally Field, Robin Wright, and Gary Sinise were. The story transported her mind away from her hurricane week.

As the credits rolled, Weston waited until he saw Savannah, "Ready to make dinner?"

True to form, Weston lined the ingredients on the old oak counter in order—like soldiers awaiting roll call. Brooke retrieved their matching aprons, and for the next half hour they prepared the delicacy like two brain surgeons. Once the layers reached the top, Weston carefully slid the porcelain dish in the oven and set the timer. Brooke opened the refrigerator and grabbed the wine.

They sipped wine while swaying in two shaded rocking chairs overlooking the rolling backyard. Chickadees darted back and forth from the old trees to the gray wooden deck, landing a few feet away. A single Carolina Wren perched atop a nearby cedar post, as if vying for attention, with its tail raised, belting, "Teakettle-teakettle-teakettle." The freshly cut grass mixed with the daisies and tulips, forming a hazy sweetness. Brooke settled in and enjoyed the surroundings like an outdoor movie.

Weston checked his wrist watch as the buzzer sounded. He jumped up, grabbed his wine glass, and said, "Let's eat."

The lobster lasagna was sensational, even better than Brooke remembered. Her daddy's comments rang true—she wasn't eating right. But tonight, her appetite resembled Tanner's after a football game. Tanner preferred a meaty red sauce, but loved the creamy white lobster lasagna. Brooke could still picture him sitting beside her, chatting with her daddy about sports while devouring three helpings. Her daddy always made Tanner feel at home.

Brooke swallowed the last bite of her second helping, then lifted her wine glass, "To the greatest daddy in the world. You make the best lasagna."

"Aw, thanks Brooke," he lifted his glass and clanked with hers, "*We* make the best lasagna—it wouldn't be the same without you."

They both drained their wine, then Weston glanced at his watch. "Oh, we better get these dishes in. It's already past my bedtime."

"Don't worry about it—I'll do 'em. You go get your beauty sleep. I don't have to wake up early tomorrow."

"Nonsense, let's do them together. It won't take us long." Weston lugged his plate over to the sink and began rinsing before Brooke moved.

"Okay, you wanna rinse, I'll load."

"You betcha. Are you staying here for a few days?"

Brooke wasn't prepared for the question and the wine dimmed her usual wit. While setting a plate inside the dishwasher, she said, "I can't. I have so much stuff to do."

Weston frowned, then Brooke explained, "I'm going to hit the job search Monday."

"We could do it together tomorrow. I have some people in mind."

"I need to be near my computer. I'm supposed to do my resume. Plus, I have to shop for an interview outfit."

Brooke loaded the last dish, squirted detergent in the small square in the door, then closed it and spun the needle to start. As she turned, Weston stood in her way, and said, "Well, I hardly see you when you're working, now I don't see you when you're not."

"I had such a nice time—I loved our dinner. I'll be back soon, I promise. Thanks for everything. I love you."

"Love you too, goodnight. If you change your mind ..."

"Goodnight, Daddy."

Brooke scrutinized her father's shuffle toward the stairs like a kid sent to bed by his parents. He reverted to his old man walk, and Brooke realized his demeanor was attitudinal, not physical. Still early, Brooke glanced at the TV, but decided against it. She didn't find many worthwhile shows, and she didn't want to disturb her father's sleep. She remembered she packed that book Shane recommended. Brooke grabbed her overnight bag and slinked up the stairs to her old bedroom.

Flipping on the light, the shocking pink walls transported her back in time like a little girl entering Disney World for the first time. Though she hated being perceived as a twelve-year-old by her father, she loved how he preserved her childhood bedroom. She gazed at her track trophies from grade school, the picture of Jessie—her horse growing up—and photos of Daddy and her at amusement parks, on a tennis court, and on the beach—happy times.

Brooke opened her double-door closet where her baby dolls were still lined up. She recalled dressing each doll, cradling them in her arms, and even bathing them. She had always loved children—of all ages—but especially the innocence of infancy. She longed to nurture her own babies. Brooke hugged her favorite doll—the American Girl replica her father bought for her ninth birthday. She could still hear him proclaiming she was even prettier than the doll.

Brooke noticed her childhood scrapbook in the closet. She carefully opened the tattered cover and laughed—Billy looked adorable in a sailor outfit holding hands with her. She flipped the yellowed pages that crackled with each turn. Memories rekindled like they were still in the present. The pictures of birthday parties and riding horses brought a warmth to Brooke. Her daddy always threw her lavish parties and spoiled her with every gift she asked for. Though he wasn't in any of the pictures, she knew he was responsible for each one—usually snapping the shots on that oversized camera with the exploding flash.

In addition to her daddy, her girlfriends were everything to her. She giggled at an early college picture of "the trio"—Amber, Brandi, and Brooke. Melissa got the prize for the silliest photo—clad in Halloween costume, dressed as Dorothy from *Wizard of Oz*. The old pictures brought back happy times, but the tattered cover of the scrapbook reminded her of the friendships that had faded.

When Brooke met Tanner, everything revolved around him.

Reaching inside her bag, Brooke pulled out the book from Shane, *The Bliss List: The Ultimate Guide to Living the Dream at Work and Beyond!* She had started it, but Dixie-dawg's office wasn't the ideal setting for concentration—especially an inspirational career book. Examining the cover, it looked different. Less daunting. Tonight, she wanted to read all of it. She flipped her pink-shaded bedside lamp on and settled beside her doll on the bed that seemed smaller than she remembered. It had been a while since she spent the night in her old room.

Thirty minutes into the book, Brooke was captivated. She could see why Shane loved this book so much. Half the time, she thought the author's voice was Shane. She even double checked the back cover. Brooke remembered the saying, "When the student's ready, a teacher appears." The central message of finding meaning in life—where time stood still—resonated inside.

She realized how far she had strayed from her core at Pharmical. Brooke had tried to convince herself she enjoyed the place—partially to keep her own sanity—only to realize now, it was an illusion. Everyone had forewarned her—her mentor Todd, her father, Shane, even Melissa—but, she had to do it her way. Not joining Pharmical after acquiring GenSense meant abandoning Tanner's cause.

Now that Pharmical was shelving leukemia research, Brooke felt helpless. She prayed to the same God who brought her Tanner.

Brooke surveyed the room. *I wonder if it's still there...*

She knelt in front of the dresser, then pulled out the bottom drawer. She reached underneath and felt it—her diary. Brooke peeled back the tape, then stared at the faded cover, realizing she hadn't read her diary in twenty years. Holding it generated a mix of amazement and apprehension. Carefully opening it, she whisked back in time.

She giggled at how she detailed her name— vintage Catholic school penmanship. She sighed, considering the time wasted on math and penmanship—now that calculators were built into everything and keyboards replaced pencils and pens.

Brooke thought it fitting that reading a book about inner discovery and dream realization had led her to her original dream book—her diary. Studying the date of the first entry, she was nine. Not surprising, she wrote about her doll: "This is the greatest birthday ever. I got a doll that looks just like me from my daddy. She sleeps with me every night and I hold her lots. Also I got this diary and a new saddle for my horse Jessie. I can't wait to ride Jessie tomorrow at my birthday party."

Leafing through, each page ignited dormant memories. She had forgotten how boy crazy she was, giggling at all the pre-Tanner crushes. Every boy she sat next to made her heart go "boom boom." She realized how her dreams had evolved—going out with different boys from eleven on, winning races, getting gifts for Christmas and her birthdays. Today, *The Bliss List* recommended writing seven dreams. She returned her diary to its hiding place, then retrieved a blank sheet of paper and began writing her Bliss List:

1. To find a man who loves me for me, lifts me up when I need it, makes me laugh, lets me do things I enjoy, and who's sexy, but faithful.
2. To live on the ocean and be able to walk the beach holding hands with my dream man at sunrise, sunset, and under the stars.
3. To ride horses.
4. To have children of my own.

Brooke glanced at her closet and smiled at all her dolls looking back at her. She realized she hadn't written anything about a new job, then continued:

5. To have a job that I love doing, where I make a real difference, and feel a sense of purpose and meaning.
6. To help ease the pain and suffering of the sick.
7. To use my money to truly help others.

Brooke picked the book back up and continued reading through the night—something she hadn't done in a long time. Near the end of the book, she took a stab at doing her resume, something she normally hated. Yawning, she glanced at her alarm clock—3:18 a.m. —yikes. *Bedtime. I'll format it on my laptop tomorrow.* Travis had placed her at GenSense without a resume, but she looked forward to dazzling him this time.

Clutching her doll, she fell asleep as soon as her head hit her familiar puffy pink pillow.

At dawn, Weston knocked lightly, then opened Brooke's door and poked his head inside. He nearly melted. His sleeping daughter evoked so many memories. He recalled her sleeping sweetly with the doll like it was yesterday. One of the first people to purchase the nifty American Girl doll, he couldn't wait to see her eyes light up beside the illuminated Christmas tree.

Brooke's eyelids fluttered, then she uttered *Tanner* while still sleeping. He wanted to kiss his sweet daughter's forehead, but decided to let his little princess dream.

— ♥ —

"You're a lifesaver."

"Thanks, Mr. Allman, I mean Chase."

The light turned green, and Chase accelerated slower than usual, "Seriously, Oksana, I don't know what I'd do without you. I totally forgot about Parker's birthday."

"I'm sure you would've remembered."

Chase said, "I don't know which way's up anymore."

Oksana held her hair down as the convertible gathered speed. He reached behind his seat and grabbed a hat, then said, "Here, this will help."

Oksana inspected the underside of the baseball cap and paused. Chase spotted the blond hair—Brooke's—and hoped Oksana wouldn't comment. Without saying a word, she pulled it over her head.

Chase said, "Thank you for going along with me today. I was thinking about getting Parker his own mini fishing pole, but beyond that, I have no idea what to get him."

Oksana laughed, "You think a Ukrainian girl would know?"

"Probably better than me."

"I called Miss Stanton at Angel Academy and she gave me some good ideas."

"That was so smart. I didn't even think about her, but she'd sure know."

"Thank you, Mr. Allman."

"Chase."

"Sorry. I guess I'm not quite as smart as you say—I can't get used to calling you by your first name. In Ukraine, is so, how you say, formal."

"Do you miss home?"

Oksana demurred, "Is different here. Ukraine, girls do not wear blue jeans, hoodies, or flip flops. We try look … sexy but classy—like girls."

Chase glanced at the twenty-six-year-old and *sexy* and *classy* were perfect descriptives. Her boyfriend was a lucky man to have such a well-grounded girlfriend with such great family values. She mailed money back to her parents each month. Chase thanked his lucky stars to have her; plus, Parker adored her.

"Parker sure loves you and I don't tell you often enough how much I appreciate all that you do—including today."

"I enjoy working for you and I love Parker like he is my own son."

"There's something else I need to discuss with you."

She turned and widened her eyes, "What is it? Did I do something wrong?"

"No, not like that," Chase paused, then, "Have you gotten any more calls from Heather, Parker's mother?"

"No sir. You told me to tell you and she only called that time I told you about."

"That's good. As you know, Parker's mother has problems—for one, she's addicted to drugs."

"I know, Mr. Allman. I found a bunch of her pill bottles in the kitchen."

Chase raised an eyebrow, but didn't want to expound. He said, "She's living in the middle part of the country—in a place called Minnesota."

"Where is?" Oksana didn't attempt to repeat the word.

"It's a long way from here. Anyway, I heard she has a boyfriend—a bad person—and I don't want to scare you, but she might try to come back here and take Parker."

"Really? Is she coming here now?"

"I don't think so, but I've hired an investigator to watch her, and apparently she eluded them. I doubt she'd come back here, especially without me finding out, but just keep an extra eye on Parker. You know what Heather looks like."

"Yes, she is so pretty. I still have the picture you gave me."

"Good. I don't know what this guy looks like but he's six three and about two hundred thirty pounds."

"How tall are you, sir?"

"I'm six three also, but don't weigh that much."

Oksana's eyes nearly bulged out of her head. Chase said, "I don't mean to worry you. We have a state-of-the-art security system at home and, like I said, I'll know if she gets near North Carolina."

They drove in silence for a few blocks, then pulled into North Hills, Raleigh's upscale outdoor mall. Chase drove down the main drag, searching for a parking spot. North Hills had over one hundred stores and boutiques, restaurants, a multi-plex movie theater—even a luxury hotel. The place offered something for everyone, including a four-year-old.

Oksana pulled out a piece of paper, and said, "We should park near Learning Express or Omega Sports if you see them."

"Wow, I'm impressed. You made a list. You're very organized."

Oksana blushed as Chase turned down another road, still hunting for a parking spot.

Chase said, "I tell you what. Before we buy Parker his birthday gifts, I want to get you something for all that you do."

"Oh no, Mr. Allman, I mean, Mr. Chase, you do not have to do that."

"Are you kidding? It's the least I can do. I probably missed your birthday too. When is it?"

Oksana giggled. "My birthday last month …"

"I'm sorry, but better late than never. I'll get you something, anything you want."

"This place expensive—"

"Nonsense. Don't worry about how much, just tell me what you would buy if you had a blank check."

Oksana frowned, "What is *blank check*?"

Chase laughed, "Never mind. What would you buy if you found a bunch of money on the street?"

They passed For Beach Bums Anonymous. Oksana stared at the store and pursed her lips. Chase stopped, put his blinker on, then waved the car behind him to pass, saying, "Did you see something in that store?"

"My boyfriend wants to take me to beach, but I have no *svimsuit*. All the bikinis are so expensive—"

"That settles it then." Just after Chase uttered the words, tail lights flashed ahead and a well-dressed woman sauntered to her driver's side and opened the door. With his blinker, Chase reserved the spot, "See, it's meant to be—we even found a parking spot."

Once inside the store, Chase excused himself to call the office. He felt uncomfortable helping his nanny find a bikini. He said, "Pick out as many as you like. Here, use my credit card. I'll be right outside."

Before Oksana could protest, Chase bee-lined for the door with cell pressed to his ear. Once outside, he glimpsed back inside the store, then dialed Brooke's number—voicemail. *Dammit.* He didn't leave a message. Her irrational response to the severance package shocked him. He feared she planned on exposing him. He dialed and once again, she wasn't answering—not a good sign. *And I only have myself to blame.*

His mind wandered; he felt like James Bond, with all the bad guys hiding around the corners. First, Heather and the blood-hound reporters, always salivating for a juicy story. Second, Henry, The Butcher, and the board of directors at Pharmical—all bulldozing him. Now Brooke, who could destroy him in an instant.

Fine work, Chase.

"Excuse me, Mr. Allman."

"Huh," Chase spun around and met Oksana's eyes.

"Sorry to bother you, sir, but the owner wants to see you."

Chase shook his head, then followed Oksana to the cashier. The forty-something clerk said, "Is this your credit card, sir?"

Chase glanced at it and said, "Yeah. It's okay. She's with me."

Oksana whispered in Chase's ear, "Is $120. I am sorry. Is too much?"

"No, buy this one and something else while you're here. You deserve it."

The clerk peered over her thick reading glasses as she lifted the credit card up. Oksana said, "No, no. This is too much. Just this one please."

Chase carried the bag for Oksana, wondering if it was empty. *Swimwear was never this small when I was a kid.* They passed his car and gazed inside each store window as they strolled.

Oksana said, "Thanks again. I would never be able to buy that bikini."

"Don't mention it. If you see anything else you want, tell me. What were the names of the stores we're looking for again?"

Oksana stopped, pulled out her paper and read them again. Chase surveyed the street and said, "Of course there is no map when you need one."

They strolled a bit and Chase realized he desperately needed to use a men's room. He hadn't noticed any signs and wondered if people who shopped upscale malls ever had to go. Not too far up ahead, he saw the Renaissance Raleigh Hotel. "Hey, I need to use the bathroom. Do you need to go, by any chance?"

"Sure, us girls always have to go."

Chase laughed, then said, "I won't be long, I hope."

Oksana giggled and they ambled up to the front entrance. She giggled again at the funny looking rotating door, "I hate these moving doors." Chase placed his hand on Oksana's back and after several revolutions, guided her into the turnstile, jumping in beside her.

Little did he know who was watching them less than fifty feet away.

15

*I*s that why he tried to call me? I can't believe it—that girl is half his age! Did he promise to show her his big package? Brooke's heart exploded, with face flaring fire engine red. *I should run in and warn her while he's getting his little room key for The Players Suite. I'd love to see his face as I expose him to the entire lobby. Was that a lingerie bag he was carrying? I can't believe I fell for his bullshit. He's such an asshole!*

Idling on a busy street, she slammed her car into park, flipped on the hazards, then jumped out. A passing truck veered, nearly running her over, then laid on his horn. With fists and jaw clenched, she stomped across the parking lot but then stopped at the halfway point; Brooke glared at the revolving door.

"You're not worth it." Brooke shouted at the top floor, then shook her head against her tightened neck. She did an about face and strode back to her car. As she wandered into traffic, a car honked at her, and she flipped her middle finger high in the air, without even looking at the driver. Brooke was beyond rage—one more honk in her face could trigger murder with her bare hands. *I gotta get outta here.*

How could I have been so stupid? I'm blocking his number from my cell. Screw shopping—I need to find a clinic that tests for STDs!

Brooke flung her car door wide open and plopped in. Though barely able to see the road through seething eyes, she screeched her tires and sped off like a rocket. What started out as a shopping trip for an interview outfit had turned into her worst nightmare.

Just when she thought it couldn't worsen, the shriek of a siren blared behind her. Then she noticed flashing lights in her own rearview mirror. *Oh shit.*

Still inside North Hills complex, Brooke pulled off the access road and came to a stop over two spots in an empty parking area. The red and yellow flashing lights blinded her. *Does he really have to keep those on?* Brooke glanced at her side mirror and after a few moments, his door edged open in slow motion. A heavy-set officer approached in bow-legged stride. *Oh great.*

Brooke froze, staring straight ahead with hands on the wheel at ten and two, praying to any saint who would listen. Her window darkened as she heard tapping. Brooke turned to see his pudgy fingers and his mustard-stained tie that stopped short where his paunch protruded well above his overburdened belt. She noticed he had a badge of some sort, but couldn't make out his name.

Brooke drew a deep breath, pressed her power window button, forged a smile and said, "Hello, officer."

"Mind tellin' me what's yer big hurry, lady?"

"What do you mean?"

"Well, ya ran a stop sign, and you been squealin' and speedin' around here like it's a NASCAR track."

"I'm sorry, officer, I've had a bad day."

"Have you been drinkin'?"

"It's only 12:30 in the afternoon."

"Don't matter. Answer the question."

Brooke could only imagine how red her eyes looked. "No, I have not been drinking."

"Step out of the car, ma'am."

"Why? Are you arresting me?"

"I asked you to step outta the car."

Brooke frowned, then pulled the door handle and pushed too hard. Her door nailed the officer in the groin and he doubled over. *Good, I mean oops.*

He backed away in a crouch position, muttering, "That hurt. Get out slowly."

"Sorry about that," Brooke said, now attempting to stand up straight without laughing. She had been driving all day and her right leg had fallen asleep—and standing on heels didn't help. She stood slightly taller than Officer Pudge. He reeked of stale Old Spice and onions—or at least she hoped it was onions. He wasn't wearing a gun or a night stick, just an ill-fitting uniform with smudged pleather shoes. She didn't feel compelled to straighten the wrinkles on her sun dress. *Mall cop.*

"Now, walk over to this line and stop." Brooke gulped, suppressing a scream—*is this mall cop going to make me walk a straight line?*

"Can I take off my heels?"

"No, ma'am, just do as you're told."

"Okay, whatever," Brooke took two steps, then caught her heel on some gravel on the uneven pavement. She braced herself to avoid falling, "I have an injured ankle and it's hard to walk on these high heels. Do I really have to do this?"

"Your ankle looks fine to me, ma'am."

"I can prove it. My doctor is Dixie, err, Dr. Dixon Carter over at Duke Raleigh Hospital."

"That won't be necessary, ma'am. Just walk along that parking line, then stop and turn around and walk back."

Brooke rolled her eyes, then did as she was told. She concentrated on each step and avoided landing on any debris. At the end, she clicked her feet together like a drill sergeant, then glanced up. She gasped—he was gaping at her breasts with a creepy grin.

Brooke cleared her throat—his eyes didn't move. She waved her hand from knee to knee, finally breaking his stare. "Oh, uh, sorry. You look fine to me ... I mean, you passed the test."

"Good, so I can go now?" Brooke lunged toward her car.

"No, not yet. You broke a bunch a traffic violations. I need your license."

Brooke sighed, then said, "Officer, after the week I've had, please don't give me a ticket."

"Whaddya mean by that?" His eyes still fixed well below her chin.

"Well, let's see, I was fired Monday, then I just saw my ... um, boyfriend walk into that hotel with some bimbo. So I guess all lousy things happen in threes, so you may as well write me a ticket." He raised his eyes to hers, then glanced away and frowned as her words rattled inside his head.

"I'm sorry, I'm just doin' my job. I need to see your license."

Brooke marched back to her car and just as she touched the door, her ankle turned—the bad one. Pains shot up her leg. She winced, but managed to climb inside her car. Brooke leafed through her purse, then pulled her driver's license and jabbed it at him as if plunging a knife into a pumpkin.

He wobbled back to his rent-a-cop car with its annoying lights still swirling and struggled to swing his knees in before shutting the door. Brooke felt numb. She squinted through both side mirrors, trying to see the entrance of the hotel—hoping to catch loverboy sneaking away from his nooner. *Ugh, she was a tad young for you, Chase.*

Mall cop's door swung open, much faster than the last time, but he still struggled to walk. Brooke peered through her side mirror; he was carrying papers in his hand—*oh great.*

He stopped beside her car like the Goodyear Blimp, hovering just inches away from the window. He handed her what looked like a ticket and gripped her license just above his paunch, "Well, Brooke Anne Hart, I'm only going to give you a warning this time, but please be more careful."

Brooke smiled, then said, "Thank you."

"Just to show you I'm a good person, here, I'll give you my card. After the week you've had, I'd like to help you—that's what I do ma'am—serve and protect. My cell phone number's on the back. I get off at six tonight."

Brooke reached for the radioactive card, relieved she hadn't eaten anything all day. Brooke feigned a smile, then raised her power window. After it clenched shut, she waved her hand with wiggling fingers, blocking his view. Accelerating, she felt a sense of accomplishment for not saluting him with her middle finger like earlier. Brooke crinkled up the warning and the card and tossed them to the passenger side floor. They landed on three pennies—*that's odd, I thought I picked those up? Weren't they dimes?*

With mall cop watching her drive away, Brooke hit her brakes, keeping her speed at twenty-five miles per hour—though she wanted to set the land speed record. She swallowed hard, fighting back the bile rising in her throat. Checking her rearview mirror, he was still standing, hands on hips, dwarfing his car's hood. With the lights spinning above his head, he looked like a chubby lighthouse. As he faded out of view, she replayed the more horrifying picture still emblazoned in her mind.

I still can't believe it. I thought he was wonderful. Why did he have to be such a jerk? I wonder how many girls he sleeps with in a week—and how he keeps track. Some guys are serial sexers. Asshole. Brooke flipped on the radio, hoping to cheer up. "Fire and Rain"—*no freaking way.* She switched to the Top 40 channel—commercial for a BMW dealer—*definitely not.* She pressed CD, then hit play—"Crash Into Me"—*I can't win.* Brooke spun the dial off, then reached for her cell—two missed calls from Melissa—*I swear she's psychic.*

"Hey, sorry I missed your calls, but I was getting strip searched by a mall cop."

"What?"

"Long story."

"I can't talk right now but I really need to tell you something. Can you meet me tonight?"

— ♥ —

"You're a lifesaver, you know that?" Chase figured Oksana saved him at least two days and a dozen headaches. He had no idea how complicated birthday shopping was for a four-year-old.

"You are easy to shop with for a man. I am surprised." Oksana giggled.

"Thanks, I guess."

"No, I am serious. I really had fun today. Thanks again for the *svimsuit.* I would never buy it for myself."

"Don't mention it. After all you've done, I feel bad I didn't remember your birthday."

"That is most I ever got for my birthday." Oksana blinked a tear.

Chase said, "I was supposed to go into the office, but I can cancel my meeting. What time do you usually pick up Parker?"

"Four o'clock sharp. I usually get there a little early. Miss Stanton appreciates it."

"Well, this time, I'll pick up Parker."

She sniffled, "Oh, he will love that. You are good dad."

"You're a good liar. I would've forgotten my son's birthday if it weren't for you."

"With everything you do with your job, and without wife to help, you do good job. Parker loves you."

"I couldn't do it without you. Oh, what about a birthday party?"

"I booked Frankie's Fun Park for ten people for the Saturday after next. I hope that's all right?"

"You never cease to amaze me."

"Is good?"

Chase laughed. He loved her accent and even her struggles with English and its goofy nuances. Though he understood a little textbook Spanish, he would be lost in Russia. "Yes, that's good. Very good. I have no idea who to invite other than Parker's friend Will."

"I asked Miss Stanton for list of Parker's friends and already invited nine of his classmates at Angel's Academy—including Will. Frankie's Fun Park is close and Mary said she would help me and you, how you say, chaperone?"

"Yes, that's right. Not an easy word. What do you need me for—you've got it all covered."

"You still have to pay for it and I am sure they all want you to go on rides with them."

"Are you kidding? That's the easy part. I'm still a kid at heart. Do they have mini-golf?"

"I think so. Oh, I will order an ice cream cake at Dairy Queen with his favorite flavor."

Chase pulled into his circular driveway and dropped Oksana off at the front door. She wanted to wrap and hide Parker's gifts. Driving away, Chase glanced in the rearview mirror and grimaced, thinking he didn't even know his kid's favorite flavor of ice cream.

Since Heather flew the coop, he felt so helpless. He had taken domestic duties for granted. Going through a key event like a kid's birthday, he actually felt for his estranged wife. It must have been hard for her to leave the modeling limelight to the mundane—cooking, cleaning, shuttling, planning kid's birthday parties, while being a model wife. *She doesn't know what she's missing. Thank God for Oksana.*

After checking voicemail—still no message from Brooke—Chase pulled into the immaculate grounds of Angel Academy. The building resembled a country club with its red and tan brick façade, manicured shrubbery, and lively flowering. Chase was impressed by owner Betsy Stanton. She had planned everything so well, positioning it as a learning center rather than daycare, targeting affluent families, and personally teaching lessons that reached young kids. If there was an award for Top Toddler Teacher, the grandmotherly Miss Stanton would win.

When Heather took off, Chase worried about Parker. Her implosion came at an awful time, as if her fall was linked to his rise. He couldn't understand how she could just walk away from so much, especially an adorable son. When she left, Chase had nowhere to turn—he couldn't go public and lose his lofty position at the company. Betsy had been a godsend—so incredibly helpful and understanding. Her extra attention made the difference. Miss Stanton treated her vocation like a vacation. She cared. She had passion for helping small children, and it showed. Parker adored her and the rest of the staff too, and Chase enjoyed listening to his son's animated recanting of her stories.

Chase parked his BMW behind the line of minivans and waited in his car. Most of the moms took notice. He wondered if Parker was the only one without a mother. *It had to be confusing to his son, knowing it still baffled him.*

The door swung open and Betsy Stanton and another teacher led the kids outside like ducklings. Chase waved to Betsy, whose eyes popped open, then smiled. Chase spotted Parker, who was searching for the familiar white SUV. Chase jumped out just as he spotted his son, then Parker looked like a kid seeing Santa's gifts on Christmas morning. Parker stepped forward, then stopped, and glanced up at Miss Stanton.

Chase lifted Parker up in the air and plunked him into the booster seat, "Can you put your own seatbelt on for me?" Parker nodded as his little fingers pulled the shoulder harness on. Chase felt someone's presence, then glimpsed over his shoulder—"Hello, Miss Stanton."

"Hello to you." She surveyed the convertible as she whistled, then eyed inside, "Parker, how fun to have your father pick you up in this nifty car." Betsy covered her mouth and coughed.

"That cough doesn't sound good." Chase noticed extra wrinkles and baggy eyes—not her usual perky self.

"I'm sorry, don't worry—it's not contagious. It's just allergies." Chase nodded toward Parker and said, "How's he doing?"

"You have a great boy. I just love Parker—he's so well behaved. Can I take him home with me?" Parker beamed and Chase laughed.

"Nope, I'm taking him to play catch." Chase put his hand out for a high five with Parker, "Right, buddy."

"Sounds like fun. You're lucky, Parker. And you are too, Mr. Allman."

"Call me Chase."

"Only if you call me Betsy." They both laughed.

Chase started up his car, "Wave goodbye to Miss Stanton." Parker swung his hand in the air as they drove off.

With Raffi blaring silly songs, Chase pulled into the driveway and said, "Wait in the car, I'll be right back." He popped his head into the front door to see if Oksana had finished wrapping. Good thing too—she was sprawled on the floor of the family room, cutting and taping.

Oksana threw herself in front of the gifts, "Mr. Chase, do not come in."

"It's okay, he's waiting in the car."

"Thank you. I ran out of wrapping paper and had to run to the store—"

"Don't worry about it. I'll take Parker and Duke to the playground." Duke jumped to the door and wagged his tail wildly, displaying his true grasp of the English language. Chase stepped out to check on Parker who was waving his hands in the air and singing "Baby Beluga." He ran upstairs and grabbed a fresh shirt and shoes—with Duke covering him like a basketball press.

"See ya soon, Oksana," Chase snapped Duke's leash on.

"I will be done soon and have dinner ready for you when you get back. Enjoy your walk."

Chase breathed a sigh of relief, glad that he didn't have to endure another Chuck E. Cheese heartburn. It wasn't exactly a normal home, but Chase knew he had it better than anything Norman Rockwell could paint.

After tossing tennis balls, Frisbees, soft-core baseballs, and nerf footballs to Duke and Parker, Chase felt tired and hungry, yet satisfied. Parker darted around, competing with Duke for more throws. Chase laughed, "Do you guys ever get tired?"

As the trio ambled in the front door, the smell of fresh bread and roast lamb wafted through the air—another delicious Oksana meal. Chase marveled at her cooking prowess, always traditional

Ukrainian. He loved the mix of Russian, Turkish, and Polish cuisine. She served homemade breads with funny names that Chase could never pronounce correctly. Parker recalled the names better than his father—it was good to teach Parker about something other than cheese pizza and chicken fingers.

Oksana was so different from Heather—who hated to cook anything that took more than five minutes. Chase had long forgotten Heather's nasty microwave messes.

Stuffed from another interesting dinner, Chase said goodnight to Oksana, then tucked Parker in bed. After saying special prayers, both boy and dog fell asleep without the usual fight. He gazed at Parker, marveling at his son—growing up too fast.

Chase felt physically exhausted, but wasn't ready for bed. He didn't feel like reading and was never much for watching TV. He headed downstairs to the rarely-used basement. He noticed Oksana's hiding spot for Parker's presents and paused, imagining his son's face lighting up as he opened each gift. This would be a tough birthday to top—thanks to Oksana.

Chase entered his wine cellar, wondering when was the last time he'd been in there. His eyes focused on a vintage cognac. Examining the bottle, he had forgotten he still had it. He released the cork, then poured a few glugs into a snifter. He swirled it three times and, as the reddish liquid lingered on the fine crystal, he inhaled the floral, nutty aroma. Then he eyed the humidor—perfect. As the cognac warmed him, he selected a cigar.

Relaxing on the deck, the sun had set, but light still lingered like dusk's shadow. Crickets buzzed in harmony ringing louder than usual into the windless air. A comforting chill replaced the day's mugginess, complementing his cognac-induced warmth inside. Without Duke by his side demanding attention, he could just sit back and blend in with the surroundings. He cut his cigar and lit it with precision, puffing gently, then sipped his cognac. *Bliss.* Gratitude filled him as he counted his lucky stars—Parker, Oksana, Betsy, Duke, the house, the place in Hilton Head, his job, car, health …

Chase's bliss didn't last long. A siren in the distance jolted Chase into his main problem—Heather. *What could I have done differently? I shouldn't have waited so long to hire a PI. And Max is about as easy to work with as a rhinoceros. I hope she's not heading back here—that would really mess Parker up. He's doing so well right now.*

Glancing at his cell, Chase felt a sudden chill—problem number two. *What's up with Brooke? I want to help her but she won't answer. And calling me names doesn't help matters. Why's she so emotional? She can't possibly think I had anything to do with her losing her job. If she'd call, I could line her up with a better job. Damn Greenberg—and Stoddard. Those cold-hearted bastards slaughtered her department. Joke severances that were more miserly than Scrooge. She blames me and I can't do anything about it. Why won't she call?*

Maybe I'll try her one more time.

Brooke clicked send and hoped Travis liked her resume—it took a long time to write it. Her mind kept drifting to Chase and boiling blood didn't help her concentration. She called Melissa—voicemail. *I better go, Melissa had sounded distressed, more so than usual. I hope she's still there.*

As she pulled into the parking lot, Brooke found Santiago's Tapas & Martini Bar was packed. Judging from all the loud banter inside, Brooke figured happy hour was still going. She winced, fearing the scolding she expected from Melissa. She stepped into the crowded room, the bar was three deep—*these morons would trample over each other to save a buck on a drink they don't need.*

She scanned the room, but didn't spot Melissa. *She has to be here somewhere.* Craning her neck to see above the crowd, a guy jumped in front of her and chirped, "Can I buy you a drink? Happy hour's almost over."

Brooke stepped back. His breath smelled like his drinks were garnished with onions. He sported that Duke look she despised— upturned collar, baggy khakis. Above his smirk, he had those glasses actors wore to look smart but wound up resembling the Verizon guy. "No thanks, I'm meeting someone."

Brooke slipped around him as he spoke, "No thanks." *Do people know how ridiculous they sound when they're drunk? I bet he's obnoxious even sober.* Nearing the bar, she stopped and did a double take.

Is that Melissa—with a drink? Brooke called for her, but she didn't flinch. A man was slobbering all over her. *I wonder if he knows she's married—and pregnant.* Like trudging through quick sand, Brooke crawled until she bumped into Melissa's chair. "Hey, you nearly spilled my drink." Melissa turned in a sneer, then smiled, "Brookeyyy!"

"Hi, I'm Donald."

Brooke ignored Melissa's Siamese twin and surveyed the counter, then glared at her. "Is that alcohol?"

"Maybe. Where ya been?" Guessing it wasn't her first drink, Brooke winced. She reached down and grabbed the half empty glass and sniffed it.

"Exactly what are you doing?" Brooke's eyes narrowed.

"Just having a little fun … with Donald here." He plopped his arm around Melissa's shoulder. Brooke pried his arm off, then said, "She's married—and pregnant. You need to leave."

"She's not wearing a ring and she don't look pregnant to me."

Brooke wiped her face, then glared at Melissa's empty ring finger. "I'm taking you home."

"I'm not going back there—ever again. He cheated on me."

"What?"

"You heard me. He cheated on me!"

"Eddie?"

Donald looked like he was underwater, trying to watch a ping pong match. He said, "Who's Eddie?"

Brooke's serve, "Her husband."

"I'm not married anymore."

"Oh, yes you are. C'mon," Brooke tugged at Melissa's arm, then he grabbed Melissa's other arm in a tug of war, "Knock it off—she's pregnant!" The bar hushed and all nearby eyes descended on them, as if witnessing a gunfight. He raised his hands in the air surrendering as Brooke yanked Melissa away.

"Where are you taking me?"

"Home." Brooke felt like she was lugging a drowning victim out of the water.

"I'm not going back to that house."

"Fine, but we're getting out of here."

"I can walk, let go."

Brooke loosened her grip but still guided Melissa toward the exit. Once outside, Brooke spotted an empty bench and they plopped down together. "What happened between you and Eddie?"

"I told you. He cheated on me—the night before our wedding."

"Are you sure?"

"I've had, like, three guys tell me. He did some bimbo at his stupid bachelor party. When I confronted him, all he did was deny it and swear at me—but I could tell he was lying. Now I know why he didn't want me on our wedding night."

"Oh my God. I'm sorry. Is that why you're drinking?"

"Yeppers. I'm not having *his* baby."

A couple paused to stare. Melissa's glare said, *mind your own business*. They scampered to their car.

Brooke said, "Look, I know you're upset and you have every right to be. But do not do that to your baby. I can't tell you how many times I cry over never having a baby. You and Eddie will work it out. It's not the first time he's done something stupid and probably not the last, but that baby doesn't deserve this." Brooke's voice cracked and her eyes stung; Melissa glanced away, then down. They sat in awkward silence.

Finally, Brooke grabbed Melissa's hand, "You can stay with me."

With quivering lips, Melissa said, "Thanks."

16

"Your call cannot be completed as dialed, please hang up and try again."

What the hell? He hit redial and pressed his ear against his cell.

"Your call cannot be completed as dialed, please hang up and try again."

That's strange. Chase wrote Brooke's number on a napkin, then tried a third time—same message. *I wonder if my phone's messed up?*

Chase called Verizon and after holding forever, he yearned to punch the "Can you hear me now?" guy in the nose; finally, a voice returned on the line.

"Sir, I think the person you're trying to reach has blocked your number."

Chase pressed the end button, then stared up at the moon wishing it held an answer for the lunacy. He shook his head, then rubbed his weary eyes. He felt his heart sink.

I hope she doesn't march into Pharmical and do something stupid.

On the drive back to Brooke's place, Melissa fell asleep. The diversion of *un*happy hour took her mind off Chase, until now. Thoughts flooded into Brooke's head. She still couldn't understand Melissa—and despised her destructive side. Drowning her sorrows was bad enough, but risking an unborn baby's life—unconscionable. Though she detested Eddie, she felt compelled to encourage Melissa to forgive and forget. Brooke yearned to be a mother and couldn't fathom Melissa's selfishness.

Melissa saved me, now it's my turn to save her—and the baby. If Melissa doesn't want it, I'll adopt. I hope he or she doesn't get too many of Eddie's genes.

Brooke pulled into the parking lot and gently shook Melissa's shoulder to wake her. She growled like a grizzly bear awakened in the middle of hibernation. Groggy and crabby, Melissa staggered inside and crawled into bed, then Brooke set a tall glass of water beside her. Within seconds, her eyes rolled back and she started snoring.

Brooke collapsed in her own bed and made the mistake of recounting the day's events. Images of Melissa sitting at that bar haunted her. Though mortified by Melissa's actions, Brooke's mind reached lucidity—Melissa's sabotaging stemmed from a deep insecurity. Brooke recognized the feeling. Delving into her friend's psyche—the root of the crisis—brought Brooke back to when she lost the baby. Before the doctor confirmed the miscarriage, she already knew.

Somehow, I sabotaged our baby. I was afraid of living alone. Now I would give anything to just raise Tanner's child and grow old together. She gazed at Tanner's picture, peering into his eyes, hoping for a twinkle. *He's gone. I can't let Melissa make the same mistakes I made.*

Brooke recalled Melissa's wedding, which turned into an amazing night. *I felt alive for the first time in a long time and now, I'm not sabotaging it—Chase is. I'm so confused. How could he go from Prince Charming to a frog in one day? I thought we had something special, but now, I'm lost. I wonder if he called today. After watching him waltz into that hotel … I'm doing the right thing—I had to block his number. Why can't I get him out of my head?*

After Brooke finally fell asleep, Tanner visited her once again. It was a college setting, but it felt like the present. She awoke and reached forward, but his image disappeared. As she tried to recall the dream, it only faded further away. She heard Melissa in the bathroom paying the price for her dangerous choices last night.

Brooke tiptoed over to the closed door and said, "Hey, you okay?"

"Arrrrrgh."

"Do you need anything?" Brooke's eyes inspected the door as if she had x-ray vision.

"No, I just threw up. I'm never doing that again."

Brooke wasn't sure what *that* meant, but hoped it was all-encompassing. Now wasn't the time to badger Melissa—she sensed this was morning sickness times ten, "I'm here. Let me know if you need anything."

Melissa growled, then wretched again.

After a few minutes, Brooke heard water running, hoping the worst was over for Melissa—in more ways than one. The bathroom door swung open and Brooke gasped. Her best friend looked stunning less than a week ago, but now Melissa could scare Stephen King. Struggling with each step, her white face and purple lips rivaled a corpse.

"Are you feeling any better?"

"I look like hell, but feel better."

"You look fine," Brooke lied.

Melissa cringed, "Yeah, right. You're a worse liar than Eddie."

Melissa plopped down on the corner of Brooke's unmade bed, ashamed. She raised her red eyes to Brooke, then said, "I thought about what you said and I feel so … terrible. Do you hate me?"

Brooke's face softened, "No, of course I don't hate you. I think I know what you're going through."

"I hope I didn't hurt this baby," Melissa glanced down and circled her hand around her belly, "I'm scheduled for a sonogram on Monday. I was gonna drag Eddie along, but not now."

Brooke didn't want to mention Eddie until Melissa seemed stable. "No, you have to bring Eddie. I'll go another time. You and Eddie need to talk."

Melissa raised an eyebrow, "Talk about what? He cheated on me. I thought you'd tell me to dump him. Now you want me to just ignore it like it didn't happen?"

"I'm not telling you to ignore anything. But I didn't stand there as your maid of honor to watch you two lose everything. Eddie screwed up, no question about it. But you love him. I don't know if I ever told you this, but I remember him crying on my shoulder once, afraid he was going to lose you. He's far from perfect, but deep down, he's got a great heart. There's not a day that goes by when I don't wish I had a husband and kids." Brooke's eyes moistened, then she glanced up.

"You must be psychic or something."

"What do you mean?"

Melissa inhaled deeply, "I had a nightmare that shook me up last night. It seemed so real. My baby was drowning in a pool and I couldn't move. It was a boy and he kept looking at me, saying, 'Mommy, I can't swim, help me, Mommy.' Then, just as he slipped under water, Eddie flew through the air and scooped him out. When I woke up, I was crying. Relieved it was only a dream, I felt this wave of compassion."

"God works in mysterious ways."

"You really do believe in God—I thought you quit going to church."

"I still go once in a while, but I don't need a priest to teach me about right and wrong. And what's right is for you to forgive Eddie. There's a reason you married him—that's love."

"Well, I hope that the God you're talking about will keep me from cutting off Eddie's penis."

Brooke giggled, then said, "Don't have your talk in the kitchen."

Melissa laughed and Brooke sensed a congeniality—quite a departure from yesterday. Brooke said, "Speaking of kitchens, I'm starving. I've been dying to go to Waffle House."

Melissa swallowed hard, "Just the thought of food makes me want to vomit."

Melissa pursed her lips together, "I'll go with you, but don't expect me to eat anything."

The blueberry waffle with bacon landed in front of Brooke like a magic carpet. She spread a pat of butter, then emptied a syrup container around the steaming waffle. Brooke sliced a few pieces; the anticipation caused her mouth to water. Melissa reached across the table and stabbed the largest piece, smiling as she stuffed it in her mouth in one bite.

"Hey, get your own," Brooke smiled then paused to watch with her mouth open.

Melissa devoured it, then said, "Mmmmm."

"Do you want me to order you one?"

"No, I'll just share yours," she muffled, still chewing.

For the next few minutes, they were in a frenzied fencing tournament until the last piece ended up on Melissa's fork. Brooke laughed, then after Melissa swallowed, she giggled. The coloring had returned to Melissa's face, and even without makeup, she looked good. Sharing the naughty breakfast, Brooke felt full—and vindicated. She had revived her friend.

Brooke said, "Now that you've got a full stomach, get out of here and go see Eddie—before we order another waffle."

"Not so fast, I'm not going anywhere until you tell me about your little rendezvous."

Brooke sunk her shoulders down the plastic backing of the booth. "Now, I'm going to get sick."

"I did some checking online." Melissa curled her lips into a devilish grin, "Chase is hot."

"Unfortunately, he boiled over and burned me. I made a big mistake."

Melissa crinkled her brow, then said, "The morning after the wedding, you were beaming. I've never seen you like that."

"Well, he turned into a creep, trust me."

"Look at the reversal—you're talking me into forgiving Eddie, but you—"

"It's not the same. You knew all about Eddie—the good and the bad. You guys have been dating longer than most marriages last. Chase, it was our first time …"

"What would you tell me if we traded seats?" Melissa crossed her arms with a defiant smirk.

Brooke just stared out the window. Melissa's words stung, leaving the woman who could speak in front of a thousand strangers speechless. Brooke wasn't prepared for Reverse Psychology 101. The waffle that tasted so good moments ago, churned inside.

Brooke said, "I don't feel so good. Can I take you back to your car?"

"Sure." Melissa resisted her urge to press further, even though she despised double standards. The drive to Santiago's parking lot felt somber. Brooke hoped to lighten her mood and the tension by clicking on the radio—"All You Need Is Love." Brooke was glad Melissa didn't touch it.

As Brooke pulled up to the parking lot, Melissa hugged her and said, "Thanks for everything. You really are a great friend. I don't know what I'd do without you."

"Ditto," was all Brooke could utter as her friend pulled her keys out of her purse.

Brooke watched Melissa climb into her car then pulled away while lifting her heavy hand in a half-hearted wave. "Time of Your Life"—

subtitled "Good Riddance"—began playing. Brooke released a nervous laugh, thinking, music is strange sometimes. She passed a Starbucks without even considering a stop, but the image lingered.

Once back in her apartment, she plopped down at her desk, and fired up her computer. After her stunning beach screen saver appeared, she said, "One day," then opened her email. Nothing from Chase, but there was one from Bodady Search Partners, sent yesterday: "Resume looks great. I'll present you everywhere I can. Hoping for a quick hit—I'd love to put you in my twofer group (LOL). Talk soon, Travis."

Chase put Parker down for a nap with Duke sprawled across his Blue Devils comforter. After playing all morning, Chase considered lying down for the rest of the weekend. With his mind racing, he eyed his guitar and scurried over. *I haven't played in a long time—I wonder if it's still in tune?*

He opened his case and gazed at his custom-made Taylor—the same one Dave Matthews plays—and pulled out his digital tuner. *Not too bad.* He played a chord progression that soothed him. As he strummed, he thought of Brooke. *I wonder what her favorite song is? Does she like the guitar? Did she play an instrument? With those fingers ...*

Chase paused and closed his eyes, imagining Brooke. One week ago. *How alive she made me feel. I've never met anyone like her. I hope we meet again soon.* He opened his eyes and opened his notepad. He scribbled "Brooke" at the top of the fresh page, then wrote the chords down. He replayed the melody, making minor adjustments as he went, then added some clever finger picking.

Right before the nap, Chase told Parker he could have a friend sleep over—guessing he'd ask Will when he awakened. *I wonder what she's doing tonight?*

Though Brooke still fumed, Melissa's ominous words clouded her mind. *What would I tell her if we traded seats?* Saturday and Sunday seemed to drag—quite a change from last week. Brooke had another vivid Tanner dream, and once again, she couldn't remember it when she awakened. Her head still knocked. She guessed it was from caffeine withdrawal—or maybe, Chase withdrawal. Brooke couldn't expunge him from her head. She was spellbound despite his actions.

Without any work-related time pressure—which still felt strange—Brooke went on a long run. She decided to go without her iPod, focusing instead on the sounds of the morning. As she passed houses old and new, playgrounds with children playing tag, a church, and even a convenience store, she heard winsome chirping from birds that seemed to line up for her like people watching a marathon. Once again, she thought about Chase. *I wonder if he runs every morning. Is he running right now?*

By the time Brooke returned, she had run nearly eight miles in sixty-six minutes. Not exactly a medal performance, but she felt energized—how a Monday should feel. Her ankle twinged a few times, but held up. *I bet I can run a half-marathon in an hour and a half. I guess I'll find out next week.*

Brooke sliced some fresh fruit into a bowl. She flipped on the TV and savored the vibrant meal while viewing a cooking show. *I'd love to be able to cook like that. But first, I need someone to cook for—other than myself.*

After breakfast, Brooke enjoyed a long hot shower. Toweling off, she slipped on a sundress and went barefoot—quite a change from a week ago. With nothing to do, Brooke decided to give herself a break. She popped in the movie *Message in a Bottle*. She hadn't viewed it in a while, and loved the Carolina setting. She pined for a place of her own on the beach. Brooke could look at Kevin Costner with the sound muted and still enjoy the movie. She kept the sound on, and midway through the Nicholas Sparks story, she noticed she hadn't thought of Tanner. Chase kept popping up.

As the credits rolled, she laughed—*I'm becoming my father.* Brooke wondered if Melissa had gone to her appointment yet, and whether or not Eddie had accompanied her. She guessed they made up—at least for now—since she hadn't heard from her friend since Saturday morning. *I hope the baby's okay. It's a good sign she hasn't called.*

Brooke dialed Shane—voicemail, then said, "Just checking in. Nothing urgent." Realizing life had become *nothing urgent*, an unfamiliar feeling set in—boredom—and Brooke didn't know how long she could do this unemployment thing. She glanced down at her pastel sundress, then remembered *I never did buy an interview outfit. Gotta do that.*

Brooke recalled North Hills Mall. Too bad, they did have cute shops there, but going back was out of the question. The image of the mall cop making her parade back and forth like a stripper right in front of *that hotel* ruled out Raleigh. She considered local shops in Chapel Hill—nah, not for business wear. Though it was further away, she settled on The Streets at Southpoint. *Between Nordstrom, Ann Taylor, and Macy's, I'm bound to find something. With a killer resume, a new interview outfit, and a superb recruiter, I can't miss.* She glanced at the cover of *The Bliss List*, and smiled, reaching for her keys.

During the drive, Brooke dialed Melissa—voicemail. I bet she's at her appointment right now. She laughed as she pictured Eddie looking at his watch more than at the sonogram screen. *Maybe Shane was right. It could be worse; I could be married to a guy like Eddie.*

With Southpoint up ahead, Brooke recalled the last time she'd been in Raleigh. *I bet the RTP Convention Center's nearby.* Her emotions felt bittersweet. *Was the night that seemed so magical to me, routine for him? Did he always reserve the same suite?* As much as she tried to distance herself from Chase, he pulled closer. *Even after all the lousy things he's done, I still wouldn't trade Chase for Eddie.*

Browsing at all the stuffy women's suits, Brooke cringed. I hope I don't have to actually wear this stuff after the interview—I don't want another company like that. She noticed how differently the various clothing displays made her feel. The playful, fun clothes reminded her of GenSense, where a sundress would be considered formal—and the culture was as relaxed as a Carolina sunset. The mundane woolen ladies suits looked so Pharmical, an inner dungeon. And no matter what she tried on, she wondered if Chase would like it on her.

Without the distractions of the fun sections, Brooke would've finished shopping for the interview outfit in no time, but this time there was no rush. *Maybe having little to do in plenty of time has its advantages.*

Carrying four heavy department store bags, Brooke passed a coffee shop. The aroma nearly pulled her in, but she kept walking. She stopped outside Strasburg Children and set her bags down at her sides. The clothing looked so cute and classy, exactly how she would outfit her baby. *I have time*, she laughed to herself.

Brooke spent more time searching for a gift for Melissa's baby than she had for herself. She loved shopping for kids clothes. Lifting the outfits like rare artifacts, Brooke lovingly ran her fingers across the fabrics. The little girl dresses were so precious, while the boys' looked funny—the kind you could get away with only while they were young.

She loved Tanner's baby picture in knickers and a cap—cute as a two-year-old, but would've cost him his lunch money later in life. Noticing all the mothers browsing with strollers, Brooke felt a kinship, a strong desire to join that sorority. I'd rather do that than a corporate sweatshop any day.

"Whenever I see your smiling face..." rang out from her purse buried in one of the bags, drawing a few glances from nearby shoppers. Brooke grabbed her cell, then glanced at caller ID and smiled, "Your timing's perfect. I just bought a bunch of interview stuff."

"We need to talk." Brooke could barely hear Travis.

"Hang on, I'm in a store. Let me go outside." Brooke pinched the phone between her ear and shoulder, then gripped the bags and plodded toward the door. She said, "I'm almost there." Travis waited. Even though it was hard to hear, he wasn't his usual chipper self.

Once outside, Brooke spotted a solitary bench—a rarity on the weekend, but just a little lucky for a Monday. She dropped the bags and plunked down as she grabbed the phone in her hand, and said, "Did you find me a dream job?"

"Ah, that's why I'm calling." His tone sounded more like a funeral director than an executive recruiter.

"You don't sound like your usual self ..."

Travis said, "I've known you for a long time. You were a great placement for me at GenSense."

"Okayyyyyyyy." Brooke clenched her jaw.

"I don't know how to tell you this—"

"It's not my resume, is it?"

"No, your resume is fine."

Travis seemed evasive, as if he couldn't verbalize his thoughts—definitely not himself. Brooke said, "You sound like you just saw a ghost."

Travis sighed, "Listen, I don't think I can help you."

"What do you mean?"

"I got shot down everywhere."

Brooke felt a thud inside, "I don't understand."

Long pause, then, "Can I ask you a direct question?"

"Sure."

"Did you sleep with the CEO?"

"Oh my God," Brooke felt faint, barely able to focus through her fluttering eyes, "Who said that?"

"You're being blackballed—big time. The word on the street is you slept with Chase Allman."

"Who's spreading *that* rumor?"

Travis inhaled deeply, "I can't divulge my sources, you know that."

"No, I don't know that. That's a pretty lousy rumor to be spreading. I have a right to know who."

"I never reveal confidential sources—no exceptions. Otherwise, no one would ever trust me. Any time someone tells me something in confidence, I always honor it. My name's my business and my reputation is everything."

"What about my reputation?" Tears stung Brooke's eyes.

"I've broken one of my rules—I've told you too much. Look, I do care about you, I know you've been through a lot, and you're not just a typical candidate. Like I said, you were a great placement for me. I'm just sorry I won't be able to place you again."

"Well, aren't there other companies you work with?"

"Not in this area, I'm afraid." Travis then listed the companies he canvassed—a Who's Who of Research Triangle Park—and each name felt like a knife thrust in a different spot, deeper each time. Brooke faintly heard Travis say, "Unless you're willing to up and move," as she dropped her cell and the tears streamed.

— ❤ —

"Eddie, slow down. You'll kill the baby."

Glancing at Melissa's wild eyes, Eddie laughed, then without slowing down, said, "Relax. I'm barely speeding. You're the most uptight person I know. Sheesh. The baby's fine—the doctor showed us."

"You took that last turn at like ninety miles an hour. You almost threw me out of the car."

"Put on your seat belt."

"It *is* on."

"Relax. And stop nagging me about every little thing."

Melissa sighed. Since their wedding day, instead of honeymooning, all they did was fight. Melissa followed Brooke's advice and forgave Eddie who displayed reconciliation with a shrug of his shoulders. Though Melissa had convinced Eddie into coming along to the doctor's appointment—through heavy guilt—she would have rather had Brooke there.

I'm glad the baby's fine. I'll call Brooke when we get home—if Eddie doesn't crash.

"Any luck?"

"I've been plenty lucky. Can you be more specific? Who is this?"

"It's Chase."

"Oh, in that case, no. Your little girl's nowhere to be found."

Chase fidgeted in his chair and fixed his gaze out his wall-sized window on the swirling clouds. "Did you get the money I wired into your account?"

"Money's in, Chief. I got the word out and nobody's seen either one of them. In case they skipped town, I put plenty of eyes on it. Even if they try to sneak into Canada, I got it covered."

"Keep me posted." Chase hung up the phone. Max sounded about as confident as his divorce attorney. He opened his door, and jumped back. "Ruth, you scared me."

"Sorry, I saw your call ended and I was going to tell you ..." Ruth stopped, scrunched her brows tightly, then asked, "Are you okay?"

"I'm fine," Chase said with an edge in his voice, "What did you need me for?"

"Mr. Greenberg was wondering if you got Miss Hart to sign her severance package. He said he sent you a few emails and hasn't heard from you."

"Not yet."

"Okay, I'll tell him. Are you sure you're all right?"

— ❤ —

I can't believe he'd do that.

After applying eyedrops three times—to no avail—she wore sunglasses for the long hike back to her car from the mall. She decided to keep the clothes even though she'd probably need new sizes if and when she ever landed a job.

The drive back to Chapel Hill felt like a funeral procession—and Brooke was driving in her own coffin.

Chase sure did a number on me. I wonder if he high-fived Dixie-dawg over it. What a vindictive prick!

Brooke could barely hear her ringtone over the music blasting in her car. She clicked the volume off, then glanced at her cell—*finally.*

Brooke drew a deep breath, then answered, "I've been wondering how it went today?"

"The baby's fine, but my marriage is a miscarriage."

"Did Eddie go with you?"

"Physically, yes. Emotionally, no."

Brooke sighed; Melissa thought it odd she didn't laugh. "That's not surprising."

Brooke's phone clicked, "Hold on Melissa … another call's coming in … can I ring you right back?"

Sigh, "Yep, I'll be here."

Brooke clicked over, then said, "Hello."

"Where have you been? I called you earlier."

"Sorry, Daddy, I've had a busy day." Earlier, it would have been a lie, but now, it was an understatement.

"I have a lunch set up tomorrow with Ron Weller."

"Who?"

"The guy you met at the club last week, remember?"

"Which company was he with again?"

"Ron's retired, but sits on the board at EID Pharma. He has some—"

"I can't do lunch tomorrow. I have an interview scheduled," Brooke lied, remembering EID's name from the Travis blackball list, feeling like a wounded seal surrounded by sharks.

"Seriously? That was fast. Who with?"

Oh shit. "Um, it's an exploratory interview … with an old colleague from GenSense."

"Well, Ron's a big wig. Can't you reschedule some *exploratory*?"

"No, it was set up by my recruiter." Brooke rubbed her nose.

Long pause, then after a deep breath, Weston huffed, "I guess I'll call Ron back. Can you do it Thursday?"

"No, Thursday's bad."

"Friday?"

"Um, nope."

"You can't possibly have anything more important than this all week." A vintage Weston statement masquerading as a question.

Brooke breathed deeply, then said, "Hold off. I've been doing a lot of thinking. I don't want to waste your time."

"I … I don't understand."

"I'm not sure I want to jump back in with another company like Pharmical. I appreciate all your help, I really do. But just give me some breathing room."

"What do you want me to tell Ron?"

Brooke strangled a shriek. She inhaled, then said, "I don't know. Tell him I'm pursuing something else right now."

"Look, the sooner you get another job, the better. That lousy severance is long gone. I wish you'd let me send a nasty-gram on my letterhead."

"No. I don't care about that. I have plenty of money in the bank. I just want to move on and not have any dealings with *that company* anymore."

"I wish you'd let me help you."

"You are. I'm grateful for you. I just need to sort things out before anyone can help me. I'll call soon." As Brooke hung up, she sensed her father's fumes—and she couldn't blame him. She hated hiding the truth, especially after all they'd been through; he deserved better. But her little tryst had blown up like a mushroom cloud in only one week. *Damn Chase Allman.* Brooke knew she could never tell her father, even though Chase deserved the wrath of Weston Ingram, Esquire. A side of Brooke wanted her dad to devastate the shark-snake.

"Your call cannot be completed as dialed, please hang up and try again."

The familiar and dreaded message hit harder this time. Panic trickled down Chase's spine like spiders descending on webs. He dug his hands into his hair and nearly banged his head on his desk.

"Excuse me?"

"Huh?"

"Are you sure you're all right?"

"No, no, I'm not."

Ruth's eyes flashed empathy. She sensed Chase was suffering, guessing his family situation had worsened. In the past, he'd opened up to her, but lately seemed so distant. She wanted to ask about Heather in the worst way. Ruth hated what that woman had done to him—he didn't deserve it. He's a good man.

Ruth paused, cocked her head, and softened her expression. Though questions peppered her mind, she suppressed them. Locking her raised eyebrows, she headed back to her desk.

"Ruthie?"

"Yes," she spun, almost falling.

"One more thing. Can you mail this to Brooke Hart?" He held out the manila oversized envelope.

"Sure."

"Oh, and tell Greenberg it's in her hands now."

Ruth frowned as she gripped the sealed envelope. As she scurried away, Chase hoped his handwritten note inside would do the trick.

— ♥ —

"I'm screwed."

"That's a bad pun."

Long pause. Shane noticed Brooke's sense of humor had darkened, morphing into a black hole. Before he could apologize, Brooke said, "I don't know what to do ..."

"Under the circumstances, you should consider legal action."

Brooke snapped a nail, then said, "Shit!"

Shane said, "Is that a—"

"No, I just broke a nail. Shit, I just had them done."

"Are you thinking about suing?"

"Don't make me break all my nails—one looks bad enough."

"A cease and desist letter to Mr. Chase Allman may be the only way to stop it."

"I still can't believe he'd do it. It doesn't make sense. I guess he didn't like me calling him names."

"What'd you call him?" Shane fidgeted in his chair.

"I might have let a few 'assholes' slip out, but nothing too bad."

"You didn't."

"He deserved it. I don't know what's worse—him firing me through his minion Greenberg or taunting me afterwards."

"Ordinarily, I'd say call him and apologize."

"Yeah, right." Brooke's tone plunged an octave.

"I'm not sure calling him and having it out will help. He's clearly a vindictive jerk who is feeling spurned."

"Why do guys have such fragile egos?"

"Hey, I don't have a—"

"Not you. You know what I mean," Brooke snickered.

"Thanks, I guess." Shane's inflection brought a second chuckle out of Brooke.

"I just feel like I'm on a rollercoaster—without enough thrill to the ride, mainly terror."

"Life is designed to have its ups and downs."

"Oh, here we go again, you're playing life coach."

"Well, that is what I do …" Brooke sighed. Shane continued, "T.S. Eliot once said: 'The end of all our exploring will be to arrive where we started and know the place for the first time.'"

After a long pause, Brooke said, "I'm sick of exploring and arriving in a bear trap."

Shane snorted a laugh, "You should be a comedian."

"Nah, Chase would probably hire hecklers for every comedy club."

"Have you read the book I sent you?"

Brooke's face brightened, "I did and I loved it. I know your next question …"

"Go on."

"Yes, I've written my own Bliss List. You know what's funny? Only one of my seven goals had anything to do with work—and it wasn't until number five."

"I'm not surprised. Can you email them to me?"

"Sure."

"What was your bliss point for work?"

"To have a job that I love doing, where I make a real difference, and feel a sense of purpose and meaning."

"That's fantastic. It sounds like GenSense."

"Unfortunately, now that I'm blackballed in the industry, I couldn't even do another start-up."

"You might be surprised. Don't let Chase Allman—or anyone for that matter—derail you. I want you to focus on you. I'll leave you with a little exercise."

"I have plenty of time."

Shane's laugh was heartier than Brooke's. "I want you to spend time exploring *meaning*. Ask yourself, 'What gives my life true meaning?' Then write whatever comes to mind. Don't restrict yourself to work tasks."

Hanging up, Brooke noticed her mood lightened, but felt burdened by the question. It was clever of Shane to change the subject, but the answer could take a lifetime to find.

17

She nervously glanced all around her, then loosened the envelope's seal. With both hands, she squeezed the upper corners and edged the sheets out. Ruth loved the familiar fragrance. Setting the papers on top of the envelope marked "Personal & Confidential," her eyes narrowed as she read.

Dear Brooke,

I've been trying to call and dying to talk to you. I feel terrible about what happened and understand how upset you must be. Obviously, I had nothing to do with it. Had I known they were going to let you go, I would've said fire her and you fire me too. I mean that. I wish I hadn't been away that day or it would have been different. When I heard what happened to you, I got in Stoddard's face. He nearly fired me and I wish he would have. This company isn't the same anymore; they value the almighty buck over people and I think they made a huge mistake letting you go.

After seeing the embarrassing severance package they gave you, I practically fired Greenberg over it. I reworked it and attached it here. It doesn't excuse the company's shortsightedness, but I hope it helps. I'll do anything I can to help you find a much better job. With your talents, it will be easy. I'm probably next to go though, so I should do it soon.

I haven't been able to stop thinking about you. Our night together was the most magical I've ever felt. You truly are an amazing person. I should have never let you leave. I tried to return your slip, but must confess I couldn't bear to. What happened between us felt so right. Maybe God intervened this

*way so we could be together. I know we belong together. Please
call me.*

    Love, Chase

Ruth couldn't believe her eyes. She reread the last paragraph and
realized she didn't need to take the risk of photocopying it; she'd never
forget it.

I have to meet Lucy, and I don't think I can wait until lunch.

— ♥ —

"The sole meaning of life is to serve humanity."

After hanging up with Shane, Brooke glanced at the corner of her
desk. She had discovered this Tolstoy quote right before she started
with GenSense. It spoke volumes to her then, making it easy to leave
medical consulting for truly serving humanity.

Brooke pulled out a piece of paper and wrote, "What gives my life
true meaning?" She had a difficult time reaching those feelings like
Shane had asked. She recalled how excited she had been while studying
child psychology in college, and even choosing it as a minor with her
business degree. Then, she discarded the notion. With conflicting
thoughts swirling in her head, one word kept popping up: GenSense.

Brooke stood and abandoned the project. She flipped on the TV,
hoping for something that could make her laugh. An ad for Hilton
Head Island caught her attention. She bolted upright and darted over
to her computer to check her rental agency's website. She located her
unit on Hilton Head and scrolled to the calendar. As she had hoped,
her villa had recently become open. Optimism renewed her like water
to a parched plant. She dialed her agency and left a message booking a
full week. Images of a change of scenery blossomed.

Brooke glanced at the framed quote on her desk. From her angle,
it twinkled like a star. Glancing up from her desk, she surveyed her
collection of old books and retrieved an old C.S. Lewis book from her
college days.

She fell asleep with the book open across her chest.

Brooke awakened to the sun's early rays before her alarm sounded.
I'm going running on the beach today, then shifted her thoughts to the
dream she was having before she awoke. Although her memory had

already faded, she recalled Tanner and Chase were both in it—an awkward first. What would Freud say about that one? I really need a break; my villa better still be available.

Brooke craved a fresh-brewed coffee, but Starbucks was out of the question—especially that one. Instead, she boiled water, then steeped three Earl Grey tea bags. Not quite a quad espresso, but the caffeine would make the six-hour drive tolerable. Brooke considered taking the temperature of the steaming mug, then laughed. Unsure if she had a thermometer, she dipped her finger in, then smirked. *I wonder if his tea has to be 175 degrees.*

Brooke grabbed a fresh Georgia peach she had purchased at a roadside stand. She flipped on TV and sipped her tea—not bad, but not espresso. A concerned but perky weather lady warned of a storm brewing off the coast of Haiti, heading toward Florida. She clicked the remote to the next channel—same news, only with a weather man. One more click—same story, only with a woman—*that's progress, we outnumber men.* She wondered if the same women would be employed in another ten years, guessing the man would.

Brooke shut off the TV, deciding to avoid the negative news and just enjoy the silence. Imagining the beach for a late afternoon run felt like she was already there. Brooke dialed her rental agency. Ordinarily, she rented the two-bedroom unit through her agency, but loved using it on the rare occasions when it was vacant.

A chipper woman's voice answered with, "It's a great day on Hilton Head." Brooke smiled whenever she heard that salutation, thinking that woman should be on TV. After confirming that her villa was available, Brooke said, "Thank you so much. It's a great day here too."

Brooke recalled purchasing it—that bittersweet day. She had so many fond memories. Brooke fell for Tanner on Hilton Head and their first kiss happened on the romantic beach at sunset. The couple had always dreamed of living in a mansion on the beach. The two of them had honeymooned there, then returned each year for an anniversary vacation. Then Tanner died.

Brooke kept her memories alive now, thanks to the GenSense buyout, by purchasing a Beachwalk villa located in the gated Shipyard Plantations in the center of Hilton Head Island. Though not on the beach as the name implied, it was only a short walk to the stunning seashore.

Brooke had not been to her villa in over a year, but figured she'd follow the same ritual of run, sun, and fun. Many of her friends invited her to Myrtle Beach, but she usually found excuses not to go. Myrtle felt like spring break, Hilton Head felt like home.

Beyond the happy memories, the island offered numerous advantages—much more appealing than anywhere along the North or South Carolina coast. Brooke loved to run, bike, and walk on the sand. No rocks, only smooth granules that eased with long tide changes. Tree-lined bike trails weaved throughout the island, blending picturesque golf courses, lagoons, and tennis courts with upscale homes and villas.

As she packed for the week away, Brooke pondered how Melissa might jump at the chance to go if the invitation was extended. But Shane's voice rang in her head, quelling those thoughts: "Brooke, you can't be Melissa's solace until you overcome your own grieving."

Brooke glanced at Tanner's picture on the passenger seat and clicked on her iPod folder marked "Hilton Head." "Carolina in my Mind" transported her to the South Carolina island she loved. "Sweet Caroline" reminded her of sing-a-longs with outdoor guitar players, something she loved to do with Tanner, even though he sang a bit off key.

After the second song soothed her, Brooke started the car and was off.

"Whenever I see your smiling face…" Brooke hit ignore. I can't talk to Melissa right now. She'll make me turn around.

The cell rang a second time—Melissa again.

I'm not answering; I hate it when she does that. Why can't she just leave a message? I swear, she's psychic.

Melissa never left a voicemail but expected Brooke to call back based on the missed call log. As expected, the cell rang for the third time. Brooke answered, "Melissa, I love you most of the time, but …" as she noticed a different caller ID number. Is she playing tricks? Brooke pursed her lips while holding the off button as if strangling her cell.

Maybe now her calls will go straight to voicemail and Melissa will get the message.

With the distractions eliminated, Brooke settled into her leather seat and clicked her iPod to "Your Smiling Face." She gazed over to the passenger seat and sang along—on key. With the song ending, she noticed the Starbucks sign ahead. Her stomach thumped as her thoughts collided with the storefront. That man keeps coming at me like a pop-up window. Then a thought hit her—didn't he say he had a place on Hilton Head?

— ♥ —

Chase scoffed at the difficulty in finding a good old-fashioned outdoor payphone that actually worked. He drove around for twenty minutes before stopping at a convenience store. Even though the phone lacked privacy, he didn't care at this point. Waiting until the coast cleared, he plunged his change into the slot and dialed. After hearing so many call block messages, the ringing sounded like a symphony. But it also meant she blocked his numbers.

With his heart pounding, he heard voicemail kick in immediately. He slumped, but just hearing her voice warmed him. He pictured her lips … ah, those lips. The abrupt beep almost knocked him over, and he started talking …

I hope I didn't sound like an idiot. I wonder if my letter arrived yet.

— ♥ —

Even with the Hilton Head playlist blaring, Brooke couldn't keep her mind off Chase. Then, "Sweet Melissa" *began, and instead of soothing her, it startled her. She squinted at her cell to ensure it was still off.*

I completely forgot I put this song on this folder. A wave of remorse set in—oh great, now Melissa's haunting me and the song's by the freaking Allman Brothers. Brooke screamed, "Why are you doing this?"

Brooke clicked off her iPod and scanned for FM signals, settling on a Top 40 station. As the music played, providing safety for now, she frowned at the gloomy sky up ahead. It was hurricane season, but this looked more like a passing shower than reason to evacuate. Brooke rolled her window down and noticed the outside air had cooled even though the sun still shined. I hope I get my run in. That reminds me …

Still about an hour away, Brooke powered her cell on and dialed Beach Bike Rentals. A voice answered like an auctioneer, then put her on hold. She furrowed her eyebrows: does anyone know the value of customer service anymore? The new voicemail alert startled her. Maybe

Melissa left one after all. Doesn't matter, I still can't call her yet—I don't want to lie.

A different voice returned, saying, "Beach Bike." Brooke ordered a mountain bike to be delivered to her villa.

After hanging up, Brooke clicked her iPod to the Dave Matthews folder, and as "Crash Into Me" began, she smirked while calling voicemail—the message startling her.

"Hi. I've been trying to call you … I, uh, we need to talk … I've been thinking about you … I hope you're all right … I'm not sure why you're—"

With lips pursing as if she bit a lemon, Brooke clicked the delete key before the message finished, then bounced the phone from the passenger seat to the floor, clanking on a dime. He's such an asshole! How could I have slept with him? Why can't I forget him?

Brooke drifted over the center line as she wrestled to reach the iPod on the passenger seat. She glanced up and veered back to her lane, gripping the wheel with sweaty palms, barely missing an oncoming truck. Brooke squinted in the rearview mirror and flinched as she struggled to catch her breath.

Suddenly, rain began pelting her windshield like stones, drowning out her soothing music. The daylight darkened, quickly and virtually blinding her. She scrambled to turn on her wipers, which failed to keep up. The pounding water caused her to hydroplane and Brooke hit her brakes. High beams glared into her mirrors. Brooke accelerated but the car drew even closer, so close that the headlights were no longer visible. She tapped her brakes to alert the other driver, but he stayed glued to her bumper. Brooke clicked on her hazards. He swerved into the other lane and blared his horn while speeding past, flipping her off.

This is sure a relaxing start to my vacation.

Brooke slowed and tried to catch her breath, watching him disappear into the rain. As Brooke pulled to the shoulder, the rain slowed. Her wipers screeched across her windshield; she clicked the bar down one notch, then the rain ended just as quickly as it had begun. Brooke heard the music once again and laughed. "Fire and Rain." The exit off I-95 to Hilton Head Island beckoned, with sunny skies on the horizon.

Traffic on Route 278—the final trek before the bridge—was its usual stop and start. Just before the safety margin, a traffic light flashed to yellow. While cursing, Brooke slammed her brakes, causing Tanner's picture to fly to the floor. With neck tensing like her seat belt, Brooke needed Hilton Head like never before.

She swore the lights had been timed so she missed each one as Brooke ascended the bridge to the island. Traffic flowed like the tide as seagulls flew lazily overhead. Brooke opened her window and inhaled the sea's invigorating mist and that feeling returned—home.

Atop the lengthy, gradual bridge, the island vista looked magnificent. She cherished the low country—especially at low tide—revealing oyster beds, which sea birds had feasted on before humans took over. Brooke turned on to the Cross Island. Even though she had to pay a toll, the new bridge cut the drive time in half. She remembered what traffic was like before they finished the project.

An elderly gentleman smiled as Brooke handed him the toll, actually saying, "Thank you, ma'am." Only in the South. Brooke noticed the clock—4:49 p.m. The trip had taken longer than usual, but there was still time to work up an appetite for a steamed seafood medley at Steamer's. Opting for the back way, she avoided the congested rotary where the brooding tourists wasted valuable happy hour time.

Pulling into the Shipyard security gate, a youthful black man in uniform stood upright, peered at her resident sticker on her windshield, then saluted and smiled. Brooke waved and smiled as her ringtone sounded—Melissa again. Brooke hit ignore; she could deceive her better from inside the villa.

Brooke realized she had never been alone on Hilton Head, and she looked forward to the private time. Driving along the shaded road, scenic Shipyard Golf Course on her left, and a waterway that joined two lagoons on her right, she searched for Tanner's picture and whispered, "I wish you were here."

Just past the golf course, a family on separate bikes had paused, pointing into the pond at an alligator's eerie eyes and back half of his tail, moving like a rusty grandfather clock. She almost yelled "be careful." Ever since she was a little girl, she had been scared of the prehistoric predators. And all spiders for that matter. Brooke didn't even like Charlotte's Web.

She drove around the rotary, an island of beauty with all the colorful flowers and palm trees mixed with oaks. Turning onto Shipyard Drive, *which led to the ocean, Brooke smiled. Her weariness from the drive shifted into spring-like anticipation.*

Pulling into Beachwalk's curvy lot, she spotted her villa. It looked the same as always. Once inside, Brooke adjusted the air conditioning to cooler, then opened her bags and fished out her running gear. Seconds later, Brooke was running on the winding asphalt path that weaved around trees, leading to the beach just ahead.

Passing the majestic residents' clubhouse, she hiked up the wooden walkway. It ramped around outdoor showers crammed with families moving around like a human ant farm—washing sand off their feet and beach toys. Beyond the wooden staging area, the tall grass in the rolling dunes waved with the gentle ocean breeze. With the tide out, the expansive beach was ideal for a run.

Brooke stripped her running shoes, then kicked sand as she loped along the late-day sun. Running with the shoreline created a serenity that invigorated Brooke. Most families had returned to their vacation nests, but remnants of their day remained scattered—sand castles eroded from wind and water. Brooke stopped at the usual spot by their tree as her heart raced.

The trees had matured, but the area hadn't changed in all the years. Picturing her first kiss like it was yesterday, she wrote "Brooke & Tanner" in the sand, then encased it with a heart. She gazed at her handiwork as tears plunked like the first droplets of rainfall. A curious seagull hovered nearby like a kite, using the wind for stability.

Brooke eyed the bird, then waved her hands in the air, signaling she had no food to offer. After a few seconds, the gull peeled away with the wind at its back, reminding Brooke it was time to return. She glanced once more at their tree, then their names in the sand, and began running back to her own nest. With the breeze and the sun behind her, Brooke recalled the wild horses she chased as a little girl.

Back at her villa, she showered with cool water to temper her overheated body. After toweling off, she slipped on a new sundress. Brooke glanced in the mirror and smiled at the rosy coloring in her face. A natural beauty, she required scant makeup: a touch of lipstick, swipe of mascara, and good to go. Since leaving Pharmical, Brooke wore her hair down, providing a seductive frame to her chiseled high cheekbones. Brooke vacillated about eating alone, but her seafood platter cravings cast the deciding vote. Checking once more in the mirror, she said to the image, "I hope I don't look like a total loser."

Steamer's was crowded with families clad in colorful Hilton Head attire. Reminiscent of the eighties, people still dressed preppy. Brooke loved how the little girls mirrored their moms in sundresses and sandals and young boys wore collared shirts and khaki shorts, as if coming off the golf course with their dads.

A friendly hostess in a lavender shirt with the Steamer's logo approached Brooke, and said, "A table outside is open, if you don't mind being near the musician. He starts in, like, fifteen minutes."

Brooke's eyes brightened, "Actually, that's perfect. I prefer to sit near him." The cute college-aged girl lifted one menu without asking the embarrassing question. She led Brooke to a small table set for two, then removed the place setting across from her. Brooke almost asked her to leave it.

While placing her napkin across her lap, a cute young man who couldn't be old enough to drink, smiled, "Welcome to Steamer's. My name's Josh, I'll be your server. Can I start you off with one of our famous frozen drinks?"

Man, do I feel old. Brooke said, "I'll have a Sea Breeze."

"Excellent. Would you like an appetizer?"

Not so fast, aren't you going to ask me for my ID? Do I look that old? So much for Southern hospitality. "No thanks, I'd like the steamed seafood medley and that's too much food."

"Maybe for a little girl like you, but not for me." Brooke laughed.

Josh returned after a few minutes, handling her drink as if it was a magic potion. Brooke gulped the Sea Breeze and sighed. It tasted superb and the alcohol immediately warmed her. *These things are dangerous. No more than two—I remember the last time I drank too much.*

When the food arrived, her eyes widened and mouth watered. She ordered a second drink, this time a Cape Codder—the logic being the new concoction would slow her down. It didn't. The food tasted as fabulous as the libations, just how she remembered—succulent scallops, a delicious whitefish she guessed was grouper, buttery clams, mussels, oysters, crab claws, and plenty of the island's specialty: shrimp.

The Cape Codder disappeared first, but she finished most of her feast, savoring every bite.

She recognized the musician as he started setting up. After placing his guitar on a stand, his eyes met Brooke's. He smiled and winked. She couldn't recall his name but definitely remembered his dimples and lanky frame—a Kevin Bacon lookalike. *Well, it's been over a year, and he still remembers my face.*

As her third drink arrived, he started singing, "In my mind, I'm going to Carolina ..." as if he had read Brooke's mind. She was going to request it, but he saved her a trip up to his stage.

Unlike so many singers, he didn't try to sound like James Taylor. He had his own style, which Brooke appreciated. He tapped a foot pedal once in a while to record himself, then harmonized his own voice on later choruses. Brooke wondered what it would be like to have a man serenade her on the beach. She frowned as she spotted a shiny new ring on his finger.

It figures. But I'm happy for him. Maybe he can sing, but he's not my type.

Brooke listened to a few more songs, then decided to leave drink number three half empty and call it a night. She hated to be at the beach with a hangover. Driving along the eerily dark and curvy road, Brooke flipped on her brights. As if designed by sea turtles, the nature-friendly, driver-unfriendly trip home could be treacherous. Tanner had always driven at night, and once again, she missed him.

Aside from inconvenient lighting, she appreciated how Hilton Head had developed without disrupting natural beauty. No neon signs or flamboyant buildings—even McDonald's had a brick front and upscale roof, sans the golden arches.

Safely back in her comfy bed, she flipped off the lamp and inhaled the silent darkness. Closing her eyes, the word *meaning* popped up, spinning her brain's wheels.

An earsplitting knock on the door shook Brooke out of a deep sleep. She glanced at the clock—8:27 a.m. *Who could that possibly be? Nobody knows I'm here.*

Brooke jumped up and slipped down the tightly carpeted stairs, landing one foot from the door. Another three knocks reverberated. "Who is it?" She wished she had a peephole.

"Beach Bike Rentals, ma'am."

Brooke inspected her panties and skimpy night shirt, and said, "I, um, just got out of the shower. Can you just leave the combination under the mat?" *Please don't tell me you need a signature.*

After a long pause, in a deep Southern drawl, "Sure thing. Have a nice day."

Brooke stretched, then returned back upstairs, giggling. She eyed her cozy queen bed, but thought, *now that I'm awake I may as well go for a ride before high tide.* Brooke pulled on her shorts and sports bra and pedaled to the beach.

Hilton Head Island boasts thirteen miles of uninterrupted beach, and Brooke considered covering it all before noon. With the already sizzling sun on her back, she started from Shipyard and rode along the shoreline to the end point in Sea Pines. Aside from a few fishermen casting from the shore, and the occasional runners, power walkers, and riders, the journey provided ample reflection time. Beyond the beauty, Hilton Head offered mystique. A warm inviting attitude matched the summer temperatures, like a visit to grandma's house.

Brooke passed a tandem bike, a sweaty twenty-something man pumped furiously while his girlfriend reclined lazily, gazing at the mansions. Brooke smiled, then slowed, nearing the spot she knew by heart. Skidding on the firm sand, she balanced a stop with both feet. Brooke surveyed the area, picturing her words in the sand buried under the incoming tide like a sunken treasure.

Closing her eyes, this time her visit felt less intense but the memories were vivid. She said what she wanted to say, then popped her eyes open, this time without tears. She spotted another old tree. It seemed like everywhere she looked, Tanner's shadow hovered like the seagulls. Brooke's stomach twinged—time to eat. She pedaled up the inland path toward another memory lane.

The Friday morning breakfast crowd was light for Skillet's. Brooke figured it would be a different story Saturday and Sunday, with new hordes of vacationers opting to eat out rather than waste their first days grocery shopping. Brooke usually ordered a fruit plate, but wafting bacon taunted her. The run and bike ride had left her dehydrated. The alcohol last night didn't help. She craved blueberry pancakes—and naughty bacon. She started with coffee, remembering that Starbucks was nearby.

I won't be going anywhere near that place.

The sinful blueberry pancakes tasted sensational, but filled her like quick-dry cement. The standoffish, wrinkly waitress lifted Brooke's empty plate and actually asked her, "Would you care for dessert?"

Brooke widened her eyes further than her stomach and shook her head. *She can't be serious.* Brooke had buyer's remorse. *Why does all food that smells good make me feel lousy? Good thing I'm not that far from my place or I'd need a wheelbarrow.*

With sluggish legs, Brooke pedaled as if heading into a wind tunnel. *I thought carbohydrates provided energy.* People now lined the beach, both on sand and in the water, and she was forced to ride even more slowly. The tide had risen, making navigating tricky. Kids darted in and out of the water like deer across a road—without looking. Boogie-boarders and body-surfers caught larger-than-normal waves. Paddle boards slapped and kites soared. The beach resembled a playground at recess, with numerous side games, laughter, and chatter.

The temperature felt perfect and rain was forecast for tomorrow. She slipped into her new bikini that had felt quite a bit looser at the store, then dug out her bag from the owner's closet, and tossed in the usual beach items. Strolling to the residents' beach house, she grabbed her umbrella and recliner from her locker. The sand felt blistering even in flip flops.

After swirling the umbrella as deep into the sand as she could, Brooke spread out on her towel and listened to the sounds—waves streaming, seagulls squawking, kids laughing, adults gabbing under closely cropped rental umbrellas. Ah, Hilton Head. With nothing to do but relax. And, relax she did, falling fast asleep despite the cacophony surrounding her.

When Brooke awakened, the tide had drifted a football field away. She shook her head, flinging sand from her wavy locks. Brooke darted across the scorching dry sand until reaching the moist and comforting packed sand. Waves rolled in lazier patterns than before. Brooke plunged into the tepid salty ocean, immersing herself under a wave, then emerging invigorated. She loved this time of day. The frenetic beach activity relaxed into the serenity that she longed for.

Brooke's stomach growled. *I can't be hungry already.* She considered calling Janine, a sorority sister from college who summered on Hilton Head before moving here fulltime after graduation. She was fun, but on the wild side. Brooke was never that close with her since she hit on Tanner sophomore year. She denied it, invoking the booze excuse, but Tanner came clean. Ironically, Janine helped strengthen Brooke's trust in him. *I wonder if she ever married. When did I last see her? I was probably with Tanner. I don't think she knows he's gone.*

Brooke dialed her friend's cell number. It had been at least four years—Tanner range—and she braced herself as she pressed send. Janine sounded excited to hear from Brooke, but was preoccupied by island traffic. The conversation flowed in small talk mode until the inevitable question torpedoed: "What are you and Tanner doing tonight?"

"Uh, I'm sorry Janine, Tanner died three and a half years ago."

Silence, then, "Oh my God, what happened?"

I guess she didn't know—so much for the grapevine. "He had a rare form of leukemia."

"I am so sorry … I don't know what to say … you guys seemed so …"

Brooke didn't need Janine to sink any further. She said, "Are you still in Forest Beach?"

"Good memory. Oh my gosh, Brooke, I'm stunned."

"I'm here for a few days and it would be great to see you. Do you have any plans tonight?"

"I do. I have a dinner date, but it's not much. I'm not sure about this guy. Hey, you can join us if you want? Bail me out if needed."

"Oh, no, I couldn't do that Janine. You go out. I've got some stuff I need to do tonight anyway."

"You sure?"

"Yeah. I'll be here a few more days. Maybe tomorrow if you're free?"

Pause, "Saturday? Actually, I have another date …"

"Ooooh, sounds serious," Brooke grinned.

"No, different guy. Not sure about him either." Hearty laughter.

"Some things never change," Brooke thought *female Dixie-dawg.* "I'll call you Sunday or Monday, unless you hook up with bachelor number three and four."

Giggles, "It's good to see you still have that sense of humor. It's good to hear from you Brooke. See you soon."

Hanging up, Brooke sighed. *She's another person I wouldn't trade places with in a million years.*

Brooke sat in silence for a moment, then picked up her phone and dialed Melissa. She was relieved to hear voicemail. "Hey Melissa, it's me. Sorry I keep missing you … I'm thinking of going to my daddy's for a few days," Brooke's eyes fluttered as she fibbed to her friend. "Hope you're doing well. I'll call you when I return. Love you." Pressing end, Brooke hoped Melissa wouldn't call back immediately.

She brought her journal out to her deck, then settled, seeking inspiration from the calm pond. No alligators or spiders within sight, Brooke exhaled. A crane stood stock still at water's edge near a turtle sunning himself. A squirrel jumped from a huge oak branch to a smaller one beneath it, causing a few leaves to descend like cottonwood flakes to the pine needles below. Brooke's forehead beaded up; she wondered if humidity bothered them. Or the frost of winter. Nature seemed to adjust to change without effort, something Brooke envied.

Hunger pangs clicked inside Brooke's stomach like an alarm clock, reminding her to shower. After one full day without a watch, Brooke was on Hilton Head time—adapting like nature. While showering, Brooke forgot what day it was. Saturday? Though she pondered returning to Steamer's, she didn't want to look like a stalker—or a total loser.

Struggling to untangle her hair from the torments of the sand and wind, Brooke frowned. *I can't go out like this on Saturday.* She craved Italian, but didn't feel like sitting solo at a candle-lit table. And pizza delivery wasn't what she had in mind. Then, looking at the floor, her T-shirt strewn on top of the unmade bed flashed like an advertisement—Salty Dog. Great outdoor pizza. Perfect.

Grateful for her insider island knowledge, she drove the back way to South Beach. Ever since grade school math with Sister Rulerpain, Brooke prided herself on applying the shortest solution. Unlike long division, this methodology proved useful in traffic. On Hilton Head, like in life, there were usually at least two ways to go.

The Salty Dog Café offered the ideal setting. Against the backdrop of the Marina, the Cape Cod–style buildings resembled honeycombs with all the bustling tourists dining, shopping, and jostling for seats around the tiki hut outdoor bar. The expansive wooden deck—cut around the palm trees, of course—served as a main meeting area to eat, drink, and be merry. Brooke rounded the corner and winced at the parking options. She remembered her secret spot, then pulled onto the grass, under a majestic oak. A minivan followed and parked right behind her.

Once outside her air conditioned Lexus, the muggy air assaulted her skin. She decided to grab a cool drink and adjust in the shade, before her sundress clung to her like a one-piece swimsuit. Ambling toward the circular bar, she heard the guitar guy singing. She spotted an opening at the bar and wedged on a stool beside a cute couple who glowed like honeymooners.

Like the night before, this performer had talent. He was playing a spirited rendition of "Rocky Top," as a table of orange-clad adults acted like kids, while their unattended children bounced around on the makeshift dance floor. She figured she'd wait to request her songs.

After missing her chance with one of the three scrambling bartenders, the taller one made eye contact with Brooke, and she panicked. Keeping her eyes fixed, she pointed at the young girl's drink beside her, and said, "I'll have one of those."

"One lava coming right up."

Brooke glared at the drink she just ordered, and the pretty patron beside her said, "Oh, these are scary good. I think that's why they call 'em lavas."

The bartender flashed an *I just had my braces removed* smile, and said, "They're a mix of Piña Colada and Daiquiri."

Brooke shrugged as she watched bottles flipping and heard two blenders whirling. The bartender filled the clear cup half way with a red icy concoction, then, with a concentration that stunned Brooke, eased the yellowish drink to the top. He presented the drink to Brooke with flair—like he just accepted his Harvard diploma, then beamed. She sipped with an audience, then said, "Good," thinking, *it doesn't taste or look like lava—go figure.* Noticing the bar was packed three deep, Brooke considered ordering another one. The first sip turned to gulps, each time flowing easier; Brooke realized why they called it lava.

The cute couple next to her struck up a relaxed conversation— where are you from, are you just getting here, where are you staying, then where did you go to school? When Brooke said, "UNC, Chapel Hill," the brown-eyed brunette beside her said, "Oh my God, me too. I knew I liked you." They both laughed as a guy with an orange cap standing nearby frowned. "My name's Christine, but my friends call me Sissy." *That name makes about as much sense as lava.* Her boyfriend caught the bartender's eye and motioned for another round for his girlfriend and Brooke—*that's nice.*

Brooke noticed the sparkling diamond ring on her finger. "When are you two getting married?"

"We just got engaged last night." Sissy gazed lovingly at her new fiancé.

"Sorry, I think I need something to eat."

The musician just finished "Every Rose Has Its Thorn"—fitting—then pacified the loud mouth across the way by launching into "Bohemian Rhapsody." Sissy spun, then pressed her finger and thumb under her tongue, and whistled, drawing a grin from the performer. She said, "Oh my God. I love it when he does this song."

Grateful for the diversion, Brooke turned and faced the shaded mini-stage. After the opening, which drew all eyes front and center, Brooke said, "This guy's good. I think I've heard him before."

Sissy stared at the singer like a teen idol, then said, "Dave's my favorite. I want him to play at our wedding." Jake nodded.

Brooke blurted, "I hope this isn't your wedding song?" Laughter. Brooke realized the second drink, sans food, was erupting inside her small dehydrated body, dropping her IQ like trees in a volcano's path.

Much to Brooke's astonishment, Dave sang the operatic section. Brooke wondered how he'd pull it off, but, as if on cue, everyone joined in like a Queen video. After the rousing riff—that actually sounded great on acoustic guitar—Dave finished to a standing ovation. Brooke heard the words "short break" and took her cue.

"I need to eat something before I pass out. I should've bought you guys a drink …"

Jake said, "Nonsense. It was great meeting you. You're welcome to join us. We're waiting for our table inside the restaurant and can easily—"

"No, I kinda feel like pizza," Brooke eyed the short line on the opposite side of the café. "Thanks, though, you guys remind me of …"

Brooke stopped herself, then grabbed her cup and toasted the young couple. She didn't need it, but Brooke downed the remainder of the drink, then waltzed away.

Her smile ended abruptly as the name of the pizza stand registered—Tanner's Pizza.

I can't win.

Dave passed by Brooke and nodded, then headed to the men's room. *Everyone here is so friendly.*

"Wake up, Daddy, I'm hungry."

"Huh?" Chase shook his head as Parker's tiny hand tugged on his golf shirt. Oksana and Dmitri, her boyfriend, formed a triangle with Parker. The image startled him. Chase said, "What time is it?"

"Dinner time. Can we go back to Salty Dog? Please," Parker finished with a cute but phony pose.

Chase rubbed his chin, then said, "Oksana and Dmitri, it's your pick tonight. What do you feel like eating?"

Oksana glanced at her boyfriend, then said, "We don't care." "Well, we were just there yesterday. Don't you feel like—"

"I want pizza, pizza," Parker crinkled his eyebrows, looking more adorable than angry.

Before Chase could respond, Oksana said, "It is okay, we can go where Parker wants. We like Salty Dog, and they have more stuff other than pizza." She glanced at Dmitri, who nodded.

"Yippee, let's go," Parker said, hoping to preempt a rebuttal.

"Give me five minutes."

Driving their BMW SUV along the winding single-laned road in heavier traffic than usual, a silver Lexus sped by in the opposite direction. Chase's eyes popped wide as he peered through the side mirror. He shook his head. *That couldn't have been. I have to get her out of my mind.*

A tapping jolted Brooke out of a vivid dream. *Huh.* She heard it again, and realized a woodpecker had perched just outside her window.

With blood rushing to her head, Brooke felt pregnant—including morning sickness. The pancakes, pizza, and lava had hoodwinked her brain, but hadn't fooled her stomach. She slowly descended back into her foam pillow and tried out several excuses not to run. She was unable to persuade her inner voice.

Running was the cure-all remedy, the one constant in her life. She realized it more than ever when sidelined by her ankle injury. Still lying down, Brooke remembered the Run for the Cure was next weekend, and it catapulted her out of bed. After swallowing two aspirin with an extra large gulp of water, she laced her shoes, threw on her running garb, and jogged down the shaded path.

Once on the moist sand, past the searing zone, Brooke kicked off her shoes and decided on running the opposite direction. It looked clear and she could stop at the Marriott for one of their poolside fruit plates. After a few easy paces, her food and lava coma subsided. With the rising sun and soft breeze, she felt lucid. The tide was midpoint and she felt centered. To her right, something moved—two dolphins arced through the air, then cut into the calm ocean without leaving a ripple.

Keeping her eyes trained right, they lunged up again as if synchronized, then two babies followed. They matched Brooke's pace. After a few seconds, the four repeated their show. Memories flooded in. She recalled her fascination, observing her first dolphin while on vacation with her father. Today, Brooke's eyes widened each time the dolphin family emerged, just like the old days. Even though the scene was just as it looked the first time, the dolphins captivated her. Suddenly, she realized she was in front of the Marriott.

Brooke watched until the dolphins faded from view. Feeling exhilarated in her runner's high, time stood still for her. Brooke puzzled—*I must be hungry.*

Brooke savored each bite of the fresh fruit medley with her feet dangling in the pool. She felt like a new woman—a noticeable improvement from yesterday, but it wasn't only the change in diet that helped. On her return, Brooke decided to lazily stroll rather than run. The tide had shifted out farther than before, revealing plenty of underwater treasures.

Splashing through the irregular ocean's edge, Brooke spotted the top of what looked like a buried conch shell. She nudged it, then gripped and pulled, until the entire shell swooshed out. Brooke examined it, marveling at its shape and color. She made sure the snail-like creature was gone, *It's a keeper.* Wandering farther, she collected an assortment of seashells.

Arriving back at her shoes she had left on the walkway, the hot sun beckoned her to stay. Low tide invited the incoming beach goers, and Brooke decided to join them. She spotted a cute little boy plunked inside an unfinished sand castle—doing more playing than building. He glanced up and smiled at Brooke, impressed with her overflowing collection. His adorable smile caused Brooke to drop several shells near his burgeoning sand fortress. His eyes widened, then he squinted back up and said, "Did you find all those pretty shells yourself?"

Brooke smiled, "I sure did." She rubbed her hands together, deciding against picking them up. Inspecting the ground, she said, "That's a nice sand castle. Did you build that all by yourself?"

"Uh huh."

"Wow. Didn't your parents help?"

"A little bit, but they're over there taking naps on their blankies." The boy pointed to the couple, who lounged on beach towels nearly fifteen feet away. Neither noticed.

Brooke wished she had a video camera to capture his enthusiastic innocence—his squeaky voice and delightful eyes. Brooke smiled lovingly and thought of her doll collection.

"Hey, you wanna play?"

"I have to ..." Brooke bit her lip, then gazed at his eyes with his long lashes, and said, "Sure, why not."

"Yippee."

Brooke giggled—*I have to find a camera*, "You want these shells to protect the castle?"

The little boy bobbed his head, considered the reach of the shells, then said, "Okay, you can use 'em to keep the big sharks out. I can teach you how."

Brooke shot a glance at the distant shoreline, then with wide eyes, asked, "Are there sharks?"

"Uh huh. I caught one with Captain Carlos."

Oh you cutie, "Okay, I'll try to protect us with these shells then." Brooke lined some shells face down around the front.

The boy scanned the first few shells, then said, "Should we dig sand for them first?"

"That's a great idea. Why don't you shovel and then I'll put the shells on top to keep the sharks out."

As the two wiled away the afternoon, they constructed a creative shark cage. Though she could spend the entire day with this delightful boy, her skin screamed for sunscreen. She feared a horrible burn enflamed her back and shoulders. Brooke had to use the bathroom and her stomach's compass pointed toward a seafood salad bar.

Brooke frowned at the boy's parents, who hadn't budged, but said, "I have to go."

The boy peered into Brooke's eyes as if staring into her soul, then asked, "Are you coming back?"

"I don't know. I've got to eat lunch and do some stuff ..." Brooke's heart stopped—his eyes could melt the sun. She continued, "I'll try to come back, but if I don't get here in time, you can keep my seashells."

"Wow, thanks. I'll get them before the sharks eat 'em up. I can't wait to show my dad."

"Good idea," Brooke smiled, then grimaced at the young man still collapsed on the towel, missing so many glorious moments. She felt a magnetic pull and didn't want to leave, but then said, "Take care." After two steps, Brooke paused and said, "What's your name?"

"Parker."

"Nice to meet you. How old are you?"

"Almost four."

"You're very smart for your age. I really enjoyed meeting you. Take care." Parker smiled, then began running his hands through the edge of the castle.

Brooke marched by Parker's lazy parents and considered kicking sand, but the blaring heat was too much to stop to pull on her shoes, so she traversed the fiery ground like a ballet dancer. Once safely on the wooden path, she tiptoed to the outdoor shower station and jumped in. Brooke stood under the refreshing water and felt her temperature ease into a comfort zone.

Brooke realized her own child would be about Parker's age.

Back inside her villa, Brooke pressed her thumb against her skin and released. She gasped, observing the white turn fire engine red. No more sun for me. Pity, I really liked that little boy.

She threw on a cover-up, then strolled across the street to the Crown Plaza's indoor restaurant. Brooke selected a plentiful plate of seafood buffet. Although the residents' discount made the price less painful, her skin matching the lobster claws haunted her.

More beach time was out of the question, so Brooke decided on a nice shaded bike ride. Hilton Head offered plenty of nifty trails, from right outside her door.

Brooke pedaled away from the beach this time. She swerved around majestic oak and palm trees on the smooth dark path. Unlike most riders, she stopped at each subdivision entrance. Tall shrubbery blocked drivers' vision. Frequent stopping was an inconvenience, but getting hit was deadly. Technically, bikes and pedestrians had the right of way—which didn't matter much.

She hadn't ridden this direction in well over a year, but she remembered the path crossed Shipyard Road up ahead. While slowing, a family on bikes had the same idea. They dismounted and waited for the busy road to completely clear—which it never seemed to do. Brooke stopped right behind a trailer with two little kids crammed in like Siamese twins.

Brooke said, "Hi, you two," then lowered her head while smiling and waving.

The mama bear lugging them glanced over her shoulder. Without breaking eye contact with the wide-eyed little ones, Brooke said, "They're so cute."

"Thanks, they're a load today. Wanna trade?" The husband in front turned and sneered at his wife.

Brooke almost blurted *sure, but only for the kids,* however, she only said, "How old?"

Just as she replied, "They're twins, nine months," the man interrupted, "C'mon, let's go. It's finally clear," thrusting his bike forward.

Brooke said, "Too cute," while mini waving and following. Once safely across—just in front of a minivan speeding well past the limit—Brooke stayed behind, smiling and waving as their little eyes scrutinized her. After crossing another street in the same order, the family caravan went straight, but Brooke turned the other direction. She wanted to follow along the roadside lagoon that led to a big pond.

Brooke passed a mother and daughter tossing bread to a swarm of turtles from an old wooden bridge. The little girl giggled each time a turtle gobbled the floating food. With the little girl's laughter fading, Brooke spotted a line of little ducks swimming in tight formation behind the adult. The clearing loomed up ahead and children cried and clung to their parents' legs. She realized what that meant. Then she saw …

The alligator was bigger than the one she spotted the other day. Although a safe distance away, he eyed the commotion with haunting steadiness. Brooke pedaled faster, running a stop sign, compounding her fright. From the other direction, a Shipyard security cop glared at her. Her two fears were gators and spiders. A cop would have to shoot to stop her this close to the pond.

During the return trip, Brooke realized something interesting— she did not miss work. Hilton Head had a way of centering her that she couldn't explain—or get enough of. She decided to take a night off, relax at home with take-out sushi, and focus on the assignment from Shane—to define *meaning*.

Thunder boomed, pulling Brooke's eyes open. She froze, unaware of her locale. Then, as her eyes adjusted, she realized she had fallen asleep on the couch in the downstairs family room. An old movie ran on the TV, the sound out of synch with the mouth movement. She pulled herself up as another thunderous growl rumbled, then detonated. Illuminated by the TV's glow, her journal had some doodling under the title word—*so much for meaning tonight.*

Scaling the stairs, Brooke crawled in to bed. The thunder quieted in the distance, but flashes of lightning continued like a frayed power line while rain pelted her roof. Despite the open shades, Brooke slept soundly.

When Brooke awoke, she heard rain trickle against her window. She flipped over, clutched the covers under her chin, and fell back asleep. Once again, Tanner visited her dreams, looking like the college days. Brooke felt a tickle and sleepily brushed her hand across her cheek thinking it was her hair, but she felt something crawl onto her hand. She shook it wildly and bolted upright, screaming.

Brooke leaped out of bed and turned on every light as she spotted a spider darting away. *I hate those stupid things!* She trembled as she searched everywhere, unable to find the hairy creature. Her body felt like a pin cushion with millions of nerve endings prickling at once.

So much for sleeping in.

Brooke craved waffles and realized she never made it to a store. Still spooked by the spider, she grabbed her shorts and a new Salty Dog T-shirt and dressed downstairs. At her front door, she ducked as she exited, and then surveyed the sky, which looked like an all-day rain. That meant one thing—mall day—probably a good thing for her skin, but bad for her credit card balance. Even though Brooke had enough money to retire, she lived frugally. Unless, it was a rainy day on vacation.

Brooke drove over to the Marriott, this time opting for the hearty inside brunch. Then she cruised to The Mall at Shelter Cove. Aptly named, it was the only enclosed mall on the island. She entered a bookstore, seeking insight on *meaning*, but ended up browsing the anorexic fashion trends—not the best thing to do after chocolate chip waffles and a three-cheese omelet.

Feeling the pull to move on, Brooke exited back into the mall and stopped at Gymboree. She found plenty of adorable infant clothes, but none that were gender neutral. Realizing it was a haul to return clothes, she wished Melissa knew the gender of her baby. After asking a clerk for help, she settled on a cute Hilton Head outfit that could work on any infant. *Baby's first Hilton Head experience.*

Shopped out, Brooke treated herself to a movie. Billed as a romantic comedy, it wasn't romantic and didn't make her laugh. The buttered popcorn didn't mix well with breakfast, but sure smelled and tasted good at the time. She drove home, stopping only to grab Chinese food for later. She was out before sunset.

The next morning, sharp rays awakened Brooke—again sleeping with the blinds open. Birds sang their joyful harmonies while dining on a surplus of worms. The Chinese food left her feeling extra hungry, but she decided on fruit. Brooke took a leisurely bike ride back to the Marriott. No dolphins in sight, but she stopped occasionally to pick up seashells. With a basket, she didn't have to worry about volume. She thought of Parker and wondered what he was playing on the beach today.

The sun had evaporated the heavy rains from the previous day, creating an ideal beach setting. She stopped at the approximate sand castle spot, but no Parker. She pedaled farther—still no Parker. Hmm, most people are here for at least the week.

A little white dog sprinted up to Brooke, followed not too closely by a little girl calling the dog's name. Brooke smiled and petted the friendly dog with the delightful furry face sprinkled with sand. The little girl yelled, "Taffy," but the dog never broke eye contact with Brooke.

"Hi, Taffy," Brooke said, causing the dog's ears to shift. "Ah, selective hearing, huh, Taffy?" Another flinch, tail wagging faster. Brooke continued petting the dog as the girl neared them, giggling, "She likes you."

A woman said, "Taffy. Get back here." Taffy lowered her head, then froze.

Brooke yelled back, "She's fine. Taffy's not bothering me." Brooke and the little girl gave the dog a full body rub, as the mother slowed to a walk. She eyed Brooke suspiciously, then relaxed her stance.

Brooke peered into the hazel eyes of the girl, and asked, "How old are you?"

The girl struggled to hold up three fingers as her mother arrived, and said, "Abbey, you know how to say it."

Abbey glanced at her mother, then with the fingers still in the air, said, "Freeee," then giggled.

Brooke glimpsed at the mother and said, "She's so precious. I bet she keeps you busy."

"They both do. C'mon, we have to go. Quit bothering the lady."

Brooke started saying, "They're not—" as the mother pulled Abbey and Taffy away.

Brooke gazed until she could barely see the child and her dog anymore. She surveyed the area—no Parker. She returned to the sand castle spot. Still no sign of the little guy. Feeling a sudden sadness, Brooke parked her bike and retrieved her umbrella from the beach house.

After setting up camp, she opened her notepad to the first page. Staring out at the ocean, she pondered *meaning*. A tennis ball banged against Brooke's bad ankle, causing a grimace. A little girl shuffled over hesitantly. Brooke heard a distant, "Say *sorry*."

The little girl flashed big brown eyes, then in the voice of an angel, said, "I'm sorry."

Brooke laughed at the intensity on her tiny face, guessing she couldn't be much older than Abbey. "It's okay. Can I throw it to you?"

"Okay," the brown eyes beamed, then she extended her hands with locked elbows.

Brooke tossed the ball underhanded. It bounced off the little girl's hands onto her forehead, then fell into her hands. She squealed, then yelled to her playmate, "I caught one!" She grinned at Brooke and said, "It's my first catch."

Brooke smiled, "Great job."

Her brother shouted something and the little girl simply said, "Bye," then ran with little legs that moved like pistons.

Brooke returned to her notebook and frowned. She understood writer's block. Brooke closed the pad, then shut her eyes. With the waves lulling her, Brooke fell asleep.

Brooke flinched. Then flinched again. She lifted her feet up as her eyes shot open. The tide ended her dream, deleting the sleepy transition time when recall was possible. Brooke jumped up, pulled out her umbrella, then grabbed her open chair and beach bag, and dragged it to dry sand.

She surveyed the area—no Parker—then folded her chair and left.

Riding back to the villa, she vaguely remembered that Shane was in her dream. Even though she didn't have any breakthrough news, she felt compelled to call him.

"Fancy hearing your voice," Shane said in his usual upbeat tone.

"I've been trying to ponder meaning, but I've only been able to assign new *meaning* to the word *beach bum*."

"You're enjoying Hilton Head, that's good in and of itself. You deserve some down time."

"This is gonna sound weird, but whenever I try to think of *meaning*, I never get anything work related. I feel this mystical pull toward something greater than me."

"What do you mean?"

Brooke glanced to the right, then said, "Well, I went to a bookstore to pick up books on meaning. Ironically, I was drawn to the magazine rack. Eyeing all the anorexic airbrushed models, something hit me—no wonder I feel so conflicted. As a woman, I'm expected to be the perfect mom and wife—which I feel like I failed; have a great career—which I was fired from; then be attractive and fit in with these ridiculous, unrealistic expectations—which not even those models can succeed at."

"Sounds like you're having a quantum moment."

Brooke chuckled, "You sound new age."

"Actually, it's age old. But that's a discussion for another day. You're onto something. You've identified the root of struggle—which is the starting point. From there, what do you value?"

"This place is like kiddie land. It gets me thinking … about what it would be like to have kids of my own. But not like everyone I've run into. I've observed so many adorable kids whose parents are totally aloof and I guess it makes me sad. Did you know that when I first started school I was pursuing a child psychology degree? Dad had other ideas and I let him push me down an entirely different path that he said was more lucrative."

"Believe it or not, I think you've gained more insight about meaning than you think."

"Really? How so?"

"Listen to yourself. You've uncovered your own key to meaning. It's simplified into three words: *be, do, have.*"

After a pause, Brooke said, "Now you've lost me."

Shane drew a deep breath, then said, "Everyone has it backwards—*have, do, be.* I'll provide an example. Let's use the universal, time-tested ambition—money. People say, 'If I could *have* a million dollars, then I could be *do*ing all the things I truly want to *do.* Then, I could *be* happy.' Then they never have it and play a lifelong blame game."

"Am I playing a blame game?"

"Not when you take a quantum leap. You told me what makes you sad, now apply the Law of Polarity to determine what makes you happy. Everything has an opposite, Brooke. All it takes is be, do, have—*be* happy, then things you like *do*ing will magically appear, then you'll *have* meaning."

"My head is spinning."

18

Quantum leap, huh? Then why aren't the words leaping on the page? Brooke's doodle now expanded to the bottom of the page. *Why does Shane always leave me thinking? I'm on vacation, for Chrissake. Alone. It's hard to be freaking happy without someone—anyone.*

I need lava.

The next morning came too soon. A loud noise jolted her out of a fitful sleep. *Did someone crash a plane into my villa? How many of those things did I drink?* Brooke steadied herself up, then wobbled over to the unshaded window—a leaf blower.

Well, it could be worse. I could have that job. I wonder if he's happy. Brooke laughed, realizing she was becoming her father—he always laughed at his own jokes. *Maybe I need to tell myself jokes. Be, do, have.*

Brooke craved an espresso and actually contemplated a trip up the road. But her inner teeter-totter landed on "no." *I wonder if they make it 175 degrees here.* Another laugh. Brooke glanced at her old Sheryl Crow CD sitting near the even older boom box. Music was out of the question right now, but a song rang in her head: "If it makes you happy, it can't be that bad. If it makes you happy, then why the hell are you so sad?" She ambled over to the bedside table and carefully lifted up the book Shane suggested, *The Bliss List.*

Brooke eased into her chair while staring at the yellow brick road cover and opened to her loose-leaf page of her Bliss list. Rereading it, she set the day's itinerary—horseback riding, then a sunset stroll by her special spot. She dressed—Tar Heels hat, Salty Dog T-shirt, and white skirt—then drove to Starbucks, whistling the song.

White cup in hand, she lifted the cover and inhaled, then sipped the 175-degree quad espresso. For no apparent reason, Brooke pictured

Chase riding a horse, both bare-back. She laughed. *I wonder if he still thinks of me.*

"Whenever I see your smiling face..." drew a glare from a twenty-something mother sitting nearby, who then peered into her stroller. When she glanced back up, Brooke mouthed *sorry.* Pressing ignore on Melissa's number made Brooke feel a twinge of guilt. She lifted her cup and sipped slowly, glad it wasn't so darn hot anymore.

Brooke dialed Melissa from the car.

"Hey stranger, long time no talk." Melissa's tone managed to mix cynical with sarcastic.

"I'm sorry we keep missing each other."

"When are you coming back?"

"Soon," Brooke breathed a sigh of relief. She hoped she didn't have to lie.

"Any luck on the job front?"

"No, don't remind me. I've been trying to forget about the w-word."

After a pause, Melissa said, "I have an idea for you?"

"Not you now. Have you been talking to my daddy too?" *Oops, I hope she doesn't pick up on that one.*

"How is good ole Weston?"

"Fine."

"Well, he probably wouldn't approve of this one, but ..."

Brooke laughed, "Now you piqued my interest."

"I thought about something you said to me that night. This is going to sound strange, but how about a preschool?"

Preschool. Brooke pondered, running her fingernails through her hair, then said, "What do you mean?"

"A close friend of my mother just found out she has cancer. She's owned a successful preschool for years. I'm not sure how much—"

"Oh my God—owning a preschool sounds meaningful. You have an uncanny way of reading my mind—even when I can't read it myself."

"Her name's Betsy Stanton. Want her number?"

Slamming the door, he said, "Sit down," then marched to his chair that he always kept higher than the rest. "I thought I could count on you."

Chase fidgeted in the tight leather seat, "What are you talking about?"

Henry's glare intensified, illuminated by the fluorescent light set against the gloomy sky behind him. He said, "I'm not here to judge you. What's done is done. Your timing couldn't be worse. We don't need this right now."

"Sir, with all due respect, I have no idea what you're referring to."

"Don't insult me. I didn't get this far because of my looks," Henry frowned, red faced. "I know all about your affair, so you don't have to lie to me. I thought you were smarter than that."

Chase gulped, his dry mouth nearly choked him. "I … I… don't know what to say."

"Don't say anything Goddammit! To anybody. Sever all contact with that *girl*. I mean it."

"Yes sir," Chase glanced down.

"You better hope I can make this go away quietly. You've put our image in danger—not to mention what this will do to your marriage. I feel sorry for your lovely, devoted wife—back home with your son— while you …" Henry drew a deep breath, "Have you told her?"

"No sir." Chase's eyes remained fixed on the floor.

"I can't even imagine what this scandal would do to our stock."

Stepping off the elevator, Chase felt as if he wore concrete shoes. Once past the security station, he vaguely heard, "Where's your raincoat, sir? It's bad out there." Without responding, Chase pulled his tie like he was hanging himself until it loosened. Then, he popped the top button off his shirt, and lurched into the downpour. The instant soaking didn't faze him—he felt like he was hiking across a lagoon with alligators snapping from every direction.

I can't believe she'd do this. I thought we had something, but that's just my luck with women. I sure know how to pick them. Now I know why she wouldn't take my calls. I can only imagine Henry when he learns the truth about my devoted wife. I have to make sure that doesn't happen.

Time to make that call.

— ♥ —

"I have something crazy to run by you."

"Nothing's too crazy for my ears. Try me."

"Well, I thought about what you told me."

"And?"

"I've been going over things and I think I'm ready to go in a different direction."

"Oh."

"With your blessing, of course."

"You don't need my blessing." Shane sounded aggravated.

Brooke said, "I'm thinking about a quantum leap—buying a preschool."

Long pause, then Shane said, "That's not a crazy idea. After reading your Bliss list, working with children fits you perfectly. It's tricky to start up your own—"

"That's the great thing. I'm meeting with a lady who needs to sell her preschool business. She's stricken with cancer and desperately wants to turn it over to the right person. She would stay on to train me and help out as long as she could. It's located about twenty minutes away."

Brooke rambled, breathless and excited, "I have no idea what it would cost and I don't have teacher certification other than my minor in child development, but I know how to run a business and I love kids. I have a good feeling about this one."

Shane inhaled, then said, "That's wonderful. Don't look at it as a leap; see it as a divine calling. When you follow your heart, doors open magically."

"You can say that again. My friend Melissa actually provided the idea and introduction, but you're giving me confidence. I figure if everything feels right, I'll try it for six months. If it doesn't work, I can always return to the corporate world."

"Don't even think like that. We're going to bury the corporate world and never look back. From this moment forward, you're going to focus on happiness and fulfillment. Along those lines, I'd like to see you use your maiden name in your new venture."

— ♥ —

Brooke Ingram drove across the bridge feeling a sense of joy that, five days ago, didn't seem possible. Swirling winds and dark clouds didn't seem as scary now. Discarding her iPod, and all its memories, she flipped on a classic rock station—"Good Day Sunshine." She surveyed the swaying palm branches and smiled.

Just past the halfway point, the radio station became nothing but static and the traffic was at a standstill. Brooke turned off the radio and opened her notebook. She flipped to her notes from the Shane sessions and a quote stuck out: "The most interesting people can spend an hour alone and be happy." *Be, do, have* in action. Brooke realized though by herself, she never felt alone. Traffic resumed and for the rest of the drive, Brooke reflected on the past few days and sensed *meaning* was one doorway away.

Pulling into the entrance, Brooke felt a sense of awe. Her heart stirred in a way that reminded her of Hilton Head. Set inside the extended branches like the heart of a flower, Angel's Academy Learning Center opened hands of compassion. Brooke was home.

Betsy Stanton had the appearance Brooke knew so well. Although by 5:30 p.m., Betsy looked as if she could sleep for the night. Brooke had a million questions. She scrutinized the feeble lady, but decided against overburdening her.

Brooke felt a divine kinship to Betsy when she said, "My husband and I were never blessed with children of our own ..." Then Betsy unwittingly sealed the deal by pleading for Brooke to keep Marsha Thomas, her loyal assistant who couldn't afford to lose her job, and the other teacher that had been with her for years.

Brooke said, "Angel's Academy is a godsend for me."

Betsy said, "Having you here now is a godsend for me. You should see how it all works. Come spend a week with us before you make any decisions. Plus, I'll be able to stay on for a while."

They agreed with a handshake—so different from the legal wrangling of the contractual corporate world. Speaking with Betsy, Brooke felt she had surveyed the mirror of time—and gazed past the cancer—and saw herself. She loved her reflection.

"I think you're committing career suicide."

"Ouch. Those are harsh words, Daddy."

"You're throwing away your chance to be a CEO."

"Technically, I am the CEO of Angel's Academy."

"Don't try to be funny."

"I'm dead serious about this." Brooke's jaw tightened.

"You should think about—"

"I've given it plenty of thought. It's hard to explain. I don't expect you to understand, but I'm a big girl now. I *need* to do this."

"Be reasonable. Listen to—"

"Hey, if it doesn't work out, I can always go back to the jungle."

"I'll make one more point. Please consider all the time you've put in building such an impressive resume."

"I have. Trust me, I have. In my heart of hearts, I know working with children is my true calling and always has been. Please support me on this."

"I've made my case."

"I love you, Daddy."

"Love you too."

As Brooke hung up, she stared at the phone. She expected her father's opposition. He sounded just like a reluctant buyer during a sales call or the debate team captain with his last comment. Now that it ended, her neck muscles loosened.

With Weston Ingram, Esquire, in her rearview mirror, Brooke went online and read everything she could on preschoolers. She soaked in each tidbit of information just like her little students—and couldn't wait to start school.

Day one of her preview week arrived with great anticipation. When Brooke entered at seven o'clock—one hour before the kids arrived—Betsy looked refreshed. After introducing Brooke to Marsha and the other teacher, Miss Charlotte, Betsy let them get acquainted. Brooke had a good feeling about Marsha as her Assistant Director. She recognized she was organized and vital to the operations, but she liked her as a person. Brooke followed her gut instinct and reassured Marsha that her job would be safe.

Marsha prepared name tags for each child. The plan called for Brooke to observe all week and, if still interested, they would ink the deal. No need to inform the sometimes uppity parents until then. At eight sharp, Betsy and Marsha opened the door, allowing the children to enter in single file. Brooke noticed several parents carefully eyeing her as she stood beside Betsy and Marsha. Brooke marveled at how polite the children acted. At three years old, the kids were more courteous than business people. Then her eyes widened.

"Hey, I know you," Brooke said while placing her hand on the little boy's shoulder.

He glanced up, stunned, then said, "You're the nice sand castle lady."

Brooke beamed, "Yeah, we kept the sharks out, Parker, right?"

"Yes." All washed up, in his cute little outfit, he looked even more adorable than she remembered.

Betsy stepped in, grinning, and said, "I see you already know Parker. He's one of my favorites." Parker beamed.

Brooke waved at the woman in the last remaining vehicle, guessing it was Parker's mother. She looked so young—and familiar. Brooke frowned. *I don't remember seeing her face—she was lying on the towel the entire time.*

Once inside and settled, Betsy said, "We have a new helper. I want y'all to welcome Miss Ingram." Brooke noticed the *y'all.*

In unison, they replied, "Hello, Miss Ingram."

Brooke smiled at the tender expressions, their bright eyes full of enthusiasm. Glancing around the room, she instantly fell in love with each child. They were her doll collection coming to life. Observing Betsy with the kids ignited Brooke's maternal instincts. Betsy had a natural gift for compassion—one that Brooke hoped would transfer. She could feel herself evolving to a world where boardrooms and money didn't matter. All that mattered was helping the dolls in the room. Brooke found her bliss.

Two days later, Brooke signed a one-page contract on good faith and little else.

A note was handed to each child on Friday announcing the news. Betsy didn't want any fuss and felt grateful her prayer was answered.

— ♥ —

I wondered what was going on, Oksana thought as she read the note. *Mr. Allman will be sad to see Miss Stanton leave. That's the last thing he needs to worry about, after I just told him about the new call from Heather. I wonder if she even knows it is her son's birthday tomorrow.*

Later that night, when she thought Parker was out of range, Oksana broke the news to Chase about Angel's Academy.

"I like Miss Ingram," Parker's eyes gleamed as he ran over.

"That's good to hear, champ. We'll have to say a special prayer for Miss Stanton. That reminds me. You've got a big day tomorrow. Time for bed."

"Can we do that ride again?" Parker's enthusiasm made everyone smile. He loved every moment of his birthday party; he rode every ride he could, usually with either his dad or Oksana—so he wouldn't upset his friends, who all wanted to ride with the birthday boy.

While Parker dragged Oksana into the famous Fun House for the second time, Mary strolled up to Chase, and said, "What do you think of the changes at Angel's Academy?"

"Parker seems to like his new teacher. I'm glad, but it'll be hard to fill Betsy's shoes."

Mary contemplated her response, "I don't know anything about this new owner. She looks so fresh and pink—and she has no experience."

"I had a suspicion Betsy was sick. I don't get over there enough, but the last time, she didn't look good. I'm going to call and wish her well and try to get the lowdown. If Betsy picked the new owner, I'm sure she'll do just fine."

After finishing the thirteen-mile Run for the Cure, Brooke began week two with relaxed confidence. She had already read the books she bought on owning a preschool. In addition, Brooke interviewed every mother she could—including complete strangers. She soaked in all the information like a child.

Brooke's favorite part of the job was reading the stories at the end of the day. Her new life blossomed. In two short weeks, Brooke felt like a seasoned professional. Even though the contract was signed and the check had cleared, Betsy still visited each day. Betsy released the reigns, staying in the background like a safety net.

At the end of the week, with two hours to go, Betsy strode up to Brooke during the end of the kids' reflection time, wrapped her warm arm around her, and said, "You are doing great. I feel like I'm just getting in the way. I'd wish you good luck, but I can tell you won't need it. I'll be here if I can help you in any way."

Just like Brooke's track days, Betsy passed the baton, and Brooke seized it, happy for the chance to prove herself. This race had meaning.

"Hold still." Duke's ears flinched and then he froze.

Hearing the beep, Chase left a message, "Max, it's Chase. Listen, I don't want to be a pest, but, she tried calling again … I hope you've had some luck … Call me if you locate her."

Chase released Duke's chain, then raced him toward Parker who was playing on the monkey bars at the park. Chase led out of the gate, but Duke loped by his owner with ease. Pulling up to a giggling Parker, Chase's lungs felt as if they were filled with napalm while Duke looked ready for more.

"Duke beat you."

"He's … so … fast."

"I'll race you," Parker swung off the metal ladder and landed beside his father; he balled his fists in the ready stance.

Chase chuckled, "Not right now, buddy. Duke tired me out. How's school?"

"Miss Ingram's nice."

"Nicer than Miss Stanton?"

Parker nodded in an exaggerated motion with wide eyes.

"That's good. How is she different?"

"She tells stories about sharks and dragons and she's pretty like Mommy."

Chase winced; Parker's innocent statement struck Chase, now bracing for the follow-up question. *I bet Parker heard Oksana talking the other day. Funny, he never mentioned Heather during his entire birthday, including bedtime—when kids thought such things. I wish she'd quit bugging poor Oksana. Why did I ever get married?*

Chase glanced at Parker and smiled, "C'mon, you ready to race?"

Parker pointed, "First one to the sidewalk."

"You're on."

Parker said, "ReadySetGo," then took off. Chase laughed, affecting his strength like kryptonite. He finally caught up to Parker, which prompted a determined look that made Chase laugh again. Parker won.

Chase's grin made his ears pop. His son's gleeful celebration was better than Olympic gold. *I wish I could spend more time with him—he's growing up so fast. Maybe, I'll surprise him at school next week.*

— ♥ —

"You look great, what are you talking about?"

"I'm fat and you know it, Miss ant-sized jeans." Melissa poked her fork at her salad.

"You're supposed to gain weight. It's healthy." Brooke figured Melissa wouldn't budge, but she couldn't agree and make her feel worse.

"Eddie thinks I'm fat."

"What!" Brooke's eyes swirled in a blaze, "Does he call you fat?"

"Not exactly. But, he doesn't touch me the same way as before."

"He's probably afraid of hurting the baby. I read that in one of my books. Eddie actually told me he loved your glow."

"When?" Melissa furrowed her brows.

"The other day, remember when he answered your cell?"

"He said that?"

"You look good. Relax, your hormones are raging."

Melissa clasped her stomach, sighed, "I heard Betsy Stanton was impressed with you. Tell me about your new career?"

"Oh my God, Betsy has a glow too—like Mother Teresa. She's taught me so much. It's hard to motivate kids to look forward to school, but she's amazing. I feel reborn. Those kids are so cute. You're a lifesaver, once again. Please tell your mother how grateful I am."

"Can you make any money in the preschool business?"

"You sound like my daddy." They both shared a hearty laugh that made the neighboring tables stop and stare. Brooke ignored them, and edged closer, "Betsy had a great manager who has agreed to stay for all that nasty record keeping. I'm going to finally apply my minor degree in child psychology. And this is going to sound strange, but I'm not doing it for the money. I'd do this job for free. It's hard to explain, but I feel such love and warmth for those kids, as if they're my own."

"Wow. Most people in daycare say the opposite."

"We don't call it daycare. Betsy created the concept of a learning center. And that's exactly what it is."

"That's a stretch. Aren't they just three-year-olds?"

"Three and four, but I really feel like I'm making a difference in those kids. They soak in everything like sponges. There's one little boy who's adorable—I could take him home with me."

With the kids in the beginning of their reflection time, Brooke had pulled Marsha aside and said, "I have to run to the insurance office and sign some documents. It shouldn't take more than a half hour. Can you cover for me until I return?"

Marsha smiled and said, "Take your time. I love reading stories and have a good one in mind. We'll be fine."

"Thanks, I'm so thrilled to have you." Marsha's eyes said ditto.

"The secret of success is to make your vocation your vacation." Brooke had heard the Twain quote before, but now she understood what it meant. She felt alive. Her nightmares had dissipated and, even though Tanner still visited her in her sleep, the dreams were now peaceful.

At the end of her third week—Friday the thirteenth—she hit her groove. Usually a bit superstitious, today Brooke felt better than a vacation. Surfing on a wave of gratitude, she picked up her cell.

"So how's it going?" Shane's zeal was better than coffee—even a quad espresso.

"I can't believe how much I love it. I have amazing kids who ask some off-the-wall questions. I have to be more alert around three-year-olds than I ever had to be in the business world."

"Sounds like you really made a fresh start. What do the kids call you?"

"Miss Ingram."

"Awesome."

"It took a short while to get used to, but I have to say you were right, as always. I don't know what I'd do without you."

"That's what I love about you. You award me credit, even though you did it all yourself."

Hanging up with Shane, Brooke smiled as she climbed into her car.

Brooke punched the address into GPS and waited as it searched for a signal. *Aren't satellites like cell phones? These things take more time than a laptop.* After three minutes that seemed like thirty, Brooke sped off just as a black squirrel darted in front of her car. She slammed her brakes and felt a thump under her tire. "Oh man, poor little guy." As she opened her car door, the spooked critter scurried away.

Brooke drove on like she was in a scary movie with one of those leave-you-hanging endings. So far, no roadside black cats running in front of the car or giant ladders to drive under. Not concentrating on the road, she missed the speed bump sign as her car heaved like a bucking bronco, then landed with a crack and a thud. She pulled to the curb and stopped.

That was a friggin' huge speed bump.

Brooke opened her door and surveyed the front—bumper intact, nothing leaking. She climbed back into her car. Pulling away, her car pulled. *Now what?*

With images of a black cat, she jumped out. And noticed something worse—a black flat. Her rear passenger tire was deflated down to the rim. "Oh shit."

Brooke surveyed the deserted block and stormed to the passenger side door just as her heel caught and she smacked face first into the grass. She froze and did a quick mental body scan. Realizing her pain was only emotional, she slowly stood while gripping the door handle. Her ankles felt fine, but her leg was smeared—

Brooke's eyes bulged as it registered: "Gross. Dog shit! Why can't people pick up after their damn dogs!"

Brooke dialed Shane, who laughed so hard he couldn't speak. Brooke chuckled—quite a bit less than Shane—and said, "Only you can cheer me up even though I'm covered with dog shit."

"I'm afraid comic relief is all I can do for you right now. I can't change a flat telepathically."

Brooke popped the hood, put on her hazard lights, and listened to Shane's instructions. She didn't even know she had a spare tire and, frowning at her dress, wondered if he could talk her through changing it. On her knees, trying to force the lug wrench onto the first bolt, she heard a snap as pain shot up her hand.

"Shit."

"What's wrong?"

"I just bent my nail all the way back."

Brooke growled as Shane attempted to calm her. She surveyed the ground, knelt back down, and struggled to remove the remaining bolts.

"I can scratch mechanic off my list," Brooke wiped her brow with the back of her hand, not realizing she decorated her forehead with war paint.

Shane chuckled, "You didn't tell me that was on your Bliss list."

"Ha Ha."

Forty minutes later, Brooke successfully changed her first flat tire. "Thank you, Shane. You're a life ..." She glanced at her cell and noticed it was dead. "Oh great. Shit!" *I guess I can't meet the insurance agent like this.*

Brooke pulled into a grocery store lot and carefully positioned her baby tire two feet from the curb under a *No Parking* sign. She flipped on her hazards and darted inside. A guy in a smock stocking bananas did a double take at her and pointed, "The bathroom's in the back, by the meat counter."

Brooke lurched like an NFL running back around gawking onlookers. Once inside the bathroom, she flipped on the light and shrieked, "Oh nice, I look scary."

I'm lucky they didn't call a battered women's shelter.

The liquid soap only spread the grease. After using the entire roll of paper towels and most of the toilet paper, she finally recognized herself. Even though she triple washed her knee, she still felt a weird sensation—like an amputee with a recently removed limb.

Dang, I'll miss the kids' send off again. Thank God Marsha's there.

On the return walk, Mister Smock smirked, then nodded. Brooke coasted to Angel's Academy with the hazards still flashing.

19

"Thank God you're here!"

Brooke ignored Marsha's teary eyes, and with her eyes popping, she gasped, "YOU! What the …?"

His head craned as if trying to crack it. With furrowed brows, Chase said, "Me? Why are *you* here?"

Brooke glanced at Marsha, whose tears streamed across her quivering lips, then back at Chase.

Chase said, "Unless you're here to help me find my son, quit stalking me."

Brooke's eyes narrowed, "What are you talking about? And what are you doing to my employee in front of my business?"

"Your business?" Chase shook his head, then glanced at Marsha, who nodded, but still couldn't speak. He glared at Brooke, "Yes, Parker is gone … Since when do you own this place?"

"I just bought it—that's not important. Where's Parker? What happened?"

"My son has been kidnapped," Chase glared back at Marsha, and barked, "Where is Miss Ingram?"

Brooke stood stock straight, "I'm Miss Ingram."

"What?"

"I'm Brooke Ingram, and unless you tell me what the hell's going on, I'm calling 911."

Chase gulped, then closed his eyes, hands running up and down his head. His eyes met Brooke's, and through tight lips, "My son Parker has been kidnapped—"

"Your son is Parker?" Brooke's knees wobbled.

"Yes, and I was supposed to pick him up. Usually Oksana—his nanny—picks him up, but I was going to surprise him. His mother, who ..." Chase paused, glimpsed to the right, then continued, "Let's just say his mother is dangerous and is not allowed to see him without my permission."

Brooke opened her cell and said, "I'm calling 911."

Chase lunged and snapped the phone shut, "No!"

Marsha raised one eyebrow and tilted her head. Chase pleaded, "No, seriously, it's complicated."

"It's not complicated to me. Parker's missing, you say he's kidnapped by a dangerous ... whoever she is. I have to call the police."

"I, I don't think Parker's in grave danger," Chase touched his nose, "This is a domestic dispute. I, um, I need to talk to my lawyer before we call the cops. Please don't call the police."

Chase imagined the headlines staring Henry in the face—right before next week's board meeting; Brooke pictured different headlines, ending her new life before the one month mark. She thought, *Shit, am I even insured?*

"I need to document this incident," Brooke avoided the word *liability*—especially to a lawyer. "Marsha, what happened?"

"I was reading the kids a story when Rache's grandmother entered with a much younger, well-dressed lady. Rache peered at me and I nodded. Parker said, 'Mommy,' and ran to the pretty woman's outstretched arms. I went back to *Snow White* since we had a half hour left until pick up. I just assumed ..." She sobbed.

Chase frowned, "Marsha, you knew only Oksana and I were authorized to pick up Parker."

Marsha fidgeted, then said, "I forgot, Mr. Allman. I was on my own for a little while."

"You're not blaming Marsha?" Brooke grimaced.

Chase said, "I know I told Betsy that only Oksana and I—"

"Who's Oksana?" Brooke cut in.

"Oksana is Parker's nanny. Haven't you met her? What kind of place—"

"Hold on, mister," Brooke wrapped her arms across her chest, "I just bought the place. If parents haven't introduced themselves to me, I wouldn't know who's who yet. I supervise each child's arrival and departure with Marsha."

"Not today ..." Chase flashed a condescending scowl.

"No, I, I'm sorry, I wasn't here, I had, uh, an appointment."

"All I want to do is find Parker as quickly and quietly as possible." Chase marched toward his BMW.

Brooke said, "I'm coming along."

He stopped and twisted his head over his shoulder in a pained expression, "You're what?"

"I said, I'm coming. Parker's in danger, I'm not stopping until he's safe."

Without the police, he needed assistance. He said, "You want to help? Fine, I accept. For starters, I could use a description of the vehicle she was driving."

Brooke glanced at Marsha, who shrugged her shoulders, saying, "I was inside reading a story when she left."

"I'll call Rache's grandma. She was right there."

Chase frowned, "What are you going to say?"

"I'll start by asking how Rache is doing with the transition and thank her for her continued support. Then I'll ask her if she saw what kind of car Parker's mom left in."

Chase agreed, "Yeah, good, good discretion."

Discretion? Brooke smirked, "I'll call them right now from here. Give me your cell number."

Chase held the phone above his head and said, "Only if you lift the call block."

"Yes, don't worry ..."

Marsha creased her eyebrows, but remained silent.

Chase headed toward his car, saying, "Call me when you're done."

Driving away, Chase called Oksana and broke the news to her. He could barely understand her—the more upset she became, the worse her English sounded. He finally calmed her enough to reason with her.

Chase said, "Grab the binoculars—in the kitchen drawer—and sit where you can see the entrances. If they show up, write down the license number, color, and type of car. Don't confront them—just hide."

"Should I call the police?"

"No! Do not call the police. Call me right away."

Chase dialed Max's number—voicemail again. *Sheesh, I wonder where he's been?* Chase's head spun. He pulled over and retrieved a legal pad from his briefcase. With eyes closed, he visualized who, what, where, and why—*why did she take him? What was she doing? Where?* Then, it came ...

Chase sped over to Chuck E. Cheese—the same place he took Parker. He skirted a red light and nearly crashed into a U-Haul. His heart pounded and his hands slipped on the steering wheel. Not taking any chances, he screeched to a halt at the entrance and jumped out. Ripping open the glass door, he scanned the restaurant like a Secret Service agent—no Parker.

"Sir, you can't park there—"

"Huh?" Chase glared at the pimply-faced teenager with the name tag "Gus, Assistant Mgr." Chase continued, "I know, listen, this is an emergency. I'm looking for my son."

"Missing child? Do you want me to call the cops?"

"No, I already did," Chase rubbed his nose, then asked, "Has a little boy with dark hair and a blue shirt come in here with his mommy?"

The kid smirked, "All the time. Look around, that's our market."

Chase sighed, then flashed a picture of Parker to Gus, "Here's my card, please call if they come in here."

Back in the car, he closed his eyes and another spot came to mind. He drove to the playground near the house—no Parker. Then, another playground—no Parker. He dialed Max again—voicemail.

Chase typed "hotels" in his smart phone's GPS and frowned. There's no way I can hit a hundred and thirty hotels. He narrowed the list by locale. *I wonder if she brought what's-his-name along? Rusty, was it? What was his last name? I bet they put the room in his name since I cancelled all her credit cards.*

"C'mon, Max, answer." Voicemail—dammit. Chase scanned the hotel list again and one name stood out—Embassy Suites: two bedrooms, in case Heather brought her druggie boyfriend. He still couldn't remember Rusty's last name. He dialed Max again—voicemail. *Where the hell are you?*

While showing the Embassy Suites manager Parker's picture, Chase's stomach roiled—Rusty would probably check in while Heather stayed in the car with Parker. Other than height and that he was a loser, Chase couldn't provide much of a description. He didn't even know Rusty's real first name. He went back to the car.

"Duke, Duke, Duke of Earl" rang out. He wiped his eyes and squinted at the caller ID—I know that number.

Chase answered, "I hope you had better luck than me. How about Rache's grandma?"

"I don't have her cell and neither parent is answering. I've left three messages."

Chase drew a deep breath, then recapped his efforts in one lengthy sentence—suppressing his frustration.

"What should we do?" Brooke's voice cracked.

"I don't know what else to do other than go to each hotel."

Brooke dabbed her eyes, then said, "Maybe we should call the police—"

"No! The police are out of the question."

Brooke said, "Then let's hit every hotel we can. One of us can search the parking lot while the other talks to the front desk."

Chase sighed, "Good idea. That would really help. I'm not thinking straight."

They decided to meet at the next Courtyard on the list. Plugging in the address, Chase drove off before the GPS lady spoke her wisdom. A flash on his dashboard caught his eye—shit, that's all I need.

He pulled to the curb and typed in "Fuel," hoping he had enough fuel to make it. His range button deflated his hope. Chase pictured himself pushing his BMW to Mobil and steadied his foot to twenty-five. The station was just over a mile away. He focused like a jaguar stalking its prey—and prayed.

With the Mobil sign in sight, Chase surveyed the starless sky, and said, "Thank you." Coasting into an open spot, he guessed he made it on fumes.

A car pulled up to the opposite pump. "Chase? Is that you?"

"Huh?" Chase turned toward the familiar voice and squinted.

"Remember me?"

"Yeah." Chase stalled for time—good with faces, lousy with names—she looked familiar. He said, "From the club ..."

She said, "I go at least a year without seeing you guys, and, here, in the same day, I see you *and* Heather."

Chase chortled nervously, then asked, "How've you been?"

"Busy carting kids around. You know the drill. Parker's grown so much," she smiled, and scanning up and down, said, "He looks just like you."

Chase's head buzzed, "Where did you run into Heather?"

"I think I saw her at Target."

Chase paused. She finally said, "I'm jealous—my husband doesn't take us anywhere fun—have a nice trip."

"Come again?"

"Vacation. I mean have a nice vacation." Chase's eyes widened. She said, "Parker told Joshua you guys were going to Disney. He's so excited. Hey, weren't you supposed to leave—"

"Oh, thanks for reminding me. I'm late. Good to see you."

"Why isn't daddy flying us to see Mickey, Mommy?"

Heather glared at Rusty, whose smirk distanced her from the answer. She inhaled, then said, "Oh, honey, I hope he's going to be able to meet us there. He has a lot of work. He told me he'd try." Parker sighed. Heather continued, "We'll have so much fun. I hope you're tall enough for all the big boy rides."

Parker's eyes widened, "Like Frankie's Fun House?"

"Where's that?"

"My birthday party. Daddy went on all the rides with me."

"Oh. The place I'm taking you to is called the Magic Kingdom."

Parker looked confused, "Is it bigger than Frankie's?"

Heather said, "It's much bigger than Frankie's. And they have Mickey Mouse. You're going to love Disney."

Rusty lit a joint and by the time Heather shot him a glare, he had already taken a hit. He handed it to Heather, who inhaled a quick hit, then passed it back.

"You shouldn't smoke. Smoking is bad," Parker proclaimed, eyes widened.

Rusty laughed, then sucked a long drag and coughed as he handed it back to Heather. She waved him off, but he held it in front of her for a few seconds. She grabbed it and took a fast hit, then said, "No more, unless you wanna drive." Rusty tucked his chin into his chest and shook his head in short sideways bursts.

Heather squinted in the rearview at the wide-eyed Parker, "Mommy's trying to quit smoking. Don't you ever start, you hear me?"

Parker shook his head in an exaggerated motion, "Will you go on all the rides with me if daddy's not there?"

"Absolutely." Heather glanced at Rusty, who ducked out on his cue to speak.

"Are we almost there?"

Rusty snickered, Heather frowned, "No, honey, it's kind of a long drive."

Parker sighed, "I wish we could fly with Daddy. Can you play "Baby Beluga"?"

"I don't think we have that one."

"How about "Shake My Sillies Out"? Daddy always sings it with me."

"Nope, let's just talk—I haven't seen you for so long."

"I'm hungry. Can we go to Chuck E. Cheese?"

Heather fidgeted, then inspected the bag on the floor between Rusty's baggy jeans, and said, "We'll be stopping soon."

—— ♥ ——

"Before I start this plane, we gotta clear the air first."

Brooke glanced away, saying, "Whatever."

"What is your problem?"

"My problem? My problem? That's a good one." Brooke's face filled with rage.

"Seriously, what is your problem?" Chase stared at Brooke.

Chase unbuckled his shoulder straps and noticed his neck tighten, and heart thump. "Why wouldn't you talk to me?"

Brooke glared into his furrowed eyes, "I did."

"No, you didn't. You called me names and hung up on me twice. I was just trying to—"

"Wait, you expect me to listen to you harass me."

"*Harass* you? We had an amazing night together, then you—"

"Let me offer you a concise executive recap. You fuck me, fire me, then joke about giving me my *pink slip*, then tell me you have a *big package* for me. Then you won't stop calling. How do you define harassment?"

Chase's eyes widened, "You can't possibly think I had anything to do with you losing your job?"

"You can't be serious?"

"I'm serious."

"So, if I'm getting this straight, you're saying that you, the CEO, had nothing to do with me getting fired right after we made love?"

"Oh, my God, I can't believe you'd actually think …" Chase's eyes darted, "Is that why you blocked my calls?"

"I blocked your calls because you were harassing me. You're no different than Dix—"

"Stop using that word! I did NOT *harass* you. I still can't believe you called my boss."

Brooke shuddered, "I don't even know who your boss is, I would never—"

"So you're denying you registered a complaint—"

"Why would I do that? Now that you mention it, I should have—after you waved the *pink slip* in my face."

"I still sleep with it and since you're acting this way, I may never return it to you."

Brooke's eyes widened. "What did you just say?"

"The sexy pink slip you left in our room. I've been trying to—"

"Oh … my … God."

"You know it still has your fragrance …"

Brooke's jaw dropped as it registered.

Chase said, "I can't believe you never signed the new severance package."

Package? Brooke said, "Hold on! The only severance package I got was a lousy two weeks."

"Duh, that's what I'm talking about. I almost got fired over the new, much bigger package we offered and I wrote you that letter …"

Bigger package? Brooke laughed out loud.

Chase frowned, "I'm glad you think it's funny that I almost lost my job."

"You're either the world's greatest con artist or …"

"Con artist, geez thanks. Or what?" Chase crossed his arms across his puffed out chest.

"So when you called me the second time, when you said you had a big package for me," Brooke giggled, "you were talking about—"

Their eyes locked as it hit them and they burst into laughter.

"Just so you know, Chase, I never received any note from you—or voicemail. And the only severance from Pharm-my-ass was two lousy weeks."

Chase eyed her with slight disbelief. She sounded genuine, as if she actually believed what she said. "C'mon, you're saying you missed the big manila envelope with my handwritten note AND my voicemail?"

Brooke hesitated, glanced to the left, then said, "Well, I probably tossed it if it had your little company logo on it and I honestly didn't get that voicemail ..."

"Or you erased it."

"Don't look at me like that. I'm not crazy. Answer me one question: how can you say you didn't have me fired? The timing was a little suspect." Brooke inhaled his fragrance—as if for the first time.

"Henry Stoddard's turned from friend to foe. I had lunch with him and he mentioned the company was looking to outsource your division. I fought with him and he led me to believe it wasn't a done deal. Then I played golf Friday afternoon—the day before you and I ... Well, Henry decided to ignore what I said. He weaseled a quick meeting with Greenberg without me and they decided to undo everything I built. I took off Sunday and Monday to take Parker fishing and then the beach."

"Fishing? Did you go shark fishing?"

"How did you know?"

Brooke's pulse froze and her head spun. "Oh my God. You're not kidding, are you?"

"No, we went shark—"

"Not that ... You must think I'm coo coo."

"That would be an understatement. Look, I know you think our magical night together was a mistake but ..."

"Shhhhhh," Brooke placed her finger on Chase's lips. He raised one brow and still looked good to Brooke. She said, "I ... I'm such an idiot!"

—— ♥ ——

The dye took longer than she had hoped—no thanks to Rusty's "medicine chest"—but Parker's new hairdo would work. And he looked so different in the new clothes.

Rusty said, "Now, you're stylin just like me."

Parker sloshed across the nasty carpet to the dimly lit motel room mirror and laughed. "I look funny. Can I be this for Halloween?"

Heather smiled, "Sure, honey, anything you want."

"I'm hungry. Can we go to Chuck E. Cheese now?"

Rusty snorted, "Little guy's got the munchies—me too."

Heather rubbed his spiked hair and said, "Sorry, there aren't any nearby, sweetie."

Rusty said, "Eat those chips I bought ya, kid. Or else, give 'em to me—I'll eat 'em. Friggin spoiled—"

"Rusty, shut up. He doesn't have to eat those if he doesn't want to."

Parker's eyes widened—*he'd never heard big people talk like this.*

"Isn't it time the little guy went to bed, so me and momma can party?" Rusty slapped Heather's backside.

Heather glared at Rusty, then faced Parker, "Honey, you should get to bed."

Parker eyed the twin beds, "Where's my PJs?"

"Just sleep in your clothes tonight. We'll get you some tomorrow. Now, just go to bed, okay, Mommy's tired." Rusty lurched in behind her and gripped her like a backpack. She giggled, Parker frowned.

Parker said, "Don't I have to brush my teeth first?"

"No, remind me tomorrow to get you a toothbrush. Now, please just go to bed."

Parker trudged over to the bed like a condemned prisoner en route to the gallows. He pulled the bedspread back, then crawled in slowly. He said, "Are we going to say my special prayers?"

"Huh?"

"Daddy always says my special prayers and stays with me until I fall asleep."

Rusty sneered, then said, "There is no God kid—"

"Shut up Rusty—you're stoned—and you're scaring the poor kid," Heather rubbed her eyes, then squinted at Parker, "Why don't you say your prayers tonight, okay, I've got a real bad headache." Rusty snickered, then wheezed.

Parker's lip trembled, "Can I call Daddy?"

"Your daddy's working and doesn't want us to bother him. Now go to bed."

Parker pulled the covers tightly under his chin, and forced his eyes shut. Heather and Rusty flipped off the light, then went outside, carrying their bag.

Though the Q & A war paused into a cease fire, battles remained. Brooke still had major questions—like the wife issue. *And who was the young chick he waltzed into the hotel with?* Though he seemed sincere, she was skeptical, unable to double-check his answers. After all, his best friend was called dawg. *I wish I could hook him to a lie detector.*

Chase still doubted Brooke's denial of blowing the whistle to Henry. He remembered *All the President's Men* and snickered. He had taken extra care to tell no one—including Dixon. That left only one person. But she seemed definitive. *I wish I could hook her to a lie detector.*

They ascended into a sky darkened by night's unseen clouds. With a storm forecast, Chase wondered if they'd make it to Orlando. They lost valuable time and fuel arguing, but it beat crashing due to their fight erupting in the air.

"So what is the plan?" Brooke decided to shelve her most pressing questions.

"I know they're heading to Disney, and I'm hoping by car. If my information is correct, they'll have Minnesota plates."

"How do you know that?"

Chase paused, "I hired a private investigator to follow my wife."

"Wife? You told me you weren't married." *So much for the shelving.*

Chase fidgeted, "I, uh, I'm getting a divorce."

"That's what they all say ..."

"My situation is complicated."

"They all are. Why'd you wear a wedding band?"

"Look, I know you wouldn't believe me if I told you the truth."

"Try me."

Chase tugged at his collar, "Oh hell, all right, what I'm about to say is highly confidential. It stays in this cockpit, understood?"

"Who would I possibly tell?"

Chase smirked, "Before I go any further, I have to get something off my chest." Brooke raised one eyebrow and froze. Chase said, "I didn't tell anyone about us. I don't understand how my boss knew ..."

"Oh God, we're back to that one again." She continued, "First of all, I don't even know your boss, never met the man. How could I possibly ... You can't possibly think I'd do that?"

"What about Greenberg? Did you tell him?"

"Let me say this clearly: I ... told ... nobody." Brooke's stomach twinged as Melissa popped in her head. She couldn't contradict herself now. *Melissa would never ...*

Chase stared at Brooke and neither one flinched. Brooke marveled at his flying prowess, able to hold a stare down, yet keep the plane steady. *Is there anything this man can't do?*

Brooke broke the awkward silence,, "You're going to have to trust me. I didn't tell Henry or anyone at Pharmical. I'm here to help find Parker." She braced herself for the qualifier.

Chase inhaled deeply, "Oh hell, all right. Here goes. I married Heather five years ago. She said she wanted children and would relinquish her modeling career when she became pregnant. Then the day she got pregnant, it all unraveled. She couldn't handle it. She hated being a mother and resented me. I had achieved my goal of CEO and didn't spend enough time ...

"Then, postpartum depression hit. I saw the signs and got her to reluctantly see a team of medical doctors and psychiatrists. They loaded her up with anti-depressants and you-name-it pain killers. She became addicted. And crashed. She tried to kill herself," Chase's voice cracked.

Brooke's eyes blurred, "Oh, I'm so sorry. You don't have to tell me any more if this is hard. Just fly."

Chase wiped his eyes, "I tried to do what I could, I really did."

Brooke placed her hand on top of his, "I'm so sorry."

Deep breath, "I found her that day just in time. She swallowed enough pills to kill an elephant, the ER doctors told me. They found everything in her system—including Stabilitas. I panicked. Not only was she sick, but with my position at Pharmical, the press would kill my career and pressure the FDA to abolish a drug that's already helped millions of people. I felt lost for the first time in my life ..."

"So why still wear the ring?"

"With our board of bible toters, are you kidding me? I had to be the happily married, stable CEO—two and a half kids, picket fence, doting wife—but it tore me apart."

"How come it never hit the papers?"

"I managed to call in some favors with some select friends. Believe it or not, Dixie-dawg's not my only friend. They kept it out of the media. Then, quietly, I sent her to the top rehab program in the world in—"

"Hazelden?"

"Yeah, how did you know?"

"Long story, plus you said Minnesota. I didn't mean to interrupt. Keep going."

"I cut a check for over sixty grand; Heather gave it all of one week and bolted. She abandoned me, her son, and the life she said she wanted. I hired a private eye out of New York and he found her in some crack house living with some creep named Rusty."

"How does she afford to live?"

"She emptied a couple of my bank accounts and has plenty of cash. The house she lived in couldn't have cost much. Supposedly, they're wanted for drugs and a bunch of other things. I tried to serve her divorce papers at that Minneapolis house, but she and Rusty fled."

"What did your private eye say?"

"I haven't been able to reach him. I think he's ticked off at me for trying to serve Heather without telling him, as if I wanted her to take off."

"I don't know what to say. Now, I understand why you can't go to the police."

"We have to find Parker and somehow stop her."

"What does Heather look like?"

"I wish I had a picture of her—I removed them from my wallet a long time ago. The hotel managers all asked for her photo too. How would I describe Heather? It's hard to be objective after all that's happened," Chase inhaled, then exhaled slowly. "Heather's attractive. Blonde, blue eyes, well built, about five eight, a hundred twenty pounds."

After an awkward pause, Chase said, "Actually, you're prettier." Ordinarily, Brooke accepted flattery with an easy Southern smile.

Desperately needing a shower since playing mechanic, she couldn't even fathom a compliment. She ignored the compliment and asked, "Age?"

"Twenty-seven."

Hmmm, he sure likes 'em young. I wonder if his nooner at the mall goes to high school. What was he doing with me? I'm like her mother's age.

Brooke glanced over her shoulder, "Do you have a bathroom?"

"A small one. I'm afraid I barely fit, but you will."

Brooke smirked, unhooked, then with her head bowed, ambled along the narrow path that led to the back. The mirror was big enough to make her wince at her reflection. Gripping her purse, she dumped its contents into the salad-bowl-sized sink. Applying what makeup she had, with the plane's erratic lunges, she felt like a plastic surgeon on a rollercoaster. She finished, then glanced into the hazy mirror, and couldn't help thinking, *I'm prettier than her... I bet.!*

Returning to the cockpit, she noticed his stare as she wiggled back into her seat. He said, "Are you okay?"

"Why, don't I look okay?"

"You look great—it's just that you were in the bathroom for ... You're not airsick?"

"Oh no, I just needed to freshen up. You're an amazing pilot. How long have you had your license?"

"About ten years. It started out as a hobby—you know, the thrill of the ride—but the more I flew, the more I enjoyed it. Do you have any hobbies?"

Thrill of the ride held her spellbound for a moment. "I love riding horses. I had one as a little girl. It's funny you asked—I actually just rode one last week. It had been so long, but it brought back a ton of memories." Brooke hummed while glancing to her right, then smiled, "I guess I enjoy the thrill of the ride too."

For the first time, they settled in as a warmth pulsed inside. Their grievances were replaced by compassion, a common purpose to find Parker. Chase slipped on his headphones and started conversing in airplane lingo. Brooke hoped it was an air traffic control tower, but it sounded foreign—except for the *low on fuel* comment. Lightning flashed up ahead against the darkened sky and she quietly prayed for a safe landing.

Chase struggled to lower the plane as rain pelted the windshield. Straight lines of lights appeared below. She wanted to ask if he could land, but decided to grip her seatbelt and try not to distract him. She eyed him and remembered those hands. With his lashes focused on landing, she hoped he didn't catch her staring.

Brooke's first bird's-eye landing was both exhilarating and terrifying. Chase looked like a seasoned pro. As the tires skidded on the wet pavement, she held it together and said, "Well done, captain."

"Sorry, that wasn't one of my best landings."

"Could've fooled me," Brooke inhaled his scent and grinned, "Now what?"

"Let me pull into the terminal. I don't like this storm."

Brooke scanned the area and didn't see any jumbo jets, "Where are we?"

"Welcome to Executive Airport Orlando. I've been here before, but it's been a long time."

A man with orange flashlights guided Chase into what looked like an old arena. He slowed to a stop, then flipped a series of switches. *It's not like shutting off a car. How does he know what to do?*

Chase said, "Sit tight, I'll help you out," then slid past her and popped open the hatch. Brooke felt a whoosh, then Chase extended his hand, and said, "Here, take my hand. I don't want you to sprain your ankle." She loved the way his eyes danced above his smirk. Gripping his strong hand, Brooke felt a tingle.

Chase stepped backward down the small ladder without losing his grip on Brooke's hand. Once she was standing on the concrete, the stench of oil and fuel lingered in the stale air, eradicating her nostrils of Chase's aroma. He gripped her elbows with both hands and faced her, asking, "Are you sure you're all right?"

She sensed a deeper meaning in his eyes, a vulnerability. Brooke lowered her voice, "Yes."

Chase looked like he wanted to say something else, but instead guided Brooke away from the small craft and into a tiny gate area— with the ambiance of a bus terminal. Chase powered up his smart phone and said, "I hope she found us a car and hotel. You hungry?"

Brooke eyed the two vending machines and hoped that's not what he meant, but said, "A little."

Chase's phone beeped. "Oh good. Keep your fingers crossed while I check voicemail." Brooke heard a muffled woman's voice through the cell pressed to his ear. He frowned throughout the message, then said, "Shit."

Brooke stood still, staring at him. Chase lowered his phone, and said, "Bad news. My travel agent couldn't find us hotel rooms or even a rental car. The closest hotel is an hour from here, and without a rental car, that's not even an option."

Chase said, "I have a pull-out couch in the plane. It's not that big, but it beats nothing."

Brooke eyed him and said, "Well, well, isn't that convenient?"

"I'll sleep on the captain's chair. You can have the couch. I'm so exhausted, I could sleep standing up."

Brooke insisted, "You're bigger. You can have the pull-out—"

"I wouldn't think of it. The bed's yours. I'm fine in the chair—it reclines."

Inside the plane, Chase set up the bed while Brooke viewed from the steps. Her heart raced, she felt a stirring and blushed, unable to control her urges. *It had been easy to hate him since the pink slip call, but his side of the story altered her paradigm. Her barriers were falling in his presence. The memories of that night came flooding in.*

"All set," Chase whirled around.

"Thanks."

"Are you sure you're okay with this?"

"Don't worry about me. I've slept in tents before."

"Good, because unless we get lucky on a car and hotel rooms, we may be backpacking to Disney."

Brooke laughed nervously, "I don't care. I just want to find Parker."

Chase kept his mind preoccupied enough to avoid worrying, but the mention of his son's name made him cringe. He said, "I'm gonna walk around and give you some privacy to get ready."

Chase bounded down the steps; Brooke glanced at the chair and guilt overwhelmed her. Brooke considered Chase's good qualities— marveling at how nice he truly was and how he kept getting more attractive by the minute. Beyond his good looks, he had a kindness that drew her in like a high-powered magnet. She recalled his patience when she hurt her ankle, how he interfaced with other people, devoid of pretense. And now, with *his* son kidnapped by the woman who deserted him, he offered her the comfy bed. He didn't fit the mold of lawyer, dukie, selfish greedy executive, shark, or snake.

Brooke surveyed outside—coast clear—she pulled off her dress, removed her bra, then slipped on a North Carolina T-shirt and grinned. Let's see Mister Wonderful when he views Tar Heels.

Brooke laid down on her side, facing the plane's door and hummed. She heard footsteps, then a knock, "It's me. Permission to enter ..."

Brooke giggled, then said, "Permission granted, captain."

After the whoosh of the door, Chase's face glowed, his smile illuminated from the hangar's dim lights. "My, don't you look cozy."

"I feel bad. You sure you don't want the bed?"

"Don't worry about me," he pulled the door shut and lowered the lock bar, "I'm fine in my pilot's chair. It'll be like the college days."

Chase broke the silence, "Just to make myself clear, it doesn't bother me to give you the bed. Wanna know what does tick me off?"

"What?"

"Seeing *that* God-awful shirt. You're gonna give me nightmares."

They both laughed, then Brooke said, "Lucky for you I had it in my bag."

"Tar Heels give me a rash."

"Very funny. Blue Devils give me ... never mind."

After a brief pause, Chase said, "I'm not even tired now. I feel like I'm a kid on a sleepover."

Brooke giggled, "Me too."

Chase inhaled, "On a serious note, thanks for coming along. You've helped me keep my mind off things."

"Don't mention it. I feel responsible for this mess and I can't even imagine what you must be going through."

Chase sighed and said, "I'm sorry about everything. I can't believe how my words came out so wrong. I'm such an idiot sometimes. I can only imagine how it made you feel."

Brooke warmed, "I'm glad you weren't the evil CEO after all."

"I don't know how long I can stay a CEO there. I feel like I'm in quick sand—I've failed as a husband, I don't spend nearly enough time with my son, and Pharmical isn't the same company I joined. I'm sorry about the way they treated you. I wish I had been there—none of this would have happened."

"That's sweet of you to say, but, honestly, it was the best thing that could've ever happened to me. I feel like a new person. I love working with children—especially Parker. He's so cute. I just adore him. You must be so proud."

Chase's eyes misted. He needed to shift gears or spend the night sulking. He said, "We've spent all this time talking about me. What about you?"

"What do you want to know?" Brooke's mouth went dry.

Chase dabbed his eyes, then said, "Why isn't a gorgeous, intelligent woman like you married?"

Deep breath, then a dry gulp, she said, "I was." Brooke wanted to change the subject.

"Are you divorced?"

"No, my husband died."

Silence, then, "I'm sorry ... I shouldn't have asked."

"No, it's okay. You told me your personal story, now it's my turn. You sure you want to know? This could take all night."

"Of course. I'm wide awake anyway."

Brooke inhaled deeply, "I married my high school sweetheart—Tanner—we went to Chapel Hill together. He played football, I ran cross country. After college, we married," Brooke's eyes moistened.

"If this is too hard for—"

Brooke continued, "No, I'm okay ... we were broke, but happy, both working hard, and in love ..."

Chase heard Brooke sniffle, then paused, lowered his voice to a near whisper, "What happened?"

"Well, I became pregnant, and we were so happy. Then a few weeks later, we got the news that Tanner had a rare form of leukemia—CML. By the time he went to the doctor, it was stage four. He lost eighty pounds so fast, I lost the baby, then he couldn't take it anymore ..." Brooke couldn't continue as a tear dropped off her cheek.

Chase climbed out of the cockpit and began caressing Brooke's hair. He slid his silk handkerchief from his back pocket and without uttering a sound handed it to her. Brooke blew into it three times, then said, "I'm sorry—"

Chase placed his finger across her lips and said, "Don't be. I can't imagine what you went through."

Brooke said, "Well, you and I both kinda went through the same thing. I'm not sure what's worse—suicide or killing yourself with drugs."

They gazed into each other's eyes in silence. Eventually, their sadness subsided, replaced by a tranquil comfort. Chase eased in beside Brooke, caressing her hair in soporific strokes, until her eyes closed and her breathing deepened. Holding Brooke, his mind drifted to Parker, who could only fall asleep with his soothing presence. He quietly said a special prayer.

He smiled at Brooke. She even looked cute sleeping. He began murmuring into her ear, "How could I have been such a fool? Why couldn't I have met you sooner?" Brooke rustled with lips curling, eyes closed. Chase froze.

After Brooke's breathing returned to a deep wave, he held her and closed his eyes.

— 💜 —

Where am I? Panic permeated, her fluttering eyes made it difficult to focus.

His arm wrapped around the back of her shirt. Brooke budged, then realization set in. Brooke relaxed and recalled the previous night. *I don't remember sleeping with him—did we?* She felt for her panties— still on—and breathed a sigh of relief.

Brooke eyed him closely. Chase's breathing was heavy and Brooke wondered if they slept facing each other all night. Brooke decided not to wake him; his large hand warmed her chilled back.

Settling in, Brooke remembered the sweet things he said—while he thought she was sleeping. He could have easily taken advantage of her; although part of her wished he had, she appreciated how he respected her. Once again, she realized she had misread him, a rare gentleman.

Chase's eyelids flickered, then popped open. He flinched, then as his pupils focused on Brooke's deep blue eyes, he grinned. Brooke said, "Good morning, sleepy head."

Chase yawned, then said, "Good morning, sunshine. How long have you been awake?"

"I just woke up a minute before you," she lied, "I didn't want to disturb your sleep—plus, you're so warm," *inside and out.*

Chase beamed while his eyelashes lazily blinked. Neither one of them moved; they just looked deep into each other's eyes. Chase finally said, "Any idea what time it is?"

As Brooke shook her head, Chase slid his hand to rest on her neck and kissed her.

Brooke pulled back, and said, "It's time for me to find a toothbrush— and a shower."

"You're perfect to me."

"You need a nose job and glasses." They both laughed.

Chase's eyes revealed a deep desire, but the task at hand weighed on him. Before breaking from their cozy cuddle, he said, "I enjoyed our sleepover."

Brooke smiled and said, "I did too."

He gazed into Brooke's eyes one more time, then slid backward out of bed. Brooke couldn't help but stare—he looked so cute with his hair tousled, standing in his boxer briefs. Thoughts of Parker flooded in and they kicked into action.

Chase pulled his slacks on, slid into his shoes, and said, "As much as I'd like to watch you dress, I'll provide you some privacy. I'll go make a few calls outside where I can pick up a better signal. Come out when you're ready."

Brooke propped up on her elbows with fingers interlocked under her chin and eyed his strut to the exit. She heard a rustling, guessing the giant door to the hangar was opening. She pulled on her dress and ran her hands up and down and sighed. *I'm not sure it's any better than yesterday.* Brooke squinted through the plane's tiny window out the large opening and fretted.

Gripping the compact, Brooke utilized a small ration of makeup. She couldn't untangle her hair, but eyed a cap beside the pilot's seat— Blue Devils—argh, *I'd rather be bald than wear that thing.*

She raked her fingers through her hair once more, still unable to ease out the snarls. In bare feet, she eased down the prickly steps to the rough concrete, then slipped on her heels and strode toward the opening. The rain had paused, but clouds remained.

Brooke spotted Chase, cell pressed to his ear, back turned. He looked mighty fine in khakis and collar-less black shirt. She marveled at his v-shaped upper torso and toned biceps—not bad without a shower.

Hearing Brooke's heels, he spun and smiled, raising his forefinger in the air, saying, "Thanks a million. You're a lifesaver."

He clicked the off button as she asked, "Good news?"

"I'll say. Grab your bag—I found us a car. A cab's on its way."

"I can't move."

"C'mon Rusty, we're past checkout time and Parker's starving."

"Get a late checkout. There's Cheetos still left in the bag. I need to sleep."

Heather sneered, "We're leaving without you—"

"I don't give a shit!"

"Nice language in front of a four-year-old," Heather scrunched her brows. "We'll be out in the car waiting. I'm gonna go check us out."

Heather slammed the door before he responded, then faced her wide-eyed son, and said, "I'm sorry, he gets that way when he drinks too much. I wish he wouldn't …" She surveyed the street, and said, "Hey, you wanna go to Waffle House?"

"Do they have Mickey Mouse waffles?"

Heather laughed, "I don't know—let's go find out. Rusty'll be a while, I bet. It's best to let him sleep."

"Why won't he answer?" The cabbie sped toward the Orlando airport. Alamo held his reservation for the one available rental car in the entire area. A Hummer—with tinted windows—and, if no hotel rooms became available, it would do.

"Who won't answer?" Brooke asked.

"Oh, my private eye. After what I paid him, he better not have run out on me."

"It's too bad we can't call the cops."

The cab driver glanced into his rearview mirror; Chase gripped Brooke's knee and she took the hint, mouthing *sorry* to Chase. They rode in uncomfortable silence.

Once inside the airport, Brooke went to the restroom while Chase stood in the line that extended beyond their rope barriers. She still had some unresolved questions. Chase seemed too perfect last night—he had to be hiding something. She resisted asking him about the woman he escorted into the hotel, but was dying to know the truth. Brooke contemplated calling Melissa—the only person she trusted with her keys—to have her open the infamous *package,* but she didn't want her to see the note. Not until she could see it first. And she wanted to see a picture of Heather. *All of this has to wait.*

Brooke thought of Parker—*I hope he's all right. His wife, ex-wife, or whatever she is, sounds like a nut case. If she hurts him, I don't know what…I can't think like that. She's his mother, after all. I wonder if there's more to the story. Why does someone try to end it and leave an adorable son, gorgeous husband, and a life of riches? My situation was different—or was it?*

Brooke left the bathroom more confused than when she entered. Even though she slept well, she needed a shower—and a toothbrush. Chase spotted her and waved. He had only inched a few spots but was at least inside the ropes.

"Feeling better?" Chase lowered his voice, though people in line stared.

"I could still use a shower—"

"That makes two of us," Chase reasoned, "I'll just be happy to find a car."

"What's the plan?"

"I was hoping to call around to all the local hotels and see if they're registered, but …"

"That sounds like a great idea. We can split—"

"Not so fast. I'm guessing the room's in his name or some alias cash deal. I don't remember his last name or even his real first name—only Rusty. I wish Max would answer."

"Max?"

Chase moved in closer, cupped his hand and said, "My PI."

"Oh," Brooke leaned in, Chase lowered his ear, as she said, "I wish we could just call the cops."

Forty-five minutes later, Chase and Brooke finally reached the counter. While Chase fidgeted, the aloof representative punched her keypad as if she was writing a novel. Finally, she peered over thin dark-framed reading glasses, and said, "All I have left is a Cadillac Esplanade for $155 a day."

"I thought I had a reservation for—"

"It's the best I can do. We're overbooked. Take it or leave it."

Chase glanced at Brooke, and said, "We'll take it."

More typing. Still more typing. Chase asked, "Does the backseat recline?" Brooke shot a glance at Chase.

Slow Alamo woman nodded, saying, "Uh huh," sounding like Billy Bob in the movie *Sling Blade.*

Chase signed the remaining paperwork and whispered to Brooke, "I think law school had less rules and regulations—and took less time." Finally, she lifted the keys up in the air, and Chase grabbed them.

The Esplanade turned out better than he imagined. It had plenty of extras, including heavily tinted windows, though Heather would never recognize him in a Cadillac. Just as Brooke said, "Where to?" Chase's annoying ringtone—"Duke of Earl"—sounded.

Glancing down, Chase's eyes brightened, "Perfect timing."

Brooke heard a woman's voice speaking rapidly. She then tried to comprehend the conversation from Chase's comments, "I don't care what it costs ... I see ... Are you kidding? ... Yes ... No ... *That's* the *only* available room?" He glanced at Brooke as he asked, "Does it have two beds?" Brooke raised one eyebrow.

Chase covered the cell mouthpiece, and asked Brooke, "What's your shoe size?"

Brooke hesitated, eyes fixed on his, "Seven." Before she could ask why, he said, "Okay, thanks. Let me know if anything else opens." He pressed end and said, "Ever wear glass slippers?"

Brooke chortled, a combination of nerves and the absurdity of the question at a time like this. "I'm afraid to ask why."

"Believe it or not, the only available room within an hour is ..." He laughed uncontrollably. She said, "You better pull over. You sound like Goofy."

His laugh intensified; Chase veered into a gas station parking lot. Tears streamed. She asked, "What's so funny? Did you get a room or not?"

The laughter continued, then sputtered enough for Chase to say, "We're staying in Cinderella's Castle Suite."

"You've got to be joking!" Brooke's stern eyes made him laugh as hard as before. More tears. He reached in his pocket, then paused, and shot a glare at Brooke. She said, "Looking for your handkerchief?"

He nodded, still acting like he inhaled a balloon of laughing gas.

"I used it, remember?" While Chase continued chortling, Brooke thought, *this'll be interesting. I heard him say something about two beds. I'm definitely not drinking any champagne. This time, I'm keeping my wits.*

Chase said, "Well, I asked Ginny to get us as close to Disney as possible. I still don't know how she pulled *this* off. I hope you don't turn into a pumpkin at midnight." More laughter; this time Brooke giggled.

He plugged Disney into GPS, still chuckling. They cruised into the Magic Kingdom lot, scanning for Minnesota plates—no luck—then found a rare parking spot near the front.

Chase said, "I miss Parker. Be on the lookout. I have no idea if Rusty's with them."

Once inside the security gate, the mood brightened. Whimsical music bounced off the walls of the quaint little village as Disney characters waved from every street corner. The last time either one had been there was when they were kids.

At the entrance to Cinderella's Castle, a peppy college-aged girl directed them inside, saying, "Lucky you." Chase was afraid to ask Ginny what it cost—she said she pulled some serious strings to procure the invitation-only suite.

"Is this your honeymoon?" asked an animated girl behind the counter, clad in Cinderella costume.

Chase eyed Brooke, and beat her to the punch, answering, "Sort of ..."

After a Cinderella giggle, the girl said, "Well, welcome to our most enchanted suite—I should know, I live there. But, tonight, it's yours. Enjoy." More character giggles.

Mickey Mouse led them to a private elevator. Just before entering, Chase lifted Brooke into his arms, chuckling, as Mickey faced them, with hands on hips. Their suite covered an entire floor. Mickey opened the door, followed by Brooke and Chase. He said, "Would you like a tour of the suite?"

Chase started to say *no,* just as Brooke said, "Yes." Mickey spun around, then chuckled, "How 'bout I give you a mini-tour?"

They admired the windows—stained glass with slippers. He led them to the bedroom: two double beds. Brooke sighed, but thought it was fit for a princess. The room had a fireplace, with an adjacent parlor and bathroom. Stone floors and walls, along with hardwood paneling, and stone columns added to the mystique of a fairytale castle.

Mickey chattered on, "The suite is furnished with a seventeenth-century Dutch desk, two antique 'slipper' chairs—used in the seventeenth and eighteenth centuries to sit on while putting on shoes—and, as you can see, support columns decorated with carved mice. Don't worry, they don't bite." He released a whimsical laugh.

Brooke eyed Chase—whose faux frown could have turned her into a pumpkin. Brooke said, "Thanks Mickey. I think my *husband* wants some privacy." Her smirk made Mickey chuckle—out of character. Mickey took the hint though and scampered away.

The door closed, then Brooke said, "Nice touch at the front desk ..."

"You liked that?"

"No." Brooke balled her fists on her hips. Chase slinked toward her. She said, "Don't even think about it—I'm showering."

"To save time, we should shower togeth—"

Brooke shut the door and clicked the lock. Then she used all the hot water in the Magic Kingdom. Toweling off and feeling reborn, she spotted *his and hers* bathrobes and giggled—*I can only imagine him in that Prince Charming robe.* She slipped on her Cinderella robe and applied the little remaining makeup she had in her bag.

"Oh shit, now what? This trip's fucked!" The old Chevy van spewed steam out of the hood.

"Watch your language!" Heather's buzz dissipated each time Rusty swore in front of her son.

Parker's eyes widened each time he heard a new curse word.

Rusty veered off the highway as a family in a station wagon pointed at the front of his truck. He shouted out his window, "I can fucking see it." Heather slapped him on his arm, drawing a scowl.

Stuck three hundred miles from Florida, Heather wanted to grab Parker and hitchhike the rest of the way—without Rusty. She had no idea the Minnesota police were calling them "Bonnie and Clyde." The dream trip with her son had turned into her worst nightmare.

"Who the fuck is this?"

"Excuse me. I'm looking for Max." Chase pressed his cell to his ear, frowning at the floor.

Brooke sauntered over to the other bed in the room while Chase fidgeted, oblivious to her grand entrance.

Chase heard a muffled voice, "He's looking for Molini ..." Then he heard laughter, followed by, "Who's calling?"

"My name is Chase Allman. I'm a client of Max Mol—"

"Max is," the man answering Max's cell stared at the lumpy rolled-up rug, "Max is temporarily indisposed at the moment." Raucous laughter, "I'll make sure I tell him you called."

Hanging up, Chase's face whitened.

Brooke, sitting with her legs crossed in her Cinderella robe, asked, "Who was that?"

Chase's eyes never left the floor, as he said, "That explains..." He paused, "Huh? Oh, Brooke—I didn't hear you come in."

"I'm out of fresh clothes, so I thought I'd try this robe out instead. Do you like it?"

Chase glanced over to Brooke, and said, "I think Max is dead." Brooke scrutinized Chase like a psychiatrist, beckoning him on with her silence. He said, "That explains why he hasn't called. Shit!"

Brooke scratched her still-damp hair, then flipped her head up, and said, "Maybe, we should go to the police."

"I can't. You don't understand. If this goes public, I lose my job and you lose your new business."

"I don't care about anything but finding Parker." Brooke's glare looked ghastly in the Cinderella mirror above the fireplace. She took his comment as a threat.

"There's a chance they're here today. We should split up and check everywhere."

Brooke shook her head, "I don't even know what Heather or Rusty look like and they probably disguised Parker."

"I'm not sure Rusty's even here. We should just focus on finding Parker. Hey, nice outfit, by the way."

"I thought you'd never notice. I'm all out of fresh clothes. I hope you don't mind me in a dirty dress. You better disguise yourself or Heather will spot you from a mile away."

"We both need disguises."

"Well, we're in the right place—I noticed a gift shop downstairs. Let's find you some goofy ears and sunglasses and I'll pick up a T-shirt."

Clad in touristy garb, they set out together. The place was packed— Sunday and right before children returned to school. Every little boy resembled Parker. They scoured winding lines, then scrutinized passengers exiting rides. By five o'clock, they had circled the Magic Kingdom at least five times.

Deciding to split, they canvassed the main exit lanes. Countless families scurried past in an array of Disney outfits, carrying stuffed characters. After the crowd dwindled, Chase found Brooke, and said, "I suppose there's a chance they didn't even arrive yet." His comment couldn't replace their feeling of helplessness.

Brooke said, "Or they could've gone to Epcot, Animal Kingdom, or even the Hollywood Studios."

"Parker loves rides. Even though he's not tall enough for Space Mountain, they have to be here. I can see him on Splash Mountain all day long. I think they'd go here first, then Epcot, but who knows? Parker may talk her into going shark fishing." Chase buried his head in his hands. Brooke rubbed his broad shoulders as he shuddered, his prayers turning to tears.

So much for the magic of Disney.

—— ♥ ——

"It's okay if we can't go to Disney, Mom."

"Oh, Parker, you're so sweet. Don't worry, we'll get there. Rusty's good with fixing things. He'll be back soon—I hope."

A couple of truckers had stopped—more to check out Heather than to actually help. Some offered rides, saying garages are closed on Sunday. Tempting. Rusty's cell phone was off; Heather guessed he ran out of juice. *I wish he would've plugged it in like I told him.*

Rusty plunked down against a giant oak and fired up his crack pipe again, thinking, *why do we have to take the little shit all the way to Disney?*

Heather and Parker waited and waited—though tempted, she didn't dare leave; Heather knew what Rusty would do to her.

A doorbell chimed "It's a Small World After All." "I'll get it," Chase said.

Brooke and Chase hadn't eaten much since they left North Carolina. Too tired to go out, they ordered room service while they planned their next move. After Donald Duck lifted the metal trays, they dug in like ravenous wolves. *Nice first dinner date,* Brooke thought.

The doorbell rang again. Chase glanced at his half-eaten steak, and said, "I don't think we ordered anything else."

Brooke jumped up, saying, "My turn." As she opened the door, one of the Seven Dwarfs stood holding another delivery—champagne.

His tag said "Sleepy," but he acted more like perky, saying, "Special gift for the honeymooners from your friends at Disney."

Brooke invited him in, then eyed Chase, who shrugged. After opening the bubbly, Chase handed him a twenty, then Sleepy skipped to the door, whistling, "Whistle While You Work." Chase and Brooke eyed each other, then laughed.

Chase poured as Brooke said, "The last time I drank champagne, I got into trouble."

Chase smiled, raised his glass, and said, "Cheers to trouble."

The alcohol overhauled their weary bodies. Chase said, "I am really sorry about Pharmical. I wish there was something I could do."

Brooke pressed her finger to Chase's lips, and said, "Shhhh. Don't be sorry. I wasn't happy there and my ouster wasn't your fault. I believe things happen for a reason and Angel's Academy was a godsend."

"I still feel lousy about the way it happened."

Brooke placed her hand on top of Chase's and said, "Do you know what you can do to make it up to me?"

Chase shook his head back and forth quickly, then raised his eyebrows. Brooke said, "Make Stabilitas—lives depend on it."

Chase frowned, inhaled deeply, then lowered his tone, "Look, I know what GenSense's gene therapy means to you. Unfortunately, I don't think our greedy board cares about saving lives unless they can make a killing first."

Brooke pulled her hand back and crinkled her brows, "If that's that your idea of humor—"

"No. That's not what I meant to … Here I go again, saying the wrong thing." Chase continued, "I'm going to tell you inside information that could get me fired."

"I'm not looking to hurt you, if that's what you mean. You can trust me. I didn't tell anybody at Pharmical about us, and I won't break your trust now."

"Okay, here goes," Chase gulped. "In the last three board meetings, more than a few people have complained about our GenSense acquisition. Our M&A team has been secretly shopping it, but haven't found any takers."

Brooke's eyes widened, "Oh my God …"

"Marvin Wixfeldt, who I call The Butcher, wrote it in his chop report. The same one that advised outsourcing your old department. I've seen enough to know if he recommends it, it happens fast."

"They can't do that. They just bought it."

"That board is only interested in the stock."

"Doesn't a scientific breakthrough that cures an incurable disease increase the stock?"

Chase bit his lip, "You sound like me. I pride myself on building businesses, even if it takes a long time. I had a nasty argument with Stoddard and, so far, lost the battle and the war."

"All it takes is approval in the U.S. for it to—"

"Unless it can be done with a magic wand overnight, they won't even listen." Brooke's eyes stung.

Chase lowered his voice, saying, "All they want to discuss is anti-depressants. Wall Street dictates focusing on our *core products*, and we're afraid to buck them."

"What about doing what's right? Making the world a better place? Saving lives?"

"I agree with you more than you know—"

"So do something about it. You're the freaking CEO!"

Chase sighed, "All my life, I wanted to be a Chief Executive Officer—the big boss. But now, I hate the job. It's all bullshit politics with chickenshit policies. You have to know I tried to do something with GenSense. Sometimes, it's not enough."

"Well then, I hope they sell it quickly, to someone with a vision."

After a few moments, she plopped beside Chase, causing the bed to bob. Well into the bottle, the bubbly buzzed them. Brooke said, "I don't know what it is with this stuff, but it makes me crazy." The last few words slurred.

"Me too," Chase grinned, "Well, without knowing Rusty's last name, there's nothing much we can do until morning." Brooke felt that familiar surge inside. They locked eyes.

Their lips met with intensity. Though the champagne loosened their inhibitions, they didn't need it; their relationship had developed new depth. A magnetic pull they didn't resist. This time kissing with lights on, as they retreated for air, they gazed into each other's eyes—as if joining souls. Like lovers for the first time, they embraced again.

Brooke felt lightheaded, marveling at his magical way of igniting her passion. She didn't want the feeling to ever end. Chase wrapped his sturdy arms behind Brooke and locked lips in another deep kiss. Their hands explored each other, launching rockets of desire. With tongues dancing, they traded moans.

Chase dropped Brooke's robe with a whoosh of chilled air. His hands warmed her. Chase kissed her neck and Brooke giggled, then his mouth warmed her.

Brooke's hand searched for his belt buckle, but landed below, causing him to groan. Brooke's eyes widened as her hand massaged his slacks. His lips sprinkled down, kissing her, tickling her. Their breathing became heavy, as they pleasured each other with a fresh familiarity.

Chase ripped open his belt and lowered his zipper. In an instant, he pulled his pants and boxers to the floor. He slid Brooke's thong down, sending a tingling sensation, then caressed her inner thigh. Their lips joined and sloppily engaged in lover's delight. With lips locked, Chase slowly lowered her back …

Brooke gasped as he entered her. Chase paused, then kissed her deeply. They moved together, then Brooke started pulsing her hips. She tightened, causing him to move in and out slowly. The unhurried deliberate pace felt titillating. Their breathing increased, matched by faster and deeper thrusts.

Then Chase pulled away and fell beside Brooke, with tiny beads of sweat forming all over his body.

"What's wrong?" Brooke asked.

"I'm sorry … I don't think I can …"

Brooke pressed her finger to his moistened lips, and said, "Shhhhh. It's all right. I understand."

Brooke reached her arm around Chase then ran her other hand through his wavy locks. Chase's eyes welled up. He said, "I'm sorry … it's not you."

"Shhhhhhh."

With lips trembling, he said, "I'm scared. I just don't know what I'd do if Parker … I've got to find him."

"We're gonna find him—tomorrow. I can feel it."

"I should have called the cops—"

"Hey, no second guessing. Live in the present." Brooke channeled Shane's coaching.

Brooke soothed Chase with her gentle voice and touch; the tears slowed as his eyes shut. Within seconds, his breathing deepened. She pulled a blanket over him and continued caressing his face until her eyes felt heavy. They cuddled until morning.

Chase awoke to strange sounds. He noticed he was naked—in a bear hug with Brooke, trembling, with eyes flickering. He couldn't understand her words, but guessed she was having a nightmare. He awakened her with a tender kiss on her forehead.

Brooke's eyes shot open and she said, "Huh …"

Chase smiled, then said, "Were you dreaming of Prince Charming or the Wicked Witch?"

"Oh, I was dreaming," Brooke decided against revealing the dream and kissed Chase on the chest and cheek.

"I've made a decision—I'm going to the police," Chase announced.

Brooke hugged Chase tightly, then said, "Are you sure? We could try for one more—"

"No, I should've done it sooner. I was a selfish coward ..."

"No you weren't." A powerful surge swept inside Brooke. Their lips met.

Brooke pulled back, eyeing Chase, as she said, "Don't get me excited. We have a big day. Today, we find Parker."

With the park opening at nine, they had to hurry. Quick showers—alone—another room service, then Brooke left to pick up a few things, while Chase made the call he'd been dreading. He punched in nine-one-one, and drew a deep breath.

After the introductory information, Chase said, "My four-year-old son's been kidnapped and I have reason to believe he's going to be at Disney World today."

"Was he abducted in Disney World?"

"No, in North Carolina, and I know who did it."

"Have the kidnappers contacted you with ransom demands?"

"No."

"How do you know who did it?"

"It was my soon-to-be ex-wife and her boyfriend."

After a pause, the female 911 operator's voice turned snippy, "Sir, this sounds like a domestic dispute. You are calling on an emergency line. You need to go through the courts."

"I have been granted sole custody through a court order. She is in violation—"

"There's nothing we can do. You mentioned it's your soon-to-be ex-wife?"

"Yes, and her boyfriend."

"And they allegedly kidnapped your son?"

"Yes."

"I'm confused. Where did they kidnap him?"

"They kidnapped him from preschool in North Carolina."

"So your wife picked up her son from preschool and is taking him to Disney—that's hardly an emergency kidnapping case. You need to call—"

"Ma'am, with all due respect, I have a court order that she is in violation of, and she's wanted for dealing drugs."

"Dealing drugs? In North Carolina?"

"No, in Minnesota."

"Minnesota? Now I'm really confused. Plus, we have no jurisdiction or access to Minnesota's records."

"Can you at least check and see? She's a drug addict and dangerous—I'm worried about the safety of my son. Please help me."

"Give me her name and I'll forward it to our non-emergency personnel. They will contact you within twenty-four hours."

Chase feared by the time the local cops called, it would be too late. He buried his head in his hands, not knowing whether to cry or scream—or both. *I've got to find him.*

"Duke, Duke, Duke of Earl" jolted him. He thought, that was fast, as he answered. It was Brooke, who said she was on her way. As he explained his frustrating call, it infuriated him further, distancing him from the task at hand. His stomach churned and it wasn't from the breakfast. He gazed into the magic mirror on the wall and wished for his son back—and a quad espresso.

At 8:45 a.m., Brooke and Chase paced in front of the main entrance. They both wished they had brought sunglasses—the Sunshine State lived up to its billing. The couple plodded like the Secret Service along the ruts they had formed—no sign of Parker. Chase's disguise of goofy ears and T-shirt caught a few stares and even a giggle, but Brooke thought he looked cute.

Just after nine a.m., they entered the Magic Kingdom and decided to divide and conquer. Even with the disguise, he feared Heather would notice him before he spotted her. Chase camped on a shaded bench near Splash Mountain; Brooke stood just inside the main entrance.

After three hours, Brooke needed to use the restroom. Chase scolded her for having two cups of tea, then snickered. While scanning the oncoming crowds, he power-walked to the front entrance and relieved her of her duty. Then she did the same—still no sign of them.

Just as Chase left his bench, Parker, Heather, and Rusty waltzed into the line for Splash Mountain. They had walked right past Brooke but with Parker's new hair color, she didn't recognize him.

When the ride ended, they exited. Parker begged to go on it again, but Rusty growled and Heather's stomach churned, so she said they'd come back to it later. Parker ran ahead while Heather and Rusty trudged along, unable to keep up. The noon sun overheated their backs, erasing their morning buzz.

Chase settled back on his bench next to an elderly couple, just missing his son. He checked his cell—still no call from the police. So much for serve and protect.

Brooke's ankle flared up and her legs hurt. She hated standing still. The crowd entering had gone from throngs earlier to a steady flow now. She thought, maybe they'll come in after lunch. She found a bench that still had a decent view of the three lines to enter and wished for a food vendor.

The afternoon dragged on. Chase checked in with Brooke every hour. He hated hanging up because hearing her voice provided his only form of comfort. He wondered what it would be like to sit beside her on the famous Splash Mountain ride—*would she scream? Or laugh?*

By six o'clock, their patience had worn thin. Hunger pangs hit both of them. They grudgingly decided to wait another hour.

Brooke stared at the boy, two steps ahead of the arguing couple. Familiar face, about Parker's height, but the blond spiked hair looked strange. Then it hit …

Purple sneakers—it has to be him! Clutching her bag, she advanced like a torpedo. Brooke punched what she hoped was the send button on her cell, but didn't have enough time to talk. As she neared, she heard the guy calling the woman a nasty word—had to be Rusty. Thank God for those shoes.

"Parker?"

The little boy glanced up and squinted. The low setting sun blinded him, but she recognized the eyes. The couple behind him continued bickering. Brooke heard her say, "Asshole," as Parker rolled his eyes.

Brooke stopped directly in front of Parker, blocking the sun. His brown eyes nearly exploded, "Miss Ingram!"

The woman paused while the guy kept yelling. She glared, saying, "Parker, do you know this woman?"

"It's my teacher, Miss Ingram."

Rusty stopped and frowned through bloodshot eyes. He shot a glance at Heather, then back to Brooke, then stood open-mouthed in a daze. Heather scowled.

Brooke stretched out her arms and said, "You're safe—thank God."

Parker stepped forward to hug Brooke. Heather said, "What the fuck?" Brooke dropped her purse and the contents strewed across the pavement. She gripped Parker in a monkey hug.

Heather glared at Rusty and said, "Do something. Don't just stand there," as she tried to yank Parker away from Brooke.

Rusty said, "Let go or die bitch." Brooke froze, gasping as she spotted the butt of the gun. Rusty struggled to pull the .38 special out of his pants. Brooke released her grip on Parker, then lunged for her lipstick. Time stood still.

Then she emptied pepper spray into Rusty's eyes. He fell hard, shrieking as his rubbing only made it worse.

Heather blurted, "What the hell ..." as she knocked the container out of Brooke's hands, then dove on Rusty.

Not realizing it was Heather trying to grab the pistol, Rusty bucked her off like a bronco, "Get the fuck off me!"

Brooke reached for the other pepper spray as Heather kicked her.

Parker yelled, "MOMMY, DON'T."

Brooke gripped the bottle, but couldn't stand. Her rib cage seared with each heavy breath. Heather gripped Brooke's throat while jamming her knee into Brooke's newly broken ribs. Heather's face shuddered in a rage.

The pain was excruciating, yet somehow, she managed to lift her hand ever so slightly ...

The spray blinded Brooke, but she felt Heather's grip on her neck ease. Brooke could tell by the screech that she nailed Heather. Then Brooke heard the voice of an angel ...

"Daddy!"

20

A crowd had begun to gather, and security personnel were approaching.

Father and son collided literally and emotionally. Parker clung to his leg, happy to see his daddy. Chase said, "I'm here, little buddy. Everything's gonna be—"

"Be careful Chase—he has a gun." Brooke swung her head back and forth wildly but she couldn't see.

Rusty propped up on one knee, wiping his eyes but unable to open them. He ripped the gun from inside his jeans, pointed it toward the direction of Brooke's voice, and pulled the trigger.

"Fuck!" He shook the gun, then clutched it in both hands, clawing for the safety switch. Just as it clicked, his eyes flicked open. He took dead aim at Chase's head.

Rusty trembled as the taser paralyzed him. He hadn't noticed the officer behind him. Another second later and Parker would have been fatherless. The guard held the trigger until Rusty fell on his side. While he shook, the guard slapped a handcuff on Rusty's right wrist; then he locked down on the other wrist.

With foot pressing Rusty's face into the hot asphalt, the guard demanded, "What's going on here?"

Heather was the first to scream, then Brooke tried to out-yell her. They both were sprawled on the ground, still blinded. Chase lifted Parker into his arms, then stepped toward the guard, who said, "Hold it right there!" and pointed his taser at Chase. Parker burrowed into Chase's chest and squeezed his arm like a tourniquet.

Chase froze, raised his free hand in the air, and motioned his head at Heather and Rusty, saying, "Those two kidnapped my son. Arrest them."

Heather said, "That's bullshit! He's my son! I don't even know the bitch who maced me. Arrest *them*."

The guard said, "Nobody move," then pressed his walkie-talkie and said, "This is Henderson. Call 911. I have a situation at the front gate."

Rusty spun and kicked the legs out from under the officer. Henderson fell hard on his left shoulder, dropping his taser. Rusty jammed his head into the guard's face, shattering his nose. Rusty kicked the taser away, then booted Henderson's stomach. The bloody officer locked into the fetal position and howled in agony.

Rusty spotted his gun, turned and grabbed it.

Chase kicked as hard as he could squarely in Rusty's nuts, and the gun fired.

Henderson's eyes popped open; he gripped his knee. Blood began soaking his slacks.

Chase couldn't reach the gun—Parker weighed too much. And there was no chance Parker would loosen his grip. Chase's foot landed once more in Rusty's crotch just as the cavalry arrived.

A police officer dove on Rusty and severed the gun from his grip. Four other officers descended on the scene. They grabbed Parker and then handcuffed everyone else and hauled them into Disney's security office.

An officer sat with Parker and asked, "Are you okay, little man?" Parker nodded.

Inside, all four detainees beseeched their innocence in a cacophony. Efforts to quiet them only worsened the situation.

Brooke was released first and immediately found Parker. She hugged him and rocked him back and forth, saying, "It's going to be all right. You're safe now."

Just as Parker asked about his father, Chase darted in the room. He bear hugged Brooke and Parker.

Douglas "Rusty" John and accomplice Heather Allman were arrested once the first of two felony-sized bags of cocaine were discovered in their possession. Marijuana, methamphetamines, and heroin added to their impending doom. That didn't include what the police would find in their car.

Rusty faced multiple felony charges: concealed weapon, use of a deadly weapon—shooting a cop could bring the death penalty in

Florida—even if the officer didn't die. Compounding the couple's troubles, the reports from Minnesota tied them for public enemy number one. Rusty stole the wrong bags from the wrong people before fleeing Minnesota.

After the police had failed to serve Heather with divorce papers in Minneapolis, they searched the house, finding stolen goods and enough drugs to supply Woodstock. To avoid felony drug trafficking time, the spurned friends of Rusty had copped pleas, pinning everything on Rusty and Heather. Then, in separate interrogation rooms, the two blamed each other. Freedom didn't look good.

Brooke, Chase, and Parker staggered outside. The sun had descended, leaving dusk's glow over the Magic Kingdom. With Parker in the middle, the three held hands, heading nowhere in particular. Chase eyed a restaurant, and said, "I could really go for a pizza ..." Brooke and Parker chimed a resounding yes.

Eating breadsticks and sipping soda together, Parker asked, "Is Mommy going to jail?"

Chase had wondered how to broach the subject that weighed heavily on him since their release from detention. Realizing that Parker was wiser than his years, he sighed, then said, "Yes, son, I'm afraid so."

Parker accepted the information as if he expected the answer, then said, "I wanna stay with you, Daddy."

"Me too."

"Will Rusty go to jail too?"

"Yes, for a long time."

"I didn't like Rusty. He was mean."

Silence, then Parker said, "Can we stay at Disney some more?"

Chase gazed at Brooke, "Tell you what; we can stay another day here. If you ask Miss Ingram nicely, I bet she'd go with us tomorrow."

"For real?" Parker's eyes brightened. "Miss Ingram, will you? I want to show you and my daddy all the rides. My mom and Rusty were too scared to go on 'em."

Brooke laughed. So focused on finding Parker, she hadn't even considered her next steps. She eyed Chase, whose face beamed like his son's, then she said, "That's so sweet of you to ask me."

"Will you, please?"

"I'd love to. Thanks to both of you for asking."

After dinner, Chase bought them ice cream and, as it melted down the cones onto their hands, none of them cared. Viewing the crowd up ahead, they found a bench and huddled close together. Jiminy Cricket's voice boomed through the loudspeakers—then the famous fireworks extravaganza began. Parker's eyes popped with each magnificent burst in the sky. For the moment, they relaxed, forgetting about the earlier fireworks.

Parker's eyes wavered during the grand finale. Chase carried him back to the Cinderella Castle under a starlit sky. Parker slept the entire way. Once inside the suite, Brooke tiptoed to the small bedroom and pulled the covers back while Chase slowly set his son down. Parker's eyes popped open and he said, "Daddy, where am I?"

"You're in Cinderella's Castle son. We have a full day tomorrow. Go to sleep."

"Can we say our special prayers?"

Brooke snuggled beside Chase on Parker's bed, feeling warmth inside and out as father and son recited their prayers together. Memories of her own childhood flooded in. Brooke cherished a loving dad. On the craziest day Brooke had ever had, she also recognized both Chase and Parker were lucky.

After the final prayer, Chase lingered until his son's eyes closed. He combed his fingers through Parker's hair and whispered, "Daddy loves you."

Chase followed Brooke out of Parker's room and closed the door. He turned and jumped—Brooke startled him. Their eyes met, followed by a passionate embrace.

Pausing for air, Brooke said, "Watching you with Parker was the sweetest thing I've ever seen." They kissed again. A powerful feeling resonated inside.

"It's a Small World After All" rang out. Chase said, "Hmmm, I wonder who that could be ..." with mischievous eyes.

"I'll get it," Brooke said, eyeing Chase as she sauntered to the door. Snow White smiled and said, "Special room service for you."

Brooke gasped, pressing her hand to her mouth—Dom Perignon, flowers, and chocolate-covered strawberries. "Chase, how did you—"

Chase's lips met Brooke's before she could finish the sentence. Snow White turned to leave. Chase pulled back and said, "Wait a second, Snow White," then handed her a fifty.

In between sips, they fed each other strawberries while relaxing in the Starry Sky tub. Brooke paused, glanced up, and said, "Let's wish upon a star."

Chase raised his glass and clinked hers, "I got my wish already."

With the grand finale still fresh in their minds, it didn't take long before they created their own fireworks. After toweling off, Brooke modeled her glass slippers for Chase. That night, they felt the magic of Disney like never before.

Lying in Chase's arms, Brooke eyed the magic mirror on the wall and smiled. She understood what it meant to have dreams come true.

Brooke's eyes flickered as morning's light pierced the stained glass slipper window. She had set her own internal alarm clock—to avoid confusing Parker. Chase mumbled, still in a dream state, while Brooke messed up the other bed in the room. Then she slinked down the hall and noticed Parker sleeping. She tiptoed back, locked the door, and surprised Chase with the most amazing wakeup call he'd ever had.

While placing last night's room service order, Chase had also reserved a Mickey Mouse– themed breakfast for eight sharp. The restaurant was a short walk; glancing at his watch, they didn't have much time. He used the time excuse to coax Brooke into the shower with him. Holding soap and wearing nothing, she didn't offer much resistance. While Parker slept, they soaped each other—and quietly made love one more time.

Chase jiggled his son, "Parker, wake up buddy." His little eyes opened with a *where am I?* look. Chase mentioned Mickey Mouse and Parker's eyes brightened like Christmas morning.

Parker asked, "Can Miss Ingram go too?"

Brooke hung up with Marsha after explaining their ordeal and making plans for the next week.

"Yippee." Parker's enthusiasm started the day on the right foot— not counting the wakeup call and shower. All three of them were starving and the breakfast was plentiful. Mickey posed with Parker, then with Chase and Brooke. The photographer schmoozed, "You have a handsome family. We should use you in our brochures." Brooke sensed her eyes were off from yesterday's mace, but winked at him.

"Oh my God," Chase said with eyes wider than their breakfast plates.

"What's wrong?" Brooke asked.

"Look at this ..."

Chase handed Brooke the newspaper and pointed to the heading: "New York PI Slain in Mob-like Hit." Brooke stopped reading after the first two words of the article—"Max Molini."

Brooke said, "I'm so sorry. That's just awful. Were you two close?"

"No, I'm not sure Max would let anyone get close to him. I never met him face-to-face. I can't say I'm surprised."

"You sure you're okay?"

Chase shrugged, "Yeah, I'm good." He glanced at Parker, who was talking Mickey's ear off, then flipped the paper aside and said, "Let's do Disney."

At nine, they hit the park like paratroopers, starting at Big Thunder Mountain Railroad. The exhilarating ride challenged their full stomachs and their vocal cords; every ride afterward seemed easy. All three of them rode every ride they could, while racing each other to the next one. The Monday crowds thinned out from the weekend. Before lunchtime, they had covered most of the park.

Needing a break, Chase suggested they try their luck at the booths. Parker spotted a putting challenge and sprinted over to it. Chase bought Parker three tries. Then three for Brooke. After six misses, Parker said, "Daddy, your turn."

Chase steadied himself on one knee and lined up the putt. Then, with a crowd gathering, he nailed the long putt on his first attempt— Parker squealed. Chase qualified for a big prize and asked, "Which one do you want, son?"

Parker's eyes brightened as he scanned the stuffed Disney characters. He couldn't decide. Parker glanced at Brooke, "Which one would you get, Miss Ingram?"

Brooke smiled, then pointed and said, "Pluto. I wish I had a dog like that."

"Okay, Pluto," Parker pointed while bouncing up and down. The man handed the big yellow stuffed dog to Parker. He wrapped his arms around it, saying, "He's bigger than Duke."

Brooke raised an eyebrow at Chase, "Really?" Chase shrugged and grinned.

"You have two more tries, buddy," the cast member handed Chase two golf balls. Chase steadied himself and narrowly missed the next two, drawing sighs from the onlookers. Parker asked him to try again, but Chase surveyed the line behind him, and said, "No, son, we have to give these people a chance."

Parker glanced at Pluto, and said, "Here, Miss Ingram. You take him."

"Ohhh, that's so sweet," Brooke's eyes moistened. "I couldn't take him—he's yours."

"We already have a doggie."

Brooke hugged Parker while gazing at Chase. She said, "Parker, you're too cute. Can I take you home with me?"

Parker smiled and then said, "What are you gonna name him?"

Brooke grinned at Chase, and said, "NC."

Parker said, "That's a weird name."

Chase buckled over laughing while Brooke placed her hands on her hips. She wondered if Chase had already brainwashed the little guy.

With Chase carrying NC, they hit one more ride, then devoured pizza and milk shakes for lunch.

The scorching afternoon sun dictated an afternoon of water rides. With NC safe in the friendly staff's hands, the three splashed and giggled. They jumped back in line and did it again, feeling the magic of the moment.

At five o'clock, they picked up their bags and strolled back to the car while holding hands, recapping their favorite rides. Chase marveled at what a difference a day made.

Flying back to North Carolina, Parker perched on Brooke's lap in the cockpit—to search for sharks and be with the big people. No sharks, but plenty of birds flew between the translucent water and the cloudless sky. The return flight seemed much faster due to Parker's second wind. He was chatty and having the time of his life—and he wasn't alone.

After a smooth landing, they drove with NC sitting beside Parker in the back seat of the convertible. Driving into the leisure sunset, Parker said, "Can Miss Ingram sleep over tonight?"

Chase grinned, thinking his son was psychic.

Brooke said, "Oh, I'd love to, but I have to get back to my house. We have a big day tomorrow. You can use NC for show and tell."

"Miss Ingram, I wish you could live at our house."

The words struck Brooke and Chase like a lightning bolt. Both remained silent, searching for the right response. It marked the first time Parker alluded to the situation and neither adult knew what to say.

Finally, Brooke said, "I get to see you every day at Angel's Academy—I'm so lucky."

Dropping off Brooke felt like a funeral procession. All three had glum looks. Chase waited until Brooke's car started—secretly hoping it wouldn't. After the Lexus over on the first try, father and son waved, then drove away.

Parker said, "I really like Miss Ingram."

"Me too son."

After a somber drive home, the travelers were greeted at the door by an anxious Oksana holding the wildly wagging Duke. Oksana's hugs and Duke's licks erased Parker's sadness. Chase tucked Parker in as Duke sprawled on his bed with his chin on Chase's knee—home. Alone in his bedroom, Chase realized he never called in—or turned on his cell. It could wait. He had a more important thing to do before calling it a night.

"I just wanted to call to tuck you in."

"Aw, that's sweet of you. Did you and Parker already say your special prayers?"

"We did. He really likes you—he told me so right after we drove off. I told him I really like you too."

Brooke giggled, "I'm lying here with NC, thinking of how much fun I had today—with both of you."

"NC's one lucky dog ... But so am I. I can't thank you enough for everything you did. If you weren't there, I would have never found Parker."

"We did make a pretty good team."

"Goodnight Brooke. I ... I miss you. Sweet dreams."

Hanging up, Chase's heart pounded like a school boy with a crush. He said his own special prayers.

— ♥ —

Though exhausted physically, mentally, and emotionally, Brooke couldn't sleep. She replayed the previous four days. Although most would perceive a whirlwind, she felt lucidity. Glancing at the breakfast picture of the three of them, her heart glowed. A week ago, she despised him. Or did she? Brooke pondered the dichotomy of love. Then a flash hit.

Brooke jumped up and searched for the letter. She remembered he said it was in a large manila envelope. It didn't take long—she had tossed it on a collection of magazines she hated to toss but would never read.

She returned to bed and carefully opened the envelope. Sliding out the letters, she inhaled and beamed. Brooke detached the handwritten note from the paper clip, and as she read, she could hear his sexy voice. Brooke even loved his penmanship—as if he used a quill pen.

Everything he had said over the last four days rang true in his letter. Then she scanned the accompanying typed severance offer with glowing eyes. *I wish I had opened this sooner.*

When she read the final paragraph—time stood still:

I haven't been able to stop thinking about you. Our night together was the most magical I've ever felt. You truly are an amazing person. I should have never let you leave. I tried to return your slip, but must confess I couldn't bear to. What happened between us felt so right. Maybe God intervened this way so we could be together. I know we belong together. Please call me.

Love, Chase

Brooke read it over and over, and giggled about the infamous pink slip—or slipup. She set his note beside her bed and hugged NC picturing Chase. She slept with warmth in her heart.

— ♥ —

Strolling into Starbucks, Chase surveyed the area—no Brooke. He didn't expect to see her, but still hoped. He had missed his favorite coffee place—and Brooke. Marcus delivered the usual amusing greeting and two steaming quad espressos. Halfway to his convertible, thunder crashed, followed by a sudden downpour. He sprinted, nearly spilling his coffees, and raised the car top. *Shit.*

Now saturated, he contemplated returning home to change. Chase powered on his cell, hoping it still worked, then the voicemail alert beeped. After hearing the first two messages, he raced to the office—where a worse storm was brewing.

Arriving first, he spotted the pink note on his desk—from Ruth: "Urgent. Mr. Stoddard needs to talk to you. He called three times. I saw the news. I hope you're okay."

The news?

Chase darted to Ruth's cubicle and grabbed the two newspapers. The headline in the local paper made his knees buckle. Then, The Wall Street Journal's blurb on the front page struck like a gunshot wound.

So caught up in finding Parker, he didn't even consider the ramifications of the Heather outing. Scanning each article, the words seared like bullets—arrested, addicted, divorce, CEO's wife, Stabilitas, and suicide attempt.

Fearing the next day's articles would read former CEO, he hiked the lonesome trek to Henry's office.

— 💜 —

"I've been dying to call you."

"What happened?"

"Where do I begin?"

Shane sighed and then asked, "Good news or bad news?"

"Amazing news!"

Shane almost said, *Is that really you Brooke?* Instead, he eased back and listened to her recount the past five days in rapid fire. He couldn't remember her ever sounding this enthusiastic. She told him he would have been proud of the advice she provided. Brooke continued; Shane sensed his client had graduated. Feeling a strong sense of accomplishment, Shane actually patted himself on the back.

When Brooke paused to breathe, she asked, "What do you think?"

"I think you're in love."

Brooke stared at the bedside table holding Chase's letter, "I'm not sure you can call it love after four days."

"You've known Chase for much longer than four days. And I've known you for a long time. You should listen to your own voice—you're head over heels in love."

"I don't know what to say."

"It's a good thing. You've been so busy suffocating yourself, let alone your relationships, that when true love hits, it feels foreign to you."

"That didn't sound encouraging."

"Nonsense. You've made a giant quantum leap. Stop the analysis paralysis and start living your bliss."

"But, it's so soon …"

"There you go again. Don't you dare short circuit your emotions. Be your bliss."

"What the fuck has happened to you?"

"Henry, settle down—"

"Settle down? The board's crawling up my ass and you want me to settle down?"

"Listen, I can explain everyth—"

"There's nothing to explain. It's all over the fucking papers!"

"I've been meaning to tell you about Heather, but you wouldn't understand."

"Try me." Henry puffed his chest out, standing toe to toe with Chase. Chase had him by four inches, but feared the old man could kick his ass.

Chase stepped back and explained, "All my life, I've wanted to be the perfect husband, father, and CEO. Then the wife I thought I knew turned into a monster."

"C'mon, Heather's hardly a monster. She's a stunning model."

"To you, and to everyone else. But once Parker was born, she changed. She hated her life, hated me, and hated herself enough to commit suicide."

"The press is having a field day linking Stabilitas *with her suicide attempt. I tried calling you all day yesterday—where were you?*"

"*Rescuing Parker. She kidnapped him.*"

"*Oh, and tortured him by taking him to Disney?*" Henry crossed his arms over his chest.

Chase frowned, "Cut the sarcasm for a minute. I sent her to rehab. I tried everything. Then she disappears and ends up with this creep. He pulled a freaking gun on me."

"Do you have any idea what you've done? I trusted you. You were like a son to me. Now this?"

"You know what? For the last few years, I've been living a lie. When my wife turned into a suicidal drug addict and took off, I went into survival mode. I didn't dare mention divorce to this company. I did the best I could raising a son on my own and trying to do this damn job. You have no idea what that's like."

Henry shook his head like a grandfather clock, then said, "I can't protect you on this one."

Chase gulped, "Are you firing me?"

"You don't leave me any choice. Read the papers. Hell, you fired yourself."

As the words settled in, Chase's angst lifted into a strange serenity. He had anticipated this for so long that when it hit, he felt relief—when the bullied stands up to discover the bully's a coward.

Chase inhaled, "I'll make this easy for you ..."

After Chase finished, Henry grinned like the Grinch. Marching away, Chase hoped Friday would be the last time he saw that face.

Sondra, Betsy Stanton's daughter covered for Brooke on Monday and, according to the glowing report from the kids, did a superb job. Still there when Brooke arrived Tuesday, Sondra made a great impression—just like her mother.

Later in the morning, Show and Tell featured NC. Brooke brought him, but had asked Parker to leave her name out of the story so the other kids wouldn't get jealous. He asked her what "jealous" meant in such a cute little boy way. Then, as she explained, his focused brown eyes made her melt.

Miss Ingram eased back and enjoyed Parker's animated storytelling. He had a knack, a confidence in front of his peers. Popular and charming—just like his father. She worried about how the weekend's events would affect him, but he showed no signs of sadness. Brooke felt akin to Parker, remembering what it was like to grow up without a mother—but with a terrific father.

Reading *Cinderella*, Miss Ingram felt a funny sensation. She paused and spotted Chase against the back wall. Blushing, she botched the next line. Brooke glanced at the bag and giggled at the glass slippers she planned to model at the story's end.

After the kids left, Chase and Parker remained. Marsha had the afternoon off. The three stood silently for a few seconds. Chase sent Parker to go grab NC, then whispered in Brooke's ear, "I hardly recognized you in those glass slippers—with your clothes on."

"I see Prince Charming hasn't lost his sassiness."

"Want a ride in my red chariot?"

Parker lumbered over with NC in his arms. He said, "Can Miss Ingram come over?"

Chase raised his eyebrows at Brooke. She eyed both of them and said, "Hey, did you guys plan this?"

Parker giggled, which triggered Chase's hearty laugh—Brooke had her answer.

Parker hugged NC in the back seat and said, "Daddy, can you turn on silly songs. I told Miss Ingram I can sing 'em."

Chase said, "Did you guys plan this?" Giggles from Parker and Brooke.

Flipping on Parker Tunes, father and son sang every song—to the absolute delight of Brooke. *Is there anything he can't do?* The ride home seemed shorter; Chase noticed his palms were sweaty. Aside from Oksana, he hadn't had a female to his house since Heather. He hoped Duke would behave. And he hoped Brooke liked authentic Ukrainian fare.

As they pulled into the driveway, Brooke's eyes widened, "Sheesh, nice house."

Chase said, "You'll have to pardon the mess—and watch out for the dog. He gets a little hyper when we come home."

"You mean Duke? A dukie gets hyper around a girl?"

"Very funny."

The garage door opened. Oksana gripped Duke's collar as they parked. Brooke rubbed her neck, thinking, she looks familiar—where have I seen her?

They exited the BMW and Oksana struggled to hold Duke. Chase said, "You can let him go. Come here Duke." Oksana released Duke, then sighed.

Brooke stared—*I have definitely seen her … then, it dawned on her.*

Chase clutched Duke, whose front paws set on his shoulders and made the introduction, "Oksana, say hello to Brooke."

Oksana wiped her hand on her apron and extended it toward Brooke. *She's the nanny?*

Inside, Chase said, "Would you like a quick tour?"

"Sure." Brooke fixed her gaze on Oksana.

Parker said, "C'mon Miss Ingram, I'll show you my room," then dashed up the stairs. Brooke and Chase followed, well behind Parker. Passing the master bedroom, Chase winked at Brooke. She ignored him.

With hyper voice, Parker showed Brooke his toys, books, and played her a few Raffi tunes. He treated Brooke like a friend over to play. Chase learned which things ranked at the top of Parker's world.

Parker said, "I got lots of Legos for my birthday. You wanna build another castle with me?"

Brooke smiled, Chase raised a quizzical eyebrow.

Before Brooke could answer, Chase said, "Not right now. We have to eat dinner soon. Parker, you need to pick up your room first."

Chase and Brooke strolled away with Parker saying, "How about after dinner?"

Brooke said, "Nice try," from the hallway and giggled.

Chase led Brooke into the master bedroom and planted a dramatic kiss. Brooke pulled back and frowned. Chase asked, "What's wrong?"

Brooke inhaled a deep breath, then released slowly. "Remember how you said you'd always be truthful with me?"

"Yes, and I meant it."

Brooke sighed, peering deeply into his eyes, then said, "Is Oksana more than just a nanny to you?"

"She cooks, cleans, does it all really. But I think I know what you're asking—is she a mother to Parker? No. He sees you as—"

"That's not what I'm asking."

"I don't understand." Chase rubbed the back of his neck.

"I'm going to ask you a direct question and if you don't want to answer it, fine."

Chase raised his eyebrows, "What's this about?"

"Are you sleeping with Oksana?"

The question knocked Chase back a step. He scrunched his brows and glared at Brooke, then said, "That's ridiculous."

Brooke crossed her arms across her chest and dove in, "About a month ago, at noon, I saw you walking arm-in-arm into a hotel with Oksana."

"That's impossible. You have me confused with someone else."

"Nope. I was close by. It was definitely you and then, when I saw Oksana today, it registered. You carried a lingerie bag and she wore a low-cut dress. You two were laughing as you entered the Renaissance at North Hills—"

"North Hills?" Chase's eyes narrowed, "I remember now. Oksana was kind enough to go shopping with me for Parker's birthday."

"Unh huh. At the hotel?"

"Oh my God, you can't possibly think," Chase's eyes darted like strobe lights, then he said, "Ah, now I remember. I had to use the bathroom. That mall doesn't have any public facilities. We both had to go—the hotel was right there. We were only in there for ten minutes."

"Did you get Parker lingerie? That's the only bag I saw—"

"Lingerie? That's absurd. Come to think of it, I bought her a belated gift for her birthday. She said she needed a swimming suit—to go to the beach with her boyfriend. I bought her one—an expensive one—at some store. I forget the name, but they only sold swimwear, not lingerie."

Brooke stared into Chase's eyes and knew—he spoke the truth. She sighed, "You have no idea how stupid I feel right now."

Chase glared, Brooke released a nervous laugh—the final piece fell into place. A wave of relief enveloped her. Brooke hugged Chase with a firm grip, then glanced at his bed—and spotted the infamous pink slip beside his pillow. Another truth revealed. She giggled.

Chase broke the hug, holding Brooke at arm's length. "My turn now."

Brooke frowned, Chase continued, "Tell me the truth about how my boss found out about us?"

"I already told you the truth. I ... did ... not ... tell ... Henry—or anyone," Brooke bit her lip, then continued, "Actually, I told my best friend Melissa. I was her maid of honor that night. But she's the only one I told. There's no way she—"

"I don't understand how Stoddard found out."

"Not from me." Chase figured she told the truth. Both stood in silence, then Brooke said, "Hey, wait a minute. I found your envelope—you know, the famous *big package*. The seal looked broken—like somebody opened it and resealed it."

Chase rubbed his chin and explained, "I personally wrote that note with my fountain pen, then sealed it myself. Afterward, I marked it 'Personal & Confidential.'"

"I know, but did you mail it yourself?"

"Yes. I handed it to Ruth, but ..." Chase's eyes met Brooke's, "she's the only one who could have ... I can't believe she'd do something like that."

"Ruth's given me the heebie-jeebies since I first met her."

"God, I've confided in her ..."

"About us?"

"No, of course not. About the situation with Heather."

"I think Ruth has a crush on you."

"You're crazy. She's married. Plus, she works for me." Brooke suppressed her thought.

"Dinner!" Oksana pierced the silence like a foghorn across a still pond.

With everything resolved, Chase and Brooke relaxed, savoring each bite of Oksana's gourmet Ukrainian dinner. Hearing about Oksana's upbringing, Brooke appreciated her more.

From the first course to Parker's favorite—Yabluchnyk, a Ukrainian apple cake—the meal tasted scrumptious. Oksana took great pride in being part of Chase's family. And Brooke cherished it.

Chase awarded Oksana the rest of the night off—to spend with Dmitri. He and Brooke cleaned up the kitchen. Afterward, Chase, Brooke, and Parker took Duke on a nice walk. Brooke marveled—*I never pegged him a family man.*

Brooke and Chase settled on Parker's bed, preparing to tuck him in. Duke whimpered, waiting impatiently to jump up on the crowded bed. Parker asked, "Can Miss Ingram help me say my special prayers?"

Brooke gazed at Chase and mouthed, *he's too cute.* Chase said, "Sure thing, buddy."

Brooke placed her hand across Parker's chest and they both recited the familiar prayers. Brooke slid her fingers through Parker's short hair. The spike had fallen and the dye Oksana used had returned his hair to its natural brown shade. Brooke hoped his dreadful memories faded like the bad dye job from Heather.

Parker's eyelids flickered, then closed; Chase said, "I love you."

Brooke turned—Chase's eyes fixed on hers. They gazed at each other while Parker's breathing deepened. Chase caressed Brooke's hair, then placed his hand in hers. She rose without breaking her eye contact, then their lips met. Duke leaped on the bed and made a funny grumbling sound, causing the couple to pause and chuckle.

Chase led Brooke down the hallway and stopped. They kissed again, this time with wanton desire. As they broke for air, Brooke gazed into Chase's eyes and said, "I love you." Their lips melded as if repeating the three magic words telepathically.

He lifted Brooke up in his arms and carried her into his bedroom. Placing her in the middle of the bed, he slid on top of her. Their eyes locked in a lover's gaze. He said, "I loved you the moment I saw you," then kissed her.

Their eyes met, and Brooke said, "Make love to me ..."

Becoming one, their desires felt delirious yet delicate. Their lovemaking reached profound depths, familiarity, knowing. The passion heightened, then they exploded in ecstasy together. Gasping for air, they collapsed in each other's arms.

With moistened eyes, Chase said, "That was amazing."

Brooke said, "I love you so much," as her tears slid onto his chest.

They held each other in silence, allowing love's whisper to ring inside. Both felt awed by their emotional release. Was it pent-up stress or suppressed pleasure? Either way, this time they had taken a quantum leap together. And neither one wanted to ever turn back. Brooke hadn't quite felt this same force before; Chase had never come close.

Brooke noticed something strange in the room. She focused, then asked, "Is that a guitar?"

Chase broke from his tranquility, and said, "One of 'em."

Brooke bolted upright, the dappled moonlight beamed off her glistening skin. "Oh, my God. Pinch me. You are the perfect man." Chase chuckled. Brooke said, "Will you play something?"

"Sure," Chase pulled on his boxer briefs, then strode over and lifted his guitar off the stand. Sitting at Brooke's feet, he played the familiar opening to "Something" by The Beatles. Pausing before the vocal part, he said, "You asked me to play 'Something.'" Brooke giggled.

Enjoying a captive audience—it had been a long time since he serenaded anyone but Duke—Chase said, "I wrote a song for you."

"Did you really?" Brooke tingled inside, reminiscent of junior high. "Like, I mean, I'd love to hear it." She stuttered as cupid's arrows struck.

Chase played the first few notes of "Crash Into Me." Brooke's laugh shook the bed, then she said, "Keep playing. I love Dave Matthews. It reminds me of," her eyes sparkled, "It could be our song."

"Do you know any James Taylor?" As the words left her mouth, she braced herself. JT songs reminded Brooke of Tanner—their first date, countless lovemaking sessions, and fond times.

Chase played the intro to "Fire and Rain." The song always brought tears to Brooke's eyes. Chase stopped and asked, "Am I playing that badly?"

Brooke sniffled, "No, that song reminds me of ..." Brooke glanced away and wiped her fluttering eyes.

"Tanner?"

"Yeah. The JT concert was our first date. That song's such a sad one for me. I'm sorry."

Chase slid his hand on top of Brooke's and said, "I understand. Believe me, I do. Music has a mystical way of touching us."

Brooke sniffled, "I'm better now. I'm sorry. I hope I didn't spoil the moment."

"Well, this probably won't help, but ..." He lifted his guitar up and pointed to writing at the base. Brooke squinted, hoping to dry her eyes enough to see it. Then it came into focus: "To My Dear Friend Chase. Enjoy My Guitar, James Taylor."

Brooke looked dumbfounded, "Where did you find that?"

"It's a beauty—the Olson guitar he actually played during a benefit concert I attended. It was auctioned off; I outbid everyone and asked him to sign it for me."

Brooke's jaw dangled open, "You actually met JT?"

"He's a great guy. Real soft spoken. You'd never guess he was a legend."

"You never cease to amaze me."

Chase chuckled and started strumming, "Don't worry, this isn't a JT song."

Brooke cocked her head, "That's beautiful. I don't recognize it though. What's it called?"

"I haven't named it yet."

"Wait a minute. *You* wrote this song?"

Chase paused, "Yeah, one night, I couldn't sleep—thinking about you—imagine that. Then this melody came to me. You like it?"

"You did what?" Brooke lunged forward, nearly knocking Chase off the bed, as her lips landed hard.

"If that's how you like it now, I can only imagine what you'll do when I finish it." She joined his lips as if giving him mouth-to-mouth resuscitation.

I'll finish another time.

— 💜 —

The alarm rang way too early. Brooke didn't plan on spending the night and realized she couldn't show up in the same dress. Chase wished Brooke's clothing filled his walk-in closet. The drive back to her car took on a serenity—like the start of a honeymoon. The sun popped, piercing the darkness just as they pulled into Angel's Academy.

Chase kissed Brooke and asked, "Can I see you tonight?"

"Will you let me sleep a little?"

"We went to bed early ..." Chase's grin illuminated with a ray of sunshine.

Brooke's eyes crinkled, "We have to find a happy medium between bed and sleep."

"Is that a yes?"

"Sleep's overrated," Brooke kissed Chase, holding on longer than usual.

Chase floated to Starbucks as if on a magic carpet. He left carrying three quad espressos. He had to make Miss Ingram laugh once more.

Chase surprised Brooke in the Angel's Academy parking lot. When he handed the still steaming coffee to her, she said, "I hope it's the right temperature." They both laughed, then after making sure no kids had arrived early, kissed one last time. A perfect way to start the day.

Inside the courtroom, Pam Moliere arrived just before nine. Chase didn't mind. There was nothing they needed to do—except signatures. Pam's clout ensured they were first on the judge's busy docket.

After a quick handshake, Pam asked, "Ready to set the record for the quickest divorce in Carolina?"

Chase inhaled, "I think so." His stomach churned. Though the divorce was long overdue, he felt queasy. His present collided with the past. As life blossomed with Brooke, it was imploding at work and with the mother of his child. Thinking of Heather—how strung out she looked—he still couldn't believe it had come to this.

Courtrooms always made him feel somber. He glanced at Pam, grateful he never became a trial lawyer. *I don't know how she does it?*

The large wooden door swung open. As the judge approached the bench, Chase braced himself. Realizing the past five years were about to be erased, sadness set in. There because of a *failed marriage*, he felt responsibility for his part of the failure. Like a zombie, he listened to Pam and some judge end his previous five years of marriage—in five minutes.

Clad in suit and tie, Chase signed the papers; later, Heather would do the same in an orange jumpsuit. Even though Pam had tried to persuade Chase to fight the pre-nuptial, he was glad he didn't. Leaving the courthouse, he held his head high, hoping to never see Pam again. He wondered how Parker would take the news—and how often he'd take him to visit his mother in a Minnesota federal prison.

Chase dreaded the office. Henry had him in a holding pattern until Friday. Chase imagined the boardroom, wondering if any board members would feel somber as they cast their severance votes. His professional life was in his former mentor's hands. Chase had never been a lame duck; the master manager didn't have any idea how to manage limbo.

As he walked toward the corner of the exec floor, things looked foreign. When he spotted Ruth, his stomach sank. He hoped he wouldn't speak his mind. Near her cubicle, Ruth said, "There you are," as she tried to inform him of things that didn't matter.

Chase stormed past her with a terse, "Hold all my calls," then shut his door. He couldn't even glance at her.

Sitting, staring out the window, his eyes defocused. He concentrated on his breathing. Feeling his pulse return to normal, Chase spun around. His desk contained the usual pink-note litter and inbox clutter. He chuckled and decided against flipping on his computer. Chase glanced at his phone. He considered dialing Dixie-dawg for a golf game, but didn't want to miss picking up Parker—or seeing Brooke.

Instead, Chase set up the appointment downtown.

The kids clutched their coloring papers, eyes fixed on their storyteller. Brooke peered up from the interactive story "Squiggles and Giggles" and smiled. Chase tried to blend into the back wall, but managed to catch Brooke's eye.

After the children found their rides, Parker showed Chase his drawing with his patented enthusiasm. Chase glanced at Brooke and suggested, "I bet Miss Ingram would like that drawing." Parker beamed, then handed it to her. Brooke clenched it like it belonged in the Louvre.

Parker said, "Can Miss Ingram come over?"

Chase raised one eyebrow and smiled, "I thought we'd take her mini-golfing."

Father and son stood at attention awaiting her response. Brooke's face brightened, "That sounds like fun." Parker bounced up and down in excitement.

Once outside, Brooke veered over to her Lexus. Chase said, "Don't you want to go in one car?"

She popped her trunk, then lifted her suitcase, asking, "Can you give me a hand with this? It's too heavy for me."

At Pirate's Cove, Parker's favorite mini-golf course, the eighteen holes played like a cartoon. They laughed and enjoyed each other's mishaps, including when Brooke splashed her ball into the water hazard. She made up for it on the next hole. Her still-damp ball dropped in the cup for the day's first hole-in-one. Parker high-fived Miss Ingram, who couldn't remember the last time she'd had so much fun.

Parker persuaded Miss Ingram to go to Chuck E. Cheese while Chase was in the men's room. After his protest was overruled, Chase called and offered Oksana the night off again.

Brooke said, "Tomorrow night, I'd like to make dinner for y'all." The image of Shane scolding her popped up, but neither Chase nor Parker minded her *y'all*. She didn't miss the days when it mattered.

After sharing a pizza, they enjoyed an ice cream, then worked off the calories with Duke. Stopping at the park, they tossed tennis balls until Duke nearly collapsed. Back home, Miss Ingram tucked in Parker.

Knowing they could sleep a little longer, they stayed up a little later, working off even more calories. Afterward, Chase cuddled with Brooke until she fell asleep. He didn't want the night to end, but sensed he had better let her sleep. Sleeping beside Brooke, he considered himself the luckiest man on the planet.

Parker enjoyed Brooke almost as much as his father did. He hadn't asked about his mother since they returned from Florida.

After school, Brooke baked her daddy's famous lobster lasagna for Parker, Chase, Oksana, and Dmitri. Chase even brought a couple bottles of Pouilly Fuissé—her favorite wine. Chase and Parker cleaned up the kitchen as Brooke phoned her father. She had thought of him while preparing dinner, but didn't have the nerve to tell him where she was.

Brooke wouldn't commit to a weekend visit with her dad, using the excuse that she had met someone—big mistake. Weston's incessant questioning rivaled the Nuremburg Trials. Brooke promised to see him soon, and with slight guilt, she hung up.

Brooke joined Chase, Oksana, Dmitri, and Parker on the deck. Parker entertained them by chasing Duke all over the yard, never quite catching him.

"Duke, Duke, Duke of Earl"—Chase's ringtone bellowed amid the laughter and chatter. It was Mary, the mother of Will, Parker's classmate, who said, "It sounds like you have company?"

"I can talk. What's up?"

Mary said, "I'm calling to remind you about Will's birthday party."

"Oh, right. I'm glad you called."

"I wanted to ask you a favor ..."

Chase smiled, stood, then finished the call inside. When he returned, he said, "Bedtime, mister." Parker put up a mild protest, but Chase lifted him up, saying, "You need your rest. You have a big weekend." He winked at Brooke, asking, "Can you get him to bed? I need to ask Oksana something."

Parker started snoring the moment his head hit the pillow. Brooke felt tipsy and started preparing for bed. She guessed Chase was still talking to Oksana. While brushing her teeth, Chase surprised her. She laughed and nearly swallowed the toothpaste. She rinsed, then stood. Chase slid his arms around Brooke from behind and leaned around to kiss her cheek. Brooke turned and their lips met.

After a long kiss, Chase said, "Oooo, minty fresh," with a sparkle in his eye. Brooke turned to face him—she could stare at his lashes all night.

Their passion intensified. Wild kissing intertwined with wilder groping as they flung their clothes across the tile. The effects of the wine worked its magic; Chase paused, awestruck by Brooke's moonlit figure, then he raised her in the air. She felt a déjà vu until he lowered her onto the granite counter. Her eyes widened. His deepening thrusts sent shivers throughout her. She moaned, not wanting the feral feeling to end. She burst a flood of ecstasy, gasping with each pulse. Chase's eyes expanded, then he moaned his release.

Quivering, they hugged. Brooke's voice dropped as she said, "Wow ... I hope we don't make this granite melt."

Gasping, with sweat beading on his forehead, Chase said, "You make me melt."

Chase lifted Brooke off the counter and carried her to their bed. The combination of wine and savage lust had the couple sleeping instantly.

Several minutes later, Brooke entered a vivid dream state.

Tanner looked healthy—just like the college days. She was sitting on Chase's lap, topless yet uninhibited. They were floating around the beach. She kept saying, "Come back," to Tanner, but he smiled lovingly, and finally said, "I never left. I'm always here, by your side—like I promised you."

"But you're gone Tanner, I can't see you ..."

"I've tried so many times to reach you but I'm running out of time."

"Come back."

"I can't come back. But I've been there every time you asked—the wind, the coins with our special dates, Angel's Academy, I even kept that spider from biting you—I know how much you hate spiders."

"Come back to me, Tanner. I'm sorry for loving Chase."

"I brought you Chase. It's okay. You need to let me go. There's so much I need to do here—but not till you let me go. Be with Chase. He loves you like I love you."

Brooke was crying. Then Tanner wiped her tears and chanted, "Read the letter. Read the letter. Read the letter ..."

"What letter? What letter? Read what letter, Brooke?" Chase pulled Brooke close.

"Huh," Brooke's eyes fluttered as she crossed over the ledge of the two worlds.

Chase asked, "Are you okay?"

"I ... I was having a dream." Brooke's eyes glistened.

"I know."

"Oh, it seemed so real," Brooke slid out of bed, grabbed a paper and pen and headed to the bathroom. She wrote everything she could recall. Satisfied she had captured the important dream details, Brooke set her alarm an hour earlier.

"I've seen fire and I've seen rain ..." The James Taylor song made Chase bolt upright.

Brooke said, "Sorry, that's my alarm. Can you take me back to my car? I have to grab something from my apartment before work."

Groggy Chase dropped perky Brooke off at her car. The sun wouldn't rise for another half hour. They kissed. Chase even looked cute with sleep in his eyes. During the fifteen-minute drive back to her apartment, Brooke recalled the dream one more time. Unable to fall back asleep, she kept replaying it.

Once inside the dark dwelling, she felt a chill. *Is that you, Tanner?* Another chill. Brooke flipped on the main light, then stood still with hackles rising. Nothing. She plodded toward the credenza, realizing she hadn't read the letter since that day. She clicked on the lamp and froze—

Three shiny dimes sparkled from the base of Tanner's picture.

Brooke lifted them up, examining each one under the light—*holy shit: the year we met, our wedding year, and the year he died.* Hackles rose again. The light flickered. "Tanner … Tanner, you're freaking me out." Brooke scanned the room—nothing.

Brooke inched the drawer open and removed the envelope. The lights flickered again. "Tanner … Tanner, knock it off. I need light to read." Then another light illuminated. Brooke's eyes nearly popped out, then she felt a strange sensation, which made her giggle. Brooke had enough proof—only Tanner knew that ticklish spot. She glanced at his picture and smiled. Her fear now soothed, she was ready.

Opening the envelope, she read each word with heightened awareness. She comprehended everything differently, like she'd cracked the code to a hidden treasure. She wrote the key phrases:

1. *A room full of children who adore you and your beautiful eyes and radiant smile.*
2. *The place we dreamed of by the ocean.*
3. *As God is my witness, I'll find a way to help you in the afterlife like that movie you and I watched.*
4. *I'll protect you and even help you meet someone who loves you, though it's not possible to find anyone who could love you more than me.*
5. *I'll try to give you the things we dreamed about.*

Brooke felt a burst of energy. Tanner had kept all of his promises. Brooke's life story began to flash, things made sense.

Travis Bodady magically found her the GenSense job. She originally thought the recruiter chased the obituaries, but now she knew.

Shane magically appeared at the perfect time.

The money after the GenSense buyout.

Buying the Hilton Head place.

Angel's Academy.

Chase.

Tanner's line resonated—*I brought you Chase.* Brooke's heart warmed. *Come to think of it, I fell for Chase the moment he breezed into that boardroom. It was as if I had been healed from blindness that day. Then the way I fell in that elevator ... I learned about Guardian Angels in grade school. After all these years, now I believe.*

She smiled at Tanner's picture and it started to shake slightly—like an earthquake's tremor. Earlier, this occurrence would have spooked her; now, she felt comforted. She slid the three dimes in with the letter and sealed the envelope.

Brooke knelt with the letter in her trembling hands. She glanced up and said, "God, I don't always understand your mysterious ways, but I thank you for helping me understand a little bit of it right now. I feel so much better. Please free Tanner to do the great things he spoke of doing in heaven. Thank you for bestowing so many blessings—Tanner, Daddy, GenSense, Shane, Angel's Academy, and Chase. Amen."

— ♥ —

Chase's last drive to Pharmical felt bittersweet. With the top up and the wipers squeaking, the weather matched his mood. Henry had set up a lunch meeting, which meant the soon-to-be former CEO's severance made the top of the board meeting's agenda.

He parked across from Starbucks and settled for a moment. Glancing at the sign, he realized he'd miss Marcus more than anyone left at Pharmical. No contest. Marcus was genuine, unlike all the corporate phonies. He recalled Dixie-dawg's line—"The higher you climb, the more people want to fuck you over." *The dawg prophet?*

Ruth's betrayal stung the most, but Henry's ranked a close second. At least The Butcher didn't hide his intentions—*I wonder if he'll be there today?* After ordering his final two quad espressos, he shook Marcus's hand and slipped him two folded hundred dollar bills, and said, "You call me if you ever need anything."

Chase wouldn't miss the corporate paranoia, but he would miss his few authentic friends.

Marching across the office floor toward the corner, he picked up on the glares that struck him like blow darts. Chase maintained upright posture, ignoring each cubicle pygmy. *I wonder how they found out?* Spotting Ruth sitting cocksure, he fixed his gaze on his office.

As Chase passed her, she said, "You want me to hold your calls again?" Her voice struck his back—fitting.

While closing the door, Chase grunted what Ruth perceived to be a yes. He plopped on his chair, then started a slow 360-degree twirl. Later today, he figured it would all be boxed and labeled. He'd take what he could—especially the Coach K memorabilia—but probably just have the rest of it shipped.

Chase wondered who would occupy his chair—probably an outsider. He ignored both his paper and electronic inbox and spent the rest of the morning enjoying his last espresso while playing Internet backgammon.

Ruth's buzz startled him. "Sorry to bother you. Henry Stoddard's ready for your lunch meeting."

That was fast. It wasn't even 11:30 yet.

Henry stood to greet Chase. After a firm handshake—reminiscent of when they first met—Henry plopped down at the white clothed table and furrowed his brows, "The board has reached a decision." Chase stared into Henry's eyes. Henry continued, "I was able to sell them on your proposed severance agreement."

I was able to sell them? Chase wouldn't be able to stomach any food if Henry kept this up. They'd have to go outdoors—this restaurant wasn't big enough for Henry's ego. Chase stuck to his plan and just listened.

Henry said, "I might be able to add an extra kicker, provided you work with us on clearing up this mess."

Chase gulped hard, again hoping to contain his rampant thoughts. He drew a deep breath, then motioned his hand into an open palm and raised his eyebrows.

Henry continued, "Joanne's PR firm is willing to help."

"PR? What are you talking about?"

"Relax. You go on a couple of the right shows … say a few good things about Stabilitas, distance it from Heather's problems."

Chase crossed his arms across his chest, "I'm not going on any TV show to badmouth my ex-wife."

"That's not what I'm asking. We don't expect you to badmouth her, just to correct the misinformation about Stabilitas."

"No TV interviews, and I'm not going to lie for money."

"For Christ's sake, Chase, why do you have to make this so difficult?"

"I'd say the severance I proposed was a gift to Pharmical, but if you'd rather play hard ball ..."

Henry slammed the table, rattling the silverware and nearly spilling the water glasses, "Goddammit, I'm not playing hardball here. You already got what you wanted—I'm just asking for you to right what's wrong."

"So long as your idea of right and wrong agrees with mine, then I'll listen," Chase stood, placed his napkin on the table and said, "Send me what you've got in mind and I'll consider it. But I'm not going on TV." Chase stood and began to leave.

"Where are you going? We haven't even ordered?"

"I lost my appetite. You can eat my lunch." The pun wasn't lost on Henry's face.

"Sit back down or the deal's off."

"Deal? What deal? You want to puppet parade me and turn my life into a public spectacle, I'll see you in court. I have an ironclad employment contract. I should know—I wrote it. Tell your board to kiss my—"

"Sit down! And lower your voice. Be reasonable here."

Chase noticed all the eyes now glued to their table like ringside at a boxing match. "Lower my voice?" Chase said—with a hushed voice.

"Sit down or else." Henry's face had turned darker than iced tea.

"Are you threatening me?"

"Of course not. Sit down. You're not leaving until you sign these papers."

"The only papers I'll sign are for the severance we discussed."

Henry's upper lip trembled. Chase couldn't tell if Henry was going to cry or explode—or both. Henry rubbed his neck and agreed, "Fine, here." He gave Chase exactly what he wanted.

Chase read each page carefully. Henry scanned the room, wanting to order, but the waiter cowered in the kitchen. Henry scrutinized Chase's signature on the first page, chuckled, then said, "I think we scared our waiter off."

Chase finished signing six papers in duplicate and grabbed his copies. He studied Henry's solemn face and then stood, "Thanks for lunch. Goodbye, Henry."

Chase strolled out the door. Henry could only grin. He always liked his protégé—Chase reminded him of himself in his younger, more rambunctious days. Henry now wondered if they were mistaken to let him go.

Back at the office, with the door shut, Chase closed his eyes and breathed. He closed the chapter on Pharmical. He grabbed a few key items—including Coach K's picture. He laughed, remembering the last thing he needed to do.

"Do you have any plans this weekend?"

Brooke smirked, "The usual. A few hot dates. What about you—now that Parker is at Will's until Sunday night?"

"Let's go to the beach." Chase reached out and clenched both of Brooke's hands.

"I might be able to break—"

Chase locked lips. She leaned back against the wall, still holding the kiss. Tingles flew inside both of them. Finally, they broke for air. Brooke blushing, said, "Let's go."

When Chase mentioned flying to Hilton Head, her heart fluttered. Remembering her dream, she smiled.

21

*C*hase's heart raced as fast as the propellers on his plane. Flying with Brooke posed quite a different challenge than when flying with Parker. For one, she looked radiant, her hair flowing naturally against her delicate skin. Watching her lips move with each syllable, he wanted to kiss her. Thankfully, the sky was blue and the winds were calmer than usual.

The landing felt smooth; Brooke marveled at Chase's touch: whether playing guitar, driving, flying—or other things. While flying, she felt carefree. Her dream kept repeating in her head and she nearly told him about it.

In the parking area, she heard the beep from Chase's remote key, then laughed, "Do you own anything other than beemers?"

"There is no substitute," Chase chuckled.

"I think that's a Porsche."

"A minor detail, my fair maiden," Chase pulled Brooke into his arms, then said, "Would James Bond drive a Porsche?"

Brooke's lips pursed, preparing to speak as his kiss landed. Their lips felt custom made for each other.

The traffic flowed well for a Friday. Brooke wanted to show Chase her villa, but couldn't wait to see his. Brooke said, "Tell me about your place?"

"It's small, but nice. Typical island décor."

As they pulled into the three-car garage, Brooke's eyes bulged— this is anything but small.

Once inside, she admired the ocean through the huge picture windows. Brooke surveyed the house like her first time inside Disney. And she felt like Cinderella once again. Chase opened the back sliding glass door and asked, "What do you think?"

"Oh my God ... It's amazing. You're right on the ocean," she giggled while gripping his arm tightly. She said, "Can we go out there? I need to kiss you on the beach." Brooke loped toward the dunes.

Chase surprised her as he gripped her from behind, nearly tackling her into the sand. Lifting her with his strong arms, he set her in front of him and announced, "I love you."

Brooke melted inside, but somehow managed, "I love you," before he proved he could kiss on the beach. A gust lifted Brooke's sundress and tickled her skin. They broke from their embrace and Brooke struggled to hold it down.

Chase said, "Don't bother—it won't be on for long." They laughed as he led her back inside to christen his home.

Brooke wanted a hand-held tour, but decided it would have to wait. They were past holding hands. As predicted, Chase whisked Brooke's dress over her head like the wind. With the sun falling, she stripped him in record time. Then they worked up an appetite, devouring each other in fresh ways.

Lying atop the rumpled sheets, Brooke turned to Chase and said, "If we do that one more time, I don't think I'll be able to walk."

Chase grinned, then rolled on top of Brooke and said, "Then, we'll order a delivery."

Afterward, Brooke crawled across the floor to the bathroom, saying, "You wanna call Domino's?" They laughed out loud.

Chase said, "That may be our only option. It's so late—I'm not sure if anyone's still serving dinner."

"I was thinking brunch." They giggled.

Brooke was in love. Chase could make her laugh at will, could make her cry tears of joy, but she hoped he wouldn't coax her into another round. As if she wore magic slippers, Chase granted Brooke her wish. He surprised her by preparing a delicious candle-lit dinner. He had lobster tails in the freezer, frozen veggies, and even chives, cheese, and bacon bits for loaded baked potatoes. After pouring a delicious Chardonnay, he cooked it all—and even set the table.

The wine warmed her. Brooke asked, "When were you last here?"

When he told her, she recalled. This was where he went with Parker—duh. It seemed like such a distant memory: building sand castles with Parker, without any idea. And to think she thought Parker had a lousy dad.

Following dinner, Chase asked, "Are you healed yet?"

Brooke's eyes narrowed as she slowly grinned.

Chase laughed, "I don't mean for that … I meant, would you like to take a stroll on the beach? I think the tide's out."

"I'd love to."

The lukewarm sand tickled their bare feet as they ambled arm-in-arm. A tepid breeze guided the fresh ocean mist, cooling the day's smolder; stars twinkled above. A picture perfect night to stroll on the beach.

The gentle waves set their pulses. Brooke noticed the familiar relaxing feeling of Hilton Head. The last time she walked this same beach, she felt as if her life was changing with the tide. With Chase beside her, she realized she was home. Then, it dawned on her—another piece of the puzzle from Tanner's letter—the place on the beach.

Back inside, they headed upstairs. The night air, wine, filling dinner—and one more lovemaking session—had tired them out. Chase considered telling Brooke, but wanted to wait until he had more energy. With hypnotic waves reverberating through the windows, they fell asleep in each other's arms.

Brooke awakened at morning's first glow. She gazed at Chase and smiled. Brooke loved watching him sleep. His tousled hair, masculine chest, and those lashes. With eyes on him, she quietly slipped out of bed and peered out the window. The crescent moon and a sprinkling of stars were still visible, but fading. She loved the first rays popping over the horizon's expansive water. Each sunrise and sunset had different nuances, its own unique beauty. She glanced at Chase, torn between watching him or the sunrise. He rustled, as if reading her mind.

His lashes flickered, making Brooke's heart flutter. Chase wiped his eyes and said, "You're awake. What time is it?"

"Come here. You have to see this."

Still groggy, he slid across the sheets. Though she wore his Duke T-shirt, he was naked. He considered asking for his shirt, but relished her in Blue Devil apparel; he grabbed the nearby comforter and joined Brooke. With the quilt covering their shoulders, they stood arm-in-arm in silence. Then, it popped.

The first rays popped—the awe of nature's stage—and the opening act proved majestic. Chase pulled her closer. The perfect way to start a perfect day. They stood silently for several minutes, soaking in the power of love inside with the power of nature outside.

Chase said, "Remember when we first met?"

"On the elevator? How could I ever forget?"

"I wanted to go running with you when you healed."

"Let's go," Brooke grinned.

The tide was midpoint, leaving plenty of firm sand for a jog. They ran barefoot at a comfortable pace as the warming sun continued its climb. In another few hours, the heat would make running unbearable, but right now, it felt inviting. Brooke still wore the Duke T-shirt—and never looked better.

Brooke noticed a splash out of the corner of her eye. Then another—dolphins. As she glanced back at Chase, he was already watching. A family of dolphins frolicked in and out of the water, as if keeping pace with Brooke and Chase. Brooke remembered the dolphins from her last trip, and gazed up, smiling.

They slowed to a walk and viewed as the dolphin family continued their own morning exercise. Brooke led Chase to the tree and kissed him.

"Wow," Chase said, "That was quite a kiss. We may have to turn back ... unless you want to ..." Brooke laughed. A gentle breeze soothed her. She knew.

Chase picked up a nearby twig and began drawing in the sand, blocking Brooke's view with his broad shoulders. After he finished, he stepped aside. Brooke squinted to read: "Our Names" encased inside a heart. She glanced back at Chase and raised her eyebrow.

He smiled, saying, "I wanted to write *our names* in the sand." They laughed together, then Brooke grabbed the stick and wrote: "Brooke Loves Chase." Not to be outdone, Chase used the stick to write: "Chase Loves Brooke More."

Chase said, "I'll race you to the Marriott. Last one there buys breakfast," then bolted.

Brooke sprinted and, much to his surprise, caught Chase. They ran together at a swift clip, until Chase yielded at the end. After jumping in and splashing each other, they enjoyed a poolside fruit platter and fresh-squeezed orange juice.

The return trip lasted twice as long, but it didn't matter. They jogged, then kissed. Then jogged, and kissed, jumping into the ocean occasionally. For the last one hundred yards, they strolled while holding hands.

Chase said, "I meant what I wrote earlier."

"The last few weeks have been magical. I can't tell you how much you mean to me ..." Chase's eyes moistened.

Brooke said, "I love you," then kissed him.

Brooke sauntered back from the house; Chase stared from his towel on the sand. Even on uneven ground, she still had a confident stride, one of the many things he loved about her. As planned, once Brooke settled onto her towel, Chase said, "Be right back." Brooke giggled, then scrutinized Chase's every step. Just past the dunes, he spun around and caught her staring.

Once inside, Chase assembled everything with the speed of a pit crew. With sweaty palms, he lifted his cooler, while holding his guitar case handle, and headed back on shaky legs.

"Wow, what did you bring?" Brooke propped up on her elbows, eyeing Chase's every step.

"Just a few goodies."

"I was going to ask you to bring the guitar."

Chase lifted the lid on the cooler, which squeaked. He fed Brooke a grape, then, with the bunch in his hand, settled in beside her. He had removed his sunglasses, and his eyes dazzled. He appeared nervous. She said, "Is someth—"

"Brooke, something's happened to me—something wonderful."

Brooke shifted upright on her towel and removed her sunglasses. Her radiant eyes locked on Chase's. He paused, then continued, "I used to think I had it all figured out. But meeting you changed everything. I feel so alive. I feel like I finally know what true love is."

Chase popped a grape in his mouth. He said, "I know I don't always say things the right way, but ... I want to get this right."

He stood, retrieving a small box from his pocket, then dropped to one knee. As he peered into Brooke's widening eyes, his voice cracked, "Brooke Anne, will you marry me?"

Tears welled up in her eyes. Her head spun with the dream illuminating and time standing still. With trembling lips, Brooke said, "Yes." She wanted to say more, so many things flooded into her brain, but her tongue locked.

Chase said, "I love you so much."

Brooke said, "This has been the greatest day of my life."

Chase pulled back, holding Brooke's elbows. He said, "There's one more little thing you should know …"

"Oh?"

"You have to help me revive GenSense. I'm no longer with Pharmical."

Brooke squinted, "What?"

"I got my *pink slip* from Pharmical yesterday," pausing for effect, "I negotiated my severance—for the rights to GenSense."

"You're not kidding, are you?"

"You're looking at the new CEO of GenSense. I want you to be my co-CEO in life and at GenSense."

Brooke frowned, "Oh Chase, you've thrown too much for me at once … I love Angel's Academy—I can't leave it now. But I'll be beside you."

"Good enough for me," Chase said as he slid the sparkling diamond ring on Brooke's finger.

"It's stunning," Brooke's eyes twinkled with the setting sun's rays bouncing off the diamond.

"Not as beautiful as you. You're everything beautiful to me."

Brooke wrapped her arms tightly around Chase.

Chase said, "Ready to celebrate?" He reached into the ice and pulled out a bottle of Dom Perignon. Her face glowed; he retrieved two crystal glasses and handed them to Brooke in exchange for the bottle. He popped the cork, letting it soar like a Fourth of July rocket, then poured.

Raising his glass, Chase said, "To us."

22

*B*rooke and Chase looked stunning. Even barefoot, somehow the wedding dress and tuxedo worked. The decision to elope was an easy one. Neither one wanted the big wedding headaches, except Weston Ingram—of course. He put up a fight, but the couple appeased him by agreeing to let him throw them a big bash in Charlotte. Chase's decision to call and ask his permission was a wise one. Just like with Brooke, Chase won Weston over.

Brooke decided to never tell Chase what her father had nicknamed him.

Brooke also agreed with her fiancé's decision not to invite Dixie-dawg—and without any prodding.

The biggest surprise arrived on the eve of their wedding. Chase answered the door and hugged him, saying, "Shhhhh, she still doesn't know you're coming."

"Thanks for inviting me, Bro." Both Chase and Billy were excited to finally have the brother they always wanted.

Chase and Billy snuck up on Brooke as Chase said, "Look who I found—."

Brooke spun around and froze as Billy proclaimed, "Clean and sober for six months."

The early October weather was perfect. Chase's beach house looked great, decorated with fresh cut flowers. Flanked by Melissa and Parker, the couple recited their handwritten vows before the popular beach wedding reverend.

Aside from a few curious seagulls, the ceremony was exactly how the couple envisioned—private and loving. After they finished their vows, Chase opened his guitar case; he fixed his gaze on Brooke, and said, "I wrote a wedding song for you. It's called "Amazing.""

Brooke's knees buckled as she recognized the beautiful guitar intro, then Chase sang:

Wedded Bliss

On this day's setting sun
I'm always there as the day is done
We are one
My love for you I cannot hide
Like the ocean's endless tide

Your blissful laughter fills the air
You answer my special prayer
A life of dreams for us to share
Crash into me and always stay
Sweet, sweet music will fill each day

Come fly with me above the land
And write our names in the sand
Please take my hand
We'll walk along the tide
And thank the Lord our loves collide

From this day as we become one
I'm always there as the day is done
We are one
My love for you I cannot hide
With you the sun will always shine.

Brooke's tears streamed off her smiling cheeks. She peered at Chase and said, "That was incredible." Parker would have preferred a Raffi song, but he liked it because Miss Ingram—*Mommy*—liked it. Melissa's tears dotted her pink dress—and pink slip. Even the reverend was touched by the heartfelt song, later telling the new couple that it had been a long time since he felt so much love in a room.

Melissa—sans Eddie—had agreed to babysit Parker for the couple's wedding night. Oksana, the newly appointed Associate Director at

Angel's Academy, was thrilled that Brooke trusted her to run things for the next week.

After a nice beach dinner, Chase serenaded everyone. Even Parker made his professional singing debut, doing a funny Raffi song while his dad played guitar.

Chase had reserved a penthouse villa in Harbour Towne for their wedding night. Penthouse on Hilton Head meant fifth floor. As they reached the lobby elevator, Brook pressed the up button. Before the door slid open, Chase reached behind a plant and presented her with the original glass slippers. He dropped to a knee and slid on the glass slippers, then whisked her into his arms and kissed her.

With a grin, he said, "No way are you going on that elevator tonight. I'm carrying you up the stairs."

♥ ♥ ♥

Acknowledgments

*A*s a male author, this book started as a dare—*guys can write romantic stories too*—and ended as a truly amazing experience. As much as I'd like to take full credit, I had several estrogen editors who helped make the story appealing to both sexes.

First and foremost, to M.A.H., my non-fiction romance and primary estrogen editor. Without her love, encouragement, and enthusiastic support, this book would have never been more than a lost dare.

To Sophie Powell, who believed in the love story from day one and whose invaluable advice gave me the prodding I needed to continue improving the book.

To Marcia Jussel and Bob Condello for their creative and practical advice once again. To Meredith Ingram for helping me with the dynamics of the North Carolina/Duke rivalry and Carolina.

To Lisa Pelto and her team at Concierge Marketing Inc.: Erin Pankowski, Jessica Eckersley, and Ellie Pelto. In addition to designing outstanding books, creative covers and interiors, CMI is great to work with.

About the Author

J.P. Hansen is an international award-winning, bestselling author of three books, a professional speaker, and life coach. In addition, he is CEO of an executive search company, and for the past twenty years, he has helped thousands of people find their dream jobs. He was the youngest vice president of sales & marketing at a Fortune 30 company (ConAgra). Previously, he successfully ascended the corporate ladders at blue-chip companies Nestle, SC Johnson Wax, and Bristol-Myers Squibb. He graduated from Boston College with a BA in English and an area of concentration in Economics.

Since January, 2010, *The Bliss List-the Ultimate Guide to Living the Dream at Work and Beyond!* and *The Bliss List Journal* have garnered four awards (two international), including:

- ForeWord Book of the Year Medalist
- CAREER BOOK of the YEAR Award winner (Next Generation)
- Excellence Award National Finalist (Indie)
- USA Book News Award National Finalist

His novel, *Pink Slips and Glass Slippers*, became the #1 most downloaded book in the world (Amazon) within its first week in September, 2012, and continues at or near the top in most rankings.

J.P. has appeared live as a "career expert," reaching over 15,000,000 people on national TV like FoxNews, Daytime TV, CBS, ABC, NBC, and FOX affiliates, on numerous radio programs in top markets, and in publications like *The L.A. Times*, *Fortune*, AOL, CareerBuilder, CNN.com, and FoxBusiness.com. *Omaha Magazine* dubbed J.P., "The Ambassador of Bliss."

For updates, visit www.BlissList.com and click "Like" on his author Facebook page: J.P. Hansen

Made in the USA
Lexington, KY
08 December 2012